THE QUARANTINE PAPERS

THE QUARANTINE PAPERS

KALPISH RATNA

HarperCollins *Publishers* India

First published in hardback in 2010 by
HarperCollins *Publishers* India

Building 10, Tower A, 4th Floor, DLF Cyber City, Phase II,
Gurugram Haryana – 122002, India
www.harpercollins.co.in

First published in paperback in 2012

ISBN: 978-93-5029-570-0

2 4 6 8 10 9 7 5 3 1

Typeset by Inosoft Systems

Printed and bound at
MicroPrints India, New Delhi

for
Mehmooda & Savithri

6 December 1992

HERO
HONDA
HERO
HONDA
MH 02 AN 1748

That first Sunday in December, while the Prime Minister of India dozed, lesser things happened to lesser people.

Opposite Madanpura Police Chowki, Mohammad Yunus doused his clothes with kerosene and struck a match. He was twenty-five.

On the terrace of Dyaneshwar Bagh, Balkrishna More quit watering his plants and went inside. He locked the door, flung open the tall French windows, and leaned out over the frenzied crowd below.

The maha-aarati had begun.

A haze of camphor hung over the street. The brassy clangour of bells steadied to a staccato and microphones prepared for a formal diatribe of rage.

The old words, the old rage. Nothing had changed.

'Stop!' he cried out to them.

Nobody heard him.

Had they looked up, they would have seen him suspended over them like a question mark.

Before he fell.

In their joyous daze Radhika and Anwar were oblivious to the nasal monotone on BBC.

Who saw it first? It did not matter, by then they saw as one.

It was there, happening right before them.

A saffron ant crawled up the black dome. Then one more. Then another. Then a swarm of them. And then madness spilled every which way.

Their eyes searched each other in silence for a long moment. Anwar switched off the television.

Radhika's eyes shone. Her stark skin glowed. They turned, hungrily again, to each other, the double helix of their entwining the only identity they craved.

It was a busy Sunday at the Arts College. The campus was being renovated. It would finally be worthy of the architecture it taught. They were meeting about relocating classes for the year ahead when a fracas broke out on the maidan.

A crowd milled outside Kipling House. Stragglers, mostly.

They were shouting encouragement, their voices flailing against a guttural rumble. They were watching a monstrous earthmover inch closer to a small defiant figure at the end of the maidan.

She was an old woman bracing herself against the fence of the decrepit green bungalow.

On the bourne, a tall man in khaki wiped his spectacles and shrugged. Several others nodded and moved off with him.

The Union would have no part in this.

In a shuttered room in Girgaum, three old men waited for an answer.

'Tai, tell us what must be done now,' the youngest urged.

Vasundhara sighed.

'Do whatever it takes,' she said. 'Whatever. Just do it now.'

Yaqub was out of breath, hurrying to reach Sakina Manzil before the police began naka bandi. Railed barricades were being stacked outside the Chowki. He'd been out in the sun since the news broke, hunting desperately for the woman. He dreaded telling his father he had failed. Their very lives depended on finding her.

But Tariq Azhar surprised his son.

When Yaqub reached home shame-faced, his father raised a trembling hand to his cheek.

'Sit down, Yaqub,' he gentled. 'Let me tell you where to look...'

In 303, Nandanvan Apartments, Ratan Oak looked out of the window and discovered he'd been living in the wrong house all his life.

His house had a raintree at the gate. He surprised himself with a word. Saman.

Samanea saman.

Never keen on botany, when did he acquire this scrap of Latin?

Bombay was full of raintrees, but he didn't remember ever thinking of them as *Samanea saman*.

Monkeypod.

Another name for the tree. That was *the* name for it. *That's* what they all called it!

The monkeypod tree.

It wasn't there now. There was nothing at the gate except the vacuous solidity of a wall.

'Where did the tree go? The monkeypod at the gate?'

He had asked the question before he remembered his father couldn't answer him any more.

Arjun Oak was having lunch. The TV was switched off. It was a distraction. Keeping distractions to a minimum made Ratan's job easier. With luck, once Arjun was into the rhythm of eating, he might keep on till he finished the meal. Distracted, he would freeze in the very act of conveying a morsel to his lips, and remain in a trance unless Ratan coaxed him back to the present.

Over the last year Ratan had learnt that talking cricket was the best way to manage that.

Now the pointless question had shot out of him without conscious thought. Torn between impatience and apology, Ratan cast about for an opening to bring cricket into his conversation.

He turned to face his father, prepared for the hand frozen in mid-air, the spilt mush, the spattered floor.

But Arjun had placed the spoon carefully back in his plate, and was staring at Ratan. For the first time in days, his eyes had focus.

'I don't know where I got the idea there was a monkeypod tree—' Ratan muttered, lamely.

Arjun Oak nodded.

It wasn't an easy movement for him. It took him a minute entire to will it. This lent gravitas, and morphed the nod into a benison.

Ratan was taken aback.

'There *was* a monkeypod here then?'

His father shut his eyes.

Negative.

There was no monkeypod at the gate. Of course there wasn't. There never had been.

What had he agreed about then, just now?

The phone rang.

A familiar colic of dread griped Ratan. The raintree, real or imagined, no longer mattered.

He picked up the phone.

His feelings for Prema were complicated. Nine parts lust and one part rage, when by all logic, the ratio ought to have been reversed. At the sound of her voice he no longer could decide what he felt. Relief? Joy? Outrage?

Did she deliberate before she dialled, or had she called on impulse?

In the past they often had nothing to say on the phone. They were content simply in the silent communion of breathing, quivering, and quickening.

Imbued with memories, he barely listened to her words. They sank in now, pinpricks of outrage. He was annoyed.

'What am I to do about it? Sorry, I can't think of anything—' Ratan hung up and returned to the table. He'd been on the verge of saying, *If you still need me to manage your life, why did you leave me?*

His father wore a stricken mask Ratan could not bear. He ached to tear it off and expose the enraged man underneath. He wanted to yell, *It's not your fault she left!*

But he'd learnt not to notice. He'd learnt to walk his thoughts past that. Besides, it was the truth.

'I can't take this,' Prema had said flatly, when Arjun spilt his food, when he slobbered, when he was incontinent. Actually, she didn't have to take any of it, for Ratan did whatever had to be done. To make that possible, he'd quit his full-time job at the hospital. These days he worked evenings at a nearby laboratory.

All the same, Prema had left.

What did that show?

Arjun's illness wasn't the real reason.

The real reason was the monkeypod tree.

He'd had moments like this all his life, moments that offered a different reality. At such moments, he belonged elsewhere. He could neither conceal nor explain them.

This unsettled her.

Like the time he said *Esplanade* instead of *Fountain* when he was giving her directions to a friend's office.

Like the time he told her, 'Don't walk, it might rain—*take the tram*.'

These things spooked Prema.

Drawing away just a little, she'd say, 'Anyone would think you lived in a different city.'

Not entirely accurate.

It was the same city.

Just in a different time.

Sometimes, after they'd made love, she'd look at him with her searchlight gaze, turn away and wedge a pillow as barrier between them. His heart would accelerate painfully a second time. This time from guilt and the knowing that as he hovered at the edge of pleasure, the face that had sent him roaring into a corridor of stars was not Prema's.

Never Prema's.

It wasn't a face he knew.

Yet he knew no face as well...

Ratan brought a fresh plate for Arjun, determined to coax him back to the meal with cricket. He prepared to launch into Azhar's debut versus Gower's pommies at Eden Gardens on the day Orwell's year ended. But his father's eyes were stricken no longer. They prickled with question.

Ratan sighed.

'There's some sort of trouble at Prema's college.'

What trouble? Arjun looked the question.

'A woman threw herself in front of an earthmover—'

An earthmover?

'They're demolishing some old structure. To make way for an architectural marvel—one more concrete urinal!'

Who is she—a student?

'Eh? No, no. Employee of some sort. They asked Prema to intervene because she's a counsellor. Counselling architecture students is one thing, but earthmover antagonists? Prema's out of her depth here.'

Let it go. You must help her.

'No. I've had enough!'

Ratan turned away.

He was sick of the situation. He was sick of Arjun always aligning his wandering wits with Prema. He was sick of Prema's determined disgust at his father. He was sick of his need for Prema. If only she'd clear out and leave them in peace!

But she never would.

'She's got a boyfriend,' he said.

No!

'Art professor. One who professes art.'

The phone rang again. Ratan let it ring and guided Arjun's hand back to its rhythm till it countered him with an iron will of its own.

Pick up the phone. Help her.

'It may not be Prema.'

It was.

'Get here, Ratan, please! I don't know what to do!'

She hung up. As always, leaving no space for argument.

Go.

'Yes, I'll get you comfortable first.'

But Arjun was no longer paying attention. His fists were balled up in effort and he leaned forward in his wheelchair in anticipation.

Ratan waited.

His father was gathering energy to speak. It would take him a few minutes to scavenge words from the mislaid vocabulary in his brain. Eventually, the words would come.

Arjun Oak's face contorted in concentration. Two words shot out of him with a kind of anger.

'Lock wood!'

It made no sense. No sense at all.

Ratan took scant notice of the idlers at the gate as he zoomed into the traffic. It wasn't four yet, but the road was jammed already. The pavements seemed thick with people, all seeking transport. Ratan weaved through the sludged vehicles, zoomed past a red light, and was onto the flyover in a trice.

At the J.J. Hospital signal there was naka bandi and two havaldars were diverting all traffic west. Ratan had to meld with the flow and claw for road space till Nana Chowk. He made his way into the Queen's Necklace. He never called it

Marine Drive. The sea slipped by swiftly, a shed snakeskin in the sun. Then past V.T. he was there.

The Arts College gate was shut. Ratan felt affronted by the rusty iron sheets recently welded onto the delicate filigree of a more trusting age. He hammered at them impatiently.

A sigh, a slow shuffle, and then at the judas window a watchman's bloodshot eye rolled like a Dalí prop. He opened the gate with a grin, greeting Ratan like an old friend.

'Long time, Sahib! I knew you'd come today.'

Ratan did not pause to ask why and cruised to the main block. If you taught here, you recognized watchmen, clerks and bureaucrats for what they were. They were the Fates. They apportioned life, decided your entrance, your tenure, your exit in glory or ignominy.

Ratan saw Prema immediately.

Correction. He *sensed* her, as he always did, with an internal gearshift.

In the past, everything had zoomed. The day changed pace.

Now his heart was a stone in the belly and his mouth a trap.

She was still far away, but he knew she'd noticed.

The bright pink blur of her kurta clarified as her shoulders straightened. She grew taller, denser. She was the kind of woman who, espying her reflection, tailored it quickly to what she expected it to be.

She waved to him.

A cheery wave. A semaphore meaning they were going to be hearty, not just polite. It was to be the unisex camaraderie thing. Khadi kurta, batik jhola, hairy armpits, kolhapuri chappals, cutting chai. Just the mindset, that is.

Her kurta was an Ethos exclusive, her clutch and shoes were from glitzy Mochi in the Taj Arcade, she abhorred tea and was always, always, waxed to the point of martyrdom.

Ratan looked around pointedly.

There was no trace of disturbance on the campus. The place was deserted, and without the taut vacuum of a curfew. People had just gone home.

She advanced to meet him, her gait deliberate, speaking before he could engage her eyes.

'What took you so long? I've been waiting for hours!'

There were a number of answers to that.

Of late, their conversation was mostly MCQs. Some days he got lucky and chose the right answer. Now he ignored all five, maybe six, possibilities.

'What happened to your chipko lady?' he asked.

'Chipko? Oh. She didn't have to throw herself under the earthmover, eventually. They left off when the news broke.'

'What news?'

'What news?'

Of late she had grown an echo to mock his words.

'Ratan, which world do you live in? You've travelled right across the city and you still don't know what's happened?'

He was no longer curious. He just wanted out.

'Babri Masjid has been smashed.'

What?

This was crazy! It was 1992, not 992. This was barbaric, medieval, the kind of thing people did a thousand years ago when war was glory and cruelty a measure of strength, not weakness. The world had changed since then.

'Broken. Brick by brick. With hammers and crowbars. By kar sevaks. Before you ask me how, they swarmed the dome and broke it. I saw it. BBC showed it all.'

The dome hadn't crumbled. It hadn't caved in. *It was broken.* Dismantled. Brick by brick by brick by brick.

Three domes.

The Babri Masjid had three domes. He remembered thinking that excessive.

Images telescoped. Lorry loads of crazed boys, flying high

on hate. Blood bursts of tilak above their blind eyes, orange scarves around their necks in twists of flame. Gunshot and noose. Doomed. Children lost to life before it had begun.

Bricks piling up in pillars outside small shrines. Jafar's laundry downing shutters in the middle of the day and Ram Narain Halwai's knowing smile. The city quickening, in suspicion, in panic. Naka bandi. Diversions. Memories of things seen but not noticed, clumped together like a slimy ball of filth clogging his brain.

Prema's voice scaled up a notch.

'We heard just after I called you! And then the developer stopped the tod-phod too. The old dame gave up her hero-giri. I phoned to stop you from coming. I called, but Nobody answered.'

At first, during the more severe dilemmas of his illness, Prema referred to Arjun as an accusation—'*Your* father.' For a while, after she'd moved out, there was a brief Arjun Uncle phase. But all that was settled now. Now he was Nobody. As in *Nobody's at home. Nobody answers the phone. What do you do all day with Nobody in the house with you*?

This afternoon, soon after he had left, the phone must have trilled angrily, repeatedly, at his father's elbow. Arjun's brain would have refused him words, refused him action. He would have sat frozen, anxious and perspiring, not knowing how to translate that sound, unable to shout out the question, *What am I supposed to do*?

Had she thought of that when she called? Or had she dialled on impulse, eager only to save him a needless journey?

'You should put the phone off the hook when there's Nobody in the house,' she said severely. 'You should get an answering machine.'

Hate showed in his eyes, he supposed. It vacuumed his insides with visceral torque. It sucked up every vestige of Prema from within him and all he had to do was to unstopper, to let it go, and he would be emptied of pain. Every now and then he wanted to do so. More often, he was prepared to kill to keep it.

He told himself she had waited. Her friends had left, but she'd waited for him. She had stayed back, trusting he'd get there.

'Come on, let's go home,' he said roughly.

As if home was a place they shared. Her parents lived in Santa Cruz. It might be safer if she stayed over at Nandanvan tonight. The thought was priapic.

'Oh, *there* you are!'

There was a lilt in her voice. She was looking over his shoulder.

'What*ever* took you so long?'

'Chalo, then! Shall we go?'

A weedy voice.

Ratan guessed without turning around. Five-four, maybe five. Pushing thirty-five. Soft jaw, soft belly. Cute hair, toupee ten years from now.

'Oh Ratan, you haven't met Cyrus!'

Her synthetic voice. Silky as pantyhose, and just as nasty.

'Cyrus, Ratan. Ratan, *Cyrus*!'

Cyrus proffered his hand like a prize. Ratan evaded it with a mildly ironic salute.

Prema shot him one of her cryptic looks. Ratan noted grimly that he was out of practice at decoding her signals.

Not that it mattered.

She was looking at Cyrus now, and there was nothing ambiguous about her look.

'*Cy*-rus!'

He jumped.

'Cyrus, *you shaved your beard*!'

Cyrus rubbed one white cheek and grinned uneasily.

'Had to! They insisted in the staff soom. Everybody thought I'd better! Sure to get mistaken for a Muslim, they said. Beard. Fair skin. Might as well, I thought—'

Jazzy staff room. Razors, shaving gel. What else did they stock? Aftershave? Condoms? Cervical caps?

'Ratan—right? Great meeting you!'

'I wish I'd got you on the phone,' Prema said again. 'Could have saved you this trip.'

Ratan smiled. He saw his smile in his mind's eye: fatuous, bemused, the punch-drunk smile of a man who had OD'd on life.

'Cyrus lives in Santa Cruz.'

'Sure.'

He waved as they drove off in Cyrus' blue Fiat. Its dented fender failed to cheer him.

Ratan lingered awhile to avoid overtaking Cyrus on the way back to Santa Cruz.

He was insanely hungry. He considered heading back through Chowpatty, but changed his mind when he glanced at his watch. It was nearly five o'clock.

Chagrin. That was the word. He wanted to shake this day off his back. It clung to him with all its mad inconsequence, a vetaal yet to pose its riddle.

As he turned away he recognized the dark mass of machinery at the far end of the maidan. There it was—the earthmover. He left the asphalt and hit the field.

Something about the iron behemoth made it seem like a victim. It had been abandoned as dead, vanquished by one frail human frame. One knock of its bossed steel was enough to pulverize every bone in the body. Yet an old woman hadn't flinched from throwing herself in its path. Presumably, this was the patch of land she had tried to protect. There were heaps of rubble about, concrete slabs and bricks from a broken wall. Beyond the rubble ran a clumsy barricade—not a definite fence, more a desultory deterrent—a few bits of bamboo with barbed wire looped between them, enough to warn off intruders from the dingy cottage within its ambit.

On an impulse he leaned his bike against the earthmover and stepped over the fence.

He wasn't quite certain why he wanted to see the woman. It just seemed necessary.

The cottage door swung open and a man staggered out wildly. He looked as if he'd been pushed out.

Very ill or very drunk, Ratan decided. He hung back in the shadows till the man passed him. As he tussled with the barbed wire Ratan caught a glimpse of his face. It wasn't what Ratan had expected to see. The man's eyes betrayed no fugue of alcohol. They were shocked and very aware, with pupils dilated in terror. He was breathing hard. He tore free of the barbs and broke into a run.

Ratan gave him five minutes. Then he emerged from his hideout, walked over to the cottage and knocked. He had no idea what he was going to say when she opened the door.

She didn't open the door.

There are moments that alter everything. We reach them unaware, not knowing what leads us, not recognizing the beginning of change.

Ratan pushed open the door.

He stepped into the darkened house. The interior was dim, nascent. The only window was overgrown with a creeper of some sort, and the room shimmered as if it awaited the first shudder of life.

It was the usual sort of room one enters in a chawl—bare, functional, scrupulously clean.

There was one unusual feature.

Slumped on the floor was the body of a woman.

She was dead.

Ratan did not have to approach her to discern this. But some habits are hard to break. He checked for signs of life, then stepped back and viewed the body.

She had fallen forward. Her long hair had come undone from the coil at her neck. A thin braid of grey trailed in a glassy pool of blood. Her face was half hidden beneath her right arm. He raised it a little. The trickle of blood from her left nostril had clotted over her lips. There was no external sign of injury—no cut, abrasion or bruise. Her eyes were beginning to glaze over, corneas murky, not yet opaque, skin still warm, muscles pliant.

She'd been dead about a half-hour.

Ratan was disturbed by her faint look of surprise, not altogether unpleasant.

Her nauvari sari of printed cotton had ridden up over her muscled calves. The left arm was extended as if to push away her assailant. Ratan knelt and raised the right shoulder a little to free the right hand. Her fist was balled in cadaveric spasm. At first it appeared as if she clutched the neckline of her blouse, but now something showed between her curled fingers. He released the fingers, unprepared for their resistance. A swift horripilation of dread swept him. He eased out the scrap of paper from the death clutch of her fingers and let her shoulder fall forward again.

Ratan retreated from the body.

He was bewildered by what he had just done.

Why had he examined the dead woman?

Force of habit.

Force of *habit?*

It *was* true. Force of habit.

He'd examined the corpse as if he'd been doing it all his life.

Ratan looked at the scrap he had removed from the dead hand. It had crumpled into a yellow ball in her desperate grasp. Cautioned by the colour, he coaxed it open gently with his index finger, using the lightest brush of pad and nail. It was friable, beginning to crack along the creases.

It was an official Permit of some sort. The paper was badly foxed, but the print was intelligible, though the handwritten words had faded to pale sepia. The date was clearly legible:

2 March 1897.

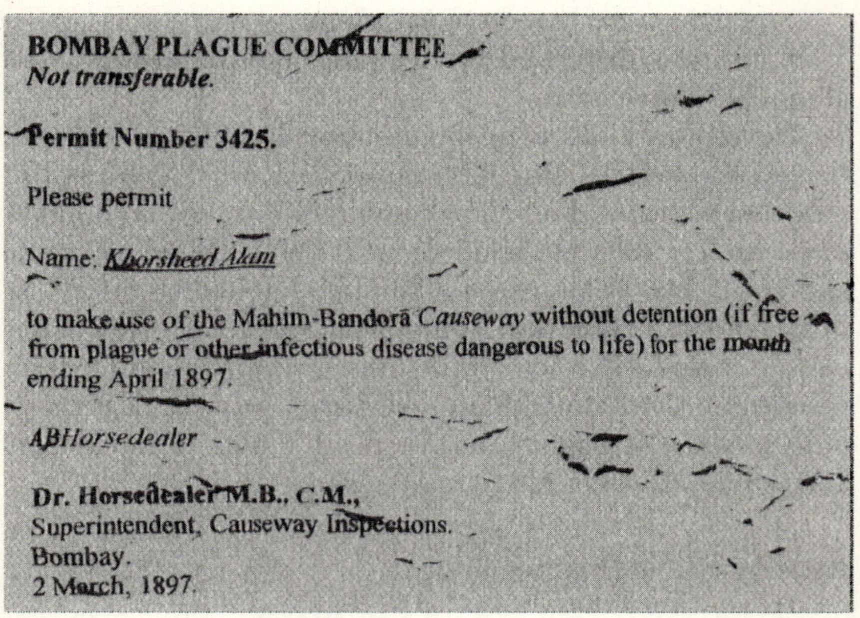

BOMBAY PLAGUE COMMITTEE
Not transferable.

Permit Number 3425.

Please permit

Name: *Khorsheed Alam*

to make use of the Mahim-Bandorā *Causeway* without detention (if free from plague or other infectious disease dangerous to life) for the month ending April 1897.

ABHorsedealer

Dr. Horsedealer M.B., C.M.,
Superintendent, Causeway Inspections.
Bombay.
2 March, 1897.

Horsedealer, Ardeshir Bomanji. M.B., C.M.

Ardha-sir Boman.

But he was half-assed, not half-brained. Reeked like a stable, even though his people hadn't dealt in horses for the last fifty years.

Till its recent mauling, the paper seemed to have been preserved flat and pristine—no line marked even a careless fold.

Preserved since 1897.

In what?

Ratan looked around for a file or a heavy book, but there was no such article around. A chair and table were pushed against the wall. A small wooden cupboard, a roll of bedding stowed neatly on it, seemed the only storage space. It was unlocked. The shelves held a few worn clothes and, in a plastic bag that Ratan opened to a whiff of mothballs, an ancient black coat and cap. He stuffed the relic back in haste.

A bracket on the wall served as an altar. It held two religious prints. But these were pushed to the back, dusty and untended, clearly not objects of devotion. Something more worthy of daily worship held pride of place. A sooty lamp glowered next to a framed photograph. A few wilted marigolds were strewn around it. The man in the picture was wearing the coat and cap Ratan had handled minutes ago. The dead husband, without doubt.

Nothing here, either.

Wait!

It wasn't just the lamp and the flowers that made the photograph so prominent. It rested on something flat wrapped in tarnished zari. Ratan lifted the photograph off, and unwrapped the rectangular package.

It was a book, cloth-bound, the gold lettering on its cover blackened with time.

Beast And Man In India
A Popular Sketch Of Indian Animals In Their Relations With The People
by
John Lockwood Kipling, C.I.F.

Of course!

It all came back to him now.

Prema had given him the grand tour in her first week at the College of Art and Architecture. The Dean's bungalow, untenanted for years, was called Kipling House. It was named for John *Lockwood* Kipling. Not his son Rudyard.

Ratan heard his father's voice enunciate the name 'Lock Wood'.

How had Baba made that connection?

Ratan opened the book with a curious sense of déjà vu. A memory flickered briefly—and was lost.

The book opened at the dedication. There was a drawing on the page. It was a glyph. A curiously patterned tiger. Or, perhaps, a leopard.

TO THE OTHER THREE

It was a glyph he *knew*.

Just as he'd known Ardha-sir Boman.

Ratan decided he must have seen this glyph somewhere and then forgotten it.

There was a line above the glyph.

TO THE OTHER THREE

The flyleaf was blank.

The book fell open promptly at page 25.

A pale rectangle enclosed by sharp yellow lines suggested something had nestled there for a long time. Whatever it was, it wasn't the crumpled Permit. A small slip of paper couldn't have caused this indentation. It had to be something thicker. Something that was no longer there.

There were two other enclosures in the book, one old, the other recent. The old one seemed of the same vintage as the Permit, but smaller. The words were handwritten in the same faded ink:

Enq No: B-192

The more recent paper was a receipt from the Bombay Archives made out to Shakuntalabai Bikaji Salwe for Rs 650 towards 'Xeroxing charges'.

That was a lot of material to have Xeroxed.

The payment had been made on 26 November. The delivery date for the material was 8 December.

The woman who had picketed the earthmover had a name now.

Shakuntala.

Unlike her original, she hadn't been ill-omened in love. The coat and cap bespoke a long affection.

Had she been ill-omened in death?

There was a battered handbag on the table. Ratan rifled through it without a qualm. It contained a wallet with five hundred-rupee notes. A plastic identity card established Shakuntala Salwe was a Class IV employee. Ratan noticed the card was past its expiry date. A bulging fern green rexine folder was stuffed with prescriptions.

Shakuntala had attended the St. George's Hospital Outpatient Clinic regularly. She was being treated for hypertension. Her last reading (a week ago) was inauspicious: 180/110 mm Hg, despite medication.

She had died, perhaps from a complication of her illness.

Cerebral haemorrhage.

The nosebleed suggested that.

This wasn't murder.

Wasn't it?

What or who had pushed her to this extremity?

He slipped the book into the waistband of his jeans. He took a quick look around to confirm everything was as he'd found it. Then he left.

He emerged cautiously through the barbed fence and revved his bike away with a great deal of commotion to announce his discovery to the watchman.

The watchman was not surprised.

She had it coming, he said.

Everybody knew Shakuntalabai was slightly loony. She'd held on to her job as caretaker of the bungalow because it was her khandani pesha. She had a letter to prove it. Her father and *his* father, all of them had served the Sahiblog. The Sahiblog were long gone, but Shakuntala's family was in charge of their land. And it's true, the watchman reiterated, it *is* the Sahiblog's land.

Of course Shakuntala's son wanted out. He ran away, didn't he? Only kept coming back for the price of a drink. Got a girl in trouble five years ago. Our maali's daughter. He was roughed up for it. Hadn't shown his face since then. He was here this afternoon, drunk like the dog he is! And Shakuntala? What do you expect in a woman of her years if she tries such hero-giri?

The watchman left to summon the GP who looked after the college staff. Ratan took his place at the gate.

He felt bludgeoned. He had acted out of character. Ransacking the cottage. Pinching the book. Handling the corpse. Or had he, for the first time in his life, acted truly in character? Why did he feel so much at ease with that cadaver? How did he know what to look for? How did he know she'd been dead for half an hour and no more? Why had he squirrelled that book away? He didn't steal books, even unread neglected books gathering dust in a library. He was—scrupulous.

Ratan stood outside while the doctor viewed the body. It didn't take long for him to make his pronouncement.

'Excitement, exertion, sudden death. That's the way it all ends, young man, get your pleasures while you can!'

He made it sound as if Shakuntala had died in the throes of an orgy.

'Cerebral haemorrhage,' he said with relish. 'Bleeding in the brain,' he added for Ratan's edification. 'Old case of hypertension.'

It was past nine when Ratan reached home.

Arjun had fallen into an exhausted sleep. Ratan checked the bedclothes and the catheter, and emptied the urine bag. He let his father sleep on without dinner.

He called Prema.

Gone out, her brother said.

'Why tonight of all nights?' Ratan asked angrily. 'Don't you know the city's about to explode?'

'She doesn't have to ask your permission,' her brother said.

'Who is it, Vivek?' he heard Prema ask.

Ratan hung up, relieved by the sound of her voice.

He was worn out, but his brain bristled with questions. He checked on his father once more and went to the balcony to sit out the hours till dawn.

The streetlights winked out. The road became a guess in the dark. Night swirled over the fringes and erased the city. Nandanvan slept.

Ratan had been on the balcony for hours. His headache had intensified. He'd fought the desire to make himself a sandwich. He was rid of that phase of compulsive eating to block out pain. It didn't work. Nothing worked. The pain kept up its nagging monologue. They were sealed in together, Ratan and the pain, in the tight confines of his skull.

The anglepoise lamp spilt its light wide of the page. He had thought of getting himself one of those booklights, advertised as the ultimate luxury for late-night readers. Right now, finances didn't allow any luxuries. Still, the light was bad, or perhaps his eyes were just tired.

He opened Lockwood Kipling's book.

There was something breathless about the title, as if the writer intended an exposé.

Beast And Man In India

A Popular Sketch Of Indian Animals In Their Relations With The People

He opened the book at random and began reading.

The Hindu worships the cow, and as a rule is reluctant to take the life of any animal except in sacrifice. But that does not preserve the ox, the horse, and the ass from being unmercifully beaten, over-driven, overladen, under-fed, and worked with sores under their harness; nor does it save them from abandonment to starvation when unfit for work, and to a lingering death which is made a long torture by birds of prey, whose beaks, powerless to kill outright, inflict undeserved torment.

Lockwood, evidently, had turned his title inside out. This was a sketch of the Indian people and their relations with animals.

Ratan frowned. He could do without a lecture now, and

it was growing harder to read. Words steamed and blurred on the yellow page. Oddly enough, the paper looked newer than it had earlier. More ivory than yellow, smooth, and only very slightly foxed. He couldn't keep up with Lockwood's indignation just now. He turned back to the dedication.

The glyph stared up defiantly, but the words engaged him first.

To the Other Three

Lockwood's family?

He knew not a thing about Lockwood Kipling.

He laughed at the thought.

His laugh was bitter, sarcastic, inexplicable. It unnerved him and plunged him into a sulphurous cavern of pain. His head roared. His eyes blinked out. His ears were lanced through with red-hot wire. Then, just as abruptly, he was past it. All that remained was a puddle of nausea.

And Prema's voice, sighing patiently.

'What a fuss, Ratan! Nobody dies of migraine, you know.'

Fuck you, he thought angrily. And wished he could.

These headaches terrified him.

She couldn't guess it wasn't the pain that frightened him. She had no idea of what came after.

He betrayed himself occasionally, by mentioning a strange name, or street or direction. She always pounced on these betrayals.

'Which world are you living in? *Laut aao*, Ratan.'

She would wave inanely before his eyes as if to sweep away a fog that blinded him.

The recollection saddened him.

How was she to know there wasn't any fog? It was at moments like these that the veil was lifted, and he actually *saw*.

He'd kept this knowledge from her, as he had from everyone else. His reading indicated it was some precious form of epilepsy. He let that ride. Neurologists were best avoided. They'd dope him with lithium, carbamazepine, amitriptylene, whatever was the newest hell in pharmacology. He wasn't going to befuddle himself with drugs.

Did it matter so much, seeing differently?

It did.

It mattered a lot. It mattered to him. He needed those rare inexplicable glimpses of another existence. He needed them as consolation. Fantasy or epilepsy, hallucination or daydream, was a name required? It was just there in his head, and he needed it.

The Other Three

He knew their names, of course. He just couldn't remember them right now because the headache was beginning another slow cruise along the inside of his face. Enough of that!

Ratan returned to the page. The glyph glared at him. Tiger or leopard, Lockwood seemed to have appropriated it as a heraldic device. It represented him – or the four of them: Lockwood and the other three.

The drawing was a rebus. The markings on the animal were words. A poem perhaps? Urdu, Persian or Arabic? He had no way of telling.

Ratan's eyes were playing tricks again. The animal on the page skewed first one way, then the other. He narrowed his eyes to a chink. The thick black lines smeared, then turned grainy, the grains growing infinitesimal shadows, like cytoplasm seen in an electron micrograph. Every one of those grains throbbed, each a scintilla of life. He told himself he was crazy, and rubbed his eyes.

When he opened his eyes again, everything was different.

When he opened his eyes again, everything was different.

The air was clear and new-washed. The glyph had zoomed into focus, its markings hard and smooth and black as wrought iron. Leopard or tiger, it looked as if it had paused, ever so briefly, in mid-stride, tail quivering in a quick arc of irritation.

The words atop the glyph gleamed like a secret:

To the Other Three.

He said their names aloud, with ease, his father's first:

Krishnarao Oak.
Darayus Dhanji 'Surveyor'.
Shaikh Mohsin Ahmad.

A whiff of newness rose off the page as his fingertip pleasured the paper. A reprint, then!

From last year, 1896.

The People's Press, Lahore.

Appa was one of the Other Three, included in the ironic message.

Ramratan called the glyph the Sign of Four. Mohsin Chacha had relished that irony when he returned the novel last week.

'Sign of Four? Very appropriate. Lockwood would have liked to be numbered among Conan Doyle's "two hundred thousand black devils" I can tell you!'

That was true. Mr Kipling's sympathies had been with the sepoys when he'd got Mohsin Chacha to draw the glyph for his book.

'Mohsin, write something appropriate. Something,

anything, to end this hate. One people, one nation. One for all, all for one.'

But Mohsin Chacha hadn't quite seen the Four as Dumas' musketeers. Perhaps he'd felt a certain injury that Mr Kipling had overlooked. For certain, he had encrypted more than words in his calligraphy.

Ramratan remembered the day he first saw the glyph. They were in the narrow verandah of Mohsin Chacha's house. The high stained-glass skylights scattered gems over the sheet of paper. The ink wasn't quite dry yet.

Mohsin Chacha's wit was ironic when mild, vicious when provoked. He had read the Persian words out mildly, the very gentleness of tone making an indulgence of courtesy.

Appa had narrowed his eyes, but said nothing. Darayus Surveyor had smiled. Ramratan had wondered if its irony would be lost on Mr Kipling.

Mr Kipling knew no Persian, and Mohsin Chacha would not translate.

'The leopard won't change its spots, will it, Mohsin?' was all that Mr Kipling said.

That was more than twenty years ago, when Mohsin Chacha could decapitate a man with one slash of his pen.

These days, Mohsin Chacha's inkpot and pens were laid out every morning, a scroll of parchment kept on the ready. Most days, he ignored them and read instead. His trembling fingers could do little more than turn the page, too slowly for eyes that devoured every scrap of print hungrily.

He would not let them draw his couch into the shade.

'I will be cool enough by and by.'

Most mornings, he drowsed in a shroud of sunlight, waiting to die.

Mohsin Chacha was the last of the Other Three. Darayus and Appa had died within months of each other. There had been no word from Lockwood.

'He has other loyalties now,' Mohsin Chacha remarked. 'Pity the man who has a famous son! He is dead already. Bury him quickly, lest he offend the nostrils of the fastidious great! Allah has been merciful to me. All my children are nonentities.'

Ramratan found himself irritated by the old man's cruel wit. He had no affection for Mohsin, holding his arrogance in contempt. He visited him every week for Appa's sake. The old man waited for these visits because Ramratan brought him the latest novels from the Native General Library at Dhobi Talao.

Mohsin Chacha had 'retired' from the Four after his friends died. Bilal would stand in his stead. Bilal was very different from his father.

Ramratan kept to the covenant out of respect for his father. It seemed childish to him; grown men swearing to a brotherhood.

An unlikely band.

Lockwood Kipling, Krishnarao Oak, Mohsin Ahmad, Darayus Surveyor.

Artist, scholar, calligrapher, geologist.

What made them brothers? Ramratan had never thought to ask, and Appa had never thought to tell. It was a given.

And now they were the Other Three. Bilal, Nusser and Ramratan. Mrs Kipling had given Ramratan three copies of the book. By this act she transferred their fathers' burden onto them.

Mr Kipling still kept his place, but at a distance. Till his death, Bilal, Nusser and Ramratan were locked with him in the promise their fathers had made.

It was a simple pact: to stop hate. No matter where, no matter why, they had sworn to stop it.

And after Mr Kipling? It wouldn't be Joseph, or Rudyard as he styled himself these days. Not him, certainly.

It was strange meeting Mrs Kipling after all these years. Twenty years? Twenty-one? She looked just the same as the day he'd first seen her in the studio, with the book of drawings...

Ramratan shook off the memory impatiently.

It was nearly 2 a.m. Time to set out.

At the thought of the silver Raleigh awaiting him at the gate, an exultant laugh rose to his lips. He stifled it quickly for fear of waking Yashoda.

Night lapped him, soft, cool and mildly damp, a flower, grape-skinned, its depth concealed in the bloom of moonlight.

Yashoda grumbled about this early shift and he'd done the decent thing with a token curse or two, but the truth was, he couldn't have asked for anything better.

Since the plague broke out, torn between hospital and home, he got no time for himself. His need for solitude shamed him. It was a selfishness he couldn't quite suppress. The early shift was the perfect solution. He did not need to be at the wharf till 4 a.m. when the first boats came in. Take half an hour for travel, it still left him with an hour and a half to himself.

The bicycle's steel struck a chill, and he rubbed his hand briskly against the tree to warm it. Appa's tree, the last one he had planted.

After planting trees all over the city, he'd realized his own gate stood unshaded. By then he was too ill to make the trip to the nursery, so Ramratan had brought the sapling home.

'Not a good choice,' Appa said thoughtfully. 'Shallow roots, large trunk, heavy canopy. But so beautiful! Grows fast too.'

He called it by its Latin name always. *Samanea saman*. Seldom raintree and never ever monkeypod. He considered the last an insult.

The tree was strong-shouldered now, adolescent and unruly, but showing already a glimpse of adult grace in the reach of its canopy.

Ramratan wheeled out his bike and swung into the saddle. He pedalled furiously, then leaned on the handlebars and let the wind take him.

The darkness changed.

Grey was dismantled within seconds. Submerged colour gleamed from dark silhouettes, revealing shapes. Walls turned rose and old gold. Edges of cracking plaster glistened metallic in the moonlight, marking enamelled patterns in brick and stone. In elbows, in crevices, secret flicks of moss held gold dust in their soft nap. The road was a lake of molten glass, a rainbow trapped in its depths. On pavements, sleeping figures turned marmoreal, their rags assuming the pointless excess of classical drapery. Branches, bathed in lamplight, shone like oiled skin. Banyans trailed tangled tresses over knotty toes. Even the scaly flagstones were silvered over like mackerels.

Ramratan was used to this change in vision.

It had begun as a teenage exercise, an attempt to possess the luscious tints of a world he had glimpsed in Mrs Kipling's sketchbook. But it had overreached itself. It had become second nature, a gorgeous retreat his vision could assume at will, when he tired of the landscape of death.

Bombay had become one vast mortuary over the last six months, and he, its overworked mortician. The dull air hid the piercings of grief like a vast pincushion smothering the city. Death roamed, a hungry dog sniffing out hunger and poverty.

The Sarkar knew exactly where the blame lay. The poor were responsible. They were filthy. Clean them up! Tear off the roofs, spray the houses, knock down walls, dig up floors, whisk them away to die among strangers. Erase them.

Twenty thousand had been erased so far. Twice that number had fled the city, some dying of hunger and exhaustion on the way.

With February came the backlash. An army of skeletons had invaded the city. They came from villages obliterated by hunger. Famine besieged the vast volcanic surge of the Deccan. Madras was a charnel house, with more than a million dead. Those who could still move, walked. With nothing but hope to fuel their muscles, they walked. They walked here, to Bombay, and spilled over pavements and hid in the crevices of the city.

They had walked here. Now they died here.

*Two hundred thousand blackdevils.*That's how the British see us, Ramratan thought. Not just Conan Doyle, but every man jack of them.

With General Gatacre's arrival, some measure of sanity had been enforced. The mindless exercise of authority had given way to some sort of strategy. Ramratan had his doubts, but at least there was a plan. He'd been posted to the wharf a month ago. He was one of the hundred doctors deputed to examine the predawn ferry traffic of farmers and tradesmen for telltale signs of plague.

It would be noon when he returned to the hospital. He would head straight for the mortuary and count the dead. Who were they? What had their lives contained? Everything was cancelled by that last exhalation.

It was as if they had never been.

He dismounted and propped his bicycle against a tree. He walked up the bridge and leaned over the railing.

A cold breeze smote him to the heart.

A cold breeze smote him to the heart.

His headache lifted, and Ratan was surprised to find himself on an empty street. It took him a moment to get his bearings. He was at the Victoria Terminus, on the pavement outside the Arts College, wheeling his bike into a small lane. He had no idea how he had got there. Surprisingly, that didn't worry him. He felt relieved, as if he had just surmounted a difficulty. Or reached a destination.

Yes, that was it—he had come here because he was meant to.

He parked his bike and swung over a low wall. That too, he was meant to do. He no longer questioned what seemed to come by instinct. He was in the college grounds now. He walked briskly towards where he was meant to go.

Shakuntala Salwe's cottage glowered ahead, a baleful yellow light flattening the windowpanes. The son was finding it difficult to sleep. Or perhaps was too sleepy or too drunk to switch off the light. Ratan wondered what the cottage felt like with its owner gone, but he wasn't headed that way. He walked away from it towards the anonymous brick wall that made up the back of another low cottage. Not a cottage exactly, this was a longer building, built like a military barracks. A long corridor, roofed and walled with zinc sheeting, led from the barracks towards what Ratan, in the diffused street light, could only identify as the back of a building. Ratan walked around the building—and was suddenly trapped in a garish fluorescent glare.

He shaded his eyes hastily. The abrupt transit from almost complete darkness to blinding white light had loosed a sharp lance of pain through his eyes. The angle of the building had cut off the light completely at the bobchee connah.

The *what?*

Bobchee connah.

The words returned.

Ratan realized the voice was not his.

It was a woman's voice. Lilting, British, aspirating the hard consonant.

BobcheeCAWnnah.

Ratan dismissed it as nonsense.

He was now facing the building. It was brightly illuminated by two fluorescent tube-lights rigged up on a tree trunk. The light streamed onto the house-front, striking it just above the verandah's overhang with a markedly surreal effect. The building, poised on a springy mat of grass, seemed buoyant, afloat on a lake of dark matter.

It seemed cut off from the rest of the universe. The startling nakedness of bamboo and barbed wire defined the permissible limits of vision.

A wooden bungalow, painted green. A stolen fragment of the hills, magicked here in the midst of Bombay's mad colonial gothic. The rusty fountain before him was dry, of course, but he remembered what a thrill its fine spray had been in May.

Till Mr Kipling turned it off because—

Ratan stopped in mid-thought.

He needed to clear his head. It was hunger, lack of sleep, exhaustion. Or, the aura of his next dislocative trance.

He walked into the empty bungalow.

The door opened at his touch.

He entered a small square room, its dimensions barely visible once he'd shut the door behind him. A scatter of light came in through the carved lintel of the verandah, and struck the skylights in the high walls. Ratan's eyes accommodated slowly as if they were unused to greyness. Beyond the square room was a raised dining area that gave on to the passage. He remembered a clever turn and a staircase.

Yes, it was right here. If you didn't know about it, you walked into a bathroom. But with previous knowledge you'd find yourself here, on the wooden staircase with a single volute to it, and soon you were at the two marble panels that Mohsin had painted for Mr Kipling—a rather glum floral design, half-hearted.

The marble panels were slopped over with whitewash. Ratan couldn't see them in the murk. His hand felt for them just next to the door. Their coolness answered his questing fingertips briefly, quickly replaced by the abrasive sting of lime.

Then he was there, in the vast glass-walled studio on that drowsing May afternoon…

Then he was there, in the vast glass-walled studio on that drowsing May afternoon…

Nearly time for cricket, but Mr Kipling had asked him to wait.

There was a drawing pinned to the easel, a pencil sketch of women at a well. The air held a faint smell of paint. It was hot outside, yet the house was cool.

Sunlight filtered in through the carved wooden trellis, curled as ferns, and spattered as leaves on the smooth red floor. It filigreed a pattern on his bare feet that shifted when he twiddled his toes. It was a good room for a game—big, and with very little furniture.

You could get a good lift to the cricket ball, the ceiling was quite high. He couldn't imagine Mr Kipling agreeing, though Appa might. If Ai weren't around.

Ramratan didn't want Mr Kipling to return quickly. He wanted to see how long it took for the patterns to change on his feet if he turned into a statue, into black glassy basalt stone.

'Ram Ratan?'

He didn't turn at once because that was not his name.

'Bad sheep,' he translated.

For that's what it sounded like: *Ram Rotten*.

Years later, when he remembered his first meeting with Mrs Kipling, the irony stung him. By then Joseph Baba had written his famous *J'accuse* in which he called himself Black Sheep. Yet, in 1870, at the height of Black Sheep's troubles (if the story were true) it was Ramratan his mother greeted by that name.

'Ram Ratan.'

It couldn't be put off.

He turned to make that quick bob of the head which passed for a bow. When he caught sight of her, his greeting changed to something easier and heartfelt.

He greeted her as he greeted his elders. He steepled his palms against his chest and bowed. It was done before he knew it.

He stepped back looking around wildly for retreat. But he couldn't get her out of his sight.

She was a skein of sunlight, a white woman in a white dress, her dark hair concealed within a white cap. There was a laugh in her eyes that caught his suppressed grin unawares, so it slipped out and the breeze licked his teeth.

What did she say after?

Did it matter? Ramratan forgot it all in the next few minutes because she was gone, leaving a book of sketches on the table.

'Take a look at these sketches while you're waiting,' she said.

Ramratan opened the book while her eyes were still on him, knowing with resentment that she would have read his action as obedience. His mother would have recognized it as politeness.

He had been aware for some years now of that wide difference in point of view.

At school, Mr Mackintosh had made things clear to the first form. 'Indians are docile and passive. Their natures have been subdued and softened by the tropical sun. The Englishman is naturally high-spirited and enterprising. If Indian boys score better marks in examinations, we must conclude that it is not by any measure of intelligence, but solely through their innate willingness to be instructed. The Indian is invaluable in taking orders and carrying them out, making him Her Majesty's most obedient subject. Do you understand that, Mister Oak?'

'Perhaps you don't like sketching, Ram Ratan?'

She broke into his sullen memory of that last day of school when Mr Mackintosh read out the marks.

'Ram Ratan?'

'Don't!'

The word was out. A pebble of hate catapulted from the rage stretched to snapping in his chest.

'Don't take my name if you don't know how to say it!'

And she was gone, leaving him with a sick and hammering heart swelling with reproach. He couldn't possibly leave now.

Ramratan looked down at the open book.

A book of sketches, she'd said.

These weren't sketches.

Sketches, as Ramratan knew them, were what Mr Kipling drew. Rapid pencil drawings or tediously shaded ones, dull as the lead employed to make them. He looked up quickly, and then returned to the book. He would never be able to look away again.

Colour seized him. Enclosed him. Bit with sharp scarlet teeth and tugged. And something in his heart came loose, beaded with blood.

Red opened its flower. From its vermilion frill to its cerise heart through a swirl of reds—cardinal, carnation, carnelian, carmine, crimson. Satin unfurled, shiny and dense, a slither on the skin that made him gasp. Then further agape, a silken billow, a swell of red blown thin, left glistening in the air to harden, a glass bubble through which the sun came in and inked the skin pink. When he blinked, it splintered and scattered in pink shards. Pink petals, turned vermeil at the edges, enamelled jewels.

Green drooped. It quelled its sunlit spaces into a scabbard of darkness till a sudden torque of the brush betrayed a shining trim of gold. Then green was everywhere, a disapproving sentinel, ribbed, veined, jointed, scaled, a chameleon guarding this tract of hues, its own rainbow clenched deep within its skin.

Everything was lit with the gold slant of evening. Skin was neither brown nor white, not pink nor black, but awash with light, wet, soft and tense as an oiled haunch. Mud was not gravel or clay, rock or boulder, but shavings of light scattered on crumbled leaf mould, red-gold, fragrant. Wood was porous, aerated and buoyant with light, and yet the sun stayed unseen.

Blue was everywhere, raised in song.

Fearfully, he touched the paper.

It was only paper, rough to the fingertip. His skin remained unstained.

Ramratan rubbed his eyes and turned a page.

Once more colour suffused him, this time in a whisper that thrummed an echo through his bones.

Everything was the same, yet everything was changed.

Colour was submerged beneath a film of marble, a clean polished table of marble, milky, murky, with a faint breath of grey and pink and blue clouding its thickness. Interred beneath were the bones of colour. Red fading into rose, revealing a stilled blue heart as it paled to ash. Green thinned to a leaf stain. Brown grown ancient as memory, a forgotten page in a lost book.

And blue? Blue that once sang with a rose in its throat? Blue shuddered from grey to flaky white, calcined beyond whiteness into a brightness of extinction.

Ramratan shut the book.

The pictures had fled from his head, but the colours had stained his soul.

'Ram Ratan?'

She had returned. Her voice now was careful as glass.

Ramratan felt the hot rush of tears. He looked up, once, and then she caught him, quickly, to her unfamiliar warmth, and let him go.

When he straightened up, and all the crooked twisted places inside him were at ease again, he heard her voice.

'Well? Did I get it right this time, Ramratan?'

She had.

It wasn't Rum Rotten either.

She caught his smile and laughed. She perched on a stool and opened the book.

'Did you find the sketches interesting?'

He was lost for words.

'My brother Edward's an artist—my sister's husband, Ned Jones. Such a common name for such an uncommon talent, don't you think?'

Ned Jones.

Yesterday he would have thought it a joke name, like John Smith. Now it was a prism. A colourless pyramid of glass that concealed and constrained all the colour in the world.

He sneezed.

He sneezed.

The room was dusty, but not as if it had been shut up for months. It was chill, too. That helped. His head felt clearer now, his eyes had stopped hurting. There was nothing to see here anyway.

The rooms behind were tall and ghostly, with a pink tinge to the grey walls. Ratan did not linger. He walked down the shaded passage to the bobcheecawnah, which was locked, as expected. He walked past Shakuntala's cottage, swung over the wall and was back on his bike within minutes. He revved up and roared off, his mind as blank and grey as the meandering road. When he whizzed through Agripada, a flare of torchlight glowed beyond the tall shrug of sleeping buildings. Ratan did not notice it. Nothing registered but the damp air and the vacuum in his head, in his soul.

As he turned into the lane, voices carried in the still air. Ratan recognized the Nepali watchman's hectoring bark pitted against Jafar's thin protest. There were people crouched in the shadows along the wall. Only Jafar stood out in the neon at the gate.

'What's happening, Jafar?'

At the sound of Ratan's voice, Jafar left the gate and came running. Ratan realized the man was close to tears. He killed the engine, trying to stifle the irritation the watchman provoked in him.

'Ratan Bhai, I have to open my laundry.'

Jafar's steady voice betrayed an iron discipline, yet his face wore incomprehensible defeat.

Jafar's laundry, located in the basement of Nandanvan, opened daily at 7 a.m. It was now five minutes to four.

Shadows detached themselves from the wall. Ratan recognized them as Jafar's family. Each carried a bundle.

'Come on, then.'

Ratan walked ahead to the gate. The watchman barred his way.

'Siplani Shaab has forbidden—'

'Forbidden me from entering my house? Is he mad? Or has a mad dog bitten you, Bahadur?'

Ratan pushed the watchman aside roughly and blocked him with his bike.

'Come on, Jafar, tell them to hurry up. I want the clothes ready by ten. Get your laundry going.'

Jafar's family moved in silently. Fear gagged them, even the children did not whimper. Jafar hurried to unlock the laundry, and they followed him in quickly. Ratan stayed a moment longer to confront Bahadur.

'I don't know, these are my orders,' Bahadur said sullenly. 'You can ask Siplani Shaab if you wish.'

'This is not Siplani's building. That laundry is Jafar's property. He has as much right to come in at 4 a.m. as I have. Go and wake up Siplani and tell him I want to talk with him.'

The watchman grinned uneasily. He wouldn't risk Siplani's ire by ringing his doorbell at four in the morning.

Ratan went into the laundry and shut the door behind him. Jafar's wife had pulled out some sheets from their bundles and was putting the little ones to sleep. The two older children, bleary with sleep and dread, cowered against their father.

Jafar lived in the lane behind Nandanvan. He had a small one-room flat above Banarsi Halwai. That side of the lane housed emigrants from Banaras and its surrounding villages. Jafar was from Banaras too, but now the lane had disowned him.

'Last night at ten o'clock, Jehangir from the Halwai knocks on my door. When I let him in, I see he's out of breath and shaking like a sick dog. "Run, Chacha!" he tells me. "Take the children and run! I just came in for a moment to tell you, I'm on my way out—'

'"What's happened?" I ask. "Sit down boy, think with a cool head. Who is after you?"

'"Chacha, the whole mohalla, the whole country is after us! I heard them talking in the rasoi."

'"In the rasoi? Did you tell Birju?" That is Brijnath. We call him Birju. He is the owner's son, about Jehangir's age. Jehangir hung his head and I understood it was Birju he had overheard.

'"What did he say then?" I asked.

'Birju had said a mandir had been broken in Dongri, and now it was war. Birju said they had to keep the mohalla safe. They didn't want troublemakers. Troublemakers! That is what they call us now, after destroying our masjid with their bare hands. They will burn our houses and kill us if we do not leave by sunset, Jehangir said. I tried to keep the boy with me, but he panicked and ran. I don't know where he's gone. Ratan Bhai, all day I asked myself, who are these people who will smash a masjid? I have lived with Hindus all my life, and I have never known one who will even think to do that. But now?'

Jafar made a gesture of hopelessness and sat down heavily.

Ratan, counted among the accused, felt the oppression of hate.

'The people in the mohalla are all dehati, they will listen to any nonsense. Forget them!' Jafar's wife said uneasily.

Jafar turned away.

'You saw that watchman. You heard what he said about Siplani Sahib. What will he say when he finds us here?'

'This is your property, Jafar. You own this space. You are registered with this housing society. Nobody can ask you to leave.'

'And if they do? Where will I go? Where will I take my children?'

His composure gave way.

'If that happens, come up to the third floor. That's your address till your house is safe for you again. Anyway, Jafar, send the children upstairs when they wake up. They can play there. No school today, I guess.'

Jafar nodded and walked with Ratan to the lift.

'We escaped Partition. Was it a sin that we weren't born then?' Jafar asked. 'Do we have to pay for that now? Do we have to pay for not knowing hate?'

Ratan was silent. In his experience, one always paid for refusing hate.

Ratan let himself in. The flat breathed with comfort. Ratan looked in on his father. Arjun was asleep, his face relaxed, eased of the lines that etched the diurnal efforts of his living. What joyous country did he roam within his eyelids? For one brief moment, Ratan wished himself there.

He was too tired to eat—hunger, though, ate into him. He barely had his clothes off when he toppled into bed and was dead to the day.

7 December 1992

Morning brought no truce. Ratan woke at six, still at war with himself. Those vivid drawings still beat in his memory as he staggered to the bathroom, half asleep. Not even the grey air of dawn could leach their exuberance. For one mad moment he wanted to retreat into that rich psychedelia, give in to that tug of colour intent on turning him inside out.

Ned Jones?

He knew no artist of that name. It was all a joke. His brain had made it up, just as it had made up the rest of those names and given them faces.

A tumour, then! The unseen projectionist within his skull, sitting crouched under some jutting overhang of brain, hallucinating in IMAX. The temporal lobe, most likely.

The thought didn't frighten him. It was—interesting.

It was a paradox. It meant death, but announced itself by gifting him a new life. How far into that alternative existence could the tumour push him? Would death simply mean he stopped fighting it, stopped pulling back, and toppled headlong into luxuriant colour?

He needed to check it out, of course. But not now. Not just yet.

Ratan stalled halfway through the simple act of making his father's tea. What would Arjun do if Ratan died? It was not to be thought of. Not now.

He made a cup of coffee for himself and carried the two mugs to Arjun's bedside.

His father was awake, waiting for the hot tea to thaw his frozen hands. Ratan tucked a towel around his neck and raised his pillows. The slurp of his father's first sip of tea returned him to childhood, to that first-day-of-the-vacation feeling.

Eager, anticipant, a little fearful, it was the sound of the air in an empty room waiting for you to enter and claim it. It was a weak susurrus, an indrawn breath, a gasp, quickly cut off by the silence of absolute pleasure. His own enjoyment of coffee was nothing quite like this.

Arjun Oak drained the cup and shut his eyes preparatory to the first movement of his day. This first was always the most difficult and always the same. He raised one hand to touch his son. Ratan had learned only very recently to read that touch. He answered it now.

'Monday, 7 December 1992. It's 6:15 in the morning. Your name is Arjun Oak and I am your son Ratan. This is your home, 303, Nandanvan Apartments.'

Arjun nodded slowly, storing away the information to navigate his day.

Ratan got the chores sorted. Planning Arjun's meals took thought. He checked the fridge. They were low on fruit and vegetables, it meant a trip to the market on his way home from work.

After Arjun fell ill, Ratan's life had changed.

He'd given up his job as a hospital microbiologist. Now he was a freelance bug detector. He went where he was called, did what he could, took what they paid him. A humiliation, really, after two years of having had his own lab. It was no sort of living, and downhill all the way. At thirty-six, even without a brain tumour, his life was over. Might as well enjoy this spooky other-life while he could. Cash was close. If Prema filed for divorce he would have to eke out alimony as well. He had to find something else to do. Fast.

His first job that morning was at MedLine, a small lab off Bombay Central. He didn't have to get there till afternoon. Nagpada next—he stopped in mid-thought, remembering those flares on his way back. The enormity of what had happened yesterday hit him.

He switched on the TV and caught a rerun of the BBC footage. Coffee bubbled up in his throat, burning with acid, acrid with shame.

How many they were! Thousands, a lakh or more, a smear of saffron against a sullen sky. And that tired old mosque looking bewildered at so much attention. He barely heard the words. The saffron rush in the background became inseparable from the prurient gleam in the newsreader's eye. *Savages. Heathens.* But it was a man's voice he heard. Mr Mackintosh took over the news from the pert British blonde. *Left to herself, India will smash herself to smithereens.*

No, that wasn't what the television was saying.

The saffron tide peaked and broke in a spatter of blood drops on the grey stone as tiny figures swarmed the three domes. They made streaks of red on the basalt, like blood they stained the smoky sky. They stood out, little stick figures, men without faces or names, swinging toy hammers, taking potshots at history. It was laughable. What dent could they make on the immense solidity of those domes? They were schoolboys carving graffiti with each widening crevice, carving magic obscenities, compelled by the unbearable lust of hate.

Did they realize there was no prey beneath their scrabbling claws? That they were breaking stones, not gods or prophets?

Incredibly, under those tapping toy hammers, the massive domes caved in. All three of them.

The crowd roared. Death was in their throats. The circus raged on.

The sun set, uncaring, as it ever has over bloodier plains.

There were close-ups of jubilant faces, spewing hatred. The utter stupidity of it all appalled him. Lakhs of people harried from their homes, dissociated from the lives they lived, all gathered in the camera's leer. What were they here for? What kind of madness drew them?

Religion irked Ratan. He couldn't stand the exuberance of temples, the stern austerity of mosques, the exaltation of churches. They were spaces that had cancelled their own meaning. But this—this had nothing to do with any kind of religion. This was about something more personal.

No man in that crowd had the faith of his fathers.

His faith was private, like DNA, a conviction so complex and so inscrutable it could be read by no other mind except his own. It excluded everything. It permitted no ethic. It transcended logic. It was anger, hunger, lust, and grief. It was beyond definition. It simply was. It was hate. There was no before or after, it was the moment. Some ancient door in the brain swung wide, and the darkness that streamed out was reptilian, older than reason, colder than thought.

Ratan debated the wisdom of telling his father the news. When he did, Arjun raised a trembling hand to his head, as if summoning a memory. His eyes scorched Ratan's face, commanding his son to voice the words that eluded him.

'Baba, I went into Lockwood's bungalow yesterday.'

Slowly, Arjun's intensity receded. He leaned back in his wheelchair. He was ready to listen.

Ratan began describing the empty bungalow, but he faltered.

'Baba, I want to check some facts,' he said urgently.

Arjun waited, alert.

'Was there a tree at the gate?'

Where?

'Not here—maybe in the house where you grew up?'

No.

That's right. Ratan knew there wasn't. His father had grown up in a chawl.

'But your father's house, where he grew up? That was different, right?'

Arjun smiled.

It was the veriest tremor of his mouth, but a wave of pleasure swept his face.

You loved your grandfather's house, I know. You've told me—

Had he? Ratan wasn't certain. Perhaps he'd read it as a boy from the look of longing on his father's face. Arjun's father had been a millworker. He had grown up hating those cement chawls, the communal way of life.

'There was a tree at the gate of your grandfather's house.'

Yes.

'A raintree. *Samanea saman*. He hated anyone calling it monkeypod.'

Surprise erupted past Arjun's confused muscles. One of the fallouts of his illness was that the facial muscles were pulled awry. It had taken Ratan months to work out these distortions of emotion. He still got it wrong sometimes.

Yes! Yes! How did you know?

'And your grandfather's name was Ramratan Oak?'

Yes.

'And he knew Lockwood Kipling?'

No! Not him.

'He knew Rudyard Kipling?'

A sneer contorted Arjun's mouth.

'I know. I've always loathed the guy. But what about Alice?'

As he put the question to Arjun, Ratan shivered.

Alice! How did he know her name?

'Alice Kipling?' he asked. 'Did your grandfather know her?'

Arjun's face shut the door. He was not playing this game any more. He made a slight movement to indicate he wanted to be left alone.

Ratan put off his plan. He would show him the glyph some other time.

By ten he was ready to leave. He looked in on Jafar on his way out.

Jafar was at the ironing table, intent on his job, his face expressionless. Shakira came out. Ratan held his keys out to her.

Usually, he depended on Jafar to keep an eye on his father. Would the arrangement hold today?

Jafar's household had adapted quickly. A kitchen had evolved around the small hotplate. The small toilet was noisy with the splashy sound of children bathing. Their basic needs were met. Jafar's face indicated it was enough.

'Go upstairs, Bhabhi,' Ratan said. 'Take the children with you.'

'For how long?'

The scorn in her voice quashed him. She spat, aiming at Ratan's foot.

Jafar reached out and took the keys from Ratan roughly.

'Don't mind her, Ratan Bhai. I'll send Salma and Faraz upstairs. They'll look after Baba. You carry on. Where to, today?'

'Nagpada. MedLine. Mondays twelve to four.'

'Be careful, Bhai. Just do your work and get home.'

Ratan stopped at the corner stall for fruit and vegetables. He brought a second lot for Jafar's family, some bread, eggs, two cartons of milk. He doubled back to Nandanvan, pushed the two lots across the laundry counter. Jafar thanked him with a look so quick that Ratan caught no more than a sheen of anger or of tears. The next instant Jafar was intent on ironing again, the ropy muscles of his shoulder and arms bunched with unnecessary strain.

'Tell Santa Cruz to stay home today,' Jafar said in a low voice without looking up.

Ratan winced.

Santa Cruz was Jafar's euphemism for Prema, after she had dumped Ratan. Jafar disliked her, perhaps more for the loss of custom than for any injury she may have done Ratan. Prema was good for at least a hundred rupees worth of ironing every week. Yet Jafar had thought of her safety, and he, Ratan, had not.

He hadn't thought of her once, not since he woke.

At the thought, his headache came roaring back, reminding him that Prema had no place in his new alternative life. A face flashed tantalizingly, and dissolved in the haze of headache. He stopped at a paan shop and used the phone.

'Prema?'

'Yeah. Yeah. Gimme a moment—'

She blocked the receiver and kept up an argument in animated Gujarati. Eventually, after he'd fed two more rupee coins into the slot, he got her attention.

'Ratan? Tell me.'

He felt that insane surge of anger which filled him when she used phrases like 'Tell me' and 'Bol', as if he were one of her vast coterie of buddies—non-denominational, asexual, non-committal nonentities.

'There's nothing to tell. Just be careful when you go out today, okay? Better still, don't go out at all.'

Prema was on her way out, he figured. She took the 10:40 fast to Dadar, and changed there to the Harbour Line.

'Yeah, I'm not going. Cyrus said better not. You know what these Muslims are like.'

She spoke into his silence.

'Cyrus says they'll be roaming about with Rampuris today, better stay home he said. First thing this morning he came here, you know. I was hardly up and there he was. He spoke to Daddy.'

Ratan heard his voice say, 'Okay, bye.'

What kind of words were these? Okay, bye, hi, tell me, bol? Why bother to say them? Why bother to say anything?

He spat, like Jafar's wife.

The roads were busy as usual, everybody rushing, everybody late. He had a vision of this mad race: all making it gaspingly to the finishing post, only to turn back on their heels, or wheels, and staggering back again. What did this crazed pendulum of a city measure, what demented scale of time or space? Perhaps an unseen clock, a grandfather clock, a Rajabai Tower weightless in ether, Magritte-like, hovered overhead. Who was watching it? A break in the clouds might reveal a clutch of curious faces—Allah, Ram, Jesus, Yahweh—jostling for a ringside view of the madness they churned up every day.

Traffic thickened near the Byculla flyover. The market seethed, foul-mouthed and halitotic, with truck drivers crazily trying to park between liquefying mounds of spoilt fruit. The flyover arc past Gloria Church was blissful, but from the summit he saw cars and buses jammed bumper to bumper all the way past the signal. There was no point trying to weave through them, there simply was no space.

At the underpass, as he tried to turn right, a taxiwallah told him to lay off Nagpada. Ratan ignored that and pushed on. As he turned into Nagpada, he found the road cut off with piles of old furniture. A wary group of boys hunkered on either side of this embankment.

Ratan caught sight of Ramzan Ali in the group, and called out to him. The boy conferred hastily with his friends. One of them came to the barricade and waved Ratan in.

'Ramzan Ali says you're a doctor. You can come in, but no trouble, okay?'

'Okay.'

The boys had hockey sticks stacked against a barrel. They looked more frightened than defiant. Very soon, Ratan knew, they too would don the intent look of the kar sevak, that pewter mask of hate. It was inevitable. It infuriated him, this sacrifice of youth at the altar of inherited hate.

He dismounted. It didn't seem right to go roaring down this injured street. He wheeled his bike slowly, suddenly overcome with exhaustion. MedLine was just five minutes away, but the bike seemed too heavy to push. Usually, the road was thick with kids on their way to the afternoon shift at school.

The foyer at MedLine was not vacant as he had expected. The patients looked wary and uncertain. At the desk, Farzana seemed distracted and kept a phone conversation going while answering queries and directing patients. Her usual bright-eyed half smile always made him feel she had a delicious secret, and today was the day she would share it with him.

She was a giggly eighteen, little more than a child. Usually, when she brought in a cup of tea for him at two o'clock, she stayed to talk about her dreams. He sensed she didn't dare tell them at home. They were bent on getting her married next year, if not now. Farzana wanted to study art. Ratan hadn't actually seen anything she'd painted, but he knew he didn't have to. The passion was there. He brought her art books that she stored covertly in his cabin.

Today Farzana's smile died halfway to her eyes.

She greeted him nonetheless, gravely.

A thick package awaited him on the desk, addressed in Farzana's distinctive brush script. He had no need to open it to know all the art books were inside. He laid a hand on the rough bindings and felt for the first time the texture of crumbling stone.

He was a block of black basalt, cracking under a toy hammer wielded by an angry child.

There was no tea at two o'clock. At three, Farzana came in with a tray. There were two cups of tea and a plate of Parle-G biscuits on a lace doily, an unusual mark of refinement. She placed the tray on the table, away from his workbench, and slipped out without meeting his gaze. Anger began a faint tattoo in his occiput.

Rahim came in. He owned the place. The lace doily was for him, not Ratan. They had been friends since college. When Arjun fell ill, Rahim had been the first to remind Ratan that his laboratory needed a microbiologist. Ratan did all his blood work too, though it wasn't strictly part of the deal.

They sipped tea silently, ritualistically—bonobo males, politely presenting their engorged red posteriors as truce.

The word truce is usually misread, Ratan thought. It wasn't so much a halt to war as the moment of calm that marked the commencement of hostilities. This cup of tea was a truce. Rahim never dropped in on him with such ceremony. Something was about to begin.

Ratan was silent. What could he say? His own emotions bewildered him. It irritated him that Rahim and Farzana and Jafar's wife and the boys at the barricade should think his injury was any less than their own. It saddened him that they should equate him with that crazed mob in Ayodhya. It angered him especially that Rahim, who had known him for twenty years, should think so. Rahim hadn't spoken yet, but Ratan knew what he was about to say.

Rahim said it.

'Ratan, finish fast and go home. Get out of Nagpada before four o'clock.'

Rahim was being practical. He wanted Ratan to be safe. But he had presumed that Ratan would be unsafe. Ratan knew that if he stayed on, Rahim would protect him—with his life, if it came to that. If he stayed, he would be an embarrassment to Rahim. He would have to be explained. Neither of them wanted that. Subtly, through this very kindness, Rahim had laid down barbed wire between them. Ratan wanted to cry out. Can we not fight this together? Can we not weep together?

Aloud he said, 'I'm done for the day. Is a morcha planned for four o'clock?'

Rahim shrugged.

'Frankly, I have no idea. Everybody is upset. There are rumours, multiplying as they fly. People are gathering in little groups in every building. Some say the women will march with black banners, and the men will gherao the chief minister. That's a big deal. I don't think they will be so organized. They're so angry they will burst out into the streets yelling. They can't be held back for too long. To tell you the truth, I feel like doing so myself, and you know me, Ratan, I am no namaazi.'

'I feel like that too,' Ratan said.

'How can you? How can you possibly feel that, Ratan? No, don't say a word. How can you possibly feel as I do?'

Ratan was silenced. Rahim would never admit that he, Ratan, had equal reason for outrage. Now Ratan had ceased to be Ratan. He was just—*Hindu*. Just as those roaring madmen swarming the masjid were. All Hindu.

'No, I cannot presume to feel what a Mussalman feels,' Ratan said quietly. 'I merely feel what any human being anywhere feels at such an outrage. I feel sadness and anger and desolation.'

'That is what all of you will say now, after having done what you have done. That's all we're going to hear over and over again. Chal, jaane de, Ratan, finish the biscuits, yaar. I'll get Mukhtar to walk with you to Mohammed Ali Road.'

'I'm done. Farzana can type up these reports, I'll leave them here on the desk. And Rahim, don't bother Mukhtar. I still know my way around here.'

Ratan clattered down the stairs, knowing he would never return.

As expected, the road outside the clinic had filled up. Whiteclad men moved around gravely, organizing the rabble. Not a woman in sight. Most of the men were little more than boys. There must have been over a hundred of them. One of them handed Ratan a black band. He tied it on, redeemed by the grace of belonging. Just as swiftly, a boy Ratan vaguely recognized untied it with an apology.

Immediately, he became the focus of their gaze. It was a polite gaze, containing neither anger nor hate. It was the gaze of courtesy. He was being tolerated.

The crowd parted a little and Mukhtar came forward.

'Sah'b, let me take you out of here, don't go the usual way.'

Ratan followed him numbly, wheeling his bike.

'Why not the usual way, Mukhtar Bhai?'

The old man shrugged.

'Gadbad, what else? Some ten fellows decide to hold a morcha and before we know it, everybody is on the road with them. Somebody said, "Chalo Police Chowki, today we will give those havaldars a taste of their own hafta." But we never got to the Chowki. Some goondas had got ahead of us. They dragged out one havaldar and thrashed him. You know these havaldars, Sah'b. They live off the pheriwallas, every week the hafta goes up. All the other havaldars got out through the back door and hid in the mohalla—'

'Where did they hide?'

Mukhtar looked irritated at the interruption.

'Where did they hide? In people's houses, of course! In the building opposite Suleiman Chowki. By then the news had spread and jeeps drove in. That's all I know. Most of us ran away when we saw the jeeps. Sah'b, once the Inspectors come, what strength do we have left?'

It would be safer to go through Bombay Central, Mukhtar said. He left Ratan near Sarvi, the kabab place. The street bore a name that belonged in a nursery rhyme. Ratan noticed the sign for the first time: Dimtimkar Lane.

Ratan got on his bike with relief and sped towards Bombay Central station. On an impulse he decided not to go over the bridge to Tardeo, but swung right past the State Transport Bus Depot into the road towards Maratha Mandir.

He couldn't have made a worse decision. A hundred yards away he caught the fringe of a fleeing crowd. Fifty. Perhaps more. From his vantage it was hard to tell. Dense black clouds billowed over the Bus Depot, giant fungi claiming the sky. All that could be seen of the blaze in the bright afternoon air was a tongue or two of orange.

Within seconds, police jeeps hurtled round the bend. Shots rang out. The road emptied. The crowd dispersed.

He was mistaken. The road was not empty yet.

The jeeps wheeled around and slowly circled the three injured men on the road. Then they revved up and drove off. Shops on either side of the road had downed shutters hastily. Nobody had seen anything.

He rode towards the fallen men. Two of them, both in their twenties, were dead. Shot in the head. The third, shot in the abdomen, was bleeding profusely. Barely conscious, he was moments away from death. He held Ratan's gaze for an instant—and died.

Ratan reached home in a daze. The day had been wiped clean from his brain except for one fact.

Each of those dead men had been shot in a vital spot. And, they had been shot by the police. No tear gas, no lathi charge. All three had been shot above the waist. All three had been left there to die.

Everything else, the insane malevolence of the kar sevaks, the violent act of tearing down the masjid, the alienation he had experienced, everything paled to nothingness beside what he had just witnessed. This wasn't callousness or dereliction of duty. It was murder.

Ratan shut off the day. He went through his chores numbly, caring for Arjun with a quiet efficiency, his mind blank. An ominous headache stopped all thought. He was quick, sure and final in his movements, eager to be rid of the lives of others. There was another life within him, impatient to be claimed, clamouring for release. He held all at bay. There was too much waiting to be done, too much of the last two days still waiting to be understood.

Meanwhile, the pain that had consumed him during his parley with Rahim hadn't let up. It was renewed when he walked past Jafar's laundry and caught sight of the family huddled around a makeshift meal.

He had a skirmish with Siplani on the landing, brief and fierce. If Siplani had anything to say about Jafar's family occupying the laundry, he could say it at the committee meeting, a month away. It was hardly enough to block off further arguments, but the best Ratan could think up short of clobbering the man.

He had just about finished when the phone rang. With the prescience that comes of despair, Ratan knew it would be Prema.

It was.

'You didn't go to Nagpada today, did you?' she asked without preamble.

Life roared back into Ratan.

'It's Monday! Where else would I go?' he answered nonchalantly, keeping elation from his voice, waiting for the wave of pleasure her anxiety would bring.

'Yeah, that's what I told Cyrus. Don't venture out till I've checked with Ratan if it's safe that side of town. Cyrus has this important meeting tomorrow. So what's it like? Can I tell him it's safe?'

Ratan heard his voice answer from a galactic distance.

'No, it isn't safe. Tell him to stay home.'

He should have hung up, but he didn't. The receiver stayed glued to his ear while she nattered on about Cyrus. Then his voice broke in, with words he hadn't planned.

'Prema, do you know anybody in the Bombay Archives?'

'Archives? What do you want with the Archives, Ratan?'

'Stuff someone wanted for the Department—'

'What Department? You're not working for them any more, remember?'

'Yes.'

Why was he doing this?

'Radhakrishnan practically lives there. You know where the place is? Elphinstone College? Same building, first floor. Shall I ask him to call you?'

Ratan let her talk for a while more.

He tried, later, to make sense of these phone conversations.

Mostly, she ran her day past him. Not those larger plans that one calls life, but the small irritations—quirky appliances, missed appointments, confusing protocol, financial snarls, bills lost or unpaid, delayed cheques, coughs, colds, small fevers. Things that had been his responsibility in their life together, things that clearly still belonged to him. Cyrus, he supposed, got the good stuff now, the bargains, the window shopping, the movies she had read about, the plays, the songs, the poems. The dreams.

She had stopped telling him her dreams long before Arjun fell ill. Once she said she had nothing left to dream about. He should have seen it coming then.

That was three years ago. They hadn't been married for six months yet. Surely, she hadn't meant it then.

Had she meant it then?

Ratan was still debating this question when Radhakrishnan called him. Ratan didn't know what to ask him, but he needn't have worried.

'Prema called. Tomorrow? Ask for me when you get there. Ask at the desk. We'll take it from there.'

The man's voice was hurried and harried, there were kids squealing in the background. One of them grabbed the phone and let fly an endless string of gibberish.

'Sorry about that.' The man was back. 'They're totally out of control when I get home.'

'How old is he? Two?'

'Yeah, two. They're all two.'

'All?'

'Three of them. Triplets.'

He didn't sound aggrieved in the least. Ratan congratulated him.

'Prema told me you were interested in medical records, right? Get there around eleven, is that okay? I'm usually there from ten to five. I'll be there tomorrow unless this madness gets out of hand—'

Too late now to retreat.

He was committed to Shakuntala Salwe's quest. Tomorrow he would present the receipt at the Bombay Archives and claim the Xeroxed documents she had paid for. Rs 650 was a lot of money. She had died clutching the receipt. Something told him she had died safeguarding it. To Shakuntala, that money had been well spent. If the documents seemed important he would look up the son. No, that would mean too many explanations. Perhaps he should make another pilgrimage to the cottage.

His headache revved up at the thought. It was nearly ten, and he was tired, but sleep was out of the question. He couldn't dismiss the dead woman from his mind.

Death from natural causes, yes. But what had precipitated that fatal stroke? Not a melodramatic question if you considered the desperate urgency of her final gesture. Cadaveric spasm.

Ratan resolutely blocked out cadaveric spasm. He hated the very thought of the dead with a virulence he couldn't explain. The very first time in the post-mortem room had been the worst hour of his life.

In his first year of Medical College, the embalmed dead in the Anatomy Hall bothered him not at all. Yet the moment he swung past the gates of the Autopsy Room, dread possessed him.

It wasn't the smell. That morning, there was no smell, except for the keen reek of disinfectant and the fetor of pigeons who made noisy and urgent love in the tall windows, undeterred by death.

It wasn't what he saw, either. Not yet.

At first glance everything was clean, dry, orderly. There were no spills.

Four corpses lay on their marble rests in decent solemnity. Nude, arms by their sides, a tag around the left big toe. He hadn't yet looked at their faces. It was not *them*.

It was something in himself that scared Ratan. He had to stop himself from walking up to the long bench along the far wall and picking up the gleaming steel instruments. He counted the plastic jars lined up, and found they were two short. He watched Mama, the clerk, make the incision in the first body with the thought: *He won't open the skull unless I remind him*. Mama didn't. And the thrilled or aghast faces around him didn't notice this omission till Ratan's, 'Kya Mama, khopdi nahin khola?'

Seconds before Mama made his incision, he heard the ripping sound of the scalp being dragged down. He saw the smooth round rock of skull emerge past the grassy scalp a full minute before it actually did. At each stage of the autopsy, Ratan was two steps ahead.

It was a case of sudden death. Mama found nothing.

He called the pathologist who was elbow deep at the next table.

Nothing.

'What about the mediastinum?' somebody asked.

With sinking heart, Ratan recognized the voice as his own.

'What about it?' the pathologist barked. 'What do you expect to find there?'

Mama held up the thoracic viscera by the trachea, and brandished it at Ratan.

The class laughed.

'Raise the apical lobes off the trachea, please.'

Ratan heard his voice make the request.

There was hushed silence.

The pathologist did as he was told.

Tucked coyly beneath the spongy flaps of lung was a pinkish mass encircling the trachea.

'Thymoma!' The pathologist laughed out.

It was his prize now. He took the dangling mass of flesh from Mama and admired it at arm's length. The students milled around him.

Ratan sneaked out, his head reeling. He ran all the way to the hostel and got under the shower, clothes and all.

Ratan never attended another autopsy in all his college life. He got out of the mandatory attendances for his MD by getting a friend to alibi for him. His reluctance was put down to fear. They made a coward of him at every opportunity, and Ratan let them.

They knew not the half of it.

He had topped his class in pathology almost without effort. He was a natural at histology. Yet the thought of spending hours sawing the dead put him off general pathology. He opted for microbiology instead. A waste, really, of his medical degree, since half his colleagues were MScs who had never seen a fever in their lives.

He had turned his education to some good by working in infectious diseases as an adjunct to growing microbes in the lab, but the work didn't thrill him. Pathology did.

He felt at home with the architecture of disease. He knew its sly territory, the stealth of its progress. He knew its codes. Only the thought of that autopsy room kept him from appropriating the skill that was naturally his. He told himself it was simply because he couldn't bear the dead. He built up the pose that it was a waste of human skill to help the dead.

Yet, Shakuntala Salwe's body had commanded the swiftest of responses from him. Why? And he'd known exactly what to do.

Pain cancelled all else from Ratan's brain. He threw himself down on his bed and closed his eyes.

Cadaveric spasm is a sign of ...

Cadaveric spasm is a sign of ...

... unusual muscular activity caused by heightened tension at the moment of death.

What did that mean? That the fear of death could make you clench your teeth and ball your fists?

An inadequate definition, he had pointed out to Professor Small.

Benjamin Small was a pale man with a quick temper and an inordinate amount of perspiration he nervously tried to conceal. Why not sweat like a man, Ramratan would have liked to ask him, but didn't.

The British had a horror of sweat. They thought it a sign of moral weakness. Like 'going native'. They strengthened themselves against it with large meals of boiled meat and many layers of absorbent cloth against the skin.

Benjamin Small did not like to hear Taylor's *Principles of Forensic Medicine* contradicted, like when Ramratan said the book failed to explain both cadaveric spasm and rigor mortis.

'Cadaveric spasm is a condition quite distinct from rigidity although often running into it,' Small read aloud from the book.

'Gentlemen,' he continued, 'Mr Taylor's masterpiece tells us this. But we humbly await enlightenment from our own Mr Oak.'

Ramratan overlooked the sarcasm. He knew

they wouldn't learn very much about the dead from Taylor.

Poor Prof. Small! He was dead now.

Dead from dysentery.

From its treatment, more likely, for Charles Morehead had treated the poor bastard.

What would Small have said if he knew his most argumentative student had made a career out of refuting Taylor?

Hardly a career yet. He was wasted in this apprenticeship: lecturing, microscopy, a little clinical work and then back to the post-mortem room where he began each morning.

For how long?

The degree he held was a mere LM, and likely to stay thus despite the furor Dr Bhalchandra Bhatavdekar had stirred up in the Bombay University Senate.

Ramratan admired his guts. The Students' Council bulletin reported it all avidly.

'In what way are we inferior to European doctors?' Dr Bhatavdekar demanded of the shocked Senate. 'Why is an Indian a mere Licentiate, while his European colleague—who invariably has poor marks in the examination—can proudly put up his brass plate with the letters M.B., B.S. engraved on it?'

Change must come.

They had come a long way since John McLennan's day. The little school he set up near Azad Maidan in 1826 was meant to train 'high-caste boys' to be assistants, dressers and compounders to British doctors. Today, just two years to its fiftieth anniversary, the Grant Medical College had Indians on its staff. The slave had risen to wazir, but would he ever be king?

What he, Ramratan Oak, desperately needed, were the letters MD after his name. What kindly genie would provide them? He had a wife and two children to feed, and no godfather to pay his passage to London or Edinburgh. Bombay must be enough for him.

Was it? Was anything enough?

Yashoda stirred beside him, waking to his silent need. The raintree scattered moonlight over them. She in radiance, he in night, with the stealth of clouds, with the corybantic abandon of branches tossed in sudden breeze.

8 December 1992

While Ratan slept, Bombay moved into history.

Like a rash, an exanthem whose arrival spells an end to a mysterious fever, the city erupted in the pattern of violence it recognized as *riot.*

Nobody alive remembered a riot. But the hardware that mapped the city—walls, boundaries, buildings, streets—these did.

Memory flooded the air.

It had all happened before. It would happen again. It was happening now.

Riot.

There was something paradoxical about its ambit. The word was too small to contain the enormity it described. It meant uncontainable. It was both locus and contagion. It hummed with unseen connectivity.

People were slow to mouth the word. To accede the word was to cede responsibility, to admit surrender, to abjure culpability. In a riot, each man stands alone. It is the hour when he may act as he feels, without fear of censure. It is the moment of fantasy.

Of all that had happened the previous day, very little would percolate to the newspapers, even less would flicker on television. Yet reporters roamed the streets, observing, interviewing, photographing. The truths they witnessed were not always printed.

Ratan rose early, getting the house organized before his father awoke, preparing for a long day ahead. Within minutes it was clear he would be going nowhere at all.

It was nearly six, still dark outside, when there was an altercation at the gate. Ratan watched from the balcony as a group of men questioned the watchman. His thin whine persisted past the menacing rumble of his inquisitors.

'Don't come running to us later saying we didn't warn you!' they shouted as they moved away.

Ratan went downstairs and questioned the watchman.

'Don't talk to me Shaab, it's all your fault,' the watchman whined. 'All the result of that Mussalman dhobi in the building.'

'Forgotten his name, have you, Bahadur?'

'What do I care? I should have dragged the motherfucker out and thrown him to those dogs. I didn't do it because of his daughter. You know what those dogs do to women?'

'So what did you tell them, Bahadur?'

'I told them there are no Mussalmans here in Nandanvan.'

'Good. Stick to that story. Don't get drunk when you get home and shoot your mouth off.'

'I never touch the stuff, Shaab.'

'I'll tell Jafar to keep the shutters down. He can take in clothes through the back door.'

'Tell him to leave, Shaab.'

'He can't go back to his mohalla.'

The watchman smiled, showing blackened stumps through a slurry of tobacco. He spat richly before he spoke again.

'They set fire to all the Muslim houses there, a few hours ago, just after midnight.'

How had he slept through that?

'They didn't make a noise. It was dead quiet. All the houses were empty. I saw the flare in the sky, or I wouldn't have known either.'

It was a warning, then! To tell those who had fled there was no coming back.

Ratan trudged back up the stairs to the third floor. He would tell Jafar later to send his wife and kids upstairs for the day. They were safer away from the laundry.

At eight Prema called.

'There's curfew everywhere.'

Her voice crackled with excitement.

'Imagine, curfew! Cyrus just called me. He says Muslims have gone crazy everywhere. You know the milk was poisoned in Kalina?'

'What?'

'Yeah, Muslims poisoned the milk in Kalina. Everybody there is vomiting. We just heard. You know that Muslim bakery down our road? There's a big crowd outside with sticks and bottles waiting for it to open. They're going to show them. Blood for milk, they're shouting! That's when we heard about the milk. Our bai's husband is in the shakha, you know? He's organized the bakery mob. He told us.'

'He told you, and you believed him? Just like that?'

'Why not? Cyrus didn't doubt it for a second. He says it's absolutely true. It's only the beginning, he says.'

'Good. I hope he's drunk a good tall glass of milk by now.'

Ratan rang off, feeling murderous.

By ten he'd about had it.

First Radhakrishnan called to cancel their meeting at the Archives and warned him not to venture out. Things were bad his side of town and his family knew from the bitter past, just how much worse they could get.

Nandanvan called an urgent meeting on the terrace. Ratan did not attend. Siplani rang his doorbell and asked him to persuade Jafar to leave. Ratan refused. He accompanied Siplani back to the meeting, ready to take on the rest of them. In Siplani's absence, the committee had reconsidered. After all, Jafar's house had been burned down. A man cannot be dispossessed twice. Nobody can refuse to shelter a man who has lost his house, Adarkar said. This family had nowhere to go, and Nandanvan would shelter them. They had decided to ask Jafar to take down his signboard—**Bismillah Laundry**—and 'put up something neutral instead'.

When Ratan went downstairs he found Jafar had pre-empted the committee. The laundry had switched identity. A muscular man in a ragged banian sat at the counter. He sported an ostentatious tilak. There was a little altar on the wall and agarbattis curled smoke before an oleograph of a gigantic blue infant gorging on a pot of curds. The signboard had been changed too. Faraz pointed proudly to his handiwork.

'I had to think of something with a "B". Then I thought of Birju.'

Birju, the halwai's son, the treacherous neighbour.

Faraz had painted **BrajMohan** in red against the deep green background that hid the **Bismillah**.

'One is as good as the other,' Jafar shrugged, emerging from behind the screen. 'This is Shiv Prasad. I think he is the right man for the counter. Look at those muscles, Ratan Bhai! Pure desi ghee.'

Mr Muscles smiled. A curiously guileless smile, as he bent earnestly over the iron, giving it all he had.

Jafar explained he was Faraz's friend. He had heard what happened in the mohalla last night and hurried over. He had brought the photo of Kishan Kanhaiyya, and offered to stand guard. He was a wrestler by profession—and out of a job.

'Till today,' Shiv Prasad broke in.

'What about your house, Jafar?'

Jafar shrugged.

'I'll have to wait to find out. Maybe it's just gutted. Your bhabhi has been crying since she got the news. "Hai my this, hai my that." Let it all go, I say, we are alive, bas, that is enough. Allah will show us the way. What about you, Ratan Bhai? Don't go out today.'

'I need to,' Ratan said. 'Send the children upstairs when you can, will you? I'll leave in an hour.'

Ten minutes earlier, Crispin Rego had phoned.

Crispin was the closest Ratan had to a friend in the Department. They were classmates who had parted ways when Ratan opted out of pathology. It was Crispin who had covered for him in the autopsy room. Now Crispin was in line for an assistant professorship. To Ratan's knowledge, he had already been superseded at least four times by political favourites.

'Get here, Ratan.' Crispin was peremptory. 'Don't ask questions, just get here.'

'What's happening?'

'Yeah, I know there's a curfew on, but when did that ever stop you? Listen, S.V. Road is closed off, come through Nana Chowk, okay? Got your old ID? Great, they'll let you through, just say you're reporting on duty.'

'I can't leave for another hour at least.'

'Fine, as long as I know you're coming.'

'I'm coming.'

Ratan left a little after eleven, and took the western route. The roads were empty but for a few trucks and cruising cars. They looked like predators, hovering in wait, poised to pounce. He was stopped several times by police patrols. They let him through once they inspected his hospital ID. He wasted no time in asking what was happening, his memory of Maratha Mandir from last night was too raw to allow polite conversation.

The exits at Nana Chowk and Foras Road Bridge were cordoned off. Army trucks rolled into view as he turned left just short of Chowpatty and sped past Charni Road Station.

The army unit moved at an amble, bristling with guns. Ratan overtook a Sikh regiment. The jawans' eyes looked bewildered despite their decorous mask of impassivity. Ambulances were parked in a ring outside Saifee Hospital, but all appeared quiet. He swung left into Girgaum, planning to cut through and emerge at Pydhonie. The army would certainly be patrolling Mohammad Ali Road, and things were bound to be quiet there.

Police vans seemed stalled in the middle of the road as he entered the maze of Girgaum. To his surprise, the curfew didn't seem to work here. Vehicles packed the road, honking madly. Here and there a handcart angled to sneak across past trucks lined up shoulder to shoulder. Through all this, pedestrians pushed past, cutting trails. There was nothing Ratan could do but dismount, walk his bike, and thread his way past obstructions.

It took Ratan fifteen minutes to round the curve of one lane. It was mildly uphill, the macadam just a cleft between two converging tenements. There was no horizon. There was no sky. The only coordinates were those buildings, spilling over onto the pavement which swarmed with urgencies – children in various stages of defecation, bhangis piling wet mounds of garbage, barefoot Jains, scrubbed and masked, hurrying for some obscure surgical rite. Marwari women, doughy midriffs jouncing between bright banks of bosom and belly, sauntered towards vegetable carts as they measured the morning with distant eyes.

There was, besides, the pavement's rooted life. Squatters, deroofed and vagrant, ready on the instant to flash territorial rights. Ear surgeons from Kathiawad with glinting tin probes on the ready to excavate piecemeal the numbed brains of their customers. Women still abed on bright appliquéd quilts, clothes tumbled about bare shoulders, trawling their filthy tresses for lice. Kwashiorkor children, balancing swollen bellies on twiggy bowlegs, as they tottered about and snivelled in misery. Old women, wall-eyed and canny, directing and despoiling lives around them. Young men picking their teeth, draped over parked cars, lazing in wait for fortune. All this in the twenty-odd steps it took Ratan to traverse the lane.

Half an hour later, Ratan had no idea where he was, except that it was Girgaum, and he was lost in its labyrinthine heart like an ant exploring a sponge. It was an interminable haze of shopfronts, dark sockets most of them, with low wattage bulbs gleaming yellow in the depths like baleful eyes. Hairline fractures glimpsed between buildings became corkscrew lanes as he got closer, snaky conveyor belts of disappearing backs and advancing bellies. Everything, everybody, was on the move in every direction. There was no place to stop, no place to dawdle, you either moved on or got mowed down.

These lanes were ripples set off by a mighty surge of energy at some epicentre. It was obliterated now without trace, leaving this careening landscape to survive without purpose. Its concentricity, like that of a maelstrom, milled around a void.

Ratan felt watched. The street eyeballed him everywhere he turned, and refused entrance. He kept walking, yet didn't seem to have moved an inch.

Every five yards or so, the street branched into lanes on either side. Each lane was a radial spoke in this tireless carousel of streets.

On both sides, shops and stalls opened directly onto the street. In crevices between them were pulses of colour: washing, perhaps, or heaps of plastic scrap, or more expendably—people. To navigate these lanes it was necessary to ingratiate, to smile and nod gravely, to accept and acknowledge favours, to co-opt.

He wasn't wanted here. Everything about him announced he had no business here. This topography was unfamiliar and these faces were anomalous. What could he be but a stranger?

Different in appearance, confused of purpose, he was the intruder, the enemy.

He recognized the flat look of refusal in eyes that met his —and these were very few, the rest all evaded his gaze. He knew it for what it was. It was the look the householder has for the salesman at the door, the look that tells the salesman he may not enter. The sullen politeness of deep fear. Fear of the other. Xenophobia.

That was the momentum of these spiralling streets. It drew them tighter still, winding closer to the unseen heart with its tremendous gravitational pull. It was xenophobia, turning the spill of life inward, closer to the black hole that throbbed with galactic energy, and defined the purpose of this life.

The lane suffocated him. This little lane was no more than a fibril. A wisp of fuzz in the dishevelled city. In lanes like this one, such narrow strips that never see the sun, it is here that the chill of hate makes its first strike.

Any small thing might set it off.

A word. A stone. A push.

Or nothing at all, nothing more than a stranger, like himself.

Ratan passed a small shrine as he pondered that thought. It was guarded by a man with a lathi. His eye met Ratan's and Ratan saw through those eyes and—

He saw himself, transformed. He was a stranger in a sacred space.

The sacred space was not the shrine. It was the street. It was sacred because it was exclusive. It became sacred by excluding the stranger.

As a stranger he need do nothing at all to desecrate this space.

He *was* the desecration.

Nobody had raised a finger against him. He had been tolerated. But the measure of hate in eyes that looked back at him was deep enough to kill. Hate lurked dormant in lanes like this one, waiting for a chance spark, a word, a shove, a glance, to awaken.

If he was still here in this street when it awoke, there would be no escaping. It would drip from every balcony of these teetering buildings, pour out of every doorway and shopfront. This street would rear up with a hiss and sting him.

There was nothing in his appearance to mark him as either Hindu or Muslim. Any moment, though, a stranger might approach and ask him to lower his pants. It had happened yesterday, just about anywhere in the city, Jafar told him.

How does one have the nerve to make a demand like that?

Ratan recalled his squeamish first month in the clinics. History taking was fine, you chatted and made friends. But it was hell when it came to asking patients to display a hernia, a hydrocele, a penile lesion. The best way to do it was brusquely, with your eyes fixed on the horizon.

He wondered if that was how the command would come.

What would he do then?

He would show them his hospital ID. It would be tossed aside. IDs can be faked.

The demand would be inexorable.

He would shut his eyes—impossible to do it with eyes open—he would shut his eyes, and comply.

What would they do next?

Who would look after his father? More immediately, who would tell his father? Who would make Arjun understand his son was dead?

How could anybody explain why a man's bareheaded prick should be the death of him?

Ratan, like a million other men, had been circumcised as a child—not from religious, but clinical, compulsion. He imagined trying to explain that here, on this street, to an impatient mob, with his eyes shut and his trousers around his ankles.

Ratan gagged.

Nobody stopped him. Nobody questioned him. He walked on, then stopped, suddenly tired.

The street was emptying around him. People were being sucked into doorways, shopfronts, crevices between buildings. Some even sought out shadows and lurked there, just out of view. Some others, ten or twenty perhaps, emerged, cutting a swagger. One of them stopped Ratan.

Where was he going?

A doctor, was he?

They were going to the next naka, maybe he should go with them. Perhaps he was lost? That would be a short cut, then!

Ratan had no choice.

They walked around him, laughing and kidding.

Ratan did not attempt conversation.

At the head of the lane, they stopped. They motioned Ratan to stay where he was. The road gaped before them, empty for the most part, or emptying—

'They've arrived. Wait here. We can watch from here.'

Ratan realized their focus was a group of three, about fifty yards away.

Two men and a woman.

One of the men had a black bag on his shoulder. Ratan recognized it as the standard kit of a press photographer.

The woman was in her twenties, small and slender, pert in a green-and-blue shalwar qameez. Something glittered at her hip, a sling bag, probably. She carried a spiral notebook in her left hand.

The other man was their guide. He had brought them here.

The woman seemed uneasy. She clung to her companion. From the urgency of the gesture it was evident he was more than her colleague.

Ratan felt compelled to join them. Like him, they were strangers here.

He mounted his bike. Immediately, he was pinioned.

'We told you to wait here.'

A white Ambassador drove up and slowed near the three. A head appeared at the window, and called out.

The photographer turned.

The woman gave a sharp cry.

Two men got out of the car and approached them.

In one swift white arc their arms swung up and a cascade of something shining and smooth enveloped the photographer.

It all happened in no more than an instant.

The flare of a lighter, Ratan's lunge forward, the woman's piercing scream as she writhed and tore free from her captor's grasp. She leapt on the roaring column of flame, the bright green of her dupatta erased by the sullen ochre sheath of heat.

Ratan ran.

His heart bursting his ribs, he sprang on them and miraculously getting a grip on flesh, he grabbed and pulled away. He'd got the girl. She was still screaming, her back on fire. He tore off his shirt and rolled her in it. Her face was badly burned, her hands and arms branded with the fabric of her qameez and dupatta. More than 60 percent burns, for sure. She would die of shock unless he got her to hospital quickly. Behind them the photographer smouldered, a charred heap on the ground, his face miraculously untouched.

Ratan caught the gaze of his dead eyes, fixed at the spot where the girl had been standing.

It was the yearning look of a child straining at the horizon, staring at a disappearing train.

The car had roared off, the man who had brought the couple here had vanished. At the mouth of the lane, Ratan's bike lay forlorn. His recent companions were all gone. The girl writhed at his feet. The street around them was empty. Not a face was to be glimpsed in the buildings on either side.

From the top of the road, police vans began moving towards them. They moved slowly as if waiting for the smoke to clear before they came any closer.

Ratan signalled frantically. He had the mad thought they might cruise past. The girl was unconscious now, her breathing stertorous.

A van stopped. Two policemen jumped out.

'Get her to hospital quickly!' Ratan shouted.

He picked her up and carried her to the van. It was his urgency that forced them to take her in.

'I'm on duty at J.J. Hospital. That's my bike there. One of you bring it along, please, I'll ride with her.'

The policemen on the pavement stirred the smoking heap with their lathis.

'Wait till he cools,' one of them said. 'We'll all choke in the van otherwise.'

Ratan, jolted in the van, held the girl's feet and kept his finger on her pulse, a futile gesture of caring. A policeman followed the van on Ratan's bike.

It took him half an hour to persuade the Plastic Surgery registrar to make a direct admission. General Surgery refused burns. They were overburdened. Ninety-three admissions since morning, fifty of these awaited emergency surgery. And it was still ten minutes shy of noon.

Ratan was walking towards Pathology when he felt an unfamiliar weight in his pocket. It was the small glittery sling purse the girl had been wearing. He remembered it glinting in the sun. It must have slipped off her shoulder when she sprang at the photographer.

He didn't remember stuffing it in his pocket, but then he didn't remember half the things he did these days. His headache was back, hammering for attention.

The bag was the usual Kutchi trinket, palm-sized, soft cotton fabric embellished with beads, shells and mirrors, red and white on black. Pretty. He opened it. It had a small hairbrush, ballpoint pen, wallet. The wallet had her press card.

Radhika Panchal.

There was a residence phone number. He found a booth and called. The police had probably informed them by now, but he felt responsible nonetheless.

A woman answered. The mother, probably.

'Panchal?'

He spoke in Gujarati.

'Are you the mother of Radhika Panchal? She has had an accident—'

The woman did not answer him. Instead she hissed with tense venom at somebody next to her.

'What have you done? You promised me they wouldn't touch her—'

Her voice was cut off abruptly.

Ratan visualized a hand pressing down on her mouth, clamping her jaw. He sensed her struggle. He waited.

Presently a man came on the line. English this time.

Ratan repeated his words.

'What? Is she serious?'

'I'm sorry. Yes, very serious. She has severe burns. Please come as soon as you can, you'll find her in—'

The man interrupted roughly, 'Was anybody else hurt?'

'The young man with her, her colleague I think, he died instantaneously.'

There was a sigh.

'Yes, yes, we are coming.' The man collected himself, and asked for directions.

Ratan could not get the dead man's look out of his mind, nor the sound of the girl's scream as she flung herself on his flaming body.

He walked to the Plastic Surgery ward and left the bag with the staff nurse. The girl was out of sight, being resuscitated. She would not last. She might die before dawn. The young man who died yearning wouldn't have to wait very long.

Crispin's head gleamed copper in the sun as he bent to comfort a grieving relative outside the Coroner's Court. Guilt came with the job. The feeling of having transgressed on grief was inescapable. Compassion or drink, take your pick, Crispin always said. And if he had a game liver to start with, a pathologist had only one choice. He greeted Ratan with relief and drew him hurriedly into Pathology.

Once inside the cool stone building, he lit a cigarette and said, 'You look like hell.'

'So do you.'

'I've been in hell, man. Twenty-six bodies since morning and I'm still on number five. Why do you think I sent for you?'

'I'm not going in there.'

'Yes, you are. Ratan, you owe me, and I'm calling in the debt.'

'Why me?'

'You have to ask? I've had five phone calls from the Dean. That fucker Mane—'

'The new professor?'

'The very same. He's in the ICU with chest pain. It hit him soon after the bodies started coming in. You know what the Dean told me? "Keep it simple." Today that translates as "report no bullet injuries, no internal haemorrhages from lathi charges, no custodial torture". He was all set to send me an assistant, but I told him I already had one. Now I do.'

'You keeping it simple?'

'Would I call you if I were?'

'So what've you got so far?'

'One liver rupture. One intra-cerebral bleed, one cardiac arrest, one subclavian tear. All, except the cardiac arrest, were bullet wounds. The cardiac arrest had multiple fractures from lathi injuries. You want chai? You look like hell, man. Ratan, what's up?'

'Headache.'

'Migraine?'

Ratan shrugged off Crispin's concern.

The truth was, he wasn't listening any more. His responses had grown mechanical and absent-minded. He simply had no attention left to spare for anything but the swirling upheaval within his head. It had overcome everything else, even his dread of what Crispin clearly expected him to do. For the next few hours he would be helping Crispin sort out the twenty-one cadavers awaiting autopsy.

Ratan followed Crispin through the swing door, propelled by a rush of pain. Strange that pain should make him so energetic.

He hurried.

Crispin's voice was a buzz in his skull. He kept trying to shut it out. It was a distraction from the pain and kept him from catching up with it. The pain sped before him, escalated dangerously, and all he had to do was hoist himself onto it and it would carry him the rest of the way. He was almost there now.

Almost.

Crispin's voice had grown fainter. Any moment now he could step onto that accelerated conveyor belt—

Now. Now.

A black rush of pain, and he was there.

A black rush of pain, and he was there.

Ramratan looked around for his knife. As usual his instruments were laid out on a green square of mackintosh. Only the knife was missing. Somebody had laid a scalpel teasingly across the naked breast of the woman on the slab.

A prank.

The students knew there was nothing he hated more than to see a cadaver treated like a table or a bookstand. It had taken him a year to break them of the habit and convince them that 'Mr Simmons allowed it' was no excuse.

Ah, there it was. Bhiku must have borrowed it earlier in the day and left it on the edge of the sink. Bhiku was usually soused by midday. Why wait till he was dead to steep his brain in alcohol?

Ramratan picked up his knife with a keen ripple of pleasure. He wiped the blade on his overall and whipped it free in a streak of light.

'All this fuss over a kitchen knife!'

Ramratan could hear Salim scoff.

'A small piddling knife like that? Is that any knife for a man? Why not use a butcher's knife if a scalpel's too fussy for you?'

Salim's delicate scalpel was too temperamental for Ramratan. It was a swift riposte to the skin's resilience. Epigrammatic, precise, steady, amidst the tremulous poetry between insult and injury. It was too nice for him. The butcher's knife was too coarse, a brutish instrument of murder.

Ramratan's knife was above this shilly-shally between life and death, above insult and injury. It was a knife for the aftermath, the blade of judgement. It incised more than skin, it pared truth down to the bone.

Could Salim's scalpel do all that?

I must stop these conversations with Salim, Ramratan told himself. Salim is dead.

Salim is dead.

Kitchen knife, did he say? Yashoda had several just like this one in her kitchen. If he slipped this in among them, she'd never know. He smiled at the thought of her outrage.

A kitchen knife?

It didn't feel like that when he held it. Against his palm it was firm as a friend's handclasp. The bone handle had a smooth rounded heft to it like the midshaft of a femur—which of course, it wasn't. He read the letters stamped on it like Braille:

Evans & Co. Old Change.

Most of his colleagues used the mortuary instruments, but Ramratan preferred his own set.

He had bought the set second-hand in Chor Bazar. An extravagance—he'd paid all of twenty rupees for it. The handsome mahogany case with its ornate silver clasp could easily be mistaken for a jewel case. Only the initiated knew it held the tools of a despised trade. This knife was the humblest of those tools. The case held, besides, a villainous saw, blunt-ended scissors, probes, skin hooks, several scalpels, rib cutters, a spine wrench, a hammer, a chisel, a skull key and a short length of rubber tubing. Ramratan never touched any of these, except the saw and the skull key to get at the brain. The knife did all his work. The box weighed as much as his firstborn, his second son, and he carried it just as tenderly.

Ramratan liked to douse his hands in alcohol before he began. It made them more sensitive.

On the slab before him was a woman of sixty. He disregarded the case notes. That was for afterwards.

He turned to the dead woman.

Death had annealed the muscles of her face into flat vacuity. Divested of clothes and ornaments, most people would think her divested of identity.

Not Ramratan.

He knew by now that only in death was the body permitted its true identity. It could finally announce with assurance: Here I am, unchanged. No matter what life did to me, here I am.

His eyes travelled the body, making mental notes. He noted the landmarks of a difficult life lived from chore to chore. All that drudgery was now meaningless to the statement on the slab, the flat assertion of identity. This is who I was, myself.

He was about to unseal the crypt of that self, to explore its chambers. Was it merely to track down disease, or was it to track down that elusive thing called identity?

'Reading too much into it, as usual.'

He heard Salim's ironic voice, and shuddered.

Salim was dead.

He raised the woman's shoulders to slip in the block. He'd thought of the block when still an undergraduate, shown Mr Simmons how it could simplify exposure by making the chest prominent and allowing the shoulder to slump away. Now everybody used the block, and thanked Mr Simmons for it.

Ramratan did not mind. He suspected that prosectors from Vesalius down had used some such device. He stropped the knife against his thigh and gathered himself for that moment of awareness, that single lucid second, when everything stilled.

The knife sank sure and unzipped the body shoulder

to shoulder in a deep V between the breasts, down the centre from xiphoid to pubis. He deepened the incision and the purplish skin sprang apart. With one sharp tug Ramratan peeled the chest flaps off the ribs. The concealed palette of the body rushed up at him.

Fat first, and scant little of it, amber globules embedded preciously, glistening kundan in silvery fascia. Nacreous ligaments flashing blue or green in the oblique light. Bone glinting secretly white beneath the pink and grey escarpment of muscle and tendon. And everywhere the rich tumble of blood vessels, opacifying in stillness, turning every other colour but red.

Most people thought of death as grey. Would he have done that too if he hadn't seen Alice Kipling's book of Ned Jones' sketches?

She had given him the book when they left. He hoarded it. He imagined how Ned Jones would look at the body laid open: as a jewel box, enamelled, filigreed, cushioned, rendered voluptuous and luxurious, yet restrained to its original purpose. The liver would be a liver still, but strangely illuminated.

In time Ramratan too had begun to see it like that. With the cessation of life, the body ceased to be erotic. It became sacred.

And he, Ramratan, was its celebrant: priest, disciple, acolyte.

He incised the neck in the midline, up to the chin, sweeping swiftly beneath the jaw to the back of the ear on either side. The knife nicked teasingly along the cut, and Ramratan slid in a finger, working it gently beneath the nicks. The skin flaps simply peeled back, uncovering the strappy scaffolding of muscle. Beneath the great columns of blood vessels, nestled in webby packing, were pale bunches of lymph nodes.

Ramratan's knife levered up the cut breastplate of

sternum and cartilage. The ribs splayed, then opened like a book, presenting the central bulge of a cold knot of muscle. The pericardium glistened like oiled paper. He was about to nick it when he heard his name called out sharply, and a door shut, cutting off sight.

The voice that had called out his name continued shouting its alarm.

The voice that had called out his name continued shouting its alarm.

Somebody held his arm. Vaguely, he recognized the voice as Crispin's.

His face was mottled with rage.

'Have you entirely lost it, Ratan?'

He wasn't shouting, but the fury in his voice made it a shout. His gloved hand hovered between Ratan and the opened chest of the cadaver.

'Look at your hand, Ratan! Man, have you gone completely mad?'

Ratan looked at his hands, trembling now, naked, bloody.

'And you a microbiologist!'

Ratan had just opened a cadaver without a latex sheath to protect him from body fluids.

'You opened the body? What for, Ratan? Mama is right here to do the job for you!'

He had opened a body. Ratan had never done that before. He had opened a body with the greatest ease using just a—

His knife! Where was that knife?

'Where's my knife?' he asked in panic. 'You know I can't work without my knife.'

Crispin didn't answer him. He stripped off his gloves and laid a hand on Ratan's shoulder.

The room reeled around Ratan. Crispin's hand steadied him. He felt the weight move away. He found his feet. Nausea stained his tongue, but he actually felt better. The headache had left him.

'You want to go on, Ratan?'

Yes. Yes, he would 'go on'. Whatever that meant. He drew on gloves and, disregarding Mama, got on.

This wasn't his knife, but he would use it nonetheless. He cast about for a syringe, filled it at the tap, nicked the pericardium and injected the cavity with water. The heart stared back grey and sullen, a mollusk in a shallow puddle. He cut into the right atrium and ventricle. No air. He drew blood samples and labelled them.

'Sah'b is going into details,' Mama said disapprovingly. 'Short cuts are okay for today.'

Ratan ignored him.

He restituted the chest flaps, felt the breasts (that drew a chuckle from Mama), returned to the cavity and set about freeing the lungs. He expected tough adhesions from old healed tuberculosis. He wasn't wrong. The trick was to get the right plane of cleavage and strip the lungs off the thickened pleura. He had them now, bunched on either side, much travelled bags of tough grey rexine. This time Mama had a jar and label ready for snippets of pleura.

He preferred an en bloc evisceration to the standard Rokitanský. For the next twenty minutes he worked with dizzying speed, using little besides the knife and his fingers.

Crispin peered over his shoulder.

'That was quick!'

'Yeah. I do it this way now. Quicker. Neater. That Austrian's been teaching me. He's much quicker.'

'What Austrian?'

'One of those Plague Commission men. Anton Ghon. You should watch him, Crispin.'

'Ghon! Always the kidder, our Ratan!'

Ratan raised puzzled eyes at Crispin and got busy again over the thoracic pluck.

He had his report ready by the end of the hour. The old woman had lived with tuberculosis, malaria and a solitary kidney only to succumb to a large cerebral bleed, like the one that probably killed Shakuntala Salwe.

The name recalled Ratan to the present.

What was he doing here in Autopsy?

Crispin was hurrying him over to the second body, a young girl this time. She had bled to death from a ruptured ectopic pregnancy.

Or had she?

He very nearly missed the bullet hole on the nape, concealed by the mussed hair, almost bloodless at its point of entry. It had cut straight through the brain stem, killing her instantaneously. Perhaps the ectopic had chosen to rupture just before the shot. Perhaps she had been shot as they were taking her to hospital. Perhaps the shock of the shooting had ruptured her tubal pregnancy.

'They were getting her into a taxi when the shooting started,' Crispin said. 'Husband's outside. Young kid, not yet twenty-five. Ratan, I tell you, this madness is not going to stop soon.'

After the next one, Crispin said he had work for Ratan in his office.

---

* **Anton Ghon** was born in Villach, Austria, on New Year's Day 1866. Educated in Graz, he would become the professor of pathological anatomy at the German University in Prague. He came to Bombay in 1897 as a member of *Pestexpedition der Wiener Akademie der Wissenschaften*, Plague expedition of the Viennese Academy of Sciences.

His name endures for his 1912 monograph on childhood tuberculosis, *Der primäre Lungenherd bei der Tuberkulose der Kinder*. It described what we now call *Ghon focus*—the primary lesion in the lung from infection with *Mycobacterium tuberculosis*. This can be seen on X-rays as a small, sharp calcification.

In an inversion of karma, he died in Prague on 23 April 1936 from tuberculous pericarditis.

Ratan's headache was back, but inexplicably, he felt jaunty. His hour with these newly dead had enlivened him. For the first time in months, he felt that unreasonable alertness which portends joy.

In recent years, sex had become a complication. All too often, desire spiralled into dread, into despair, and worst of all, into occasional disgust. It had become a beast of the groin, a shame to be concealed. He had almost forgotten what it could be like: the fizz on his taste buds from a mouthful of water, the liquid depth of a stranger's laugh, the shrill flare of colour in a twist of ribbon, sunlight on a leaf, the air on his skin. The day, tumescent, was restored to him now. Despite his headache, which in a perverse manner, was pleasure too.

I'm turning kinky, he decided. I can't explain this any other way. It's morbid.

'What's morbid?' Crispin demanded, settling down in his chair, and Ratan realized he'd thought aloud.

'That I should feel so good after mucking about with cadavers.'

Crispin looked closely at him.

'That's exactly what worries me, man. You got a secret life or something?'

It was a slap of wet cloth on his cheek, burning, yet cold. How could Crispin know? When even he, Ratan himself, did not?

'What do you mean?' he asked, with more anger than he'd intended.

'Hey, take it easy, man. I asked because I was watching you in there.'

'And?'

'You were too much at home in there, Ratan. I know you hate autopsies. Remember, I covered for you. Always. You were good in there. You were fast. You were sure. You were a natural, Ratan. You've done this before. Where? When? So, do you have a secret life?'

'All I have is a headache.'

'Not true. You have a headache and something more besides.'

'I think I have a brain tumour.'

There! He'd said it out aloud. Now he might as well go the entire mile.

'It starts off as a headache. And then—it's like I'm somewhere else. I'm—I'm almost someone else. Antecedent hyperthymesia. A temporal lobe tumour, that's what I'd say.'

'You'd say? Are those diagnoses? You've seen a neurologist?'

'Nope.'

'Psychiatrist?'

'Hah!'

'So you do the smart thing, think one move ahead, and walk into my office for an autopsy?'

'Consider my table booked.'

'Back to where we started, then. This time I agree. You are being morbid.'

'Got to live with it somehow,' Ratan said roughly. 'I'll break your neck if you ever refer to it again.'

'Only in my notes, I promise you. Now let's go.'

'What, back already? I thought we had something else to do.'

'Absolutely. We're getting you a CAT scan.'

'Forget it.'

'You'll have to fight me on this one, Ratan.'

Crispin was a boxer. Ratan wasn't. Crispin won out.

Ratan wondered if he'd wanted all along to be led like this, unresisting, to the truth, had been too scared to go it alone and needed a friend to hold his hand.

The next hour was bizarre. He was like a band of elastic, endlessly stretched past its logical snapping point, yet without any hint of fatigue. He floated in a wordless state till confronted with the pictures on the viewing monitor.

With imaging like this, they'll soon stop opening skulls.

The thought made him inexplicably angry. He realized he was more worried about those cadaver skulls than his own. Those dead, hermetically shut boxes, jammed with strange brains mattered more to him than these black-and-white slices of his own mysterious brain.

Temporal lobe tumour, he reminded himself, and forced his eyes to render three-dimensional sense to the flat images.

'Nothing,' said the radiologist.

'Nothing?' Crispin shook his head.

Ratan was vaguely alarmed by the disappointment in their voices.

'Nothing organic,' the radiologist elaborated. That was worse.

Ratan now was officially a nut case.

Timorously Crispin suggested an EEG.

The radiologist smiled, shrugged, and backed away.

'I told you it was a migraine,' Ratan responded with needless malice.

Crispin changed the subject.

'Let's get something to eat, I haven't had any breakfast.'

'How's Lillian?' asked Ratan.

'Won't let me near her. Says I stink of the dead.'

He laughed, but Ratan wasn't fooled.

'She's got that on her brain. She won't sleep with me any more,' Crispin said.

'Shit.'

'Actually, it doesn't matter. I just don't care about that any longer.'

'Lucky you.'

'Like that, huh?'

'Like that.'

They walked on in silence.

They had Punjabi samosas and filter coffee at the Central Canteen and walked back to the Autopsy Room.

At six o'clock, Crispin said they'd done enough.

Ratan had opened three bodies in the last three hours, Crispin had done two. All five had died of bullet wounds. The wounds were all above the waist. Four had also been shot in the skull.

The police van would drop them home, Crispin said. Ratan could leave his bike parked here—no point risking the roads now. He needed Ratan back on the job next morning anyway. He seemed to take it for granted that Ratan wouldn't refuse. Ratan did not.

On their way out, Ratan stopped by the Plastic Surgery ward to enquire after the girl. Still dicey, the house surgeon said. She was still on the ventilator. He didn't think she'd make it.

Ratan tried to recall her face. All he could remember was her lover and that last look of yearning stilled on his face.

Vasundhara tapped her walking stick imperiously on the floor. She was too exhausted to raise her voice. It took her a while to recognize she was striking the floor in time with her jerky, unpredictable heartbeat. That won't do, she decided angrily and began to beat a taal which couldn't be faulted. The stick could take over what the heart, after eighty years of hard work, could be excused for shirking. She kept up the taal. Eventually, someone would hear her.

One by one her brothers appeared. The boys, she called them.

Ananda, Vinayak, Gopal.

How young they were, yet they walked like old men.

Gopya would be seventy next year, the little monkey!

As always, her eyes roamed beyond them for an absent face.

He would be eighty-six now, if he'd lived.

But Narayan, dead at twenty, was perennially young.

They misread her impatience.

The murmur outside was growing louder by the minute. They shut the windows, but they couldn't shut out the street.

'You must find it,' Vasundhara directed.

'Tai, the woman is dead.'

'He won't stop at that. The boy—'

'The boy! He's touching sixty!'

'What is his voice like? Sweet?'

'He wheezes and creaks like wet leather.'

'But deep?'

'No. How does it matter, Tai?'

'The boy will find it if you don't.'

'I don't think so.'

Vinayakrao sat down next to her.

'Tai, it's over now, you must let it go. Gopal got there in the nick of time. He's done what had to be done.'

The youngest of them, a man of nearly seventy, Gopal glared at his sister with a stubborn pugnacity that caught at her heart. He was still the ten year old she remembered, her ally, her champion and torment all in one.

This was the scowl he had specifically reserved for Tariq as he'd sit between them, tone deaf, waiting out the riyaaz.

Vasundhara smiled. She wondered if Gopal ever realized how his frown would melt and his trusting eyes widen with wonder as Tariq began singing.

You had to have steel inside you not to weaken. And she did. She never gave an inch. She gave as good as she got. Always.

She could let her voice soar like a kite, leaving the flimsy flutter of lesser throats far below. She could hold her breath longer, swoop lower but, and she could admit it now, never, never could she wrap her throat like oil around each note the way Tariq could. Never could she make the sargam speak its soul.

When he fell silent, Tariq withdrew into politeness. Every week he would hand Gopal a coloured transfer saved from Pears soap, usually an exotic bird, crested and vibrant, and tell him the Latin name, spelling it out carefully. Gopal kept these transfers in a dictionary. He never stuck them, never peeled off the gummy membrane by floating them face down in a saucer of water …

'Gopya, remember how you tagged along for my music lessons?' Vasundhara laughed. 'Three hours every morning, and you deaf as a post!'

Gopal grinned. That same boyish grin of crooked teeth, eyes disappearing into creased lids. He pushed his cowlick back. Just as he used to.

'I hated it,' he confessed. 'I wasn't all that deaf. Once we got there, I had to listen, there was no escape!'

'Just our luck,' Vinayakrao said. 'I had to do the chores and Ananda the milk run. You? You got the music of the gods every morning for free!'

'And no ear to hear it with,' Anandrao pointed out. 'It all equalizes, my brother!'

Silence overcame them, intense, joyous, too intimate for words. All four remembered the sunlit hour, their mother's voice vibrant in the air.

Running through the verandah, catching their father's chuckle behind the rustle of newspaper, and everywhere the long liquid notes of music …

'Nobody sings any more,' Ananda grumbled.

'Noises. They all make noises, now.'

'Enough! Everybody sings. We're just not listening any more!' Vasundhara exclaimed. 'We've all become deaf like Gopya here. Let that go, children. Back to work now. Gopya, you were going to tell us?'

'Yes. Yes. What is it you want to know?'

'Everything! You haven't said a thing except you couldn't find it. That his son was there, and the woman was dead.'

'That's what happened. What more can I tell you?'

Vasundhara sighed. Gopya was going to be difficult. The other two were relieved, actually. They wanted no part of this. They had never been any part of this.

'It finishes with us, Tai,' Vinayak said firmly. 'It must. The woman is dead.'

'He will not let it go.'

'Then he must do it on his own,' Ananda snapped. 'None of us remember anything about it. We weren't there. None of us. Not even your ustad.'

'Baba told us.'

Vasundhara saw from her brothers' faces that he hadn't told them. Baba had told *her*.

'That's right,' she said aloud. 'Baba didn't tell you. He told me. I wish now I hadn't left it this long. I didn't think it would get so bad. I didn't think. And now I cannot afford not to think. Even tomorrow may be too late. I am old, children! Old!'

'Tariq is older,' Gopal offered.

'But I may go before him. Besides, he could be ill.'

'Maybe. Or he may be in danger. He's more at risk than you are.'

'And therefore he will risk more. I must go.'

'Go?'

'To him.'

Vasundhara rose with difficulty. Her hip protested with a thunderclap of pain. It was only by being light as a sparrow that she could coax her legs to carry her.

'I will be ready in ten minutes,' she said at the door. She didn't expect them to argue. All their lives, her word had been law. 'It's madness outside!' Anandrao said. 'How will you go?'

'Take my Pajero,' Vinayakrao said.

Gopya smiled.

So it was a given that it would be Gopal again. In all her mad ventures—and there had been many—it was always Gopal.

Vasundhara returned. There was a tremendous roar out in the street. It was followed by a cough on their doorstep, and a cautious knock. Motioning the others back, Vinayak stepped to the door.

He recognized the man at the door, one of the goondas from the local shakha. Behind him, two boys held a flaming censer.

'Namaskar, Rao Saheb. We have come for your blessings.'

Speechless with sudden rage, Gopal could only stare at the gate. The street was choked with orange—banners, turbans, tilaks, and everywhere pots of flame held aloft—a rustling crematorium on the march to claim its dead.

Vasundhara spoke from behind Vinayak, her voice resonant in the sudden silence, 'You have come for our blessings, but it appears we must wait for yours! Clear the road, please. We have a crisis in the family, someone is seriously ill. Let us pass, please.'

So imperious was her tone that the men stepped back. She waved her stick angrily and looked haughtily past them, as Gopal backed the car out of their garage.

The tide of orange rippled back. Two of the boys helped Vasundhara into the car. Gopal eased the car out, inching his way past the bristle of resentment that emanated from the crowd on either side.

At the main road they were stopped by the police. Gopal stuck his head out, was recognized, and waved past the barricade.

Vasundhara glared stonily ahead. Still expressionless, she spoke once more.

'Tell me exactly what happened on Sunday,' she asked.

Gopal, who'd found it so difficult before, now easily recounted everything.

'I must have got there at four. I was about to knock on the door when I heard voices raised in argument. One of them was hers. I pushed open the door and entered. There was this burly man in there. He was breathless, red with fury. He turned on me and barked, "And you, I suppose, are Joshi. She wants money, money! Reason with her, tell her this is not barter! Tell her what's at stake!"

'The Salwe woman wouldn't give me a chance to speak. She kept shouting. Then she waved a piece of paper and screamed, "Here it is, then! Here's everything! And you're not going to get your hands on it!"

'By now I realized the other guy must be Tariq's son. He looks nothing like what I remember of Tariq. I think we both lunged at her. I meant her no harm. Neither, I am sure, did he. But she slipped and fell. We didn't help her up. That is the truth, Tai. Both of us stepped back—'

'Men!'

Gopal shrugged and continued.

'How can I explain? I think we were both overcome by horror. Horrified not by her fall, but by her avarice—or perhaps her ignorance. Anyway, next thing we knew, we were outside the house. She was dead. Anybody could tell that.'

'Since when are you a doctor, Gopya? What if she just had a heart attack? Or a stroke? What if you left her to die?'

Gopal drove on doggedly, very fast on the deserted road. They would be at a barricade again any minute now.

'Yaqub said that too, as we walked out. "We've left her for dead," he said. I had—I have, no such qualm. Yaqub is not an educated man. I cannot expect him to know the implications.'

'What about the paper?'

'She had it clutched in her hand. Nothing we could do about it.'

'Then it isn't over, Gopya. You see that, don't you?'

Her voice was gentle, but it still hurt like hell. He had failed her again.

'Yes, I see that,' he said sullenly.

He braked hard. The road flamed ahead of them, a roar of raging orange. He turned the car back silently. Vasundhara sighed.

'So the time is not come yet. Gopya, will it come before I die?'

Gopal didn't answer. He kept his eyes fiercely on the road, hiding the tears he wept for her.

It was dark in the van. The sliding windows were opened to a mere chink, the glass grimy as sin. The protective wire mesh was painted dark blue. The paint had dripped and dried in webs that clogged the mesh. The floor was littered with empties—cigarette cartons, tetrapacks of juice, banana peels, orange pips and curls of rind, plastic bags. Tinsel from crushed wrappers winked at Ratan like grounded stars. He kept his eyes down, trying to shut out the shapes that crowded his space—Crispin, and the two policemen beside him, the thick head and shoulders of the driver.

'You okay, Ratan?'

'No. I'm going to throw up. Ask them to pull over, Crispin.'

The driver hurried to comply.

Ratan shot out just in time to direct his bile into a convenient gutter. He squatted at the filthy edge, doubled over with pain as his gut squirmed and griped.

Please, no diarrhoea, not yet, he prayed.

The Almighty had taken full responsibility for Ratan's sphincter since he was ten when he had been stricken in the middle of a cricket match. On that occasion, prayer had conducted him to the bathroom in time. It did not fail him now. His bowel changed its mind. Only the waves of nausea kept up their ceaseless assault at his diaphragm. One of the policemen bullied a glass of water off a restaurant. Ratan rinsed his mouth out, and splashed some water on his face.

He felt empty and frightened, the inside of his head as dark as the van. They jolted off again.

'There's only so much a man can take,' one policeman said.

The others grunted in assent.

Crispin was startled by Ratan's rejoinder.

'Not to be here,/not to be anywhere,/And soon; nothing more terrible,/nothing more true.'

'Why do you say that?'

Crispin sounded frightened.

Ratan laughed.

'I didn't say that. It's from a poem about the fear of death. Listen:

This is a special way of being afraid ...
... this is what we fear—no sight, no sound,
    No touch or taste or smell, nothing to think with,
Nothing to love or link with,
The anesthetic from which none come round.'

'Scary.'

'Not as scary as finding out it isn't true.'

'Huh?'

'Just my head, Crispin. Pay no heed. Drop me off at the naka, okay? I'll walk from there.'

'Sure. Today of all days.'

The drive lasted half an hour more, half an hour of being trapped in a black cube of dread.

When they reached the naka, Ratan let Crispin have his way. Crispin walked him into the lift at Nandanvan, shut the door and disappeared.

Ratan fumbled with his key at the door and almost fell into the house. It sucked him in hungrily and shut out the day. He slumped to the floor shaking with distress, back to the wall, fingers clawing at his scalp.

The paroxysm abated. Ratan rose, remembered guiltily he hadn't looked in on his father yet. The truth was, he hurried to his father's bedside not to comfort but to be comforted. The thought that Arjun might not recognize this lanced him with fresh pain.

Arjun Oak was awake.

Jafar's daughter was doing her homework on the balcony. Her face lit up as she turned at Ratan's step, then turned grave, infected by his anxiety. An awareness of the day, of the madness outside, flooded her young face. Ratan would have liked to comfort her with a touch on her shoulder, but he was suddenly aware of the smells that clung to him—disinfectant, vomit, smoking flesh, death. He carried all this as contagion.

'Have you eaten, beta?' he asked. 'You can stay and finish your homework, if you wish. If you want to go home, I'll be here now.'

'Daade-abba won at chess again.' She smiled. 'You better help me play next time, Chachu. And I made lunch today! Daade-abba loved it!'

Arjun looked happy.

As usual, the children had delighted him. Ratan interpreted his father's glance at the fridge. There was a cache of chocolate he kept for them.

'You're sure Faraz will like chocolate today?' Ratan quizzed Salma.

The girl giggled.

Faraz almost never got his share. Salma's usual excuse was 'Oh, Faraz hates chocolate—*today*!'

After Salma left, Ratan pulled up a chair next to his father. He had given Arjun's comfort no more than a cursory glance, even failed to check the urosac. His own need was far more urgent. And having got here, next to his father, Ratan could find nothing to say.

With great difficulty, Arjun advanced a trembling hand towards his son. Ratan guided it to his cheek and leaned against the thin hand, soft as a fallen leaf. He remembered with grief a time not long past when that hand had been hard as a slat, muscular and sinewy from a lifetime of labour.

Ratan was no longer thinking of the events of his day. They had rushed away like scenes glimpsed from a train window. He was hurtling towards something immense and central, a knowledge that drew him and yet receded like the horizon. In silence he tried to ascribe a name to it. *I.*

I.

That's what it was all about.

The I-ness of him, the thing that had been given a name: Ratan. Was he Ratan? Was he Ramratan?

Whose was the face in the mirror?

Ratan Oak, thirty-five, jobless drifter, once associate professor of microbiology, erstwhile husband, anxious son—

Or

Ramratan Oak, age unknown, address unknown, husband of Yashoda, pathologist, prosector, father of–of—of—

Siddharth.

Gnyaneshwar.

A tidal wave of longing battered Ratan's soul as he said those names at last, names that had eluded him for weeks. Siddharth. Gnyaneshwar.

Arjun's hand tensed against Ratan's cheek. Ratan covered the trembling hand with both of his own, and met his father's eyes. An unreal feeling overcame him. His father's face had altered. It was a child's face, but the eyes, grave, full of expectation, were eyes he had known all his life.

Ramratan had refused, as always, to cast the child's horoscope. Gnyaneshwar demurred. He said the name Arjun was not propitious, the stars ordained a name that began with *Sha*—

How did a son of his get such fool notions?

He noted in his diary.

Arjun Gnyaneshwar Oak, born 5 May 1925.

It was more than sufficient.

He wasn't as sanguine when Arjun was left in his care.

Six days old, and already he looked the world in the eye.

Ramratan knew this child was different. Arjun would make his own sufficiencies. He, Ramratan, could only prepare him.

Was that enough? He remembered worrying, but he was already feeble by then—how old, how old was he? Where did he go? How end? How begin?

Aloud, Ratan addressed Arjun.

'Baba, there are some things I must tell you. First I want to show you a book.'

He went to fetch the book, hurrying so that the moment should stay, willing his father's attention to continue past their brief separation. Once Ratan was home, Arjun had a way of drifting off to sleep. From sheer relief, Ratan suspected.

Arjun, too, had prepared himself when Ratan was away from the room. He looked alert, the way he did when he was summoning his dodgy vocabulary.

Ratan opened the book at the dedication, that maddening glyph he could make no sense of.

Arjun took a swift look at it and smiled.

It was more than a smile. Arjun's face was charged with life. He put the book away with a flattening gesture, and transfixed Ratan with the cunctation that signalled he was about to speak.

'Trunk,' Arjun said.

Ratan knew his father meant the iron trunk that was called the 'steamer trunk'.

The steamer trunk was part of Ratan's childhood. It was opened only very rarely and with great ceremony. He had never actually investigated its contents, but suspected it held lives squirrelled away till he should be old enough, or tough enough to examine them.

When his parents moved into Nandanvan twelve years ago, Ratan was in New York. The first time Ratan entered the flat, his mother's touch was everywhere. *She* wasn't there.

He pushed the thought away angrily. He had lost her as he had lost everything else in his narrow life. All he had left was a fistful of odds and ends. Darned if he would let them go.

This other brain within his, this parallel circuitry of memory clamouring for notice, deserved a hearing.

Where had she put the trunk? It was too large to be stowed away in the kitchen loft.

Yes, of course! It was furniture now—flat-topped, sturdy, the size of a small table. Ironing table? Settee?

It was the settee in the passage. Covered over in Lepakshi kalamkari, its quilted seat had worn thin these twelve years. A convenient parking spot for laundry, last week's papers and shopping bags, a perch for a snack in a hurry, for an argument with Prema in the kitchen. It had been right here, back to the wall, all these years. Hidden in plain sight, unexpected steganography, grimoire perhaps to his chancy other life

It wasn't even locked. The hasp relented with a touch of oil. The lid almost defeated him, it was so heavy. Luckily, there was enough space away from the wall to ease the lid up and he was saved the labour of having to drag its deadweight. The trunk was lined with wood, cedar from the smell. The lid had a label stuck inside, almost worn away now, just a few vestiges of colour and the tail end of a word in Edwardian curlicue.

Ratan recognized the soft cotton cover within as an old sari of his mother's. He winced at the stab of distress it inflicted.

Swiftly he removed the familiar contents without noticing the days, the years, the torments and joys they contained. These were layers of his own life—infancy, childhood, boyhood.

All familiar, all useless, all lost.

He ignored them. Beneath, wrapped in his mother's wedding sari were mementoes too private for his eyes. He lifted off this bundle of silk carefully and carried it into the living room, leaving it on the sofa until he could return it to its cenotaph. He was now touching the bottom of the trunk, and he had found nothing. Nothing of what he sought, nothing of what he thought Arjun meant.

He was wrong. That was merely the top tray. The trunk went deeper. The tray was fitted with beautiful precision, so it lifted off easily. The scent of camphor mixed with cedar, a complex accord he could only identify as age.

Books. A spectacle case. A fob watch.

And then—

His case. His necropsy case. His instruments.

His fingers caressed the mahogany lid, finding lost landmarks. Here was the scratch Bhiku made when he put a pair of curved scissors wiped in alcohol face down on the smooth wood.

Ratan's mouth was dry, his tongue rasped against his palate as his fingers searched for something else. Something on either side of the hinge, etched with the tip of a surgeon's scalpel. The moment he found that indent in the wood against his fingertip, darkness rushed into him, and put out the day.

The mark Salim had made.

The mark Salim had made.

'This is going to fade by next year,' he said. He dabbed a sting of mercurochrome on the thin scar on Ramratan's arm, all that remained of an infected cyst.

'Come, Salim. I expect you to leave a more lasting mark.'

'No, I'm like that consumptive poet. Remember his epitaph?'

'Here lies one whose name was writ in water? Do you know he was one of us?'

'Meaning we're poets too? That we are, Ramratan, that we are.'

'No. He was a medic. Like you and me.'

'Poor chap. Must have monitored his end, day by day. Since I can't scar your skin, let me scar your soul, eh? Give me your instruments—the box, man! I don't need your savage cutlery! Give me your necropsy case. I'm going to scar your soul.'

'Poetry, Salim?'

'No! You're the only human being I know with a tangible soul. *This* is your soul. This box fashioned from a tree you never saw, by a man you never knew. You are like the heroes of the Mahabharata and Ramayana, completed by your weapon, because the weapon only works from your soul. This is your soul, Ramratan, and I'm going to leave a scar on it. How else will you remember me?'

'Where are you off to?'

'Who knows? I'm taking the box with me, you can have it tomorrow.'

Tomorrow came.

Salim was carrying the box when they hid in the labyrinth of Madanpura. He was still holding it when he crumpled, felled by a bullet in his neck.

The scar Salim had left on his soul.

The scar Salim had left on his soul. Ratan's fingertips traced the scar.[•]

ہم نے مانا کہ تغافل نہ کرو گے لیکن
خاک ہو جائیں گے ہم، تم کو خبر ہوتے تک

The silver clasp was tarnished, but it gave willingly.

Here it was, his knife!

The instant he picked it up, Ratan's headache receded. The knife completed him.

Salim had been right. He was all right, he would be fine tomorrow morning. He could open the next heart like a flower with his knife, and not go snipping at it like a tailor!

Whistling, Ratan shut the box.

[•] **Mirza Ghalib**:
transliteration:
Hum ne maana ke taghaaful na karoge lekin
Khaak hojaaenge hum tumko khabar hote tak.
translation:
You won't miss my funeral, I doubt not at all
Alas, my dust will witness your coming.

The trunk was emptied. The spectacles and the watch were for later. For now, he would put them away where they belonged—in his desk.

Ratan turned his attention to the books.

The *Beast* again. This copy of Lockwood Kipling's book had a cover different from the one he'd pinched from Shakuntala Salwe. This had a caparisoned elephant kneeling against a Prussian blue background stamped with a faint pattern. The frontispiece had two birds glaring at each other as if an invisible mirror were transposed between them. These birds seemed similar to the rebus of the dedication.

This was a first edition, 1891.

There was no inscription.

Facing the dedication was a verse by Walt Whitman. The dedication, the tiger with its complex calligraphy, and the birds were acknowledged as the work of Munshi Sher Muhammad.

Why had Lockwood done that?

Mohsin Ahmad had made the drawings. Yet, Lockwood Kipling had ascribed the drawings to this stranger, this *Munshi Sher Muhammad.*

Who were these people, anyway? What were they doing in his head, cluttering up his life?

There were two more books. One, a flat brown ledger, he recognized instantly. Like the spectacle case and the watch, it belonged in his desk. He opened it briefly to reassure himself with a glimpse of the first page. The ink had faded a bit. Waterman's blueblack. He had always used Waterman's. For the price it ought to keep its blackness.

His irritation receded as he read the single word on the yellowing page, remembering with keen pleasure the sharp strokes and slashes he had inflicted on the page in what Salim called his 'slapdash hand'. The word held all the speed, all the brio it conveyed to him.

NECROPSY.

The other book …

Ratan's chest thudded like doom, low and heavy and meaningful, every beat an augury. He carried it, with the ledger and the glasses and the watch, to his desk. He placed the book on the desk, and carefully stowed away the rest in the drawer after emptying it of things that no longer mattered.

The instrument case found its own place on the shelf. It looked as if it had stood there all his life.

He put the other things back in the trunk, brought the top tray back from the living room. He tucked the sari over it, refusing once again the remembered scent of his mother's touch. He shut the trunk. It soon lost itself again under the cumulus of banality—quilt, cover, cushion, dog-eared magazines. Adsorbed by life, it became a scar, a stain. Provenance erased, it was a settee once again.

The next hour passed in a blur. He felt an urgent need to make certain of the tangible, the immediate, the visceral, and convince himself of his own necessity.

Ratan launched himself at what remained of the day. He cooked, fed his father, ran the washing machine (a recent luxury he couldn't stop gloating over), stripped and made Arjun's bed, even though this was usually a morning chore. Then he forced himself to eat, distracted bites and hasty swallows, between washing up and waiting for the drinking water to come to a boil. He finished with the kitchen for the night, picked up two bottles of iced water from the fridge, and joined his father.

He settled Arjun in bed. Neither father nor son expected that to mean the day was over. For both of them, it was the beginning of a long night.

Ratan had considered this moment for years. If he were ever to speak of the parallel life that absorbed him, he knew it could only be to his father. Not just because he saw Arjun as a sort of bridge between his two lives, a flesh-and-blood connect with –

What?

Imagination? Hallucination? Memory?

Ratan could put no word to it, neither define his feelings nor his fears. A growing sequence of events was rapidly mapping another life for him. Different, and yet entwined with the life he lived in Nandanvan.

What would this parallel life do to Arjun?

Ratan had never seen his father as a man whose brain was corroded by slow decay. He was Baba, the man who had all the answers, and more often, all the questions. Nothing could change that.

Ratan did not care what his parallel life might do to Arjun. His own need overpowered any shred of altruism. He needed answers, and Arjun held them.

This other life had smouldered in him for as long as he could remember. Stray sparks often flew out and burned like cinders in the eye. Not until two days ago had it clamoured with such imperium. It had been a presence, a memory. Now, it was a life.

No. That wasn't true.

It had always been a life. His own life, verso.

He had never owned up to it, that's all.

Arjun may have known it all along.

Ratan had hidden it desperately from his mother, fearing her snap diagnosis.

'Just memories of your last birth. All of us have them!'

She'd had a very structured view of the afterlife. Now that she was dead, it no longer amused him. Death was a blank wall. Once you got at it, there was nothing.

Besides, this wasn't memory any more. It was now.

Arjun didn't take to labels. Arjun's universe was never a finite galaxy. Ratan remembered their conversations on the terrace with hope, Arjun's voice urging him to look at the night sky beyond the stars he could see.

'The Milky Way is such a small galaxy, Ratan. We must get ourselves a bigger place!'

Now that he was here, and this was the moment, what would he say to his father?

That he was Ramratan? That he shared Ramratan? That he remembered Ramratan? That he, Ratan, son of Arjun, was actually his own great Ramratan? That he had—impossible thought—held his infant father, Arjun, against his middle-aged heart? Each notion was more insane than the last.

'Baba, sometimes I think like Ramratan Oak,' Ratan divulged eventually.

Arjun's response was immediate. He must have prepared these words a long time.

He too had waited for this moment.

'I know.'

'I feel I'm living his life, as well as mine.'

'Stop.'

Pause.

There was more to come. Long pause.

Wait, I'm finding that word for you, it was just here, a moment ago, just on the tip of my tongue. Darn. Slipped away again, but I'll find it. Wait. Don't distract me. Don't speak. My word. I will find it. On my own. My word. Yes.

'Stop. Fighting.'

Pause.

'It.'

Ratan took that in, and echoed it.

'Yes, Baba, I'll stop fighting it.'

This echo played Arjun false. Anger stung his eyes. Ratan looked away. He had learnt that Arjun could feel challenged by his gaze, and withdraw completely. He must give his father the ease of time.

Ratan kept his eyes on his toenails. They needed trimming.

What was the earthly use of toenails? Another atavism the body could junk with ease. Except, the thought of toes without nails was somehow disgusting.

'You have stopped fighting it.'

The sentence shot out like a prophecy. It meant not just what it stated, but what it would do to the rest of Ratan's life. It was an announcement of victory, not doom.

Ratan's immediate feeling was of reprieve. Baba thinks it's okay.

Then he noticed the corollary with the reprieve.

'So what are you going to do about it now?'

'Nothing. I'll take it as it comes.'

His father smiled.

Ratan felt an immense weight lift off him. It's all right. I'll take it as it comes. I don't have a brain tumour. I'm not going to die. I don't need to worry about Baba. I'll be around to care for him. I don't have to feel bad about feeling good over autopsies ...

It was like the time he came home from school with a bad report card. Once he was past the telling, all was right.

Ratan grinned. He felt about ten years old.

'There are so many things I need to ask you—' he began with a rush, and was stopped by the bafflement in Arjun's eyes.

Of course.

Arjun had been twelve or thirteen when Ramratan died. He, Ratan, knew much more about Ramratan than Arjun ever could. There was little, really, he could ask his father.

'Baba, now that you know how I feel, I'm not frightened any more. I can take my time to understand,' he said earnestly.

Perhaps you never will.

'Yes. I may never understand. I'll discover it's not that important to understand. Perhaps, I'll grow content to just be what I am. Two men in one skin.'

What a burden to have to bear, Ratan!

'Yes, it is a burden, Baba. *You* know it is a burden, because until I took charge of it now, you carried it for me.'

He brought the books, and opened *Beast and Man in India* at the dedication.

'Do you know what this means, Baba?'

No.

'I will tell you. The other three were Krishnarao Oak, Darayus Dhanji "Surveyor" and Sheikh Mohsin Ahmad. What?'

Arjun looked puzzled. Ratan caught his thought.

'That's right. You remember "the Other Three" as Nusserwanji Surveyor, Bilal Ahmad and—Lockwood Kipling?'

Yes!

'With Ramratan, the Sign of Four. Like the Sherlock Holmes story?'

Yes! Yes!

'Ramratan read you that story?'

All. All.

'All the Sherlock Holmes stories?'

Arjun laughed. Sheer pleasure erased every crease of worry and torment from his face.

They didn't speak any more that night, but sat a long while in silence, revelling in what wasn't said.

Ratan woke in the middle of the night. His father was fast asleep. The room blazed with light. He felt stiff and cold. His mouth tasted poisonous and his feet were numb.

The digital clock face pulsed 3 a.m. in eldritch green. He had slept two hours, cramped and upright in the bedside chair.

He put the light out and tiptoed out of Arjun's room. He brushed his teeth, brewed coffee, and carried the mug to his desk.

He moved the ledger to one side and reached for the third book he had taken from the trunk. He could put it off no longer, though the thought of opening it made his chest tighten with dread.

Ratan switched on the anglepoise lamp. It pooled a bright splash on the faded brown canvas cover, gilding it with the light he remembered. What if it was nothing like that on the page? What if the book opened to a world that had died and shrivelled, leaving behind nothing but fossils, parched twigs, and bones like tombstones?

What if it was nothing like it had been? What if it had never been anything like that?

Ratan switched off the lamp. As he stepped out onto the balcony, a voice echoed in his skull.

'What are you going to do about it?'

'What are you going to do about it?'

Mohsin Chacha cut a swagger like the man on the frieze as he continued.

'I've quenched your thirst with my urine and fed you my shit. I carry god in my asshole. So what are you going to do about it?'

His companions roared with laughter.

'Why are you laughing? That is exactly what he's saying. You don't think the sculptor saw it like that?'

They were looking at stone figures that seemed to have stepped out of the wall. From Ramratan's vantage, it appeared as if the sculptor had seen the fat man and his wife exactly as Mohsin Chacha put it.

How old was he that day? Eight? No, nine.

It was a birthday gift, that trip to the Kanheri caves. He had never forgotten it—touch, smell, vision—and above all those words. So mysterious at nine, and then, like invisible writing popping up magically with time. His memory of it now was even more real than the actual experience of it.

Ramratan wasn't supposed to be here. They had left him playing in the sun, but he'd tired of that long ago. He had loitered in and out of caves till he'd caught up with them. They hadn't noticed him yet.

The wall looked like stone but was, in reality, a membrane of finely crenellated silk, thin, like a sari. Within lurked a secret world where people were curious about *him*. They pressed themselves against the membrane, so they could see him better through their blind, silk-covered eyes. They were close, so close, Ramratan could feel their heat. He was afraid to touch them, of course. But he was also afraid to look, lest they catch him staring, particularly the women who didn't have too many clothes on.

When he came in from the sun and into the shadowy corridor, that silk between them seemed so tenuous, he could have ripped it with a breath.

Would that let him in?

What would these two swaggering couples have to say to him?

There were four of them, two fat men and their wives, standing insolently as if they owned the place.

Darayus, his finger inching across an inscription, said, 'It says here that these are the donors who paid for the sculptures. The arrogant new rich!'

'Flung the sculptor a coin, perhaps. That must have hurt,' Appa added.

'No, no, Krishna, I assure you he was the soul of courtesy! How are you, my man? How's Vahini? How are the kids? Tell me if you need anything. Your bhabhi remembered you on Diwali. *That* kind of courtesy. Sweet talk is what the sculptor heard. But when the man was no longer before his eyes, *this* is what the sculptor saw.'

'Come, Mohsin! He might have simply wanted to

make their figures human—compared to the divine perfection he had to pull off on the others!'

'It was rage, I tell you! What? You don't think the sculptor felt rage? Look at this man's attitude, paunch one pace ahead of the rest of him, chest puffed out, chin tilted up, defying not just you and me, but the towering Buddhas on either side of him. Look at him, Krishna, and tell me truly you cannot feel the sculptor's contempt for him!'

Ramratan couldn't but agree. It was easier to understand if you put clothes on the stone figures, but Mohsin Chacha had it right. This man was gloating. Spine arched back, belly flopping free of his dhotar, ready for a belch. He might scratch his balls in irreverent ease any moment now. His companion had been erased, gouged out by vandals long ago, but she couldn't have been much different.

'Still, Mohsin, he's done a good job, you must admit. He didn't let contempt get in the way of art.'

'Get in the way? Contempt *is* the art here, Darayus. Feel this man, come here, put your hands here.'

Mohsin placed a palm on the man's belly. He rubbed it as though trying to still its rumbling, and belched sonorously. To Ramratan, the belch came burbling out of the stone belly and the dhoti looked visibly looser. To complete the illusion, Mohsin crumpled his thin face in disgust, holding his nose.

Ramratan could almost smell the fart.

'You don't want to touch him, do you, Darayus? You're even more frightened to touch her, eh?'

'Not frightened. Hesitant.'

'Why? I'll tell you. The moment I touch one of these figures, I wilt. As long as that is flesh, I am rock. When I look at this man's belly, it makes me want to fuck. Consider this, Darayus. This mound of fat settled in the hollow of the hip, the navel like a thumbprint, all this is rock. Coarse, unpolished rock. Pitted, weathered rock. But when the sun lies aslant this belly, it is flesh. Beneath its surface life is shouting out to be heard. I want to put my ear to it, to hear yesterday's hunger, today's glut and tomorrow's shit. But I won't. I will keep my distance, and my erection.'

'That's a man, in case you didn't notice. What does that say about you, Mohsin?'

'Arre Darayus, keep your labels for your fossils. The living respond to *everything*. Man, woman, animal, thing. Subject is irrelevant. Joy is everything.'

'Joy?'

'What else? A window flung open somewhere, and all the world comes racing into your veins.'

'Ah that.'

'Yes, *that*.'

They fell silent.

Somehow so did the four figures. They seemed to shrink back into the wall. Perhaps that was because Appa moved, and Ramratan, for the first time, caught sight of what stood at the far end of the corridor.

An immense figure, gracious, commanding, aloof. The calm face forgiving the coarse swagger of these four boastful mortals. Forgiving, but not overlooking. Enduring, but not censuring.

'We should have brought Lockwood along,' Darayus said. 'Mohsin would have shocked him.'

'No.' Appa sounded sad. 'Lockwood cannot be shocked. He is above shock.'

'I think he's a poor judge of art, even if he is a professor of art.'

'Let's say he professes art.'

'You can say what you like, Krishna. Lockwood Kipling is no judge of art. He is its executioner.'

'That's too harsh, Mohsin.'

'Harsh? Have you seen his drawings? Perfect corpses! Lineaments without life! He should be an embalmer.'

'You dislike him, Mohsin.'

'Yes! Yes! I dislike him! But I love him because he is my friend. He's asked me to draw some pictures for his book. "Mussalman art," he specified. "Please Mohsin, it must be Mussalman art." There is no Mussalman art and Hindu art and Christian art bhaiyya, I tell him. Art is art.

'"Oh no, that's where you're wrong," he tells me. "Islam will permit you to draw a flower but not a woman."

'You are right, I tell him. There is one difference. Mussalman art can make a flower look like a woman. And Hindu art can make a woman look like a flower. Put that in your book.'

'I don't think he will, Mohsin.'

Again, Appa sounded sad.

Ramratan felt a clutch of dread.

'He'll put his thoughts in that book, not yours or mine. So what have you decided to draw for him?'

'I will draw exactly what I feel. Just like this sculptor here squeezed this hillside into the shapes in his heart.'

Mohsin slapped the fat man's stone belly. Appa, without turning around, grabbed Ramratan and swung him onto his shoulder. Mohsin reached up and settled his cap on Ramratan's head, and they went laughing out into the sun.

How old was he that day? Nine?

And how old is his memory of that day? Thirty-five?

Why did the memory flash up from the abyss?

Ratan, thirty-five, standing in the dark in 1992 felt the hot sun bite his neck as he bounced on Appa's shoulder down the stone stairs of Kanheri.

How did he know it was Kanheri? He had never visited Kanheri. So he shouldn't know the fat stone man, the overpowering Buddha, the monkeys chattering in the sun.

But he did.

He knew them as he knew Appa's comfort, Darayus' kindness, and Mohsin's bile.

Ratan picked up Lockwood Kipling's book. The elephant on the cover looked moth-eaten, wrinkled, bundled in its caparison but coming apart.

A pair of stylized birds were fashioned in mirror-image Nasta`līq calligraphy. The esoteric symbol below these was a sham, a mere arabesque of the publisher's name, MacMillan & Co.

The enantiomeric birds spelled the benediction.

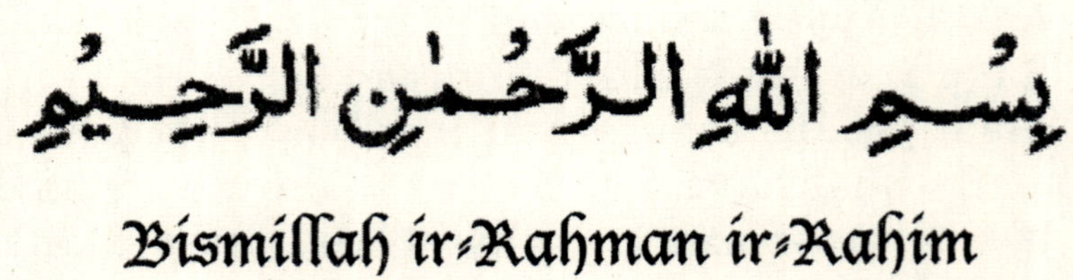

'In the name of Allah, most Gracious, most Compassionate'

Ratan traced the Arabic with a trembling finger. It was the one line of Arabic Mohsin had taught him.

'Words enough for you to assimilate the world, beta. All the wisdom in all languages, the true essence of all religions, is in this one line'.

Ratan closed the book. He found pencil and paper, and shut his eyes as he tried to write the unfamiliar script.

As his pencil moved...

It was like running backwards.

It was like running backwards.

Running backwards with the wind in his hair, exhilarated as he sensed the fathom in unfamiliarity.

He heard Mohsin's voice.

'Not bad. Now your name is justified.'

'My name?'

'Don't you know why your father named you Ramratan?'

'No.'

'Never mind, Krishna will tell you himself someday. You know the song?'

Ramratan shook his head and Mohsin sang in a cracked high voice.

'पायोजी मैंने राम रतन धन पायो,
मीरा के प्रभू गिरिधर नागर,
हरस हरस जस गायो,
पायोजी मैंने, राम रतन धन पायो!'*

As always with Mohsin Chacha, in those early days, it ended in a romp with both of them singing in mad discordance.

Ram ratan dhan payo.

Ram ratan dhan payo.

Ratan opened his eyes as the voices faded from his brain. He compared what he had written with the markings in the birds. The letters seemed to match, but he couldn't be sure if they made sense. He'd ask Jafar in the morning.

Right now, there was something else he had to do.

Ratan's hands hovered over the third book.

Of his other life, imagined or remembered, the strongest imprint was contained in this book. That life took colour from these pages. It would fade with them, grow pale, foxed and indecipherable, its richness reduced to a stain.

If I open the book now and find it's all different, then it's all a lie and it was never like that.

The thought induced a terrible sorrow. Like a loss, a displacement. Not to be ruminated over.

He couldn't face it now.

What then? Live a lie?

---

* Transliteration:

Payoji maine Ram ratan dhan payo,
Meera ke prabhu giridhar naagar,
harash harash jas gaayo,
Payoji maine, Ram ratan dhan payo!

translation:

'My jewels, my affluence, my esteem, all derive from him,'
carols Meera of her Lord.
Her hum, her hymn, her hymeneal, it is always Rama.

That voice again!

When had she said those words?

Yashoda's voice. Angry. Bitter. Crying out to him beneath the fury.

Take this thorn from me!

Ratan was homesick for that voice, those words, the scent of her skin.

What had Crispin said?

Says I stink of the dead.

The words brought back a moment …

… in the yard, beneath the raintree.

In the yard, beneath the raintree …

… a pail of water waited for him, to lave his feet after their daylong imprisonment. He liked to walk home barefoot across the grass, straight to his bath. He insisted on washing his clothes himself, fearful some mephitic vapour might offend Yashoda.

The bathroom was at the back of the house. Until the pipes were put in, it had been a long walk from the pump in the backyard. Now Yashoda wouldn't have it any different. The bathroom and the lavatory had no place within the house. She wouldn't let him get 'as British as all that'.

Just wait till you're old, he shot back. Then let me find out how British you've grown. One day they'd have enough money to settle this argument.

When the boys were three and five, he had put in a pane of stained glass in the ventilator. In the gloaming the stone flags flared scarlet, viridian, gold, and he treasured that bit of magic every evening.

She would appear with a fresh white dhoti as he finished, the bathroom steamy from the hot breath of the huge copper cauldron. He could feel that heat now, on his skin, in his soul. He ached with yearning.

'I don't stink of the dead, do I, Yashoda?'

She breathed him in, deeply, not replying.

'Yashoda?'

'You know what they call me? Dead man's wife, married to a man who makes his living off the dead.'

'And?'

'None of them know a live man, do they?'

'They don't?'

'No. They don't. Not *this* live.'

'No. Not *this* live.'

Ratan, his hands still uncertain on the book, felt his blood recede as the moment passed. Another overtook him, and brought sadness, not lust.

Again that lilting teasing voice.

Have you ever been able to walk away from a book, any book, without opening it?

'Have you ever been able to walk away from a book, any book, without opening it?'

Laughing, he had conceded her point.

But there was one book he had never opened, the diary she kept so carefully locked away.

It hurt him that she locked that drawer every time.

Eventually, thirty years into their life together, he dared to ask her why.

She had laughed.

'Have you ever been able to walk away from a book, any book, without opening it?'

He had laughed too, but the injustice of it had stung him. The key was always there on the ledge. He could open the drawer any time he wanted.

He never had and never would.

He told himself it was habit that made her do it, nothing else. It hurt him, nonetheless.

When he was younger he'd wanted mercy. As he aged, all he craved was justice.

As he aged, all he craved was justice.

In today's idiom, Ratan thought bitterly, that quite defined his own marriage.

He was done with wanting Prema to be nice to him. All he wanted was for her to be fair.

Perhaps his moments of injustice to Yashoda, recalled without name or instance, had made him scrupulous with Prema.

Or so he believed.

He understood Yashoda's need to lock away her diary now, as Ramratan never had. It was habit, born of Ramratan's unfairness to her in their early years when she was still the widow he had married, and not yet his wife. He had never voiced it. But implicit in all his instants of hesitation was the question: *So was it like this with him?*

The black ice of doubt rimed Ramratan's pleasure. And each time Yashoda would overlook insult and pain and thaw it with her mercy.

Did Ramratan ever see that?

Ratan did.

That's what this was all about. Why had he to accept this other life? *Because it was incomplete.* Now, it was his to complete.

Ratan opened the book.

His eyes blurred. His eyes cleared.

Nothing had changed. It was all as he remembered.

That slow wakening of colours, their breathless rush and sullen retreat.

All was as Ned Jones had left it, backlit with radiance.

The pictures grew with each viewing, all through Ramratan's life.

9 December 1992

Woken at 7 a.m. by Radhakrishnan's phone call, Ratan tumbled out from oblivion into chaos.

All he could hear on the phone was the hullabaloo of toddlers. The harried father shouted over the din.

'Ratan? Don't try and make it to the Archives, okay? If you can give me the reference number on the phone, I'll get you the papers.'

It took Ratan a long moment to place Radhakrishnan, the Archives, the reference number and the riots, all in perspective. He'd get the papers? What was the man talking about, wasn't there a curfew on?

Somebody took the kids away. Radhakrishnan's voice came down ten decibels.

'They have a toy phone, but it's no use,' he complained. 'They only go for the real thing. Can you hear me now, Ratan?'

'Yes, I heard you before, too. Would you settle for a toy when you can get the real thing?'

'Eh? Of course not. I see your point.' He laughed.

'You can't possibly be going there yourself. There's a curfew on,' Ratan said.

'I'm on some kind of vigilance duty. They need someone there, and I volunteered, so that I can get on with my work. They're sending transport, so that's something. And there's extra pay. I may be holed up there for a day or two.'

'What about your family?'

'They'll be okay. I hope. My brother lives across the landing, so we're practically the same household. We've been through this before, you know.'

'Elsewhere?'

'No, right here. In the sixties. Things don't change with time. Only the target changes. Then it was Tamils, today it is Mussalmans. Tomorrow it will be someone else.'

'You must have been a kid then.'

'Twelve. My father was forty-five. They beat him to a pulp. Five of them. Caught him as he crossed the street to the milk booth at six in the morning. Thrashed him with lathis. He bled to death right there before we could get to him.'

Ratan didn't know what to say.

The man's voice betrayed no pain. He was simply stating facts. He was explaining why this was the only way he could live his life, by keeping the day going while the city around him ground to a halt.

'I don't know why I'm telling you all this, depressing you before the day's begun. It's all done with. Like I said, I'm going to be right there, so I can collect your papers for you if you'll give me the name and number?'

Ratan looked hastily through the papers on his desk. Both the papers were where he'd left them—in Lockwood's book, the copy he'd lifted from Shakuntala's house.

'I have a receipt for the Xeroxed papers,' he said cautiously. 'Quite a lot of papers. Someone I know asked for them. Her name is Shakuntala Salwe.'

'Wait a moment! You don't mean our Salwebai, do you? Sixtyish, nauvari sari, persistent as a—sorry, some relative of yours?'

'No, no. A friend asked me to look into the matter. Yes, I think we mean the same person.'

'If you'd told me earlier, I would have saved you a lot of time. She led us a regular dance, I can tell you. Kept at it till she finally found what she wanted. I admire her gumption. She came armed with some family papers, and demanded we trace names and addresses. You know that isn't our brief. The Archives are meant for researchers, so the guys at the desk bounced her out. Unfortunately, she met me.'

'I thought you were a researcher – that's what Prema told me. I had no idea you were on their staff.'

'I've researched there for so long, I'm furniture. I translate, transcribe, do all sorts of things.'

'Tamil? In the *Bombay* Archives?'

'Marathi. I'm what's called a medievalist. I'm out of my period in the Archives. But for the last two years I've been stuck in the mid-1700s. So anyway, Salwebai and I got chatting, and the upshot was that I did the ferreting for her, and it wasn't easy. Eventually, everybody got involved in the search. For once we were looking for people, real people, not just ghosts. That's always thrilling.'

'About the plague, I gather ...'

Ratan let his voice trail off. He didn't know how long he could keep this up without blurting out that Shakuntala Salwe was dead. How was he to explain where or how he came in?

'Yes. Quarantine papers, mostly.'

'Quarantine papers?'

'Mystified? She was, too. Couldn't understand how they could isolate a whole city.'

'That happened? Bombay was isolated?'

'In a way. It got split up into compartments. Walls came down hard between people. You're a microbiologist, aren't you? Then you know all about it, better than me.'

'No,' Ratan said hastily. 'I don't know anything about what happened here. And I need to, if I'm going to help her with these papers. Do you have something I can read?'

'Sure. A cartload. I wouldn't wish it on you. Tell you what, give me a call around two in the afternoon? I'll see how I can get the stuff to you. Where will you be?'

Ratan's eye caught the clock.

Half past seven! Crispin would be at his gate at nine.

Radhakrishnan cut through his explanation with a hurried, 'Call me', reeled off a phone number, and rang off.

Crispin was on time.

Ratan had just got Arjun comfortable for the day when the watchman delivered that message – with a newfound respect, explained by the police van waiting at the gate.

'Just as well,' Jafar remarked dryly as Ratan stopped by at the laundry. 'Who knows? Today the watchman may call me by my name again, seeing that my protector has police protection.'

Jafar's irony was not misplaced.

Over the last two days, everybody had forgotten his name. He was called *tum log* now – 'you people'. The walls had come down hard.

It was the hour for the morning exodus and Ratan tarried a bit at the gate to see what blessings might come his way. Sure enough, Siplani appeared out of thin air to ingratiate himself with Ratan's uniformed companions.

'Day or night, the police is there for us. No matter what rumours we hear, common man survives because of police. Doctors also, don't think I do not appreciate you doctors, even test-west doctory is something, eh Ratan? Very good. And today you are on special duty. Blood test, urine test, everything is done officially. I understand. I admire public service, I really admire it. We are here to look after your father, Ratan, you go for duty without tension.'

Siplani's oily smile spread its slick over Jafar.

'Ratan can count on us always, eh Jafar Bhai, what do you say?'

Jafar sprinkled water on the hissing iron and ducked under a convenient cloud of steam. Ratan, hating himself, endured Siplani's pleasantries and climbed into the police van.

It smelt worse today and the havaldar had opened a window.

Crispin looked pale. They didn't speak. The tense air in the van held all the words they needed to say.

The havaldar ripped open a sachet of paan masala. In the murky interior, the foil leapt from his fist in a flare of silver and blue like the trick of an arsonist. A shrill current of ersatz rose shocked Ratan's nostrils, and his breakfast lurched against his ribs. Crispin looked away.

The havaldar's chaw could not cancel the truth that fouled the air.

The van smelt of fear. Fecal, halitotic, sweaty. The odour human beings exude when threatened.

'There will be quite a few this morning,' Crispin remarked.

'Yes Sahib, better do them fast or they'll pile up,' the havaldar chuckled.

'What do you mean?' Ratan asked sharply. He felt Crispin's restraining hand on his shoulder.

The havaldar smiled. He had perfect teeth, pearly in their dazzling symmetry.

'It is just beginning. Let's see what these hooligans can do first. Then we'll show them. You'll hear the news by afternoon.'

Ratan fought for breath. Words rushed and were lost. On his shoulder, Crispin's hand compelled like iron. Under its pressure, Ratan's shudder of loathing subsided, slowly.

'What's that you've brought, Ratan?' Crispin's voice reached past his rage, and recalled him to sanity.

A plastic bag rested on Ratan's knees. He had his box with him again! Ratan thrilled at the thought. The wood felt like a lover's skin to his touch. Every cleft, every pore, was a day in their life together, every knot in its grain a homecoming.

If Crispin was surprised by the box, he offered no comment. There was no recognition in his eyes and he displayed no more than a polite curiosity.

'Antique piece?' he asked.

How could Crispin guess what that box meant to him? Crispin was a friend, yes. But he wasn't Salim.

The havaldar drew their attention to a thick funnel of smoke unravelling in the east and smearing a grey pall over the skyline.

'Asalfa.'

Ratan hadn't a clue where Asalfa was.

'Off Sahar airport. Ghatkopar side,' Crispin explained. 'It is a long way off.'

Ratan pictured it.

A road run berserk, traffic snarls matted and choked in exhalations of their own filth. Broad-backed gutters, their oily scum a glacial glint in the sun. Tidal webs of garbage washed up against buildings like end moraines. Buildings erupting past the hairline, breakaways from the grid of roads, lanes, parks, pavements, lunging into the traffic. Peopled long before they were plastered or painted, numbered or named. Concrete structures extruding like warts, flat-topped, scaly, confluent, prurient with urgencies. Walls like slow bruises changing colour after seasons of abuse as old Bollywood posters peeled off, and returning finally to their natural pigments of earth and excrement. Pavements spilling over with lives that began faraway and were headed elsewhere. The taste of dust and onions, the musk of freshly hewn wood, and the sting of burning plastic squeezing the lungs.

And through all this flux, a rootedness—a shrine beneath a peepul, a garland on a cross, a woman winnowing wheat on a ragged charpai. Pickles in glass jars set out on sills to trap the sun. The intent faces of children, picking their way to school past jungles of scrap metal, bamboo and PVC spilling from makeshift factories and warehouses. The plaintive azaan lurching heavenward over the visceral throb of stereos in parked cabs.

All this had been cremated.

The pillar of smoke rose solid like a buttress holding up the empty highway of the sky. The ashes would disperse with the first sea breeze, and not one wayward cinder would squeeze tears from a stranger's eye.

'Something caught fire?'

A stupid question, but if Crispin hadn't asked it, Ratan would have.

'These things happen. If you ask for it, these things happen! You are doctors of the dead and you are used to looking for reasons, so I expect you'll understand. Shops and godowns were torched last night. Some boys ran up Kajupada hill and threw down fireballs. So? Can you blame them? They were angry. Wouldn't you be angry in their place? On Monday night these people break the Ram Mandir, break the murti, even! How can our boys keep quiet? Tell me. So Tuesday morning they burnt the masjid on Pipeline. They burnt also one-two shops. Nothing much. Just to teach those gaandus a lesson. Still they do not learn. They bring a complaint to us! That one of their women living in Narendra Chawl was driven out with her children. Why come to us? Why not look after your women? What she was doing in a Hindu chawl, I ask? First you give me answer. That shut them up, doctor. But only for little time. Then they said something, and our boys reacted. But natural. They are young, hot blood. They went up Kajupada and threw down fireballs. Now all the people whose shops and houses are burning come running straight to Saki Naka Chowki. I am from that area, so I know the inside story. All of them are shouting. Police are not helping. Police are supporting troublemakers. Arre baba, if the troublemakers are from Ghatkopar, what Saki Naka police can do? If fire brigade is not coming, what we can do? Police is supposed to do everything or what? Words are not working with these people. Only lathi is the language they understand. One good beating and they all ran away. Except those who fell down, that is. And except those we pushed inside.'

'Inside? For what crime?' Ratan asked. His voice was cold, polite, and interested. But it wasn't his voice, not his voice from now. It was the voice that told him: Ramratan, you have a job to do. *Do it!* Talk to this monster and remember he is a man.

'Crime? Aha! You are a doctor of dead men, you won't understand. A doctor who keeps men alive will understand.

We push them in not because they have committed crime, but to stop them from committing crime. It is called preventive arrest.'

'So all this happened last night? Why isn't the fire out yet?' Ratan persisted.

'What? With only one fire engine? Doctor Sahib, one whole basti, 300 houses, more shops, many more than that, and then all those godowns! Something explodes every five minutes! All sorts of chemicals they have there, who knows what their plans are? Don't tell us those Kajupada boys did it, the Inspector told them. Your own people have done this to you. Your own greed is feeding the fire. No Sahib, this fire will blaze till it burns itself out.'

Crispin had to pull Ratan out when the van lurched to a halt outside the Coroner's Court. Ratan heard him thank the driver, and utter a few friendly words to their voluble companion. But all this was happening far away. He clutched the box to his ribs. It was his only anchor in a world that had imploded, and left him in free fall.

The stink of burnt flesh stung his throat as he stepped into the corridor. His instant reaction was to bolt. That other voice urged him forward.

This is my job, this is what I do.

Then a deeper thought.

This is my dharma.

Ratan was stymied by that.

Dharma? Religion?

The words meant nothing to him. They were common cant in politics and films. An identity badge, used to discriminate and incriminate. Words he abhorred. What were they doing in his rational brain?

'Dharma isn't religion,' Ratan heard his voice argue. 'You could call it ethic, I suppose. But it goes deeper than that, Crispin. It is the stain on your soul.'

'What's that, Ratan?'

'Nothing. Sorry. Look, the Kajupada lot has arrived.'

'Impossible! It happened last night, the havaldar said. The bodies won't turn up till tomorrow. They never send them directly here. Lord! It'll worsen.'

'What's that?'

Ratan pointed to the fracas at the far end of the corridor.

A hearse had discharged its load onto the stone flags.

Usually, the air stilled when corpses were brought into the morgue. White noise ceased. Voices were throttled, feet arrested. For perhaps no longer than a minute, the dead held centre stage. Every eye was riveted on them.

In this warehouse of mortality, death was the paradox. The odour of putrefaction was inhaled and exhaled without protest. The door to the Autopsy Room swung open every hour for exits and entrances that were never noticed.

Trolleys with rubber-sheeted occupants jolted past without ceremony. They carried the newly dead. Absorbed into the system, they were part of the landscape, and did not challenge the eye.

But the corpses that a hearse discharged were different. They were open to question, and must be sized up. They were noticed. When the first one struck the stone courtyard with a cold soft heavy *thwock,* everything stopped. Everything stilled. That corpse, the first one, commanded silence.

Not today.

The alarm that ripped through the small crowd was cut off by the strident bark of policemen. Hastily, in an attempt to hide the dead, havaldars formed a sullen shifty wall.

Mama came trundling out of the mortuary with a trolley and pushed his way around the khaki barricade. Then an unearthly yowl tore from him and he backed away in terror. Trolley abandoned, he ran back into the building.

Ratan and Crispin hurried over.

'Ah, D'Souza. Take a look!'

Ratan looked at the man who had addressed Crispin. The voice reeked of mouthwash and aftershave, the face was suave, fiftyish, smooth. The ACP, probably.

Ratan stared at the tangle of bodies, bent, broken, bloodied, and vomited from the maw of the hearse. Judging from the reek, they had been shoved into it long hours ago. Torsos lay collapsed over invisible heads. Faces stared up blind and passive, framed by angled arms and legs. There were no individuals here. This was one dead organism, many-backed, multi-limbed, hydra-headed.

But not quite dead yet.

Ratan gasped as the flaccid mass stirred. It shook, rumbled, slid. Face, limb and torso twitched as if a galvanic stimulus had revived its traduced heart. The havaldars drew back to a man with strangled curses and mutters of dread.

Here it came again.

Stronger, and lasting longer this time.

As they watched in horror, the soft belly of an old man quivered above his bloodied pajamas. Losing anchor, the corpse slipped onto its side and dragged into view a child's body. The little face was half hidden by a glistening fragment of bone. The bullet had burst through her skull and avulsed the scalp which now hung over her face like macabre orange peel.

A pulpy mass of brain and pulverized bone had dried into glair. The child's mouth gaped, pale lips parted, silenced midscream.

Two large rats, red in tooth, claw and matted hair, streaked out from the mass of bodies and blundered around looking for passage past the police cordon. With inadvertent choreography, one heavy boot and one rifle butt smashed them into squelch.

The policemen guffawed. They didn't notice it wasn't over yet.

That holon of the dead twitched again.

Ratan felt the twitch like a flashburn before he moved.

He dived into the heap.

Instantly, the dead engulfed him. He was in them and among them before he quite knew what he was doing. He hadn't realized how many they were. He was plunged neck deep in corpses. Bending, stooping, squatting, he strained every muscle in lifting, pulling, and frantically thrusting aside bloodied limb and torso.

Speed was paramount. He had to move them off what lay twitching and heaving beneath their deadweight. He lost count of the bodies he moved. There were at least twenty-five twisted in that heap.

At least twenty pairs of gleaming boots ringed him, and not one of them moved forward to help.

Ratan paused at the body of a middle-aged man shot in the neck. There was something alive beneath it.

A boy. Face-down in a spread of dark ooze.

He convulsed, in a brief sustained spasm, and subsided.

Ratan and Crispin lifted him.

A glistening slither of intestines spilled from him. His arms flailed, his hands sought what his eyes could no longer see. His heart beat an unreasonable tattoo against Ratan's palm, desperately refusing quietus.

After that, all was bustle.

A stretcher materialized, and was pushed silently next to the boy. Mama had returned, with reinforcements. This was only an injured boy, there was nothing to fear any more.

Mama and his men lifted the boy onto the stretcher, draped a sheet to cover him and raced the trolley to Casualty. It was all done before Ratan could disinter himself from the entanglement of dead limbs.

There was no trace of khaki now. The ring of policemen had dispersed. The courtyard was empty, except for Ratan and Crispin. And the remaining tangled dead.

The fug of burnt flesh still choked the air.

Ratan and Crispin walked to the Autopsy Room.

The smell had them by the throat now. Crispin hawked and spat several times. Ratan breathed easy, but his hand strained the box painfully against his chest.

There was a small knot of men waiting beneath the mango tree outside the office, every eye fixed on the corridor.

Relatives.

The stench kept grief a safe distance away from the dead.

'The Police Surgeon's available if we need him,' Crispin said.

Ratan grinned at Crispin's circumspection. What he'd meant was, *I know you're at ease doing autopsies, God knows how or why. But what the fuck do you know of forensic detail?*

Resenting the smile, Crispin spat out, 'Ratan, what do you know about forensic detail?'

'What do you know about forensic detail, Mr Oak? Or is it plain Doctor?'

The voice carried him to a chill room. Thin grey light filtered in through the tall grimed windows.

A room. A voice. A name.

Bakhtyar.

It conveyed nothing to him. He knew no one of that name.

A blinding slap of pain thumped his left temple.

Bakhtyar!

The voice would be heard. The name would be noticed.

Ratan permitted the name.

It shaped itself into three words in broad-nibbed pen.

Waterman?

No. A Swann's nib.

In painstaking cursive, a clerk's hand.

Bakhtyar Rustomjee Hakim

The pain passed.

Crispin expected an answer.

'I won't know the new stuff. But you'll be around, won't you?' Ratan glibbed.

'Any time, man,' said Crispin with relief.

The source of the stench confronted them. A charred mess loomed on the marble slab, unidentifiable as anything human.

It had been left on the first table, closest to the door. It lay on its back, defending itself, arms and legs bunched in a clench of clumped muscle, tensed to avert a barrage of punches. The pugilist's pose assumed by bodies burned to death.

Foetor. That was the term for such smells.

Cracked, cindered, blistered with the expected post-mortem blebs, the skin could still shock his eye with its bizarre tattoos of melted plastic. The deep crimson intaglios made Ratan think of mehndi on a bride's hands.

A flash memory of crimson tracings—

Did it tell of who had once lived within this cindery shell?

There was no face left for recognition. The lidless eyes were sunken and wrinkled, the corneas muddy and dull. They seemed to hold traces of a terminal yearning.

Ratan had seen this look before. He had looked into these eyes before the roaring tongue of flame cloaked them. How long had he burned there on the pavement, a human torch in the noonday sun?

With the spark that ignites, every onlooker becomes a conspirator. Past the first lick of flame, there can be no protest. Does it matter then, how long it takes to char the bones?

Ratan began his examination of the body at the cephalic end. The cranial bones had cracked, within the vermiform confines of their sutures. The fragments buckled, lifted and stretched apart by the heat were now stuck as mosaic over the rendered brain.

Get on with it, a stern voice ordered.

Collect blood from the heart.

Clip fragments of cloth, if you can find any.

That trickle of melted red stuff. Take that!

Do not rely on the morgue photographer. Take your own pictures.

What? No camera?

'What? No camera?'

'Really, Ratan! Do we need one?' Crispin said testily.

He was well into his first corpse, and looked askance at Ratan's table.

'Collect blood for cyanides and carboxyhemoglobin. Besides the usual, of course. Check for ligature, bullet or knife marks. In case this is a post-mortem burn—'

'No it isn't. I was there. They doused him with petrol and set him alight. I watched. Yesterday.'

'Oh-oh. He was with the girl?'

'Yes. She threw herself on him. I pulled her off, but too late, probably.'

After a moment's reflection, Crispin offered, 'We can switch, if you like. If it's too much—'

'No. Just the camera?'

'Sure.'

After he had photographed the body, everything was

quick. The yellow parchment skin, burnt through its thickness, split in long fissures. Much of the periphery—arms, ears, genitals, and most of the face—was burnt away. The feet radiated fragile metatarsals from a shrivelled stump. After this havoc, the internal organs looked surprisingly fresh. The rosé of carboxyhaemoglobin. The bronchioles were peppered with a dusting of soot. The spine was brittle, burned to palest grey and splattered with dried webs. This oozing smelt had once been a plexus of nerves, clever with electricity. Blobs of cartilage had floated off and hardened elsewhere like gum. Pared down to the marrow, all that was left of him was ash.

Crispin hurried Ratan over to the body waiting on the next table the minute his notes were done. His hurry had little to do with the pressures of time or backlog. There were just four bodies left to autopsy. They wouldn't be starting the new load today.

Ratan tuned his attention to the boy waiting on the slab. He had died quickly. A bullet had sliced through the left carotid artery, ripped the soft tissues of his neck in one clean long burn before shattering the jaw. Fragments of teeth were embedded in the boy's face.

The cause of death?

Having looked at that mutilated face, who would ask?

Yet, that question would be asked, five, perhaps ten years from now, in some courtroom filled with bored people who had never seen a corpse.

Some lawyer, unacquainted with blood, who had never nicked himself shaving, would declaim with disbelief, 'Are you certain, Doctor, that the death was caused by a bullet injury?'

Hadn't he heard that question before?

'Can you say with confidence that *this* bullet caused the death of the victim? Is it not a fact, Doctor, that the carotid sheath was merely grazed? That the jugular vein was intact? Yes, there was grave injury to the face. But was that sufficient enough to *kill*? Have you or have you not, Doctor, seen patients recover after such injuries? Would you consider such an injury to be uniformly fatal?'

'If by uniformly fatal you mean that everybody so injured will die, the answer is no,' Ramratan replied.

'I believe that is what I meant. I believe that's generally meant by the term uniformly fatal. However, I crave the indulgence of the court in repeating my question, in simpler words, for the native gentleman here. Dr Oak, can every patient with such an injury to the face be expected to die?'

'No.'

'And Dr Salim Sattar died. We can only conclude that something else was responsible for his death. Did you find any other feature on autopsy that could be held responsible for his death? Did he, for instance, have any other disease in a major organ?'

'The heart showed acute dilatation.'

'Would you please explain to the court what "acute dilatation" means?'

'The heart was enlarged.'

'Remarkably enlarged?'

'Yes.'

'What does that indicate? A strong heart? A weak heart? A stopped heart?'

'It is the appearance of a heart that cannot contract effectively. The purpose of the heartbeat is to propel blood into circulation. A dilated heart lacks this propulsive force.'

'And therefore cannot pump blood into the circulation?'

'Yes.'

'It is therefore a failed heart?'

'Yes. Or, more correctly, it is a failing heart.'

'Which in itself could have caused death?'

'Perhaps. But it failed only when the bullet hit him.'

'The witness will confine his testimony to answering the counsel's questions.'

'Dr Oak, could a failed heart be the cause of death?'

'Yes.'

'No more questions, milord.'

'Thank you, counsel. You may stand down, Dr Oak.'

'I will be heard!'

Ramratan's voice rang out in the shocked courtroom. He spoke rapidly in the tense air.

'Yes, Salim Sattar had a failing heart. And yes, the bullet did not cause injury enough to kill. Nonetheless that bullet did cause his death. He was standing on the first-floor balcony when the bullet from a police rifle hit him—'

'Dr Oak, you have been warned. Stand down, Dr Oak.'

'No, I will not! The direction of the bullet track is irrefutable. The point of entry is on the left, at the lower third of the sternomastoid muscle. The wound track passes upwards and obliquely. The exit wound is over the right mandible, shattering the face. The shock of impact caused the sudden cardiac dilatation and failure. Dr Sattar was in good health before he was hit by the bullet. I was standing beside him on that balcony—'

'Very well, I hold you in contempt. Havaldar! Remove the witness, please. Clerk! The last part of his testimony should be struck from the record—'

Where had they been standing when Salim was hit?

Peerbhoy Mansion, Pydhonie.

They were standing in a first-floor balcony. They had escaped the melee and were watching the tidal surge of backs fleeing the police.

Ramratan saw the policeman's face as he swung his rifle in their direction. It all happened in a blink. One moment he saw the policeman, the next he fell, hitting his head against the wall, and Salim toppled over him.

How little blood there was!

Ratan forced himself to confront the dead boy on the table.

This was not Salim Sattar.

Not the thirty-three-year-old body of the man who had lived as madly and joyously as he had died. He had hurled himself in the bullet's path. Salim had shielded his friend from instinct, not design; from love, not rationality.

This wasn't Salim.

But this boy too had been shot in the same manner.

From below …

An hour later, Ratan's notes on the boy were done.

But that other bullet wound continued to trouble him.

Why had the policeman shot at Salim?

Peerbhoy Mansion.

Peerbhoy Mansion.

The policeman was on horseback.

They were all on horseback, thundering through the stampede, shooting in the air. Here, there, everywhere.

'They've lost control,' Salim said. 'They're on a rampage now, Ramratan. Better go inside.'

'Wait a moment, Salim. Let's see how this goes, they're firing blanks, they—'

And then he saw the policeman—

Ratan shook his head, walked to the sink, washed and disinfected his hands.

Crispin was waiting for him in the corridor. They didn't talk, but walked out the back way, risking mortuary odours rather than facing the outrage of the bereaved out front.

Ratan asked to use the phone.

The phone on Crispin's desk was dead.

'Let's try the cops,' Crispin said. 'They're sure to have a line open.'

The police had commandeered the only decent room in that wing and spurned the office allotted to them.

The Inspector at the table greeted Crispin with a cheery, 'How's it going?'

'Four down, three to go.' Crispin was equally breezy. 'What's the news outside?'

'Terrible. Mahim side. Machhlimar. You know? Near the Dargah? Everywhere these people are, nothing but trouble. You saw that burnt body?'

'I saw him burn,' Ratan said tonelessly.

'Muslim boy, Hindu girl. What can you expect? Relatives were here just now. Boy's people. Came with the press. No photographs, I told them. Please, eh, even if they ask you, no photographs. We don't want inflammatory pictures in the papers. As it is, the press has been very irresponsible.'

'He *was* a press photographer,' Ratan said.

'What a photo-op he missed!'

The Inspector roared at his own joke. He sobered quickly when they did not smile.

'Only joking. Poor fellow. All for love. Girl is dying, I heard. Must be dead by now. You want to phone? Please go ahead.'

Radhakrishnan picked up the phone at first ring.

'I was waiting for your call, Ratan,' he explained. 'I've got all the papers. But how do I get them to you? Where are you?'

Ratan asked him to hold on while he checked with Crispin if they could possibly make a detour on their way home. The papers were terribly important, he said, family papers, legal stuff.

He was lying well today. He would have to lie much more when he met Radhakrishnan.

The Inspector interrupted.

'Where do you want to collect from? You tell them to keep the papers ready and I will send my man. No problem, van is on its rounds.'

Ratan thanked him, surprised by the sincerity in his voice. A week ago he would have refused the offer. Now he was prepared to do anything to get what he wanted. It was an ugly feeling.

'A police van will come by to pick up the papers,' Ratan said into the phone. 'Where can you leave them?'

Radhakrishnan seemed relieved.

'I'll leave them downstairs at the gate. The police have set up a cell there. You take a look at them, Ratan, and give me a call later. I'm here now, till things settle down. I'll be glad if you call, it can get hellish all alone in this mausoleum. This place is full of ghosts.'

'Listen, you wouldn't know anything about—'

Ratan stopped himself, recollecting the presence of the Inspector in the room.

'About what? Oh-ah. You're with the cops, I understand. Something about the riots then, right?'

'Right. Nineteenth century, early twentieth.'

'1874, 1893?'

'The last, I'd think.'

Now why would he say that?

'I have those reports right in front of me as we speak because I've been looking them up myself. It is uncanny. Practically the same events. In the same places. And, we'll probably discover later, engineered in the same way.'

'In Pydhonie?'

'Why, yes! That's where it started in 1893. You know all about it then.'

'No, but I need to.'

'I'll add on a few more Xeroxes then, no problem. Will your cops get here by five?'

The Inspector nodded when Ratan checked with him.

'Wife and kids okay?' Ratan asked, mechanically.

'Yep. So far. Just spoke with them. What about Prema?'

Ratan did not know. He hadn't thought about her in two days.

Seven autopsies for the day. Six gunshot wounds—three to the head, two abdominal and one cervical. The charred photographer was the only one who had died differently.

A havaldar brought a thick celadon canvas envelope for Ratan just as they were leaving.

As Ratan and Crispin walked past the Coroner's Court, two men fell in step with them.

Without breaking stride, one of them spoke.

'Dr Oak? We're Anwar's colleagues. The police say you were there when it happened.'

Anwar.

He had a name now.

'Yes. I was there.'

'You rescued Radhika.'

'Not much of a rescue. She's in a bad way. Was in a bad way. That was yesterday. We're on our way to see her now.'

They walked the rest of the way in silence. Once in the hospital building, the noise and confusion in the foyer offered protection from being overheard.

The two men now introduced themselves as Arun and Kashi. They were both in their late forties, out of condition, soft-bellied. Desk jockeys. They were here with Anwar's family. They had been told the body would not be released today, what could they do to expedite things?

'It's a police case,' Crispin said. 'The Police Surgeon's opinion is necessary. I don't think he'll be in this afternoon.'

Crispin was buying time.

Anwar's murder would get buried under the heap of bodies piling up in the streets. It was just one act of hate amongst many others.

'Anwar's family has told the police they don't want to register a case. They just want the body.'

'Why?'

Even as he asked the question, Ratan realized his folly.

'Let it go,' Arun said. 'These things happen.'

Who was he to let it go? Had he lost his life, his happiness, his dreams? The only person who could let it go was dead.

'Anwar's father is a heart patient,' Kashi said.

'So are we all. All heart patients in these times,' Ratan said roughly. 'Even if they let it go, we cannot. *I* cannot.'

'What will you do?'

All three waited for his answer.

Ratan had no answer.

They misinterpreted his silence. The tension drained out of them. He was entered in the ranks of the shocked, the baffled, the defeated.

'Have you given a statement? Made an FIR?' Arun asked.

'No.'

Nobody had asked him to. Not the police, not the CMO, not the Plastic Surgery registrar.

'Not yet.'

'Radhika's family may want to shift her to a private hospital,' Kashi said.

They had reached the Plastic Surgery ward now.

Ratan went in. Arun and Kashi stayed outside with Crispin.

Radhika was alive.

Still in the ICU, but off the ventilator. Deeply sedated.

Her lungs were clear, the resident said.

So far, so good.

About 60% burns, at least 25% of them third degree, on the neck and chest, and second degree on the face and arms.

The moment flashed through Ratan again. She had hurled herself onto those flames. Quicker than thought. He in contrast, had taken too long, far too long, in pulling her away.

'Are you family?' the resident asked.

'Friend.'

'Oh. Okay. Nobody's turned up yet from her family. Are you in touch with them? Sister tells me she's tried calling, nobody's answering.'

'Her friends are here, colleagues from the paper. She's a journalist.'

'We'll need blood, antibiotics. You know. She's still critical.'

'I understand. I'll talk with them, and I'll be around for anything you need. I'll leave a number. I'm here through the day, the next few days at least.'

'Is it true her boyfriend was burned too?'

'Yes.'

'And?'

'He's dead.'

'What was it, a gas cylinder burst or something?'

'Not quite.'

'There are no details. The policeman said he didn't have any details.'

'I have details.'

'You were there when it happened?'

How often would he have to answer this question?

'Yes. I was there. I watched it happen,' he said heavily.

The police van dropped them home.

Ratan clutched his box and avoided Crispin's eye. Not that Crispin noticed. He seemed lost in worries of his own.

Radhakrishnan's thick envelope lay between them on the seat. The streets outside could have been aflame for all they knew, nothing penetrated the tense chill of the van's interior.

'Nine o'clock then,' Crispin said as the van stopped for Ratan.

'Nine o'clock.'

And for some reason, they shook hands.

The day receded.

He became absorbed in the life of the house, learned what he could of his father's day, and tried to tamp down the guilt over having left him alone all day.

Jafar's kids had cheered Arjun. That roused a faint twinge of envy. Ratan quelled it. He was grateful to Jafar, and to his harridan wife whom he'd begun to loathe.

Finally, the day was done and the kitchen cleared.

Arjun and Ratan drowsed through an old movie on television.

The hot shower, a good meal and the quiet hour with his father had leached the iron out of him. All day, his head had been like the interior of that police van, cut off from reality. Now it felt as if that dirt-encrusted grille had been prised off and there was a little patch of sky he could call his own.

Ratan opened the canvas envelope and retrieved the two slips of paper concealed in Shakuntala's book. He switched the anglepoise and began reading the Quarantine Papers.

The Xeroxed pages bristled with yellow Post-it notes untidily scrawled in blue ballpoint.

Radhakrishnan's contribution.

The first page had two columns of names. Most were written in Urdu, a few in Gujarati. Every name was transcribed in English in the margin.

One name had been circled in blue ballpoint.

Sheikh Ishaq Ahmad.

Radhakrishnan had scrawled in the margin here.

Pl. tell Salwebai this was the closest I could get.

Ratan had let Radhakrishnan believe he was helping Shakuntala Salwe with the Quarantine Papers.

How long could he keep up the deception?

Was it deception?

He was doing what Shakuntala Salwe had set out to do.

What had she set out to do?

Why did she need these names?

Sheikh Ishaq Ahmad.

The name conveyed nothing to Ratan because he didn't know what the list was about.

Shakuntala Salwe had known, and so he, Ratan, was supposed to know too.

The next page was in English, in a thin crabbed clerical hand.

Another list. Addresses, this time.

Luckily, Radhakrishnan's ballpoint had been active again, and Sheikh Ishaq Ahmad's address blazed out at Ratan.

Room 17, 4th Floor, Sakina Manzil, Pydhonie.

There was another note here from Radhakrishnan.

Some of these old houses are still around! Worth checking out!

He now had a name, and an address.

But what was he looking for?

The next ten pages were evidently from a ledger. These were handwritten in English. They began with a list of complainants, classified according to grievance from **A** through **H**.

A = People sent to Plague Hospital without previous medical examination.

B = Persons unnecessarily or improperly turned in to the Segregation Camp.

C = Persons made naked.

D = Persons forcibly examined.

E = Sanctity of temples violated or images broken.

F = Wanton destruction of property.

G = Persons assaulted or ill-treated.

H = Modesty of native ladies not respected.

There was one name that Radhakrishnan had circled under **A** and two under **B**.

The first was *Avdaji Pundalik More*.

The other two were women.

Shantabai Avdaji More and *(Miss) Chitrangada Avdaji More*.

Ratan paused. There was something wrong here.

Something worth a quarrel.

It was worth a quarrel.

'Why do you write Miss in brackets before her name?'

'Why, what's wrong? Should it be Mrs?'

'No. It should be Doctor.'

'That is not the custom.'

'Make it the custom then!'

How many times had he quarrelled over that?

Time and again every list on the noticeboard read the same: Mrs Julia Alfonso, Miss Prabhavati Madhukar Shinde, Mrs Freny Daftary.

Dr Chitrangada Avdaji More, she had written with a flourish across the flyleaf of *Middlemarch*, his gift on her eighteenth birthday.

Two years later, when he borrowed the book from her, he found beneath that proud flourish, a hesitant line in pencil.

Dr Chitrangada Khursheed Alam.

And then, with a little more assurance, the script was more deeply indented.

Dr Chitra Alam.

And after that another hand had taken over, less timid, more square and swift, with a broad-nibbed pen.

Dr Khursheed Alam More.

Dr Khursheed Chitrangada More.

Could a love story be more succinct? Or more complete?

Chitrangada.

The name flooded Ratan with a sense of loss.

What had Shakuntala Salwe wanted with that name?

Chitrangada and her mother had been 'unnecessarily or improperly turned in to a Segregation Camp'.

How could that matter to Shakuntala a hundred years later?

The question induced a queasy feeling of guilt. It should have mattered to *him*.

Had it mattered to him?

Try as he would, the wall wouldn't give.

He returned to the papers, still distracted by the sadness the name induced in him.

Chitrangada.

And by quick association, Arjun. The mythical hero who had claimed the warrior princess Chitrangada.

Arjun.

Arjun.

He had named the baby Arjun because it was a boy.

Arjun, the name forever linked with Chitrangada.

This shocked Ratan. Had his father, born in 1925, been named for *this* Chitrangada? This girl, who was sent to a Plague Camp in 1897?

He knew, or remembered, three facts about her.

- Chitrangada Avdaji More was a doctor.
- She was, at some point in her life, in love with a man called Khursheed Alam, also a doctor. He was in love with her too.
- Chitrangada, and her mother Shantabai, had been 'improperly or unnecessarily turned in to a Segregation Camp'.

How could this happen to a doctor? Couldn't she have spoken up with authority? What had happened to her there?

The next lot of papers answered his questions, or at least hinted at where the answers might lie.

It was a ten-page complaint by Avdaji Pundalik More, ironmonger. Translated from the Marathi by Gangadhar Raoji Khare, 'Oriental Translator to Government'.

As he read it, Ratan grew testy and impatient with Avdaji More's self-centred whine even as he conceded the justice of his grievances.

24 March 1897 was an important day in Avdaji's household. It was the thirteenth day after his father's death.

'Certain cooking arrangements (in connection with the ceremony to be performed) that day were made in my house.'

Avdaji's family had been cautioned not to start cooking until after the Plague Inspectors had made their visit. Knowing how early they called, Avdaji had opened his shop at 'the earliest dawn'.

The Inspectors arrived. They broke open locks and safes in the adjacent shops. Soon one of them approached Avdaji, and claiming to be a Plague Inspector, demanded to examine him. Finding a few insignificant lymph nodes in Avdaji's groin, the Inspector marched him off with an armed guard to the patients' van parked in Bohri Lane.

Avdaji now made loud complaint. Nothing would induce him to enter that foul carriage! He would willingly walk with them wherever they wanted him to go, all the way to pataal if necessary, but enter that van, he would *not*. He was put in charge of a sowar and taken on foot to the Plague Hospital.

Ratan had a mental glimpse of this indignant man, hurrying to keep up with the sowar who cantered alongside at a sedate pace, supremely indifferent to Avdaji's outrage.

At this time (wrote Avdaji) *the state of my mind was exactly like that of persons who are led, under a guard, for being hanged. Just as prisoners under sentence of death think that they must leave the world in about half an hour, so I, being under the impression that those entering the Plague Hospital never return alive, thought that I would have to leave the world that evening or the next morning. The sowar appeared to me like the messenger of death.*

Outrage turned into terror when Avdaji reached the Plague Hospital.

He was given a bed – the fifth in a room with four mortally sick patients. He begged to be allowed to pace the corridor, to stand outside the room, to do anything to avoid breathing the air of that foul cubicle.

Authority, as quoted by Avdaji, coldly answered:

'You must stay in that very room. If you complain, you will be seized by the neck and pushed into it.'

Avdaji's anxiety (he took his temperature every half-hour) was not lessened by the knowledge that just two hours ago, a municipal worker called Chintu Belapurkar had died in the very bed now allotted to him. The sheets and bedding had neither been aired nor changed. It stung Avdaji that the Plague Committee should countenance this injustice.

When any patient or corpse be detected in any house in the town, all the inmates of the house and all the persons who might have come to inquire about the state of the patient are, without paying any heed to their objections, taken to the Segregation Camp ... how is it then that healthy persons are kept in the rooms of the Plague Hospital next to plague patients who are on the point of death or restlessly rolling about in pain?

Even after a hundred years, Avdaji's predicament in the Plague Hospital made gruesome reading.

The ironmonger watched helplessly through the night as his two closest neighbours in the cubicle convulsed, bled, vomited, gasped for breath, and eventually died.

Avdaji was released from the hospital at 11 the next morning.

The rest of his report dealt with his devout thanks at having escaped Yama's clutches despite the agreement that inexorable god had compacted with the Plague Committee. Somewhere in this breathless effusion, Avdaji had remembered to mention that his wife and daughter had been dragged away to the Segregation Camp. He had no further information about them.

Ratan picked up the next paper in that sheaf.

This was a letter from the chief medical officer of the Modikhana Segregation Camp.

It stated that Miss Chitrangada Avdaji More, inmate of the camp since 24 March, went missing on 25 March. She had left 'on her regular employment' on the morning of 25 March, but had failed to return to the camp that evening.

The next letter was signed with a name that made Ratan quiver. His eyes burned as they strained across the abyss of a century, searching for a face he could no longer recall.

He fumed in silent frustration to see the Xeroxed page filled with a hand he knew so well. An unusual hand, square and left slanted, using a thick nib and *green* ink.

Nusserwanji Fakirji Surveyor.

Nusser.

Dear Sir,

In answer to your enquiry dated 28th March I have the honor to bring the following facts to your notice.

Dr(Miss) Chitrangada More is a trusted colleague and member of our staff in the Sir Dinshaw Petit Laboratory, working under the supervision of Dr Waldemar Haffkine and myself on the production and purification of a vaccine against the plague.

You ask me what her daily employment is.

I can best answer that by describing the numerous delicate and complicated steps that make up the process of culturing and isolating the organism of plague. But such an answer will scarcely address the purpose of your enquiries. I will, therefore, confine myself to saying that Dr (Miss) More's daily employment consists of complex and accurate scientific work.

To your question about her likely whereabouts at this time, I have, alas, no answer.

I mentioned in my earlier communication to you, dated 27th March that Miss More did not report for duty on the morning of the 25th. This occasioned no small anxiety in our laboratory, as Dr More is entirely responsible for one particular phase of production. I must say I was disturbed at such dereliction of duty on Dr More's part, having known her so far as a worker of the highest integrity and dedication.

On the following day, I was approached, in my capacity as her supervisor, by a well-wisher of her family, Shri Shankar Buwa Joshi Saheb. It was then that I was apprised of the circumstances under which she was missing.

I would like to strongly voice my protest not only as Dr More's senior colleague at the Petit Laboratory, but also as a member of the Plague Committee, at the high-handed and violent means of removal of Dr More and her mother Sowbhagyavati Shantabai More.

Dr More, as a doctor specially trained and interested in plague, would have been the first to report any signs of illness in her family. That she should have been so segregated, without any respect for her professional opinion, is outrageous to say the least.

However indignant her colleagues may be at the disrespect shown to Dr More, we are even more anxious to offer our utmost cooperation to you and your men in tracing her. I am sending this by messenger, and have arranged for this same man Bhiku Tulpule to call upon your office twice a day so that you may be spared the trouble of sending out to the Laboratory. I request you to waste no time when she is found, but to send for me immediately. I will attend Dr More in person. I am presently in charge of our laboratory, and have sole access to the remedies for this illness.

Believe me, Sir, to be at your service at any hour to further your search for Dr (Miss) More. Shri Shankar Buwa Joshi Saheb has assured me of every assistance in this matter.

I have the honour to be, sir
Your obedient servant

Nusserwanji Fakirji Surveyor
M.D., M.A. (Bombay); M.R.C.P. (London)

Poor Nusser!

Not his kind of trouble. He was your man when the sterilizer blew up, or the centrifuge wouldn't budge, or even when the jailbirds in Correction House looked sceptical about inoculation.

Hadn't he drummed up twenty undergraduates to roll up their sleeves and take the shots like good men, right under the convicts' doubting eyes?

Waldemar Haffkine* got all the credit, but Nusser did most of the work.

This letter was *as far as Nusser was prepared to go in public...*

What more had Nusser known?

The next page was a letter from Shankar Rao Mangeshnath Joshi, to the police commissioner. He introduced himself as a well-wisher and family friend of Shri Pundalik Avdaji More and expressed his anxiety at the disappearance of Miss Chitrangada More. He offered to place his 'not inconsiderable personal resources' at the commissioner's disposal to aid in tracing the missing lady. The note was written on his personal stationery and bore a Girgaum address.

This letter had been routed to the Plague Committee by the commissioner, with a handwritten comment:

It may be noted that the above signed Shankar Rao Joshi is a member of the Cow Protection Society.

---

* Joseph Lister, who ushered in the era of modern sterile surgery, called him 'a saviour of humanity'.

Waldemar Haffkine (1860-1930) not just developed vaccines for two dreaded diseases, he tested them first on himself. Nine years after Robert Koch's discovery of *Vibrio cholerae*, Haffkine produced a cholera vaccine. He injected himself with it on 18 July 1892 and two weeks later reported his findings to the Biological Society. During Bombay's epidemic of bubonic plague, he worked in Grant Medical College and readied a vaccine on 10 January 1897. Again he tested it on himself. The Plague Laboratory he set up in Bombay was named the **Haffkine Institute** in 1925.

The antiseptic mouthwash Listerine, by the way, honours Lord Lister.

Ratan was so puzzled by this note that he nearly overlooked Radhakrishnan's Post-it which said

Ratan, 1893

There were still some more pages to read. A list of figures, and an official letter of some sort. He was inclined to skip it—and then he caught sight of the signature.

STATEMENT

Of Plague Seizures and Deaths in the Town of Bombay

			Seizures	Deaths
Total during	October	1896	389	276
Total during	November	1896	333	268
Total during	December	1896	1,655	1,160
Total during	January	1897	1, 791	1,444
GRAND TOTAL			4,168	3,148

MEMORANDUM on the Plague by Medical Practitioners of Bombay

We, the undersigned medical officers and members of the Special Research Committee, are of the opinion that the bubonic plague now prevailing in the city is, under certain conditions, only slightly contagious or infectious, and the facts observed in connection with individual cases and those associated with the general progress of the disease, warrant us in concluding that its incidence is greatly due to local conditions.

We are emphatically of the opinion that the only practical method of dealing with the outbreak and of arresting the progress of the disease is by removal of the inmates from those houses in which a case of the disease occurs.

We quite appreciate the practical difficulties attending the adoption of this proposal, but in such an emergency as the present, these difficulties can and must be overcome. The Municipal Corporation will no doubt provide huts, free of rent, for the accommodation of the different classes, and we understand that mill companies and other employers of labour are prepared to erect huts for their different employees. The experience gained in the melas at Allahabad and Hardwar will be available, as to the construction and arrangement of huts.

There will thus be no difficulty experienced in providing sufficient and suitable accommodation for the evicted, and it requires only the concurrence and sympathy of the leaders of the different sections of the native community to render the scheme a success. If houses in healthy localities are available for occupation, there is no reason why they should not be utilized.

The steps leading up to removal would be the report to the health officer of a case by a duly qualified medical officer. The health officer would then notify the occurrence to the municipal authorities, and would at the same time, submit his recommendations for the removal of the inmates in the particular home, and if he considered it necessary, those also in the immediate neighbourhood. The municipal authorities would then take the necessary action and indicate the huts available.

Carts, if necessary, should be provided free of cost for the removal of the goods and chattels of the inmates.

The person attacked would either be removed to hospital, or remain in the house with his or her relatives until recovery or death took place. The house should then be completely vacated, and taken possession of by the health officer for purposes of cleaning and disinfection, and he should be invested with full powers, in consultation with the executive engineer, for removing all partitions, erections or portions of house walls that impede or obstruct ventilation. After an interval to be determined by the health officer, the house would be reoccupied.

There can be no question as to the necessity for the adoption of the measure we now advocate, and we trust that, in the interests not only of Bombay, but also in those of the whole of India, it will be at once accepted and acted upon, more especially as the untiring energy displayed in the thorough and systematic cleaning and disinfection of the affected parts of the city has as yet failed to arrest the progress of the disease.

K.N.BAHADURJI
JAMES ARNOTT
TEMULJI BHICAJI NARIMAN

ISMAIL JAN MAHOMED

BHALCHANDRA KRISHNA

E.H.HANKIN
L.F.CHILDE
ACCACIO G. VIEGAS

N.F. SURVEYOR
THOMAS BLANEY
HENRY COOKE, M.D.,
Surgeon Major General
JAMES CLEGHORN
Director General, Indian Medical Service

T.S.WEIR

SYDNEY SMITH

I am of the opinion that, as there are facts showing that the plague is spread by people coming from infected localities, the measures compelling the inhabitants to leave those localities ought to be accompanied by others calculated to control their further movements.

W. M. HAFFKINE

This was followed by a long note that ended in a paragraph which Ratan saw half as print and half as memory.

NOTE
by
Director General, Indian Medical Service,
dated 16 January 1897

I beg to submit copy of a note signed by those medical practitioners of Bombay, who have had the greatest opportunities of becoming practically acquainted with the present outbreak of bubonic fever, and along with it, to prevent any future misrepresentation, a memorandum of the remarks I made to those gentlemen before I submitted the note for their approval and signature ...

The whole city is now under the inspection of the Health Department. All latrines, drains and gullies are being flushed; houses, as far as possible, are being cleaned, disinfected, and whitewashed, and in those parts of the city not drained, surface drains of excellent construction are being made in connection with the house pipes. The importance of this will be understood from a description of the houses. The chawls or tenements may run up to seven stories and the unit of construction is a long corridor with rooms opening on either side. In the corridor, either at one end, or in the centre, is situated a water tap with a bathing platform, and alongside it a latrine, with two or three seats. The whole tenement is built up of a congeries of these corridors and rooms, and contains 500 to 1,000 individuals. The only space between each tenement is a gully sufficiently wide to admit a sweeper. In most of the corridors and rooms, either from the absence of openings, or from the obstruction of the existing ones, there is absolutely no light admitted, and consequently, no ventilation. The Health Officer has informed me that he estimated that 70 per cent of the population live in such houses. The corridors, before being taken in hand by the Health Department, were the repositories of filth of all kinds, and it is surprising that the mortality under such conditions has been so small ...

16 January 1897 J. Cleghorn

That explained it all—the inspection, the internment in hospital or camp. He couldn't even begin to imagine those camps, and yet he seemed to remember them so well …

It was close to midnight and Ratan was dizzy with exhaustion. The name Chitrangada beat incessantly in his brain and all he wanted was to be rid of it.

What depressing baggage he had accumulated!

Three women.

Missing, dying, dead.

He was still clueless about the quest Shakuntala had set him on.

Chitrangada?

A ghost on a cloud of unexplained sorrow.

She mattered so much to Ramratan, he named his grandson for her.

Her disappearance from the Plague Camp shook the phlegmatic Dr Surveyor out of his reticence.

Ratan knew Nusserwanji Surveyor was reserved to the point of seeming arrogant and unfriendly. He was distant with his staff, and famously non-committal on paper. Ratan had this previous knowledge, without knowing how.

From another man, that letter could be dismissed as a formal expression of concern. Nusser was a hermit, punctilious and exacting. Unforgiving.

'Nusserwanji Surveyor, you are an unforgiving man,' Waldemar Haffkine often grumbled. 'Learn to forgive yourself, at least now and then!'

Nusser could not.

These things Ratan simply knew.

He also knew Nusser wasn't moved by a softer emotion for his young assistant. Nusser did not have that in him. Yet, here he was, not merely concerned, but atwitter with anxiety, thrusting his services on the police, ascertaining nobody else was called upon to treat Chitrangada, whatever the state she was found in.

Nusser was rattled. Nusser was frightened.

What could have got him so terrified?

And now, a third woman.

This miserable Radhika, battling for life after having witnessed her lover incinerated.

Could she not have warned Anwar?

What did she think would happen? Didn't she know what her own parents were like?

Why did she expose him to such danger?

Ratan heard her mother's words rustle in his ear.

'What have you done? You promised me they wouldn't touch her...'

The girl must have known just how deep ran their hate. She should have shielded him.

Ah, the irony.

She *had* shielded him.

With her body.

With her life.

The police hadn't asked him to make a statement. No FIR had been filed. Who was to say it had happened the way it did?

What would Radhika say if she lived? If she died, what dying declaration would she make?

Nemo moriturus praesumitur mentire.

The words surprised him.

A dead language, not one he knew. But the meaning was obvious.

'No man dies with a lie upon his lips.'

No woman either, presumably. Ratan wasn't sure.

But Radhika might die without saying anything at all. Or she might choose to live and tell a different sort of tale. Either way it would be up to him, Ratan, to describe the murder as it happened.

The phone rang again. It was Radhakrishnan.

Ratan gave him no chance to get a word in.

'I saw a man burnt to death yesterday,' he said. 'They drenched him in petrol and set him alight.'

'Shit.'

'Did the autopsy today. No, yesterday.'

'Oh God.'

'They haven't asked me for a statement. Nobody's filed an FIR.'

'You were the only witness?'

'No. His girlfriend threw herself on him. They say she'll live.'

'My God. Poor kid.'

'Which one of them? Tell me Radhakrishnan, which one of them is the poor kid? '

'Call me Raki. The girl. Of course, the girl. The boy's dead, he's escaped. The girl has pain, suffering, sorrow, disfigurement, reproach, hate, rejection. It's all there waiting for her. She'll probably die.'

'Her folks did it. Do you know, Raki, they hired a thug to kill the boy? They couldn't have timed it better. It can't be called murder now. It's just part of the landscape.'

'What are you going to do, Ratan?'

'I don't know. I'm hoping you'll tell me.'

'I?'

'Yeah. How did you live past all that?'

'My father, you mean? It was a long time ago, Ratan. But it was also yesterday. And it is now. You know what I mean? You don't live past it. You live because of it, you're always in it. This boy was Muslim, and the girl Hindu or vice versa, right?'

'Wrong. The boy is a lump of carbon. The girl will soon be a map of scars. That's who they are. Their families can't object now, can they?'

'But what about you, Ratan? I heard about Prema. She called my wife yesterday.'

'Oh.'

'She wanted a recipe from Vani. That's when she let it slip. I'm sorry.'

'For her or for me?'

'For neither of you, actually. I'm sorry about the hellishness of things in general. That's all one can do, apologize for the Fates.'

'I thought Destiny was single and singular.'

'Fates, not fate. The Greek things, winged harpies who peck your liver out every time you want to eat. Harpies.'

'Those. Yeah. Those I know.'

'Me too. So you didn't get a chance to read those papers'

'No, I did. I have been reading them, but haven't finished. This whole thing about Segregation Camps, quarantine and—'

'Hard to believe it all happened. Imagine Bombay city cut off from the outside world. It almost happened.'

'Almost?'

'Couldn't be sealed off, could it? Not when British bread got its butter off Bombay! And there were Europeans too who caught the plague, remember.'

'I do remember. You bet I remember.'

'You do?' He sounded puzzled.

'Say, Raki, can I see the originals if I turn up there tomorrow? Is that possible?'

'Sure. But why?'

'That letter. I must see Nusser Surveyor's letter. The one in green ink.'

'That one. Ah. Okay. Afternoon? Call me and tell me when. But how will you get here, Ratan?'

'I'll get there, don't worry. Two o'clock.'

'Any time's okay by me. I have the run of the place these days.'

'Thanks, Raki. I'll see you then –'

'Hey, wait a moment! How did you know it was in green ink? How did you know if you haven't seen it?'

'Waterman's dark green. Nusser always used that.'

Ratan rang off. Before he could be asked to explain.

Also, Raki was wrong.

Very few Europeans had got the plague.

Very few Europeans had got the plague.

Manser was the first.

He was the first European Ramratan saw on the slab. Sheeted.

Bodies were placed naked on the slab. That was the rule.

This one was hidden beneath a fresh white sheet. Matron, Sister Marie Evangeline, was short of sheets. Then he noticed it wasn't one of Sister Marie's. There was embroidery on the edges, the sort Yashoda called broderie anglaise.

He was puzzling over that when they stepped up to him. They had been waiting all this while. His eyes on the veiled body, he hadn't seen them.

Nusser, Haffkine, Childe.

Bhiku raised the sheet, ceremonially.

European male, aged between forty and forty-five.

Surgeon Major Robert Manser, first physician and professor of medicine, Grant Medical College. President, Committee of Experts on the Plague.

'I have sent a message to Dr Heinrich Albrecht,' said Haffkine. 'He will send his assistant.'

'Dr Oak does not need assistance,' Nusser swiftly interjected.

'But Albrecht is preparing a report,' Childe added. 'He has more than fifty plague autopsies. We need all the data we can get. Dr Oak?'

'Of course. I will wait for Dr Albrecht's assistant.'

Nusser avoided his eye. Ramratan had only five plague autopsies.

The word on the street was that hospitals were cutting up dead people for practice. The Dean had called a moratorium, and the only plague deaths autopsied were unclaimed bodies.

In summoning Albrecht, Haffkine wasn't worrying about the moratorium. He was trying to soften the outrage of a native opening up a European corpse.

An autopsy, after all, was a judgement of sorts.

Ramratan did not know Manser except by sight and reputation.

Like Nusser, Haffkine, Childe and Hankin, Manser was an expert on the Plague Committee.

At Ramratan's end of the epidemic you did not hear much about the course of illness. You weren't told how many recovered. You only knew how many died.

From the blisters on Manser's skin Ramratan anticipated that the deeper organs would be deliquescent. It meant the last few days had been hell for Manser. He oozed blood from little abrasions everywhere. He coughed up blood. He shat and pissed blood. He roared insanely, or was abruptly silenced, by a gush of blood in his brain.

The swollen knees told Ramratan that Manser had walked out his anguish as the fever raged, his delirium a diorama of illusions that sent him stumbling about blinded, until his heart gave out.

Apart from the blisters, Manser's body had only a few external signs of plague. On either side of the spill of pubic hair, the groin was flat and vacuous.

The neck was devoid of pebbly nodes. Axillary skin retained its lax crepe. But for a small, barely palpable node, there were no swellings submerged in there. No bubo anywhere.

Without a bubo it still could be the plague.

The two-ended bacillus could streak through the body like a burning fuse and explode in bloody spatter within hours.

Manser had been sick for two days. Very few held out that long.

'Dr Anton Ghon, gentlemen.'

Ramratan stepped back.

Ghon barely acknowledged him. He was a burly man of about Ramratan's age and height, his features hidden by a profusion of sandy hair.

He had brought his own instruments. He laid them out now on the trolley.

Bhiku had silently removed Ramratan's own kit and wheeled the trolley over to Ghon's side of the table.

It was an insult Ramratan never forgot.

Ramratan picked up the block and readied it at the head end of the table. He cradled Manser's shoulders and lifted them.

'Do not touch please!'

Ghon's voice was icy.

'You will find it makes your job easier,' Ramratan said as he pushed the block into place. 'Just enough hyperextension to expose the mediastinum.'

'Very good.' Ghon smiled, revealing bad teeth. 'You will assist me then?'

'If you wish.'

They worked silently, ignoring their watchful audience.

As Ramratan had expected, beneath the skin the body was a haemorrhagic mess of engorged flesh.

Everything had burst past its confine of membrane and now bulged, purple and pulpy.

The mouth was a dry cavern of cracked and shriveling slough, peeling thickened palate, cushiony tonsils, bloodied tongue. The skin gaped under the knife, a violet jelly wadded the muscles underneath. There were pockets of clotted blood, stellate splotches trapped beneath tense membranes.

Ramratan preferred his knife, but this man used his fingers, teasing, stripping, uprooting the stilled machinery from its cladding of muscle, skin and bone.

Ramratan prided himself in releasing the organs with one clean movement from neck to pelvis, but Ghon didn't do that. He had the organs laid out in neat physiological array—the heart and lungs in one block, the liver and biliary tree with the stomach, duodenum, pancreas in another, the kidneys and adrenals along with ureters and bladder in the next.

The stomach and intestines were studded with splinter bleeds. As expected. The liver resembled a blood-filled loofah, the spleen melted into purple smears on the fingertip.

Left now was the gaping shell of the corpse, its scaffold and plumbing glimpsed dimly past a shallow black puddle of blood.

When he sponged out the blood, Ramratan found the emptied cavity was like a hidden vineyard. Lymph nodes were bunched along the great vessels like clusters of purple berries.

Usually Ramratan played the heart like a violin and unravelled its furled secrets by drawing his knife with tenderness across its cold clench.

But Manser's heart shuddered at his first touch, and a squelch of liquefying muscle coated the knife like slime.

When they arrived at the lungs, they paused.

Pneumonia.

Violet islands raised over the spongy tissue, fenced in with crimson flares. Ghon's thumb on the bronchi pressed out a pink froth. The pleura was a sticky carmine web. Plague was rooted in here.

Manser hadn't just 'caught the plague'. He had breathed it in. The bacillus had appropriated his lungs and whatever it engendered had invaded the rest of Manser's body. His brain had haemorrhaged because of it, his heart had turned flaccid because of it. It had clogged up his airways and cut off his air. It was all here, revealed in the crimson and grey islands of the sectioned lung.

Neither Ghon nor Ramratan had seen anything like this before.

Ghon said it first.

'This is a new sort of plague. I have fifty-four autopsies. Bubonic, most. Septicemic, some. But this is new. This is *pneumonic* plague.'

This first European autopsied for the plague had something that set him apart from the thousand others who had died that week.

It was apt that it should be Manser.

Till 6 January 1897 very few Europeans had died of the plague.

'Very few Europeans have died of the plague, and only a few more have caught it,' Ramratan wrote in answer to Alice Kipling's note.

'With the precautions you've taken, you should be safe. I would advise you all to be inoculated. I will arrange it, if you only give the word. Certainly, it will be a pleasure to show Mr Phillip Burne-Jones...'

His hand stopped.

Phillip *Burne-Jones.*

He couldn't write that name. He crossed it out. It would look stupid now, to write *your nephew*. He crumpled the paper, flung it across the room. And began over.

Certainly, it will be a pleasure to show your nephew the city. I must insist though, that he be inoculated first ...

Philip Burne-Jones.

Her note had been formal, even cold, but he knew her kindness of old, and was not surprised by the postscript.

Dear Dr Oak,

I trust you will not find it tedious to be reminded of an old friendship. I am visiting Bombay in the company of my nephew Philip Burne-Jones. We are guests of Mr Sinclair in our old home in the School of Arts, and Mrs Sinclair would be delighted to receive you. My nephew is of your age, and is interested in seeing the city through native eyes. This has turned out a most unseasonable visit, with all our excursions curtailed by the plague, but Mrs Sinclair assures me we prisoners are quite safe here within the School. Do come, if you can, to tea, and bring me news of the world outside.

Sincerely,
Alice Kipling

P.S.:

John was deeply saddened by the loss of his dear friends Krishnaji and Darayus. These long years in Lahore have not provided the camaraderie he treasures so much. Perhaps you can tell me of Mohsin Ahmad's whereabouts. Do you remember our afternoons together? They were always good times for me.

A.

Their afternoons together were spent in Lockwood's studio, that summer vacation when Ramratan was eleven. She let him wander around, his sketchbook neglected, while she sat reading or sewing. Those days he had never thought of asking why.

Why he was there so often, why his pretext of learning to draw was never challenged, and why she sat there, pretending to read.

'My boy is just a little older than you,' she said one day, surprising him.

It always surprised him to discover Europeans had lives, like everyone else. They kept these lives hidden, revealing only as much as the moment demanded.

It had shocked him to discover Mr Kipling had a wife. And now here she was, telling him they had a boy! A hidden boy, a secret.

Ramratan felt honoured by her trust, though he wondered why she kept the boy hidden.

'Would you like to see a picture of him?' she asked, and went away to fetch it, without waiting for his answer.

The boy was very like her, but with something more besides. A cast in the lighted eye told Ramratan he would be the very devil unsupervised, and a perfect angel to the world otherwise. And, from that moment, Ramratan loathed him. He felt sorry for Mrs Kipling, but the best he could do was to make sure he never mentioned her boy.

Now, of course, everybody mentioned the Kipling boy.

The papers were all full of him.

Ramratan had read '*Baa Baa Black Sheep*' and learnt the truth Mrs Kipling had kept hidden that summer. Rudyard (the Joseph conveniently forgotten) had even supplied a verse or two for his father's book.

Neither Mohsin Chacha nor Appa wrote to Lockwood after reading *Beast and Man in India*. Nusser said his father had, but couldn't be certain what he'd written. None of them could have found anything to say beyond the politesse of disdain.

Ramratan wondered if Lockwood's long wait to publish had been intentional. The book was written when he was twelve, he recalled the afternoon when Mohsin Chacha showed them the glyph. That was 1874. Appa had bought three copies when the book came out in 1891.

He remembered that Saturday afternoon.

Saturday afternoons were sacred to the four. A chair was always set out for Lockwood, who was never there. That Saturday, Mohsin and Darayus had arrived well before their set hour of half past three, summoned by a hasty upswell of the past.

How old were they then?

Appa was—what? Only sixty-four? He seemed so much older! He had let them know he would make the trip to Higginbotham's after lunch, and it would be three before he returned.

Here they were, at the stroke of three, taking their usual seats on the porch—Darayus in the tall cane chair, and Mohsin on the stone flags, cross-legged on his jaa namaaz in the strip of sunlight that spilled through the trellis at this hour.

That afternoon, Yashoda's silver tumblers of ginger sherbet stood untouched.

Not a word was exchanged.

At the sound of the approaching gharry, both of them sprang to attention.

They walked gravely to the gate to await Appa.

When he appeared, parcel in hand, they hurried back to the house, breaking into a run, Appa shouting for scissors, Mohsin impatiently snapping the tarred twine with a loud *thtup* and with one brute tug stripping off the brown paper, and the books leaping like a blue light into their cheering arms.

'Twenty years I've waited to see this elephant!' Mohsin laughed. 'It was a young elephant when it left me, look at its wrinkles now!'

'That glyph, Mohsin. You remember what you wrote in it?'

'I must have been bilious that day. Read the introduction, Krishna. Maybe he read the words after all! Allah! What am I going to say to him now?'

'Wait a moment, Mohsin. What's this? Here in the list of illustrations there's no sign of your name.'

'Are you sure?'

'Look for yourself. It says Munshi Sher Mohammad.'

A heartbeat of silence, no more. Then Mohsin Chacha said carelessly, 'Oh, that? That's all right then. *That's* my name.'

'Since when?'

'You know how writers have a pen name? This is mine. My *takhal-lus.* I told him to use Munshi Sher Mohammad.'

What made Ramratan certain that Mohsin was lying?

Appa and Darayus thought so too. A sudden quiet overcame them.

Then Darayus, temporizing as usual, said, 'Read the introduction aloud, Krishna. Let's hear what Lockwood has to say.'

The silence deepened as Appa read.

There was no further cheering that afternoon.

Eight years, two editions. Not bad, considering the reviews. Mohsin had read out George Birdwood's comment with glee.

'*It is not for Europeans to establish Schools of art in a country, the productions of whose remote districts are a School of art in themselves, far more capable of teaching than being taught.*'

'Give me one such European, Krishna, and we see eye to eye. But Lockwood! We have been friends all our lives, and look what he has to say about me!'

Mohsin flung the book on the floor and stalked off.

It wasn't likely that Mohsin would want to meet Alice now. The Kiplings had been away a long time.

Ballard Pier, 5 September 1875.

Three o'clock, the sun drawing brambles across the eyes, making them bleed. His eyes are sunk fiercely in the desperate crinkle of their lids. He moves a little further into the heat where a tub of tar stands smoking. Its fumes will do to explain the sudden prickling of his eyes.

The four of them linger at the quay. Alice has gone on ahead, she is stepping into the boat when she turns back and comes hurrying towards him. She has a package with her, flat and square, wrapped as if he didn't know what it was.

'You keep this, Ramratan. It's yours now.'

She is gone before he can thank her. He stands dry-mouthed, his heart drumming on the knife-edged cardboard against his ribs. To hold it like that, never to let it go again, it's almost too much to bear.

And now, twenty-two years later, he was to see Alice again.

How old was she now—sixty?

The first time he'd seen her was also the first time he'd seen the book. He picked it now, this book of mordants. Its colours dyed his world. He kept it wrapped in an old silk shawl, away from light, for fear the colours would fade. Nobody touched it but him. Yashoda, surprising him at the book one day, had looked away. He wondered what she thought it contained. But he kept it secret.

Ned Jones was now Edward Burne-Jones. Sir Edward as of last year. No longer such a common name. That the man was uncommon, he had no doubt at all.

What would his son be like?

What would his son be like?

The words and colours blurred on the page, they swam into each other, making new hues.

Ratan shut the book and switched off the lamp. He stood in the balcony, staring at the dark.

He desperately needed sleep.

10 December 1992

Crispin clapped Ratan on the shoulder, a boxer's greeting that left him wincing. The police van smelt of something more than dread this morning. Something polite—sheets smoothed down, skirts straightened, flies zipped. It was the smell of complicity.

Crispin seemed oblivious to it. He was whistling softly, the same three notes under his breath, over and over again.

Ta-ra-ta, ta-ra-ta.

He broke off when he noticed Ratan's smile.

'Something funny?'

'Just a thought.'

'What?'

'I think here's a guy who doesn't smell of the dead any more.'

Crispin grinned.

'Bloody psychologist, ha?'

'A good one, you admit.'

'Yeah. You have no idea, man. No idea.'

He ran his hands through his hair, then looked up red-faced, and broke into an embarrassed laugh.

'It's done you good,' Ratan observed. He wondered, sadly, if Crispin realized he would have to pay.

In his own marriage, now defunct, sudden passion was always suspect. Not very long before the break-up had he learnt the bitter truths of post-coital etiquette. There was always payment, of some sort or the other. The realization had shocked him and his future had loomed grey and anhedonic. He could write a riposte to Dr Alex Comfort and call it *The Joylessness of Sex*. Or he could get out. Perhaps Prema felt the same. They never talked about it.

Did anybody?

It was easier to blame it all on Arjun's illness. Ratan tasted the acrid surge of self-loathing in his pharynx.

It wasn't always like that ...

Ratan beat back that voice.

It had always been like that, only he hadn't noticed. Every time after, he ended up doing something he didn't want to. Every fuck. Every single fucking time.

No. Remember. It wasn't always like that. Remember.

Well, he didn't remember. He wouldn't remember. It hurt too much!

No.

'No.'

It was Yashoda's voice, sated with pleasure.

'What? I didn't say anything. I didn't do anything.'

'No! To what you're thinking.'

What had he been thinking, flat on his back, supremely content? What does a man think of at moments like these?

Ah yes!

Perhaps the boys ought to go back to Father Morris' class, perhaps he should overlook last week's incident. Yashoda felt the boys should brave it out. Ramratan wanted no more of Father Morris in their lives. They should not have to take any more jibes.

But if Yashoda felt so strongly about it ...

'No.'

In the clear light of morning, he would look her in the eye and say the answer was still 'No' to Father Morris.

'No' felt safe. 'No' felt clean. It cooled him like a long draught of water.

'No it is then,' he said, drawing her closer.

Her fingers, dexterous, intelligent, told him she understood.

It hadn't always been like this.

It hadn't always been this—

The havaldar was saying something that needed an answer. Ratan put away his memory and brought his eyes to focus. The man was asking him about the papers.

The Quarantine Papers.

'Yes, thanks, I got all the papers I wanted,' he said rapidly. 'Was it you who went to get them?'

'Yes. The watchman there seemed quite surprised that anybody should want old papers urgently in the middle of the riots. Life doesn't stop because of mandir–masjid maramari, I told him! What do you say, Sahib? Let them fight, how does it bother us? Call him Ram or call him Allah, what do I care, it's still my arse torn to shreds.'

'I couldn't agree with you more,' Ratan conceded. 'Tell me, any chance of getting a ride there today?'

'More papers?'

'Family crisis, very urgent.'

'After lunch, Sahib? At that time report to HQ, so I can drop you there. Pick you up on return trip? About one hour?'

'Crispin, that suit you?'

It did, and Ratan felt his oppression lift. It would be good to see Nusser after all this time. Then he reminded himself it was just a page of writing.

'Something going on at home, Ratan? That brought on the migraine?'

Ratan heard himself lying.

'Guess what, the CAT scan cured me of that.'

Crispin bounded ahead of Ratan into Pathology. Ratan dawdled in the corridor, grateful for the sun on his back.

Relishing his solitude he tarried, not wanting to say a word, not wanting to move.

He wasn't alone any longer. A woman stood near him, waiting for his attention.

She was old and tired and gave off an odour of exhaustion and fear. Yet there was something grand about her. Her hands, clenched over a plastic bag, were wrinkled from a lifetime of scrubbing clothes, floors, other people's dishes. Her teeth were broken and crooked, black from Qaimganj tobacco. Despite all this, she projected a grandeur that Ratan recognized as grief.

'They said I should ask here. Will you look for my son.'

Ratan nodded.

'Is there somebody with you, Maaji?'

'You mean to find him for me? No, I have nobody with me. Take me inside with you and I will find him myself. How can anybody else tell if it's my son?'

'Tell me what to look for.'

Her hands unclenched, the plastic bag fell. He saw that she found it impossible to comprehend that small event. She cast about, not knowing what to do. Ratan picked up the bag, and was handing it to her when she sagged and sat down, dazed.

Ratan got a glass of water from the cooler and sat down next to her.

She wet her pallu in the water and wiped her face, poured the rest on her head and tamped down her hair.

'It seems like I've been waiting here all my life. But it was only yesterday. No. No, it was the day before.'

'What happened, Maaji?'

'I am not making a complaint. I only want my boy.'

'Yes, I understand.'

'They came in and started shooting, just like that. My boy Hanif, he was having his breakfast. He got up, made for the door. I said, let them be. The police is always up to some goondagiri, you eat your roti, beta. But he said, "No Ma, let me just find out what is happening," and he looked out of our kholi. He just looked out and—Ya Allah! Straight in his stomach they hit him. Hanif fell into the gali. I ran out crying for help. The gali was empty. Emptied in the blink of an eye. Empty! Except for all the bodies twitching and bleeding. How many? Who counts us, Bhaiyya? My son was past help. I ran back in to my girls cowering inside, I lay down on them, shielding them. I swore I would kill them myself before those filthy men could touch them. You understand? Death is better than that. How will you understand? You are a man! The same devil grows between your legs. Never mind, it's not your fault. It's Allah's wish that men should be devils and women their prey.'

'What happened to Hanif?'

'What happened? After some time the black van came. And the police. They picked up all the bodies. All of us women, mothers and wives, stood around wailing. They laughed and poked us with their lathis. Our breasts and bellies and thighs, and every one of us knew they meant something worse. Never mind. Forget I told you. Just find my son.'

'Drink your tea, Maaji. I'll go look for him. How old did you say he was?'

She cried, anguished by all the years she'd held the child, all the years she'd let go. Wonderingly, she whispered, 'Twenty?'

Ratan stepped into the mortuary. Past the door, foetid air issued like a filthy rag, damp and foul. The air conditioning had either quit, or was utterly inadequate. The fluorescent light was garish, flattening everything. He saw tan and ochre stripes, bodies stacked against the wall and strewn about the hall. Which of these had once been Hanif? They all looked ageless in the equity of death.

How would he possibly locate one particular corpse here?

Many of the bodies were bloating already. Most were naked, a few were partially clothed. It was futile relying on *last seen wearing*...

He could go find Mama, but Ratan feared once he got out, he wouldn't come back in again. It wasn't just the stench and the horror, he was beginning to feel the lack of air. But he had to look, and fast.

If it had happened the day before yesterday, he reasoned, Hanif couldn't be in the pile against the far wall. He was probably among yesterday's corpses.

What if?

Ratan ran out, gasping as fresh air knifed his lungs. Not trusting his voice, he motioned to the woman that he'd be back and ran all the way to the hospital. That boy must be dead by now.

The emergency ward, surprisingly, was always the least chaotic in the hospital. No resident in sight, the ward was dotted about with student nurses earnestly handing out pills. He had walked in on a coffee break. He found the pantry. The staff nurses were all in there, ceremonially ringing the steaming coffee pot. Sister presided, red-belted, supreme. Her cup froze in mid-air when she saw Ratan.

'Please wait in the ward, Doctor.'

Humbly, Ratan retreated. There was nothing else to be done. They took longer than usual. Eventually, a staff nurse emerged, giggling. Ratan asked his question.

She dimpled innocently.

'Expired, I think! Staff Patankar will know. I'll ask her, please wait.'

Ratan heard her.

'Patankar Staff! That abdominal wound expired?'

There was some hurried whispering.

Then Patankar, fortyish, parading a sturdy paunch, thrust her bland face out at Ratan.

'Patient is relation?'

Ratan could have strangled her.

'I'm Dr Ratan Oak from Pathology,' he answered in Marathi. 'I want to know about an admission of yesterday. A young man shot in the abdomen, he was rushed in for emergency surgery. Is he with you?'

'I'll see. Please wait.'

More whispering.

Now sister emerged from her lair.

'What did you say your name was, Doctor?'

'Oak. Dr Ratan Oak.'

'We don't have any Dr Oak on our staff here.'

'I'm from Pathology.'

'I see. Why are you making these enquiries?'

'I know the boy.'

'I will tell the Inspector. He will take your statement.'

'Statement? Whatever for?'

'It is procedure. This is police case, Doctor. What I can do?'

Ratan thanked her and went looking for the resident. That took another half-hour.

The surgical residents were all in the operating theatre.

Finally, the registrar emerged in bloodstained green scrubs.

'What? Is he alive? Will he make it? How am I supposed to know, yaar? You guys keep shooting down people and throwing them in here, and you expect us to do the dirty work? Fuck off, man. I don't care if you're from Pathology or from the morgue, just get the fuck out of here.'

Ratan clung grimly to his patience.

'I found him in a van full of dead bodies,' he said slowly. 'The kid had been trapped in that van all night. Under a pile of corpses. He survived that. I hope he's made it through surgery.'

'You hope? Yeah, he's in the side room, Ward 18. We

shifted him out of Emergency to get him away from those fuckers. You know whom I mean.'

Ward 18 had a kinder staff nurse.

She led Ratan in to the boy without a word.

He was asleep—sedated, probably. But breathing comfortably, guyed up on polythene tubes threaded in and out of him.

Outside, he asked for the boy's papers. He was listed simply as Billa #222.

Ratan returned to the woman still crumpled against the pillar outside the morgue. There now were two men with her. She said they were relatives.

He took one of them back with him to the ward. The man accompanied him hesitantly, warily, ready to flee at the sight of a policeman.

But it *was* Hanif.

The man stood trembling at the threshold of the side room, gibbering wordlessly. Ratan had to steady him.

The woman stumbled after them when they told her, dazed and disbelieving, readying herself for a terror greater than what she had lived through.

Crispin was waiting impatiently at the mortuary door. His smile did not reach his eyes.

'Ratan, you're free. No more police cases for you, you can escape all of yesterday's lot.'

'What do you mean? I can't just stop now!'

'You've been stopped. Orders from above! I'd switch places with you in a minute if I could.'

'Do, then.'

'What? You're not serious?'

'I am.'

'Sorry, boss. Can't be done. Official designates only. You can help out with the rest, if you wish.'

'How about I do them and you write the notes?'

Crispin hesitated. And looked away. He'd been warned against Ratan—no departmental caution, this. Just post-orgasmic epiphany. Why?

'No can do, Ratan. Tell you what. There's a simple suicide waiting. You want to get your hands dirty? Do that one for me.'

Are suicides ever simple?

Crispin expected this one to be.

An old man, prematurely aged, probably not older than sixty, spare and neglected. Face contused, burst wound over forehead. Frontal impact injury. Compound fracture of frontal and right parietal bones, possible cervical spine injury.

The man had jumped to his death from a third-floor balcony.

Pathetic. At his age!

Why?

Was it less tragic when the young killed themselves?

Ratan walked to the foot of the table and viewed the body.

There could be no mistake. Despite the injuries, Ratan knew this man.

Govardhan More.

Govardhan More.

Avdaji's nephew.

That oaf?

He had his eye on Chitrangada. Shankar Buwa twisted his arm. He went crying to Tilak, but that worthy wouldn't want to make an enemy of Shankar Buwa. Govardhan hadn't thought of that, had he?

Govardhan More.

Govardhan More.

The papers said Balkrishna More, but the address was the same. Ratan knew it even before he read the clerk's laboured hand.

Try as he would, be could remember nothing further about Govardhan More.

He wrote up his notes rapidly.

Across the room, Crispin struggled with his workload, flitting from table to table as Mama laid bare, eviscerated, stitched up. Ratan wondered if Crispin proposed inventing his notes later, in the comfort of his office.

Crispin looked up.

'Lunch, Ratan?'

It was almost one o'clock. He wanted to look in on Radhika before the havaldar called for him.

'I'll pass, thanks. I have to go out after lunch.'

'Yeah, those papers. You go on. Back by five, you think? I'm closing shop then. Tomorrow I'll have to start on the sections, with all the HP piled up, and no technicians. Can you blame them? Who wants to risk their neck leaving home, except fools like us?'

Histopathology!

Ratan's heart bounced. How long, how very long, since he'd held a microtome!

Crispin (or his wife) could have no possible objections to letting him handle dead bits in formalin. No political terrors there.

'I can do that for you,' he said rapidly.

'What? Make sections? Ratan, you're a microbiologist. Cutting open cadavers is one thing, but what do you know about making blocks, cutting and staining sections—leave alone looking at histology slides?'

Ratan shrugged.

'I've been doing it all my life,' he said and walked out.

Open-mouthed, Crispin stared after him.

Although he wanted to check up on Radhika, Ratan didn't plan on actually seeing her. He was too filthy from the mortuary to go anywhere near the burns ward.

He stopped at the nursing station. They welcomed him with some relief, and handed him a long list of things they needed urgently. Disposables, antibiotics, dressings.

'Surely we have all this in the ward, Sister?' Ratan asked in puzzlement.

The staff nurse looked embarrassed.

'Better you buy it all from outside, Doctor,' she said in a low voice. 'That way we can be certain the patient gets it.'

The pharmacy was downstairs and it took him thirty minutes to get back.

'You can go in if you wish,' the staff nurse said as he handed her the box with his purchases.

Ratan explained why he'd rather not and asked if Radhika was still heavily sedated.

'Actually, no,' the nurse replied. 'But that's what we're telling the police to give her some peace. What a life for her, poor thing! Just lies there, staring at the ceiling. Her boyfriend's name was Anwar, and that's all she says. Only that name. No matter what you ask her, she only answers Anwar.'

'Somebody's sitting with her?'

'Who? Her friends are working. Her family said, "Sister, please don't call us, please don't phone us, we have nothing to do with her." She's too serious for us to put her in the general ward, where at least other patients will talk to her. The nurses are too frightened.'

'Frightened of what?'

'I don't know! But we're all frightened.'

'Tell your girls not to be frightened, Sister. I'll be around from tomorrow.'

'Maybe then she'll eat something. Our doctor has advised a light diet, but she just refuses everything. And burns cases, you know, need high protein.'

'I'll persuade her.'

The staff nurse smiled.

Ratan walked away from the burns ward with the feeling he'd left behind something vital. He had to restrain himself from returning, and he couldn't explain away his unease. He'd promised to see her out of a sense of duty.

It was the least he could do for Anwar's stilled eyes.

The constable's name was Kamble. He sat in the van with Ratan.

'The things one saw on the roads these days! Enough to give a man a headache for the rest of his life! Of course, Sahib saw the worst of it in the dead house.'

The driver shouted out to them that he was going to take Mohammad Ali Road. Smoke or no smoke, at least no pitched battles had been reported there.

'The smoke should have died out,' Kamble said. 'The fire's two days old now.'

'You can still smell it.' The driver hawked phlegm out of his window. 'Makes my eyes water. Gives me a cough. All that burning rubber.'

A row of linoleum shops had been torched on Tuesday. The tall rolls stacked outside in the street smouldered, long after the blaze had been put out.

The driver was right. The smoke lingered and made them cough.

The road was deserted as far as Pydhonie, but past the traffic signal, a crowd milled on the sidewalk.

A smoking BEST bus answered all their questions.

Their driver was accelerating past this gaggle, when Ratan espied a familiar blue dupatta.

'Stop!' he yelled. 'Stop quickly! Please!'

He was at the wire grille, clawing it like a madman.

Kamble shouted at the driver to stop, but Ratan had

already flung the door open and jumped out. He crossed to the sidewalk in two bounds and dragged Prema out from the ruckus. He pushed her into the van, oblivious to the clamour about him.

Kamble got out to reason with the people now surrounding the police van. He would send somebody within an hour. Here, he was making the call right now—

'Prema! Are you out of your mind?' Ratan was furious. 'Why are you here? Where are you headed?'

'To college, of course.'

'College? Everything's closed.'

'Cyrus said—'

'Ah! Cyrus!'

'Oh, if you're going to be like that—'

'What did Cyrus say, exactly?'

'He said he'd meet me in college. He's gone ahead to get some papers done.'

'Papers? In the middle of a riot? Who's going to process papers for him? And he can't ask you to come right across town for whatever mad scheme he has. You could have burnt to death on that bus.'

'Nah. We all got out well before that. They were quite nice actually. They asked us to get off the bus. The driver and the conductor ran away. *Then* they set fire to the bus, and vanished. When they saw us here, the few people on the road disappeared too. What cowards people are!'

'Why were you just standing there? Couldn't you walk away? Who did you expect would turn up and rescue you?'

'You did!'

She gave him the look. It liquified his bones.

Damn her!

She still had that hold over him!

He asked Kamble if they could make a stop at the Arts College. He would take Prema to the staff room, and if that miserable Cyrus wasn't there, he'd see her home himself.

She hadn't let go of his hand yet. Or, he hadn't let go of hers.

'Ladies should stay at home,' Kamble pronounced, disapproval writ large on his face.

Ratan endorsed this, a little too heartily.

Prema caught his eye in a conspiratorial gleam.

Kamble conferred with the driver. They could drop them at the gate and come back in half an hour after looking in at the Bazargate Chowky. Would that do?

Ratan nodded his thanks. Suddenly elated, his hand tightened around Prema's and he thrilled to her answering pressure.

The watchman at the gate was someone new. He let them in without greeting, with profound disinterest.

The place was empty. The ugly Gothic buildings seemed suddenly very secret and far away. They walked rapidly towards the squat building where Prema said Cyrus would be waiting.

The offices were shut. There was no one about.

Ratan saw the heart go out of her.

'Come on!'

He broke into a run, knowing she would follow breathlessly, trailing questions.

'I've something to show you!'

He'd never meant to tell her. Never meant to bring her here to Alice Kipling's house. Never meant they should stand here in the leaf-strewn verandah, waiting ... as he had once waited, for the tall doors to open.

Here they were, and the door had opened, and they were inside.

He shut the door carefully, as he always did.

He stood waiting for her to emerge from the gauzy recess at the back of the hall.

'Ramratan, is that you? Go upstairs, then. I'll join you!'

Sometimes it was just her voice.

'What is it, Ratan? What are we waiting for?'

Prema drew close to him, pressing against his arm, her voice a whisper.

'Why this place, Ratan? It's Kipling House. Why have you brought me here?'

'Come on, I'll show you.'

He was whispering too.

He led her to the stairs, and up.

At the landing, they stood very close. Her breath steamed against his throat. He brushed her hair back gently from her face. How could he have forgotten how beautiful she was? Their feet grew slow and languid. He pushed the door with his hip, and lifted her over the threshold.

'What is this place, Ratan?'

The atelier.

The atelier.

Where the sun striped the floor. And the room opened to the sky.

There were shutters now.

No matter. He'd let them stay shut as he settled against her softness and heaviness. He'd hold the sun at bay.

They entwined urgently. Her fingers clawed his back as he inhaled her familiar scent, a scent now alien and strange. This was new, this swift anger to his lust. It frightened him. But Prema seemed elated as she closed in on him. Past that, Ratan was lost.

All that mattered was the tremble, the din in her, in him.

With an old and easy familiarity she found him as he

pulsed past her fingers. She cleaved to him as he curved to her. Frantic, fierce, furious, they tangled together. He knew she was there already and at the brink of his own he ceased in a searing column of pain. Still pulsing about him, she broke free, and pushed him away.

Bereft, naked and stung, he again felt the wonted sadness.

'You're crazy. Ratan! Crazy, you know? You're crazy!'

She moved away.

He shrugged and helped with her dishabille. She went to the window and looked out through the wooden slats. He trailed her sillage, kissed her shoulder, attempted to rest his cheek against her neck.

'Let's go home. I have to get some stuff, then let's go home,' he whispered into her back, hopeful and exigent.

How easy it all could be. How very easy. If only she let him be.

'There's Cyrus!'

She shrugged him off, disciplined tendrils of hair now damply askew, smoothed her qameez, settled her dupatta, tapped her right foot to straighten the folds of her shalwar where the fabric clung wetly to her thigh.

'I told you he'd be here. There he is!'

Ratan caught a blue gleam at the gate. The fucker had brought his car.

Prema pushed her way past Ratan.

She clattered down the stairs, her heels slapping the protesting wood. She was out of the house and running.

The door slammed in the wind, rusty clumps of leaves flew up into the grey December air.

'How stupid of you to take the bus!' Cyrus barked. 'The trains are running normally. Why didn't you take a train?'

Prema had barely finished a breathless recital of her adventure on the bus.

Cyrus peered at Ratan suspiciously.

'So how come *you* found her?'

Ratan pointed to Kamble at the gate.

'I was passing by. In that police van there.'

'What? They've arrested you?'

Cyrus burst into a guffaw of laughter. Prema joined him appreciatively.

Ratan thought he couldn't bear it a second longer, but it took longer than a minute. Then it was over.

He was rid of them. He was rid of *her*.

Ratan climbed back into the van.

'Rough times,' Kamble said. 'Who knows what's round the corner?'

The platitude served to blur the moment.

They made two more stops in the short distance they had to cover. Ratan scarcely noticed.

Indian men, she said, my dear, you have no idea…

'Indian men,' she said, 'my dear, you have no idea ...'

She said it sotto voce to Mrs Sinclair.

He was glad he hadn't got rid of his moustache over the weekend as he'd meant to. It made for an effective disguise, if one had a twitchy *levator labii superioris alaeque nasi*. As Prof. Peet breathlessly predicted:

The Indian physiognomy is an exercise in hyperbole. The facial muscles are overdeveloped due to the tendency to dramatize and exaggerate the most trivial response. The common native expression of distaste, the canine snarl, can be solely attributed to the superficial fibres of *levator labii superioris alaeque nasi* aligned coronally and placed anterior to the circular fibres of *orbicularis oris*, which civilized muscle is largely overshadowed by the hypertrophy of the upper lip tractor brought about by persistent and aggressive displays of primitive rage.

Mrs Sinclair was alone when Ramratan was shown in. She was a small spotty woman in her forties, uncertain of Ramratan's place in the hierarchy. Ramratan put her at ease by taking the best chair, greeting the bearer as an old friend and complimenting her on the elegance of her embroidery, thus breaking three rules of native etiquette in one go.

She responded as expected. She drew up her chair and prepared for a quick tête-à-tête.

This frightful plague had them all upset! And with dear Mrs Kipling so energetic about knowing what was going on in the city, she was almost at her wits' end!

Mr Burne-Jones, her nephew, was here too. Perhaps Dr Oak had heard of his father? But this was Mr Philip Burne-Jones, down from London, and he was going right back to London from here next week, and Mr Sinclair was absolutely certain it would be impossible for him to sail out if he went exploring the city, specially the native quarters that people said were *simply dreadful*. Of course, everything in here was perfectly safe, and there was no need really, to get inoculated.

She stopped for breath.

What did Dr Oak think? She didn't like to say this, but as Dr Oak was such an old friend of the Kiplings, perhaps he'd understand. It was all proving very *difficult*.

She stopped once more to touch her nose delicately with a scrap of lace.

Ramratan realized she was trying to keep back her tears. 'I'm afraid dear Mrs Kipling thinks us all a little common,' she said resolutely, going from querulous to angry. 'Our simple enjoyments are not to her taste. If you can amuse her, I'm sure you're very welcome! And as for Mr Burne-Jones, all of London knows only too well how he amuses himself. If you ask me, Dr Oak—' here her voice sank to an urgent whisper, 'he came to India just to escape. A shameful affair, simply disgusting!'

Unburdened at last, she sank back on the cushions.

The bearer returned, with a salver of Benaras brass—a dented lota of water on it, for Ramratan.

'Take that away and bring Doctor Sahib a proper glass!' Mrs Sinclair said with a semblance of irritation. 'Oh, can I offer you a glass of sherbet, Doctor? Or will you wait for tea?'

'Tea will be fine, thank you. And Meeta Kaka remembers my tastes, I see. Surahi water in a lota, my preferred tipple.'

Ramratan drained the lota.

The bearer's eyes widened slightly, but he betrayed no other sign of recognition.

Ramratan did not expect to be recognized. Butlers and bearers considered Indian visitors to be upstarts. It was infra dig to serve them. Meeta had shown him his place by bringing him water in the lota kept for servants.

There was the sound of voices outside. Ramratan's heart raced. Would she know him?

He remembered his first glimpse of her, a white woman in a shaft of sunlight, holding out a book that held sealed between its white covers all the colour in the world.

She came in as if he had never been away, as if all the years had been compressed into a day's absence, no more.

'Ah, there you are, Ramratan! I'm glad Mrs Sinclair has made you comfortable. Don't loom, Philip! Yes, do cool off dear, we'll have tea in ten minutes.'

The shadow at the door, Philip Burne-Jones presumably, wafted away.

'Can't bear the heat, poor boy! He'd best get cooled first or he's perfectly capable of going native on us and coming down to tea in muslin pyjamas.'

Mrs Sinclair gave a little scream. Alice ignored her and turned to Ramratan.

'I've just been with Mr Cleghorn. You know Mr Cleghorn, I understand.'

'Very well.'

'The poor man is completely at sea with natives. That's simply not the way, I tried telling him. Why, Philip, I'm glad you decided you were cool enough for company.'

Introductions were made.

Ramratan saw a plump man with shrewd, humorous eyes that seemed a little out of place in his vapid countenance. He was dressed in the many layers of white that comprised the visiting Englishman's India costume.

He shook hands with what the British generally described as 'a manly grip'. It meant he had been to the right schools.

'I was just telling Dr Oak about Mr Cleghorn's fiasco. Really, Ramratan! How can people be so unreasonable? Have you ever been to those hovels in Null Bazaar? Mr Weir showed us pictures. I had no idea it was this bad, and so close to the Esplanade! I suppose you're well aware of all the mess there. No matter what Mr Cleghorn's men have been doing, washing and disinfecting and scrubbing and sterilizing, there are still pools of stagnant water from taps that drip all day. Water isn't free! I wonder if those people know that. I'm sure they don't pay a water tax! It was totally thoughtless, sending piped water into Black Town! Now they've done it, the least they can do is to show people they can't waste it! Her Majesty's water doesn't come for free.'

Ramratan had a bizarre vision of Queen Victoria's urine being hawked in the streets of London at two shillings a vial. He could have sworn Philip shared his thought.

'I completely support the action taken, I told Mr Cleghorn.'

'And what action was that?' Ramratan asked.

'Why, to cut off the water, of course! The most sensible move, by far. You should have heard the protests! A memorial signed by three hundred people, no less. If you ask me, none of them knew what they were signing. You must understand the native mind, I told Mr Cleghorn. It's a chameleon. It just takes the colour of the company it keeps! We know that, don't we?'

'Do we, Aunt?' Philip asked airily. 'Do tell, I'm interested in chameleons.'

'You should be, dear boy. They know so much more about colour than you do.'

To Ramratan's dismay, Philip looked as if he was about to cry. Alice continued, unperturbed.

'We must keep at it, I told MrCleghorn. The British Empire must keep on. And then I did something Rudy will never forgive me for—'

Ramratan expressed interest.

'I keep forgetting you've never met my son, Ramratan. But you've seen his pictures.'

'I've also read all his books.'

'Really? Then you'll understand I did something

unforgivable. I let Mr Cleghorn in on a new poem. As yet far from publication, I assure you, and I had absolutely no right doing it. But it was so appropriate, I couldn't help it. I shall plead a mother's pride if Rudy ever hears of this!'

'Perhaps, since you've erred once, you'll err again, Aunt Alice?' Philip said. 'Let Dr Oak judge for himself how appropriate it was.'

That was the first time Ramratan heard 'The White Man's Burden'. It would haunt him for the rest of his life.

Strangely, it did not affect him then.

Not as much as Mrs Kipling's concluding words.

'So there was an end to the matter, I told Mr Cleghorn. Call in the protestors and have the lot chawbucked. That will clean up the place for you!'

'I'm sure Dr Oak agrees with you,' Philip observed drily. 'Mrs Sinclair, will you rescue a dying man and ring for tea?'

Tea was a more elaborate meal than Mrs Kipling served twenty-five years ago. In those days Ramratan's treat was a dry, slightly stale shortbread out of a blue and gold tin. It tasted like a notebook cover, sticking to his palate in a dry wad. He loved it. It made her happy to see him enjoying it, safe in the knowledge that her pleasure needn't mean another biscuit.

Today they had cucumber sandwiches, a great treat as Mrs Sinclair had cut them herself, the mysteries of the cucumber being utterly beyond the cook.

Alice appreciated this.

'Never trust 'em with the keys to the kingdom, that's always been my policy. John thinks I fuss, but the khansama, my dear, is so often the Consumah!'

Mrs Sinclair was having trouble with her servants too. The Portuguese ayah had left.

'Surely you can't mean Ignatia?' Ramratan asked.

Mrs Kipling had sent her children away, but she kept their ayah on. Ai found it completely insane. Ramratan recalled being furious with his mother.

Had Ignatia stayed on for another twenty-five years? She was a sad woman with a large family in Bandra waiting to burden her with their endless troubles. Ignatia wanted to educate herself, and had taught herself to read. Ramratan would loan her his schoolbooks, but Ignatia never had time enough to really put her mind to them.

Mrs Sinclair stared at Ramratan.

'Why, yes, I believe that is her name, now that you mention it. "Plague in the family," she said. You know, Alice, they all say that these days. The first excuse is always plague in the family!'

'And she's gone to nurse them?' Philip asked. 'That's heroic of her.'

'Heroic? You wouldn't say that if you knew these people. You should read John's book. Nobody knows India like John, I always say. Oh, Ramratan! I have copies for you. And for the others. I'm sure you'll be interested.'

'Appa bought copies for everyone the day the book was released,' Ramratan said.

'Oh.'

'But your copies are most welcome.'

'So, Ramratan! Tell me. Is what John told me true?'

'If I remember Mr Kipling right, whatever he said was generally true.'

'Oh. I meant about your marriage?'

'I am married. Yes. We have two sons.'

'You must show me their pictures sometime. Is it true that your wife is a widow?'

'Surely not, if I am alive.'

Mrs Kipling refused the snub.

'A child widow?'

'She wasn't a child when I married her.'

'That's right. I remember now. John told me a few years ago. Krishna wrote to him that he had arranged your marriage. To a *widow with a child*. I suppose the child didn't survive.'

Ramratan concentrated on his sandwich.

'How long have you been married now?'

'Ten years'

'And how old are your sons?'

'Gnyaneshwar is eleven, Chaitanya nine.'

'What difficult names, Ramratan! I suppose they mean something profound.'

'Jolly good idea to know what your name means,' Philip interjected. 'I've always wondered about mine.'

Alice ignored him.

'So the elder boy is—'

Ramratan refused to complete the sentence for her.

'—from her first marriage,' Alice finished.

'I have two sons,' Ramratan said.

'You are a lucky man,' Mrs Sinclair spoke up bravely.

'I think so too.' Ramratan smiled at her.

'I think it's marvellous,' Alice said. 'Your father was very brave to get you married to a widow. He saved the girl from certain death. I hope you take good care of your wife, Ramratan.'

'Perhaps not as much as she does of me.'

'Then you must improve. I was telling Mr Cleghorn just that this morning. We were talking about the Vicerine's Fund, and I was obliged to give him the most distressing details. Most distressing, I assure you. One of our dear friends in Lahore, a Miss McAllister, has been doing zenana work. And, my dears, you simply will not believe half of what she told me!'

'Oh yes! I believe there's a lot of consumption,' Mrs Sinclair said, sighing.

'Consumption would be a mercy in most cases,' Alice said grimly.

She turned towards Mrs Sinclair to hand her a cup of tea.

Her back to Ramratan, her voice a low rasp, she continued, 'Indian men, my dear. You simply have no idea! Such savage lusts.'

Ramratan, who was listening to Philip's story of his lost luggage, had difficulty suppressing a grin.

'Are we all to be inoculated, Dr Oak?' Mrs Sinclair quavered.

Ramratan wasn't quite sure whether her trepidation was founded on the plague or on savage lust.

'It would be safest if you were,' he said.

'And is your family inoculated, Doctor?'

'Certainly.'

'Even the children?'

'Especially the children.'

'But I am sure your wife refused,' Alice said. 'It seems to be the usual attitude of native ladies.'

'Not at all. She wouldn't let me inoculate the boys till she had convinced herself it wouldn't be too hard on them!'

'Well, she's just persuaded me,' Mrs Sinclair declared. 'And I'll speak for my husband. So, Doctor Oak, tell us when it can be done, and we'll be ready.

After that, if she will receive me, I would like to thank your wife in person.'

'Yashoda will be delighted to see you.'

'Aren't you being a little hasty, dear? Perhaps we should talk this over with Robert first. And Philip really has quite a delicate constitution, so I advise you don't include him in your plans, Ramratan.'

'All the more reason then for Mr Burne-Jones to get himself inoculated. And you too, Mrs Kipling.'

'We shall see, Ramratan. And now I have a real treat for you. I'm going to read you this beautiful ditty. Rudy wrote it for Lady Dufferin. Rudy has always felt deeply for Indian women. He heard all of Miss McAllister's stories. Women like her have done zenana work for years. London is now against medical missionaries. The ladies are all demanding scientific lady doctoresses. I never heard of such a thing! The Miss McAllisters of this world have done more good than a little chit from a London school ever can. If Indian women are ill enough to need a medical doctor, there are doctors enough in India. And when they're really ill, it won't matter if the doctor's a man or a woman. There is absolutely no need for women doctors in India. I'm sure you agree, Dr Oak.'

'Most vehemently—I disagree.'

'Well—I must remind you of what Mary Carpenter told me when she was our guest in Bombay years ago. "Mrs Kipling, there is work to do for every lady who employs native women in her service in India." Have you heard of Mary Carpenter, Ramratan?'

'The Ragged Schools lady, who was so appalled by the scanty Indian wardrobe? Yes! I've read her.'

'Well, we must forgive her little peculiarities, and look to the larger picture. You know Mary Carpenter would never have stood for nonsense like women doctoring around. She knew that the main problem India faced was its women.'

'If you believe that, surely, you must also believe in solving the problem by improving their lot,' Philip put in.

'Certainly. But educating women to perform a role that is absolutely inimical to the gender is not the answer.'

'Personally, I should love to have a lady physician take my pulse when I am ill,' Philip persisted.

'Oh you are a quiz, Mr Burne-Jones!' Mrs Sinclair cried.

'Do read us the poem, Mrs Kipling!'

After the poem, the ladies retired. Ramratan, left alone with Philip Burne-Jones, was at a loss.

'I hope you were not offended by my aunt, Dr Oak,' Philip said without preamble. 'I suppose she means well. So does her son. So does my uncle. So do they all, the entire British Empire.'

'And you, Mr Burne-Jones?'

'Oh, call me Philip, everybody does. The pater was plain Jones to start with, you know.'

'I do know. Your name, by the way, means "a lover of horses". And, I know your father well.'

'You've met my father?'

'No, indeed.'

'Ah! The usual, then. You know his pictures.'

'Right.'

Philip rose abruptly and walked over to the window.

'I'd like to look around. On my own, you know. So maybe I'll get that inoculation sooner than later.'

'Tomorrow morning?'

Philip paled a bit.

'So soon? Can it be managed so soon?'

'Yes, why not? Tomorrow, at eight. I will speak to Dr Surveyor. Another old friend of Mrs Kipling's. She'll be glad to meet him.'

'Oh, no! I'd prefer if we kept this quiet for the moment. Ramratan? Is that the way you say your name? Can I call you Ramratan?'

'Of course. Turn up at eight then, and I'll get you fixed.'

'And just where are you taking my nephew at eight, Ramratan?'

Alice was back, the old Alice in her smile.

Ramratan smiled back.

'We talk of our adventures after they're done, don't we?'

She laughed.

'It was good for us, those years. Philip, do you know Ramratan was my son when Rudy and Trix were away? Ramratan, do you remember the book I gave you?'

Ramratan nodded.

'My father's sketches?' Philip asked. 'Mostly watercolour? I've heard him mention it. Do you mind showing it to me sometime? I've seen very little of his early work. I dabble a little myself, you know.'

Ramratan was familiar enough with British idiom to understand that Philip thought a great deal of his work.

'Oh, Philip is the coming man, make no mistake,' Alice said. 'But I'm glad to say he has a proper respect for his brush, unlike those scandalous French. I never did understand why you spent all that time in Paris, Philip.'

'Like pimples, Paris is a particular phase in a young man's life, Aunt Alice.'

'This is your Bombay phase then, Philip. Perhaps you will get some pictures out of it.'

Philip made no reply, and for the first time Ramratan saw in his pale eyes the uneasiness that marks the artist. Lockwood did not have it. His pencil was so sure. And Mohsin? He was anguished by it, his entire life a grimace of uncertainty.

Ramratan saw more than uneasiness in Philip. He discerned fear. Philip wasn't uncertain about his talent. He was *afraid* of art. Philip would never reach out and grasp that thorny branch. It would hurt too much.

Radhakrishnan was waiting for him at the entrance to the Archives. After a solemn handshake he led Ratan through deserted stone corridors. He walked very quickly, a little ahead of Ratan.

The stairs were unlit, unventilated. The air was rancid with memory, sweat, urine, pigeon shit.

'All they have to do is open a window. But, can you believe it, that's against regulations,' Raki said without turning around.

He unlocked the tall doors and led Ratan into a vast hall partitioned with bookracks. None of the books looked particularly old.

'All the old stuff is in the basement. I brought up several ledgers you might need. We can go look for more.'

He switched on the lights and they flickered into uncertain life. The room grew only marginally brighter. Cavernous shadows lapped at the tables. Thin wavers of sepia motes filtered past grimy windowpanes, and left wet slicks on the stone floor.

Raki pulled out a chair for Ratan.

'All the originals? Or just that green ink letter?'

'Just the letter.'

'Here you are. I'll be across the room, if you need me.'

No questions, no explanations. The man was gone.

'Raki, hold on a minute. Mind staying for a bit? I want to look at this with you.'

As Raki pulled up a chair for himself, Ratan switched on the small lamp at the edge of the table. It cast a diffuse glow, but would serve.

Nusser's steady backslant stared up at him from the foxed page. The ink was as he remembered it, a deep viridian. It hadn't faded a smidgen. The stationery was standard hospital issue. The departmental stamp black, not today's violet.

'Listen to this, and tell me what you think. It's a letter to the police commissioner from my friend Dr Surveyor.'

Ratan read out the letter, trying to keep his voice from trembling. The page was bound securely into the ledger, else his fingers would have crushed or crumpled it as they clawed at the signature. And then he couldn't stand it any longer. He stopped fighting and felt the blessed relief of tears.

Raki gently moved the ledger away. After that he was just there. When Ratan ceased sobbing, he was still there.

He got up a little later and went away.

He returned with a paper cup of cold water, and a moist hand towel. Ratan pressed the towel gratefully to his face, drained the water and wondered where he should begin.

'You knew the writer, Ratan?'

'Yes. We were close friends.'

'What happened to him?'

'He died.'

'Yes, I know that. But what was happening to him when he wrote that letter?'

'I don't know. I thought you'd know.'

'I?'

'Yes. Because you didn't know him you can read this without prejudice. Before I explain further, I want to hear what you think. What was in this man's mind when he wrote the letter?'

Raki took his time replying.

'At first reading, it seemed just a formal answer to an enquiry. He doesn't know anything about this Chitrangada More. He's irritated by her absence from work. No, he's angry about it. But looking again at the way he's phrased the letter, I think this is more than a polite expression of concern. He's more than the dutiful employer. He offers to send a man to the commissioner *twice* a day. Also, he offers to get there within the hour, in case there is some news. By this I presume he means *if she is found alive*. He then offers help—to cure her, and to comfort her. As if he wants to be the first, and the only one, next to her. I'd say he was in love with her and afraid to show it.'

'Suppose I told you he wasn't.'

'Oh? Then I'd say he was extremely anxious about her. Maybe they were close friends. A teacher-pupil relation? He definitely cared about her. Perhaps he cared about all his employees like this? Perhaps he was just a nice responsible guy.'

'He *was* a nice responsible guy. But he didn't care for her in any special way. I did.'

'*You* were in love with her?'

'No!'

'But she was dear to you.'

'Very dear. I'll come to her in a moment. Keep thinking, Raki. If I told you Surveyor didn't care particularly for her, if I told you he was a kind employer, but distant. How then would you read the letter?'

Radhakrishnan pondered this.

'Then I'd still say the same. That he wanted to be sure he would be the first and only one near her. Of course, now that means something else altogether.'

He looked uncertainly at Ratan.

Ratan shook his head impatiently.

'Go on, Raki. What does it mean now?'

'It means that he was shit scared.'

'Exactly!'

Ratan hit the table so hard, his wrist protested.

'He was afraid somebody else would get to Chitrangada before he could. He wanted to be the first one the commissioner called. Is that what you think, Ratan? I mean, considering your knowledge of Surveyor as a man.'

'Yes. That's what I think. He was scared out of his wits.'

Raki was silent.

'Yes, I do know it all happened in 1897,' Ratan said. 'You don't have to remind me.'

'I did not.'

'You think I'm insane?'

'No. I already knew you had a fair knowledge about the writer of this letter. You expected the letter to be in green ink. That said two things. Either you knew the writer always used green ink, or else you'd been told to look for a letter in green ink. The first explained your request to see the original. It meant you knew the writer personally. That's commoner than you expect. Most history nuts are like that. They know every personal foible of their dead heroes. So I thought, aha, this is Ratan's dead hero. But things are more complicated than that, aren't they?'

'Yes. Very much more complicated.'

'You want to tell me?'

'You want to listen?'

'Let's get something to eat first.'

'Let's get something to eat.'

Ramratan and the boys had just returned from the beach. They were monkeying around with the hose, glorying in the cold spray. The sand was just an excuse. They did this every Saturday morning, beach or no beach. And then they would run whooping into the kitchen, all three hungry as bears.

Today Yashoda came hurrying out of the house. 'Who wants a hot chirote? Only two left!'

The boys rushed. The tin of flaky pastry on the shelf would last them a week, but these last hot crumbly cakes with the sugar just melting were quite simply, boy heaven.

Ramratan's laugh was stilled by Yashoda's troubled eyes.

'Nusser's in your study,' she said. 'Something's wrong. Very wrong. He's been waiting nearly an hour and not a word to say. I took some sherbet up to him. All well at home, he said. It's something else. You'd better hurry.'

Ramratan changed and went upstairs to the study. Nusser was slumped over his desk, head buried in his hands. His topi and cane were tossed carelessly on the floor. The glass of sherbet stood untouched.

Ramratan put a hand on his shoulder, and drew back when he found it shaking.

'Nusser?'

Nusser raised his head, but kept his face averted. His voice was lost in the tangle of his beard.

'What is it, Nusser?'

'They're gone!' Nusser almost screamed out. 'They're gone!'

His voice rose as he repeated the word.

'Gone! Gone!'

He shook off Ramratan's hand impatiently. He was incoherent with rage.

'Don't console me! Do I look like a man who needs consolation! Help me, damn it! Ramratan, we can't waste a moment! Do something!'

'As soon as you tell me what to do or who is gone.'

'Oh.'

He fell back in defeat. His ashen lips stopped their gibber.

'I've been here all this while, and never once told you?'

'I just got here, Nusserbhai. You've been here for an hour, lost in a reverie. What do you say to a cup of strong coffee? Yashoda is making some for me. Now, begin at the beginning and tell me.'

'Don't tell Yashoda. Promise me you won't tell her. No matter what happens you won't tell her. She mustn't know. Nobody must know. Not yet.'

'Yes, Nusser. Whatever you want. Now pull yourself together while I get you that coffee.

Yashoda was waiting at the foot of the stairs.

'Is he all right?'

'No. Make some coffee, will you? Don't bring it up. Just call, I'll come down.'

'It's that bad?'

'Yes.'

Nusser was pacing the study when Ramratan got back. The topi and cane were now neatly placed on a stool. He had regained his composure. His pince nez gleamed, he looked deceptively suave. His ears no longer blazed like beacons of distress. Even his beard looked less unruly.

'Now, Ramratan, sit quiet and hear me through, or I'll never get this off my chest. First, tell me, how much do you understand of what we're doing in the lab?'

'Making the vaccine? Or the curative serum?'

'Neither. I'm talking about the plague bacillus itself. About its cultivation and harvesting. How much do you know?'

'Nothing, frankly. All I know is what you've shown me under the microscope.'

'All right. Then let me explain how it's done. You take Warden's bouillon—'

'Which is?'

'Bouillon. Broth. A special broth. A kilo and a half of mutton, cut up small, and infused for three days in three litres of water with 125 cc of hydrochloric acid added to it. Heated to 160ºC for three hours, then filtered, and neutralized with caustic soda. We now add distilled water to make up a volume of four-and-a-half litres and then heat it again. This time for only half an hour. When you filter this you have Warden's bouillon. We take this stuff, mix it with ghee—'•

'Ghee?'

'Yes. First-class desi ghee. But made in the lab. From buffalo milk. Coconut oil works too, but I prefer ghee. I'll come to that presently. As I was saying, Warden's bouillon is mixed with ghee and put into flasks, sterilized and inoculated with *Bacillus pestis*—'

'Directly from the patient?'

'No. After several passages through rabbits. In forty-eight hours we can see tiny flakes beneath the globules of ghee. After two more days these flakes grow down as stalactites—'

'O worthy son of a geologist!'

'Don't joke, Ramratan. These stalactites grow down, and—well, they break off and fall to the bottom of the flask. This continues for five to six weeks. Then it slows and stops. That's it. The supernatent is clear. If

---

• *Experiments are being made in my laboratory with regard to the growth of plague microbes in one particular product of milk largely used by the native community—ghee or clarified butter. The addition of ghee to artificial cultivations increases greatly the fertility of the medium, but we are investigating now to what extent the microbes grow in ghee itself, in the form in which it is used for food.*

—from **M.W.M. Haffkine's** deposition before The Indian Plague Commission 1898–99 at the Secretariat, Bombay, on Wednesday, 30 November 1898.

you inject this subcutaneously, the patient gets fever, but nothing shows up at the site of injection. If you take those flakes and inject their inspissate, what you experience is pain and swelling at the site of inoculation and an enlarged lymph node in the drainage area. The rest you know.'

'I stood by you solemnly as you inoculated left, right and centre. And you were giving shots of ghee all that while! You are a good Brahmin, Nusser! Wait! The coffee should be ready. Let me get it and after that I promise you, I'll be dead serious.'

Nusser drank his coffee in a quick draught and returned to his story.

'Ramratan, what I told you just now is the official version. That's what Waldemar will say in all the reports, but—' Nusser threw up his hands helplessly.

'Oh I know the first lot of inoculations, mine included, were done without sterilizing the stuff with carbolic acid! There's nothing criminal about that!'

'Oh, not that! That's unimportant. Ramratan, this is something else altogether. A grievous wrong. And I did it. I am responsible. Those first few lots of serum we used were fine. You know we've inoculated 8,167 people till now. That's a lot of prophylactic serum.'

'Get to the point and I'll absolve you like Father Placido! After two Hail Marys you can go away shriven.'

'The worst of hells will be paradise compared to this. Here's the truth, then. One batch, B-25, had thicker stalactite growth than is usual. Khursheed noticed this first. And we isolated those flasks—'

'Khursheed Alam? Quite your right-hand man, isn't he these days?'

'He is the best. Where was I? Yes, we isolated these flasks and tested the stuff on rats. Nothing drastic happened, all was as usual.

'We were about to send it out for inoculation when I had an accident. I dropped a pipette in the animal house. It shattered. It was full of this B-25 stuff, and it spattered all over the floor. That day I was wearing a mask—usually I don't. But I had a heavy cold, and didn't want to sneeze all over those poor rats. I sluiced the floor with our standard disinfecting solution, our usual practice. All told, Ramratan, that shattered pipette must have lain on the floor perhaps fifteen minutes before I hosed the place down. Fifteen minutes, maximum.

'Then I locked up for the night. I had no specific cause for worry, but I was uneasy. These things worry me, Ramratan! Clairvoyance? I don't know. Who can tell? I spent all that night awake, reading in my study.

'Why did I go to the lab at dawn? It wasn't yet five o'clock, and I was already at the lab, pushing open the door.

'The first thing that hit me was the stink.

'God! I've never smelt anything like that, not even in the mortuary. Not putrefaction. No. It was the smell of raw meat pulverized, and liquefying. Think of a human body put into a gigantic stone crusher and pulped. Blood, bones, brains, guts, shit, piss, all mixed together. Raise that by a power of twenty and then you'll have some idea of what I smelt that morning.

'I lit the lamps and ran to the cages.

'The animals had burst out of their skins. Simply exploded into blood and slime. They're all dead, I thought. Those pathetic little bodies were just wet pelts wrung out, lying in horrific puddles of blood and excrement. Then I heard the squeaks. I rushed in that direction. Two were still alive. Dashing about their cage in a panic, squirting blood from orifices, frothing at the mouth, attacking each other. Demented! They were crazy with terror and anguish and rage.

'What had happened? What infected them? It must have come from that pipette—what else? I could trust nobody to clear up the mess. I did it myself. I took samples and sealed them. Sluiced the place down once again with disinfectant and water after clearing the cages and emptying them into the incinerator. No, Ramratan, before you ask, I did not autopsy those rats. I was too scared. Many of them had ruptured abdomens. They'd torn each other to death, I suppose, in their madness. I saw what the organs were like inside. Purple, congested, haemorrhagic. I didn't look further. Not much of a scientist, am I?

'I examined those samples and—What do you think I found? Every sample was teeming with bacilli. Were these the familiar Gram-negative safety pins we've got used to identifying as plague bacilli?

'No! Ramratan! These bacilli had spores!'

'Good God, Nusser! What made them sporulate? Something in the medium?'

'A-ha! You're thinking of the spore as a modification, a defence to tide over a crisis. Like lack of oxygen or a nutrient? An old-fashioned idea, Ramratan. I think spores form soon after a growth spurt. The thick sediment of stalactites told me how fast this culture had grown. So the sporulation was not a complete surprise.'

'I'm not convinced. How does growing a spore help the bacillus? It isn't going to bud into another bacillus and grow faster still!'

'No. But it may grow *further*.'

'Further?'

'Yes. You know plague isn't as contagious as it should be. How many autopsies have you done on plague patients, Ramratan? How many have the Austrians done? A hundred?'

'Officially? Ninety-seven, all inclusive.'

'And how many of you contracted the plague? None. Except, that unfortunate attendant at Arthur Road. But then, he *already* had plague in his household before he handled an infected body. I'm not sure how the bacillus spreads from person to person, and it isn't very quick in doing so. Look at the speed here, Ramratan. Among these rats! All of them dead within a few hours of exposure to that shattered pipette. How long was that exposure? Less than fifteen minutes. The only way the bacillus could have got to those rats was aerially. These spore-bearing bacilli were breathed in.'

'*Manser!*'

'Exactly! We found the pneumonic plague in Manser. He died too quickly for the pneumonia to be secondary to the usual progression of the plague. Manser's plague *began* in his lungs. Manser *breathed in* the plague.'

Ramratan frowned.

'But, Nusser, you looked at Manser's samples. I remember how long you took, and how many sections you stained. I saw them too. Just ordinary safety pins, those bacilli had no spores.'

Nusser sat up with alacrity.

'Absolutely, as poor Manser used to say! Manser took two days to die of an indisputably pneumonic plague. My rats died in a few hours. The difference lies in the spore. It travels far. A little breeze lifts off a lungful of bacilli. After that, the spore probably has a whole bag of new tricks. Perhaps the bacillus itself is different! Think of it, Ramratan! How much longer this spored bacillus could survive!'

'How long does the usual *Bacillus pestis* survive? What do you think?'

'I don't think, I know! Forty-eight hours maximum, on a dry surface. But spored? It could survive for months! For years! It would be practically indestructible! Immortal! Maybe it is all around us now as I speak. All it needs, all it awaits, is some sort of switch within the body to turn it on!'

'Easy, Nusser! Easy, man!'

'Easy, nothing! You'll shortly have to be looking for these answers, Ramratan! Where will we look for answers? In dusty corners of forgotten rooms? In the soil of our city? In the Arabian Sea? Where does the devil lurk today? Where will it turn up tomorrow?'

'What did Waldemar say?' Ramratan asked.

'He doesn't know.'

Nusser's words, muttered into his beard, were so indistinct, Ramratan thought he hadn't heard right.

'I didn't tell him, Ramratan,' Nusser said calmly. 'He's a Home Department employee. He can't keep from telling them about it. They'll have the army out in the streets. Who will explain to the idiot British that you can't shoot panaceas out of gun barrels?'

'You remember what Wellington Gray—'

'—said to Salim's father after the funeral? *Console yourself, Mr Sattar. A few good men must die for thousands to live.* Funny, how these good men all invariably have brown skin.'

'Let it go, Nusser.'

'No. I will not let it go, Ramratan. I cannot let it go. Because what I have told you so far is only the beginning of my crimes. I didn't destroy all the samples. I *grew* them. I grew it. I cultured a pure growth of spore-bearing *Bacillus pestis*! Which, I had quietly named *Bacillus pestis horribilis*. I grew it on a special medium of 80 per cent buffalo ghee. You should have seen those colonies, Ramratan! Sleek! There was enough in one Petri dish to wipe out a nation—What?'

Nusser stopped, raising his eyebrows questioningly.

Ramratan shook his head.

'I don't believe you, Nusser.'

'After all this?' He swept his arms in a circle about the room. 'You don't believe me? Do not say that, Ramratan, you're my only hope!'

'Oh, I believe your story. But I don't believe you didn't tell anybody, Nusser. You should have heard yourself just now. The pride in your voice! You were *bragging*!'

'May God forgive me, so I was. Yes, I was. I was coming to that, Ramratan. I didn't do all that alone. Khursheed was in on it too.'

'He's a good man.'

'He was horrified. He begged me to get rid of it. But I couldn't. Ramratan, I just could not! I prevailed on him in the end. I said we needed it for posterity. I don't know why he fell for such a foolish argument. If anything, it is the best preventive for posterity. Khursheed wouldn't admit it, but he was as fascinated as I was. You know, Ramratan, what I mean.'

'Yes. I know.'

'The lust of it, the animal lust of it, Ramratan! After a while, it becomes the expense of spirit in a waste of shame. We couldn't fight it off any more. We drew up the pure culture in pipettes and sealed it off. We made two lots of six pipettes each. Together, there was enough to wipe out the entire planet.'

'How long would it survive?'

'It was something we wanted to test out. Khursheed said a year. I say forever.'

'But *Bacillus pestis* is aerobic. It needs oxygen to survive.'

'Not *Bacillus pestis horribilis*.'

'You've made rogue decisions, Nusser. But that's no crime—'

'The crime is yet to come, my friend. Do you know that ever since '93, I've been approached at least once every month by various factions?'

'Factions? What do you mean "factions"?'

'Oh they have new names every week. Some Hindu. Some Muslim. Some Parsi. What do they want? They all want just one thing from this mad scientist. They want a weapon. Imagine, one of them told me, a weapon that just gets rid of *inconveniences*.

'The Muslim thinks the Hindu is inconvenient, an idol-worshipping, blaspheming heathen, full of lies and greed. The Hindu thinks the Mussalman is an arrogant tyrant who will slaughter every Hindu in sight. *Qatl-e-aam*. Like in Tughlaq's days. Hunt them down for their soft brown hides. And the Parsi? Oh, all the Parsi wants is to kill them both, Muslim and Hindu, and then bargain with the British for the land. The beauty of it all? These are all civilized peace-loving folk. Educated. Rich. *And the British know all of them*.

'After all this, you still ask me why I didn't tell Waldemar? Do you know what the man has suffered in Russia? You know what Europe has done to the Jews? What's left for him to believe in? He believes in us, Ramratan. The idiot thinks Indians are not capable of hate, "not by European standards of hate" he told me once. Who am I to take that illusion away from him?'

'I know things haven't died down yet and all these Cow Protectors get my goat. If that's not enough, I have to listen to Mohsin Chacha's rant every week. I used to discount that, but now what you tell me is worse than any of the old man's terrors!'

'Mohsin was never wrong, Ramratan. Your father was detached. Mine was an optimist. Only Mohsin saw things for what they were.'

'And Lockwood?'

'They would never have amounted to anything without Lockwood. Lockwood was the medium. Inert, but nutritive. Stupid, but good.'

'I'm not so sure about the good bit. Quite a streak of malice in that man, if you've read his book.'

'Mrs Kipling is here, I believe.'

'So I hear. I am to see her soon.'

'You were fond of her!'

'Yes. But get back to your story.'

'That's all. Except that the pipettes are gone.'

'*Gone?*'

'Yes. They're gone! Somebody has taken them! I'm the only one with a key. Not even Khursheed has a duplicate. They're gone! Vanished! I'm giving myself forty-eight hours, if they do not turn up—'

Ramratan didn't ask what Nusser would do.

It wouldn't matter what he did, whether he put a gun to his temple or shot his veins through with plague bacilli. The method was unimportant. The act was inevitable. He would take a day more, perhaps, to settle his affairs, and then it would be ... *finis*.

'You discovered it all this morning?'

'Yes. I waited for Khursheed, but he's late. So is Chitra. You know how that matter stands, Ramratan. They're in love. What can I say?'

'Nothing. It's their affair. I hope they're happy.'

'They won't be for long. Chitrangada says her father is very orthodox. You know what that word means.'

'Bigot.'

'A-ha. And Khursheed's mother is no better. She's the one who set that dog on to poor Mohsin Chacha.'

'The dog being the maulana?'

'The entire mohalla, more likely. Apparently, now art is an offence to Islam.'

'So what do they want him to do?'

'Oh, that I don't now. But I know what Mohsin Chacha wants them to do! Jao Jahannum!'

'Jao Jahannum!'

Radhakrishnan's face came slowly into focus. Ratan was surprised by it. He had been talking to someone else, hadn't he? That's right. He had been talking with *Nusser*.

'You okay, Ratan?'

The voice was not Nusser's. Nusser wouldn't know what okay was. Where was Nusser?

'Sorry, I don't know what came over me. I must have passed out.'

'No, you didn't! You were telling me a story. But it's not a story, is it?'

It occurred to him, then, that the time for concealment was past. There was no need to fight it any more. He cast about for words to explain. Raki stopped him.

'It doesn't matter. It is real to you. And it is real to Salwebai. Is this why she's asked you to help? Because you have this—this vision?'

Here it came now, the plunge.

Ratan took a deep breath.

Radhakrishnan held his gaze.

'She didn't ask me to help,' Ratan said. 'Salwebai is dead.'

'Dead?'

'Yes. I found her body. About an hour before I got there, she threw herself before an earthmover to stop it from digging up her property. Not that it's her property. Technically, legally, the land belongs to the Arts College and they are in the throes of a restoration. But her people have lived there since forever.'

'How did you get into this?'

'I was just there. I went there because Prema called me about this woman's heroics. As College Counsellor she was expected to talk Salwebai out of her madness. It didn't work, so she called me. When I got there, everyone had left. I saw that earthmover standing there abandoned. I kicked around a bit. Walked towards the cottage at the edge of the grounds. I knew the place. I can't explain how. I just knew. It was the most natural thing for me to push open that door and go in. And there she was, dead on the floor. I had never seen her before. I didn't even know her name. And yet I knew—I knew, I just knew, what I had to do.

'That too will take some believing. I know. I'm a microbiologist, not a pathologist who examines the dead. But I knew exactly what to look for in the body. She was not murdered. No. She had collapsed from a cerebral bleed, most likely. Later I discovered she was hypertensive—'

'You went through her papers?'

'Yes. You find that repugnant?'

'Yes.'

'So do I. But that didn't stop me. Then I found *these* papers. And I also found a plague pass issued to cross the Mahim–Bandra Causeway, and I knew immediately what it was. Can you beat that Raki, a plague *pass*? I had no idea there was such a thing. Not only did I recognize it, I also knew the guy who'd signed it. A.B. Horsedealer. No, I'm not making that up. It is a real name, and I know the man. Then I found the enquiry slip—you have the papers. And then Lockwood Kipling's book.'

'Rudyard Kipling?'

'No. Lockwood. Rudyard's father. He wrote a silly book called *Beast and Man in India*, and I found that in Salwe's house.'

'She couldn't read English.'

'I don't think it was for reading. It was a keepsake.'

'From whom?'

Ratan shrugged. He was not yet prepared to talk about the Kiplings.

'It was their house, you know,' he said, instead.

'Salwe's hut was the Kipling House?'

'No. The hut is attached to the bungalow.'

'Salwe's people were Kipling's employees?'

Ratan dismissed this with a wave.

'They aren't important. But these people in the Quarantine Papers, they were important to Shakuntala Salwe. Chitrangada More and Khursheed Alam. Also perhaps, Avdaji More and Shankar Buwa Joshi. Why did she want these papers? And, Raki, can you imagine quarantining a whole city? How did they ever pull that off?'

'By brute force. You know about Rand's murder.'

'No. Rand? Who was Rand?'

'For god's sake Ratan, don't you know *any* history? The Chapekar brothers murdered the British Plague Commissioner Walter Rand in Poona on 22 June 1897. Rand's extremism was merely an excuse for a larger political agenda, of course. Avdaji's letter is no exaggeration. The Plague Inspectors broke into homes, summarily removed anybody they found having a fever. You should read the reports of those British officials—I have them all here for you, in fact. I thought it was the plague you wanted information about! Wonderful stories of concealment and escape. The quarantine was ingenious. It even dealt with Bombay's railways and roads. Plague passes were issued for people who wanted to go from Bandra to Mahim. That's the paper you found. Inspectors were stationed along the causeway. If you boarded the train at Bandra, the carriage doors were locked shut till you reached Grant Road or Mahalakshmi. There you were jumped by the Plague Inspectors, and whisked away to a hospital or a Segregation Camp. They learnt and perfected it here, the British. It would be their model for the Concentration Camps in South Africa that Alfred Milner would establish two years later during the Boer War. This was Queen Victoria's Diamond Jubilee! Hitler was just a copycat. It all sounds sane at this remove, but imagine it happening to you!'

'Imagine *plague* happening to you!'

'Of course the plague pass was only for third-class passengers. Never first class. Those were Europeans only, remember? They were the rulers, they couldn't possibly *carry* plague. Divinely above, and immune, to all pestilence. But they must—they *had* to be guarded from the plague at all costs!'

Raki kept on, but Ratan knew it all, already. He broke in with a question that mattered.

'Why did Shakuntala Salwe want these papers? What did these names mean to her? Did she tell you anything?'

Raki frowned.

'Not that I remember, Ratan. I see this is *your* fight now. I don't want to know why. But I do need to know this. Will you see that these papers reach Salwebai's family? One son, I gather, and a no-good drunk. I owe her that, Ratan. If you won't give these papers to the man, I must.'

Ratan nodded thoughtfully. There was no denying the truth of Raki's statement—the papers belonged to the dead woman's son.

'Besides, she paid for them. A good amount of money.'

'I could leave them for him at the college gate. He's hardly ever at the cottage, the watchman said. But there's something else. Raki, tell me, what was the Cow Protection Society? What happened in 1893?'

'Almost the same that's happening now. Unbearable hate. Xenophobia. The brutish herd loosed upon the outsider. It took my father's life, don't forget—1893, 1966 or 1992. Do dates really matter? The tone never alters, only the words are different. "Andugundu" they'd shout. The word was a mystery to me the first time I heard it. "What does that mean?" I asked. I was eleven. The boy shouting that was much older, much bigger. I was a skinny kid, small. "You tell us! That's the jungli language *you* speak! Andugundu, Andugundu!" I flung myself at that boy and smashed his nose with my pebbly knuckles. But I didn't stop there. I sprang on him and clamped on his fat slug-like neck. I nearly strangled him. My father came running out and yanked me off the boy. Then he walloped me right there, with the whole street watching. I don't know whom I hated more. That rabid boy or my father. I still don't know.'

He made no effort to hold back his tears.

'Every day I think of that. Every single day. How stupid I was not to understand. How stupid I still am not to understand. The anger doesn't leave me, Ratan! Nothing, not even the sight of my father bleeding to death on the pavement, has filled me with so much hate as that word Andugundu.

'Now they're back at the same game. Yesterday you saw that boy burnt. I saw an old man kicked by a havaldar. This guy with me, a man I've known all my life says, "Marne de laandye ko." *Laandya.* Tomorrow I may be stopped on the road and asked to lower my pants. And you know what? I'm circumcised too. What will I do then? Will I cry out, "Don't kill me, I'm a Hindu who once had a tight foreskin?" You think those bastards will listen? I don't know what I will do. A plastic surgeon I know tells me circumcised men queue up at his clinic, begging for foreskin transplants. I would have laughed at this earlier! I can't do that now.'

'Yet you're a Marathi scholar—'

'That's because of my mother. She made me do that. She said if I didn't, I would end up despising their language as much as they despised mine. Then how would I be any different from my father's murderers? Now I love the language, I think in it, I write love letters to my wife in Modi script. But sometimes, Ratan, when I'm all alone with a language I'm so familiar with—a fear overtakes me. What is this terrible familiarity? Why is it so close to me? Is this love? Or is it—hate?'

Raki went to the next table and brought back two ledgers.

'There's plenty about 1893 here. Read this official report first. There are personal accounts that are more interesting. And all this, remember, is fifty years after Ellenborough's sandalwood gates!'

'Sandalwood gates?'

'The Proclamation of the Gates. In 1842. Governor General Lord Edward Law Ellenborough's battle cry in Afghanistan. The Brits had made fools of themselves in the Anglo-Afghan Wars, and then Ellenborough appealed to the British Army to route their return through Ghazni. So they could bring back to India the sandalwood gates on Mahmud's grave. Ellenborough declared those gates had been looted from Somnath and this act would assuage a thousand years of Hindu anguish. The gates were brought back, and found to be devdaru, not sandal. And also of pretty recent vintage! You should read Macaulay about that fracas! You'll learn how the British rationalized "Divide and Rule". Perhaps Ellenborough was less hypocritical. He accomplished the British agenda after all, didn't he? After those gates, Hindus and Mussalmans claimed to be natural enemies. In 1893, the trouble was all about Somnath. Prabhas Patan, it was called then, the site of Krishnadehavisarjana. The place where a hunter shot Krishna, mistaking him for a deer. The end of Krishna avatar. Prabhas Patan then, Babri Masjid now. What's the difference? Enough!

I'll leave you to read this. I'm going out for a smoke.'

The first document Raki had put before him was an official letter from the police commissioner.

Ratan looked at it without much interest. Then its words peppered him like shrapnel. *This* was what had happened in Pydhonie. *This* was happening as Salim crumpled, his face shattered, his heart stilled.

14. Looking now for the cause of the riot, I have not the slightest hesitation in ascertaining the origin of the ill-feeling between the two races to the anti-cow-killing agitation of the Hindus of which I have reported in other papers. The Bháttiás, Lohánás and Gujarátis have by their street preaching on the subject excited the Musálmans and the riots in connection therewith in other parts of India have added fuel to the flame, and lastly came the Verával Pattan disturbances, the sustained agitation on that account by several classes of Hindus, chiefly the Bháttiás under Lakhmidás Khimji. The Musalmans of Verával Pattan have been writing and telegraphing to their co-religionists in Bombay for help, and a meeting was held yesterday in the house of Mr. Husein Zainulabudin at which large subscriptions were made to defend the Musalmans now on their trial at Junágad. But at this meeting only respectable members of the Moslem community attended and they did nothing to instigate the riot.

15. Only the lower and lowest classes of the Musalmans took part in the riots and to-day's doings are clearly due to them; but in a measure the cow-protecting societies of the Hindus goaded them into their evil doings by their senseless preachings, from which, in spite of many warnings, they would not desist.

16. Perhaps the foolish article in the Gujaráti newspaper, of which I lately made mention elsewhere, has also had something to do with it.

I have the honour to be,

Sir,

Your most obedient Servant,

R. H. VINCENT,

Acting Commissioner of Police.

The personal accounts, both marked **Private & Confidential**, were more revealing.

The first was the narrative of one P.B. Joshi, recorded in Girgaum on 22 August 1893.

The real cause of the riot, I believe, is not the cow killing agitation, but the Prabhas Patan matter. Yesterday, a respectable Mussalman told me that Mr Lakhmidas and two Marwari Shetias are responsible. Lakhmidas said that he would get the Musasalman offenders (in Prabhas Patan) punished, but this would get the State of Junagadh in trouble. The matter was personal, but the presence of men like Mr Javerilal, Mr Dikshit and others made Muslims believe that Hindus were against them.

Dr Deshmukh made matters worse. At the suggestion of Gujerati shetias he made arrangements to hold a public meeting at Thakurdwar of Maratha Hindus. One Waman Shivram Sudhale and Narayan Trimbak Vaidya went from house to house to urge people to sympathize with Prabhas Patan sufferers. I don't know what happened there as I didn't attend the meeting, but Mr Sudhale makes inflammatory speeches in public. Justice Telang has often chastised him in meetings of the Hindu Union Club. On Saturday (the 2nd day of the riots) he either encouraged or organized a band of Malwans.

As far as persons who looted Bohra shops, the most prominent part was taken by Parsees. At Bhuleshwar, several Parsees encouraged Hindu mill hands to beat up Mussalmans.

On the 3rd day of the riot I went to Bhuleshwar Library. There I saw several Bohra shops looted. A Bohra boy of 10 years had concealed himself behind a Hindu shop. A Parsi gent carrying a heavy umbrella saw the boy, dragged him out and beat him mercilessly. The boy was saved by a Hindu neighbour who dragged him into his house and made him pass out to safety through the back door.

Mr Javerilal's son told me that one Mr Bomanji has sent a sensational telegram to Dadabhai and other Members of Parliament.

On the Mussalman side, a large meeting of Muslims, especially of the lower class, was convened on the morning of the riot at the house of Haji Kasam Haji Ismail in Abdul Rehman Street. About 1000 persons who couldn't be accommodated were standing out in the street from 7 to 8. They were paid to riot.

The Anti-Cow Killing Society is managed by an influential Committee consisting of educated Hindus and Parsis. The President is Dinshaw Petit. There are two secretaries, one Hindu, one Parsi. Supporters: Kavasji Shroff, Javerilal, Malbari and Dr Deshmukh and a good many Gujerati shetias. The old Hindu Shetias know very little of the inner matters, but pay handsomely when asked to give for Gomata.

The Ghatis know very little about Gorakshak Samiti and are indifferent to Mussalmans eating beef except for agitators like Dr Deshmukh, Dr Bhalchandra and Martand. Most of the agitation is carried out by Gujerati Vaishnavs and Jains.

With the exception of a section of the Gujerati Hindus, neither Marathas nor Ghatis, Malvanis or other Hindus knew anything about the designs of Muslims to attack Hindus. The attack on Friday (12th) was so sudden that none of the Hindus in Girgaum knew anything in the morning. But Lakhmidas Khimji knew, and posted Ghatis and Pardeshis there.

As far as I know, none of the richer class of Hindus have paid anything to these people, but 10 or 15 Pardeshis who were near the Bhuleshwar temple on Saturday (2nd day of the riot) have been paid by Shetias. On Sunday I saw 70 Marathi Ghatis armed with sticks, loitering in Kandewadi. I asked if they had been paid, but they bitterly complained of being cheated by the Shetias and Mr Vibhovandas.

The second account was introduced as

Notes of a conversation with a Maulana, regarding the cause of the riot

The cause of the riot is the sustained action, over the last 10 years, by educated Hindus who go abroad and are filled with hate towards Englishmen.

Is the cow sacred in their eyes?

No more than a pig!

I know of one of the Cow Protection Sabha members Chandawarkar eating beef and pork with great gusto, as his ancestors relished their puran poli! The Cow Protection agitation is only a means to an end—

First, they published pamphlets and handbills and went about taking signatures of people. Then, as the lower classes took no notice, they printed and distributed pictures.

The pictures depicted a cow looking gharib and becharah, being milked by a handsome matron in the dress, mind you, of a Dakshini Brahmin. A plump healthy child, the very picture of cow milk-drinking health played nearby. In the background is a Brahmin, in reverent posture, worshipping the cow. On the other side is a Mussalman 'mleccha' of a butcher with a hangdog villainous face, brandishing a long knife and looking sinisterly at the cow as if he were to say 'How many pounds of beef will it yield, I wonder.'

You will find such pictures in all Hindu shops, supplied at cheap rates by the League.

And then I heard of Sikh Division and Malwani Hindus shooting down inoffensive Mussalman bystanders and passersby. And the next day Mussalman sepoys bayoneting Hindus, both rioters and innocents ...

And so Salim had died. And so Hanif had been shot. In a hundred years, not a thing had changed.

Raki was back, a question in his eyes.

'Why, Ratan? Why did all this matter so much to Shakuntala Salwe?'

Ratan broke off his reverie to listen, but Raki wanted *him* to talk.

'Tell me what Shakuntala Salwe was like,' Raki asked.

'I only saw her dead body!' Ratan protested. '*You* knew her.'

'Tell me.'

Ratan was lost.

'Late fifties, early sixties? Used to heavy physical work. Overweight, plethoric, hypertensive—'

'No, no! That's her body. What was *she* like?'

Ratan visualized the neat spare cottage.

'Frugal. Devoted. A strong sense of duty. That's all I can think of.'

'I'll add one more. Resigned to having a drunk for a son. Answer this, Ratan. Why *now*? Why did she try to get these papers now? You reckon this cottage and its contents are a kind of shrine. Yes? So she's always had these papers, she's always had that book. Why now? Why did she try to find out more now? Why these addresses? Did I tell you she insisted I track down these names and signatures? Ratan, these people may be real to you, but for the rest of the world they are *dead people*. Of what possible use can they be to anybody now? Of what possible use to Shakuntala Salwe?'

Raki paused, mulling this over.

'How many women of Salwe's kind—uneducated, barely literate, domestic—how many such women do you think would have managed to hunt down these papers? Most educated people in Bombay don't even know we have these Archives.

Few would ever guess we have papers here that are more than a century old. Fewer still realize that anybody can walk in and demand to read them. *She* knew. Salwebai knew. She found out by plodding from office to office, and she started out by going first to the BMC's Ward Office. Eventually she got here to the Archives—only to be turned away. She wasn't a scholar, they told her. The Archives were for "research purposes only". Undeterred, she applied for information and came back here armed with all the right directives. How many PhD students would persist like this in tracking down a primary source? So Ratan, tell me. What compelled Salwebai to do all this?'

'Curiosity?'

They both knew that was no answer at all.

Ratan did not share Raki's admiration for the dead woman's enterprise. Shakuntala Salwe had been hell-bent on guarding her turf. Was it hers to guard? Like women of her kind, with very little education, Shakuntala Salwe was street smart. She was a survivor. She would have known her rights and obtained alternative accommodation, if she was to lose her cottage. This was happening all over the city with new buildings planned in every street. So the face-off hadn't been about losing her home.

Unlike Raki, Ratan visualized Shakuntala as a practical, even venal woman. An unfair judgement perhaps. Something about her compulsion convinced him there was more than just sentiment involved. He felt a twinge of shame at the thought, but he couldn't will it away.

Before they parted, Raki asked, very hesitantly, if he could talk to Ratan again about 'earlier times'.

'It's much more real when you tell me about it,' he explained. 'You fill in the blanks for me. It is almost as if—as if, you were there.'

'I was.'

Ratan spoke with a conviction he hadn't admitted before.

'It's a great relief not to pretend any more.'

'What will you do now?' Raki asked.

Ratan shrugged. He had no idea what he should do.

Prema called.

She spoke breathlessly, saying almost nothing worth the effort. He struggled to listen to the silence within her words.

Finally, he asked tiredly, 'What is this about, Prema? Just say what you have to say.'

'We're going to Australia!' she blurted out. 'We're going now, right away! The day after tomorrow, to tell you the truth. And then we'll take it from there. Cyrus has a job, and I'll look around to see what's on offer.'

'You're going with Cyrus?'

'We're—We're travelling together, Ratan. Nothing more. Not at present.'

'You don't have to explain.'

'Actually, I have to. There's paperwork. You'll have to sign stuff.'

'Sure.'

'Cyrus thinks it will be easier if you deal directly with the lawyer. He'll send the papers to Nandanvan, and you can take it from there.'

'Whatever you want, Prema. Whatever you want.'

He was about to hang up when she shrieked, 'You don't give a damn, do you? You're such a loser, Ratan! What are you going to do for the rest of your pathetic life?'

He let her rant. He'd heard it all before.

A heaviness lifted off him as he realized he wouldn't have to hear this ever again. Could he be so callous? Yet, there it was. A sense of relief. A liberation. He found himself whistling as he hung up the receiver.

His father was happy these days. Jafar's kids comforted him by their mere presence, as they played or read in his room. Jafar, deaf to Ratan's protests, had taken over the task of caring for Arjun through the day. This meant Arjun saw a little more of the world than before for Jafar prised him out of the wheelchair, carried him into the balcony and spent an hour chatting with him in the sun. Ratan should have been relieved, but he found himself increasingly resentful.

'I'm getting a divorce,' he announced.

Arjun stared at his son.

'Too bad if you disapprove. I've had as much as I can take.'

Arjun's eyes flashed. He grimaced.

Do what you want. Why ask me?

'Prema is serious about this art professor, I told you. It's been going on for more than a year.'

A lie. But it might absolve his father of guilt.

Arjun was trying to summon up words, but they kept eluding him. Finally, his hand swung out in a flat slap on empty air. It was a harsh gesture of rejection.

'Let her go?' Ratan interpreted. 'Gladly, Baba! Gladly. Gladly gladly shall I let her go.'

He was still whistling when he got to his desk an hour later.

The truth was, he didn't have time for Prema any more. He didn't have time even for his father. All that impelled him now was concealed in those fading Quarantine Papers.

11 December 1992

'They're gone! The whole family! Every family in the building. All dragged to Modikhana to die. U-H-H. Can't you see? Don't you know what that means? U-H-H?'

The voice, bitter and mocking, paused for a phlegmy rattle in the throat, guttural hawk and spit.

UHH?

Did he know what that meant? It was an acronym for—what?

Unfit for Human Habitation.

Sakina Manzil.

The words sprang into focus.

Room 17, 4th Floor, Sakina Manzil, Shuklaji Street, Pydhonie was UHH. Unfit for Human Habitation.

Not because it was dark, unventilated, and filthy, as the British imagined all native homes were. It was unfit for human habitation because it had the plague.

Ramratan and Nusser were standing outside Khursheed Alam's house. It was two days later, and that batch of *Bacillus pestis horribilis* was still missing. Khursheed Alam was the only other person who knew about *horribilis*. Where was he?

The street seemed asleep. It wasn't too early. People were waking before dawn and leaving for work before seven. It was one way to dodge the Inspectors...

It was one way to dodge the Inspectors...

Ratan woke with a start.

He had nodded off over the Quarantine Papers.

Sakina Manzil, that's right. Shuklaji Street.

Shuklaji Street.

UHH.

The sign dangled from the hasp like an insult.

They were about to enter the dark doorway when a voice called out from across the street.

'Come for the doctor, have you?'

A loutish man of about fifty, with filthy clothes that reeked ten yards away. His loose-lipped mouth gleamed red. He spat on a patch of sunlight and squinted down at the splotch.

'Just paan, nothing more, don't worry. But these Inspectors, do they know the difference? One look at this, and it will be off to Modikhana with me too. I ask you bhai, what difference does that make to a man like me? No food in the belly, no clothes on my back, barely the price of a paan in my pocket, what does it matter where I die?'

Ramratan refused the overt dangle but Nusser reached into his coat.

The man's eyes glistened.

'We're not looking for plague patients here,' Nusser said. 'Take us to Dr Khursheed Alam Saheb. We will make it worth your trouble.'

'Lo! You already have the information for free, and now you want to pay for it! All you Angrez doctors are humbugs and idiots. You want to cure diseases? Learn hikmat. Become a hakim, I told that boy. Did he listen? Instead, he turns on me and tells me about my own son! Maybe Asadullah is not smart like you, maybe he doesn't know your Angrez doctory, but he has studied the only book that matters. Not all the books in all your libraries in all your colleges in all the world have as much knowledge as there is in one single line of my Qur'an Sharif. This I told him. And listen, don't think we elders are blind and deaf,

I said. Every good proposal sent to your mother you have wilfully rejected. You have insulted the father of every virtuous daughter in this mohalla. We know the reason why.

'You are his friends? You tell me—am I not right? He has some chakkar with a kafir aurat, hasn't he? I told Asadullah, "Go and warn the Doctor Sahib's mother that he has some such situation brewing." She is an honourable lady. If her heart must be broken, let her be well prepared for it. That is what I told my son, but you know what he's like! Always busy with Allah's work! Still, he did speak with the Doctor Sahib and was insulted for his pains—and lo! See what happens! The Doctor Sahib himself is taken away to the camp! His mother and all her pesky relations, every one of them. The wrath of Allah may tarry, but when it arrives, it is sure and swift.'

Ramratan put a coin in the man's fat palm to shut him up, but Nusser stood his ground.

'And your son? Where is he? Can we meet him?'

'To what purpose? You are from Khursheed's hospital, aren't you? Maybe an inoculation man, like him? Yes? Then you are working against the will of Allah, and Asad will have nothing to say to you.'

'To Modikhana then, Ramratan.'

They were on their way when Ramratan remembered he had to fetch Philip Burne-Jones. They turned the gharry back to the hospital. Philip was there, waiting by the Clock Tower.

Introductions were made.

Philip seemed awed by Nusser's gravitas, or else his beard.

Nusser was living on borrowed time. He had kept

the promise, and extended his deadline to a week. There was a glimmer in his eyes now, not quite the luminance that betrayed the dreamer in this pragmatic man of science. But there was hope. Once they located Khursheed at the Modikhana Camp, those lost pipettes would be explained.

He took charge of Philip with his customary genteel authority. For a bacteriologist, Nusser possessed an excellent bedside manner. Ramratan suspected he had cultivated it as a hedge. Pleasant enough in its neat geometry, it really was an impenetrable barrier against intruders. Nobody watching him now would suspect that he was close to collapse.

That morning Ramratan had found Nusser waiting at his gate when he wheeled out his Raleigh at 2 a.m.

Nothing had happened, Nusser said. Nothing new. He just couldn't sleep and he was coming to the wharf with Ramratan. He had brought his brother's bicycle, and quarrelled with it all the way to the docks.

It was a welcome diversion when he fell off the first time. It took their minds off the horrors that seemed infinitely more tangible in the yellow mist of the street lamps. After the sixth fall or so, he managed to stay on the bicycle with a reckless obstinacy in defiance of all the laws of physics. He bumped into lamp posts and stayed on, he rolled down stairs and stayed on, he skidded off the road onto a dirt path, sheer downhill, but he managed to twist the handlebars around in time—and he stayed on.

Ramratan was a wreck by the time they got to the wharf, but Nusser looked supremely calm.

For the next hour, as Ramratan and his group examined boatloads of men and women, Nusser stood vigilant, his intense eyes raking each face as if they would discern every man's most secret thought.

At dawn he suggested they look up Khursheed.

Modikhana might hold all the answers, but it presented a new puzzle. As they waited for Philip, Ramratan pondered this.

Why had Khursheed allowed his family to be whisked away to the Segregation Camp? And himself? Was he ill? Khursheed was inoculated. So was every member of his family. Three days ago, Khursheed had been in excellent health. What had happened since?

Philip came out grimacing after his inoculation.

It wasn't the pain, he said, it was the thought of what Aunt Alice had waiting for him. A flannel liver pad. Holman's was the very best, she said. Couldn't Ramratan tell her it would interfere with Dr Surveyor's injection? Yes! She had wormed it out of him! Intercepted him as Meeta was letting him out of the house. He'd been dosed daily on Deshler's AntiPeriodic pills since the day he landed in India, and Alice never let him sit down to a meal without ruining his appetite with a large dose of Shepherd's Sarsaparilla.

Had Ramratan heard of these remedies? They were all American, sent to Mrs Kipling by her son from Vermont in his newfound felicity at being American. These days Alice, loyal mother that she was, swore by John Gunn's *Domestic Medicine*, the American matron's bible. He had but recently escaped the tyranny of Carter's Little Liver pills urged upon him by a high-strung father. Personally, the only drugs he was inclined to sample were the famous Indian remedies. He supposed these would not interfere with Dr Surveyor's treatment.

'And what remedies are these?' Nusser asked absentmindedly.

'Those recommended by Sir Richard Burton. In his more recherché publications, sir, which no doubt you have read in the native tongue. Remedies responsible, I believe, for the legendary prowess of sultans and maharajahs. Indeed, Burton leads the reader to suppose the common Indian is no mean competition to his royal patrons. Burton particularly recommends a compound called bhang. This I am most anxious to try out. Perhaps you would recommend a suitable supply?'

Nusser allowed himself his first smile in forty-eight hours.

'Not on your life, my dear sir. Strict continence for six weeks after the inoculation is absolutely mandatory.'

It was the first time Ramratan had heard this injunction.

Philip, in true bulldog spirit, took it on the jaw and moved on to his next request.

Dr Surveyor had mentioned they were on their way to the Segregation Camp—

Could he possibly tag along?

Philip had a great curiosity to witness this magnanimous British effort that had Aunt Alice all agog.

'She feels it's a most fitting tribute to the queen on her jubilee,' he explained.

'The Plague effort?' Nusser asked innocently. 'Or the plague?'

The gharry jerked to a stop. They had reached Modikhana.

Modikhana.

It didn't exist. There was no such place. He had dreamed it up. The whole thing was a fantasy. He had to prove himself wrong. Right away. He couldn't possibly squander his life on this delusion. It had cost him Prema. It might cost him his life.

It had to stop.

It had to stop.

'Why can't you sort this out, Ramratan? Why must you leave it to them?'

Them was the rest of the world. Yashoda pitted her husband against *them*.

Yashoda, in the kitchen doorway, arms akimbo, her hair like smoke, eyes afire. 'Why?'

One syllable. A pebble dropped on glass. Hard. No inflection to the sound, but the shatter in the glass.

Why was the stone she threw at him. He was that sheet of glass. All their years together, what had she brought him but tumult? Not even an illusion of peace.

'Don't you see, you can't leave it now.'

She hadn't moved, but he was racing towards her, magnetized.

'No matter what it costs us. We can't let it go.'

'We?'

He never doubted for a second that she had inherited the pact from Appa as much as he had. Nusser's wife Nergish kept out of it, as did Mohsin Chacha's son Bilal. Bilal's wife Fehmida had enough curiosity for twenty cats. Luckily they hadn't needed her yet.

'You, Nusserwanji, Mohsin Chacha, the Kiplings. I, Nergish, Bilal's wife, Fehmida. We can't let it go.'

'We can't let it go.'

Her voice, distinct almost tangible—why couldn't he see her face? He looked past her into the familiar space of the kitchen. The grinding stone gleaming wet, a bowl of batter on the floor beside it. A sunbeam flashed on the scimitar blade of the veli. There was a keen green smell. Chillies, coriander, cumin. Fat crocks of tamarind, salt, kokum and pickles stared back at him gravely, brown and white witnesses watching his next move.

The kitchen was her creature. Like her, it was waiting for him to act.

Rice came to a boil on the stove. Its simple breath of plenitude filled his lungs, filled him with a surge of longing.

He took a step towards her, knowing it was futile.

She was gone.

The kitchen had claimed her back into its aromas.

It should stop—but how could he stop it?

'You give me no peace,' he shouted.

She was gone, now, when he needed her. He could go to her, though, towards that tumult which offered not the faintest semblance of peace.

'Is that what you want?' her voice called out to him. 'Peace? Inertia? Uniform motion in a straight line? *That*? Or *this*?'

This roared in him, a torrent within his skin. He thought of his last afternoon with Prema with nausea. *That* was no more than an itch, urgent, embarrassing. *This* was what he wanted. *This.*

He could go now, right now. He could go to her, he could ride the wind, the thunder in his thighs, he could wheel out his bike and be gone before he had another thought.

He was out of the house, and running.

The city slept, lost to its frightened huddles, lost to the flares on the horizon. The chill wind stung his lips as they cried out her name.

The staff nurse was dozing with her head on the ledger. Ratan didn't wake her. He strode in impatiently to claim—*whom*?

A small lamp with a green shade made a ring of light in the side room. The rest of the room was in deep shadow. The canopy crouched over her like some predator. The dark silhouette of her head was all he saw. He couldn't see her face, but he knew she was watching him.

'Can't sleep?'

'No.'

'You'll sleep now, Yashoda. I'll stay here. Can I stay?'

'Yes.'

'Shut your eyes then. There.'

'Yes.'

After a longish silence she said, 'My name is Radhika.'

'I know. I'm Ratan.'

'I know. You called me Yashoda. I'm not the woman you're looking for.'

Ratan laughed.

'What's funny?'

'That I called you Yashoda.'

'She was someone you knew?'

'Long ago. In another life.'

'But you'll always know her, right?'

'Right. I'll always know her. I thought you were supposed to sleep.'

'I've been waiting to talk to you.'

'So have I. All my life.'

'What?'

'Nothing. We'll talk in the morning.'

'You'll be around in the morning?'

'Yes. I'll be around.'

Ratan left the hospital a little after five. He was at peace.

He planned to look in again on Radhika before Crispin allotted him his work for the day. There was no altruism in his work for Crispin. He felt at home here. It had nothing to do with the years spent, first as a student and then as a microbiologist. They were meaningless.

What mattered was this submerged life, the life he'd denied for so long, the life he held in trust, the life that wasn't his own. The life of Ramratan Oak.

He should have gone back to Nandanvan. He went to Modikhana instead.

He found it easily, despite the absence of road signs.

The chill had yet to lift off the morning air.

Why was it so cold?

It was February. All along the Esplanade the coral trees loomed bare, their branches complex intaglios of wrought iron. By next week, harsh and bleeding with red wounds, these gnarled trees would burst into flower. Soft pink clouds of paral already floated above the green treetops.

The trees ignored the necropolis they were rooted in. They would celebrate the advent of spring this year, too, like every year.

Business as usual.

What did the trees see? Did they see what he'd seen with Nusser this morning as they crossed the causeway?

Eyes. Red-hot pinpricks in the dark, glowing blood drops. Moving towards them in silent waves.

Nusser had seen them first and wobbled on his bicycle, clutching Ramratan's arm wordlessly. He stayed on, as they wheeled into the shadows, staring at the faint stipples of light. The ribbon of luminosity grew brighter as it neared. It flowed past them, hurrying north, but not before they had registered what it was.

Eyes.

Millions of eyes afloat on a narrow belt of darkness. Punctate galaxies of intent eyes, streaming out of the dying city in panicked pulses. The unseen feet that carried them made a machinery whirr as they passed. The darkness hid the bristling ripple of fur. All they could see were those eyes.

Rats!

Where did these rats go to die?

Was there some sylvan oasis they hoped to reach? Or would they end in just another stinking maze choking with human waste?

'They're off to Bandra,' Nusser prophesied. 'Next week Bandra will be swamped with cases, just you wait.' Both Ramratan and Nusser believed rats controlled the plague. Few others did.

A sick rat meant an outbreak. Nusser's school friend Lewis Godinho called them 'listless rats'. With him it was obsession, he tracked them from street to street.

Torn between myth and science, people quickly manufactured memories of ratfall.

Ramratan had accompanied Nusser on his very first plague forays into Mandvi. He recalled the stench of dead rat. All those ground-level granaries were thick with dead rodents. Jain merchants had them swept out only when they could no longer bear the vile reek.

On the perimeter of these granaries there pullulated a second city. It nourished and sustained the commerce of merchants and manufacturers. The denizens of this conurbation were drawn from the hinterland. They bore a catch-all identity, *Pardeshi*.

Pardeshi. 'Of another land'.

Pardeshis arrived from as near as the Sahyadris and as far as the Himalayas. They knew no other home but these pavements, landings, verandahs. At the very best it was a cramped ramshackle room with fifty others of their ilk. Some lived for months on railway platforms, working long hours for a pittance. They sent most of it home, retaining the veriest fraction to keep body and soul together. They made no account of fevers or aches. The plague felled them as they worked at the docks or on the factory floors. Often, their corpses lay untouched for hours.

Pardeshis weren't the only dead to be abandoned. Families fled, leaving behind their dead and dying. They disappeared into the city's vast penumbra before Plague Inspectors could whisk them away to a camp or hospital.

The British blamed it all on caste. They had a hierarchy all worked out. They slotted all their observations into that grid. In time, Indians fell in with it too ...

'Picturesque,' Philip pronounced, waking Ramratan from his reverie. 'Though I must say my countrywomen find your robes most disconcerting!'

He turned to stare at a group of women bargaining over fruit.

Nusser used the moment to whisper, 'Ramratan, step back. Something's happened.'

They moved behind a pillar.

'The lab has been burgled,' Nusser said in a low voice. 'I found out just now, when I went in for Philip's inoculation. The cupboard has been forced, and the lock's broken. *That* cupboard, Ramratan. Where I stored those pipettes.'

'But—'

'Exactly! The thief was too late. When he didn't find the pipettes, he smashed everything else in fury. Did I mention how exactly I'd stored them? Each sealed pipette contains a growth of *Bacillus pestis horribilis* in pure ghee. There are two lots of six pipettes, each lot in a screw-topped jar of blue glass. The thief knew where the jars would be—no other cupboard has been disturbed.'

'Who knew about *horribilis* apart from Khursheed and yourself?'

Nusser shrugged.

'Chitrangada perhaps. I cannot think of anybody else.'

'They might steal for each other, but they'd never compete!'

'Maybe they did do this for each other—he one day, she the next, without knowing he'd already taken them.'

'Because Khursheed was removed to a camp? Possible. Let's go find him.'

Nusser's face creased with misery. Ramratan felt no such sadness. He was furious. In that fervid moment his contempt for both Khursheed and Chitrangada was almost British in its cold certitude. Mad dogs had slipped the leash—brutish and amoral, what else could they do but run amok? Bitterness billowed in his throat. He retched against the wall as Nusser looked away.

'You're too quick to condemn!' Nusser said. 'There, but for the grace of God—'

'You? You would slit your throat before you did something like that!'

'Perhaps I will. Eventually. But suspend judgement until we know the facts, for heaven's sake! There's already too much hate around us.'

Philip, meanwhile, had found company.

Pretty Miss Billimoria had quite forgotten to stand on her dignity, and was tossing her curls with abandon as she dimpled and smirked.

'*Doctor* Billimoria, will you show Mr Burne-Jones around the camp? Please?' Nusser asked, with trenchant inflection.

Philip looked mighty pleased as he trotted away.

They checked the register.

Dr Khursheed Alam and family had signed in on the 24th morning. He had signed out 'for duty' on the 25th. At 7 a.m.

'Contacts are permitted to leave for work and return. In time for the evening inspection, of course!' the medical officer explained.

He was British. One of the recent imports, in answer to an anguished appeal from the Indian Medical Service.

K.C. Bahadurjee had pinned a copy of that appeal on the college noticeboard. Ramratan and his colleagues had read it with a clench in their hearts.

'*Our medical subordinate here is the assistant surgeon. He is a native, shaped by native intelligence and with native limitations. He is, therefore, a limited produce, and cannot be expected to cope with the present demands of energy and expertise...*'

Assistant surgeons all, they had been on twenty-four-hour 'Plague Duty' for three months now. This was in addition to meeting their formal hospital obligations. That included all their duties, from dissecting cadavers to setting fractures, from delivering babies to repairing hernias, from treating fevers to reviving failed hearts, from cultivating microbes to formulating ways to exterminate them. They accomplished it all. But they would never ever be anything more than assistant surgeons. *Medical Subordinates.* And here was one of those they were expected to assist. A young graduate who had never even seen a case of plague, never before been in a city swamped with the despair of famine.

He seemed genial enough, and answered Nusser's query with alacrity.

'Ah yes! Dr Alum! I remember him! Aluminum Potassium sulphate! He said he worked in a hospital. Amusing, though this is hardly the place for a joke. I'll recommend you to Sweeney Todd, I said. You know? Dr Alum, the barber's assistant! He didn't get it. He was very grave and told me again that he worked in a hospital. In a laboratory, he said. Now that was even more difficult to believe.'

'Why?' Ramratan cut in harshly.

'Eh?'

The medical officer had so far addressed only Nusser. The colour of his skin had rendered Ramratan invisible.

'Why was that so difficult for you to believe?' Ramratan asked.

The man flushed, then laughed easily.

'If you must know, he said he was a bacteriologist.'

'And what's so strange about that?' Nusser demanded. 'I'm a bacteriologist myself.'

The Englishman lost his smile. His lips pursed, his eyes hardened.

'Then perhaps you will tell me where your colleague is? He didn't report back on the evening of the 25th. And he hasn't been heard of since.'

'We're here to find him,' Nusser said heavily. 'If you would be kind enough to direct us to his tent, sir, we shall keep you informed.'

'Boy! Juldi! *Juldi!*' He clapped his hands, and an attendant appeared with the dispatch of a genie.

'Take these men to Alum's tent, and come back! On the double!'

The attendant turned uncomprehending eyes on Ramratan. Nusser translated.

'Why does the fool have to yell like that?' the man said sulkily.

Khursheed's mother was alone in the tent. Her sons had left for work, she said, expressionlessly. Ramratan could not blame her reticence, she had met neither of them before.

Nusser began gently.

'Khursheed works with me. He hasn't been at work for the last two days. He hasn't returned here to the camp, I know that too. Surely you know where he is?'

She shook her head.

Ramratan could see fear in her eyes.

'I understand he asked you to say nothing. But we need to find him. We need his help.'

'Everybody needs his help!' she burst out angrily. 'Hunt him down and kill him then, if that's what you want to do! That's what I told Asadullah, and that's what I'm telling you!'

'Kill him? Hunt him down? What are you talking about?' Nusser asked angrily. 'We're doctors, not murderers! What Khursheed is doing is very important. His work can save all these people dying in the city. You should be proud of the work your son does.'

'Whatever he does, it is not Allah's work. Why else would he be on the run?'

'Is it not Allah's work to comfort the sick?'

'Not if it means comforting the ungodly. That is what Asadullah says, and who am I to contradict him?

It is the truth. My son spends his days in the company of kafirs, and now he must pay for it. Go look for him if you want to, but look elsewhere.'

'Is that what Asadullah told you? That Khursheed must pay for it?'

'Yes.'

'Then you had better not tell him where your son is.'

'Am I a fool? My son may have done wrong, but he is still my son.'

'What about Khursheed's brother?'

'He doesn't know anything.'

She had nothing more to tell them. They were out in the sun once again, walking dejectedly towards the gate, when a woman called out to them. She was a darker smudge in the shadow of a tent, a slender figure in a burqa.

They hurried towards her, not quite knowing why.

'You're looking for Khursheed?'

'Yes. You know where he is?'

'He's with *her*.'

'Chitrangada?' Ramratan asked urgently.

'Yes, Chitra. Don't tell Ammi, or Asadullah will kill them both.'

'Don't be silly,' Nusser said brusquely. 'We're not in the middle of a Laila–Majnu story. Nobody kills people. You're just a child—who are you, anyway?'

'Please, sir!' she spoke now in English. 'Please believe me. I'm not joking. Please, help my bhaisahab!'

'I believe you,' Ramratan said. 'We're Khursheed's friends. We'll do anything to help him.'

'My husband knows where he is. They're brothers He won't tell me because he's afraid of Asadullah. Also, he's afraid of Ammi.'

'Will he talk to us?'

'I don't know. I will ask him—if I can. Ammi doesn't let us alone.'

'We'll be back tomorrow—if we don't find Khursheed before that,' Ramratan said. 'What is your name?'

'Sharifa. My name is Sharifa. My husband is Suhail. He is with the press. *Times of India*.'

'Don't worry, Sharifa, we'll find Khursheed.'

'Find them both,' she said earnestly. 'But do not bring them back here. Asadullah will kill them, and Ammi says we can do nothing about it.'

'The devil!' Nusser exclaimed.

Not given to profanity, the devil was the worst Nusser could invoke.

'Let's look for Chitrangada.'

'No.' Nusser stopped and faced Ramratan. 'Send out a feeler. Don't start off an alarm.'

So, finally, he had to tell Yashoda.

Ramratan had the greatest respect for duty. Dharma was his word for it. It went deeper than discipline, farther than mere duty. It was—

'Conviction. Your own conviction, Ramratan. That's the only rule to play by,' Yashoda said. 'What does your conviction say?'

She had heard Ramratan and Nusser, and now she had a question for her husband. What did he propose to do about it?

Uncharacteristically, it was Nusser who spoke in the silence that ensued.

'Ramratan has forgotten one detail, Vahini,' he said. 'I've kept the theft of *Bacillus pestis horribilis* a secret. I have till Thursday. On Friday, Waldemar Haffkine will be back. I cannot keep him in the dark after that. Khursheed must be found before that. Even if we don't recover the *horribilis*, we must learn where it is. Or I will be forced to tell Waldemar that it might be used as a weapon.'

'You should tell him anyway, Nusserbhai.'

'No. He has borne too much already, Vahini. In Russia, in Europe. That degree of hurt can blight a man unless he finds something he can believe in. He found us. Bombay showed him that people with different beliefs can live without hate. It will destroy him if he learns there is another little Europe right here.'

'Oh don't talk to me about European standards of hate, Nusserbhai. Consider first our Indian standards of hate. Forgive me, but you are wrong to think Mr Haffkine will not understand. He's Jewish, isn't he? Unlike the two of you, he does understand hate. Because he has suffered under its ignorance. I understand hate. This girl Sharifa understands it too, and for the same reason. All women understand hate. Ask Nergish, she'll tell you.'

'You are unjust, Vahini! Surely we are loving husbands, Ramratan and I.'

'My world is more than my husband! I can assure you, Chitra feels something very close to death at this moment. Even if Khursheed is with her, she can still feel the bludgeon of hate. Yes, since you ask, your friend here is a very loving husband. But not even he can protect me from the hate of others. And what is this hate all about? It is about ignorance. It is dread. It is the terror of the broken rule.'

'So what is the solution, Vahini?'

'The solution to hate? The only solution is refusal. We must refuse to hate. Because you see, Nusserbhai, hate is a gift.'

'A gift?'

'Oh yes. It's a gift. A gift you don't ask for, a gift you don't want. If you accept it, after some time it belongs to you. It's there, in your lap, and you look at it day after day after day. It seeps into you and oppresses you, and the only thing you want to do is give it away. So you make a gift of it to everyone you meet. Only, what you give away is now twice what you received. It is easy to be generous with hate. The easiest thing in the world is hate.'

'I never considered it in this manner.'

'You are fortunate. Perhaps you were never hated.'

Ramratan noted the crumble in his wife's voice and trembled for her grief. He could neither comfort nor assuage it. A prescience guided his words.

'So you've had a visitor this morning.'

'Sulabha Tai. Nusserbhai knows them?'

'No—let me explain. You know Shankar Buwa Joshi, Nusser?'

'The philanthropist?'

'Every man is a philanthropist if he gets to choose which of his fellowmen to love,' Yashoda interjected.

'Peace, Yashoda. Shankar Buwa's brother, Damodar, is a friend of mine. Damodar and his wife Sulabha are related to Chitra's father Avdaji More. Damodar and Sulabha have no children of their own. They have looked after Chitra since she was a baby. Chitra was a remarkably bright child, and Damodar persuaded Avdaji to let her study. I don't want to list all the battles he had to fight. Shankar Buwa is much older to Damodar, more father than elder brother, I'd say.'

'Can't imagine you having anything to do with a man like Shankar Buwa Joshi,' Nusser said with surprise.

'I don't know him. I've never spoken with him. Damodar is a very different sort of man. Besides, Appa loathed Shankar Buwa, though I never learnt why. Enough! Tell me Yashoda, what did Sulabha Tai say?'

'She told me something incredible. But now it's all explained. Nusserbhai, you know Ramratan and I are not invited for many family ceremonies—'

'Surely not now, not any more! After all these years, Vahini?'

'Surely so, Bhaisahab! Surely so! In our time, and in our children's time, and their children's too. Time can change pain into bitterness, but it doesn't change the quality of insult. There is silence when I enter a room. Women tremble for their mangalsutra at the sight of me! Am I ever invited for halad kumkum? Not even by my sisters! My brothers would like to visit me on Bhau-beej. Do their wives let them? Hate has a very long reach.'

She turned away, trembling. Nusser, distressed, looked helplessly at Ramratan. Ramratan knew from long experience he must let her go past the moment on her own.

When she returned, Yashoda was quite composed. 'Never mind all that now. Nusserbhai, listen. This is what happened to Avdaji—Chitra's father.

'It was Chitra's grandfather's thirteenth-day ceremony on Wednesday. The Plague Inspectors chose that very morning to march Avdaji to Arthur Road Hospital! All he had was a mild fever. They took him away from his shop, and shut him up in a room full of plague patients.'

'But did anything happen to Avdaji?' Nusser asked.

'Not a chance! Your *horribilis* took fright at the

sight of him,' Ramratan interjected. Yashoda's eyes had regained their sparkle. 'The next morning Avdaji returned home, only to find his wife and daughter missing. He's trying to trace them in the Segregation Camp. I learnt this from Sulabha Tai. How could Chitra let this happen? Now, of course, it's all clear as day!'

'Is it?'

Both men had spoken in unison.

Yashoda clucked her tongue pityingly.

'What would you do if you wanted to escape with a girl?'

'I certainly wouldn't take her to a plague camp!' Ramratan exclaimed.

'It isn't a bad idea,' Nusser said thoughtfully. 'Much easier to get away from the camp together—which perhaps is what they've done. Good luck to them! Except that they have the *horribilis* with them!'

'*If* they have it with them,' Ramratan corrected him.

'Oh, they have it with them all right,' said Yashoda. 'You see, I know all about this new plague. And now you've even told me its name. *Horribilis.*'

The two friends stared at her, incredulous.

'Sulabha Tai again. She told me,' Yashoda continued, unperturbed. 'Govardhan More provided Shankar Buwa with this information. A new sort of plague was being developed in Chitra's laboratory. He demanded that Shankar Buwa use his influence with Chitra, and obtain it before the Mussalmans got whiff of it. This Govardhan is big trouble. He's had his eye on Chitra for a long time, and Chitra—sure enough—turned him down. That hasn't stopped him from harassing her. She told me about it the first time she was here with Khursheed—'

'What? She was here with Khursheed?' Ramratan was flabbergasted.

'No need to get all excited. Of course! She wanted to show him off. It's only natural! A nice boy, I thought. Very grave. But Chitra will take care of that.'

'She told you about Khursheed?'

'Somebody had to tell Sulabha Tai. Chitra picked me.'

'And Sulabha?'

'She hasn't yet told Bhauji.'

Damodar wasn't the kind who'd stand in the way of Chitra's happiness, but Sulabha would have the final say. Ramratan knew this, only too well.

'I thought we should do something about the other side too,' Yashoda said.

'Other side?'

'Khursheed's family. So I made Mohsin Chacha's favourite, soft boondi laddoo, and looked up Fehmida. She knew all about Khursheed's family. It was Fehmida's idea to invite Khursheed's brother here, so that we could talk things over. Khursheed's brother will stand by him. But the mother's a monster, says Fehmida. I tremble for Chitra. Better if they run away together. Nergish was here with me, Nusserbhai. We too need to do our bit.'

Nergish. Fehmida. Yashoda. Bhagini Varg, the sisterhood. They had valued the old men's dreams.

Ramratan no longer heard what his wife was saying. It was Appa's voice he heard, hollow with grief, as they walked back from Salim's house.

'We've failed, Mohsin and Darayus, I can see that now. How we've failed! We were too uncertain, too weak. Our sons are alive, they have escaped hate, but what can bring back Salim?'

Their daughters had heard them. They were stronger, less uncertain than their sons. More watchful.

They understood hate, and moved quickly to stop it.

'Sulabha Tai was to meet Khursheed this week. And now this! What am I to tell her now? I'd dismissed Govardhan's nonsense. But you say it's true.'

'So what do you think happened, Vahini?' Nusser asked.

'I think Govardhan bullied Chitra to get him this *horribilis*. Terrified, she told Khursheed. So together they took the *horribilis* and ran. If there's a Govardhan after Chitra, there must be someone after Khursheed too, believe me.'

'Asadullah!'

'Asadullah!'

Ratan sprang up—and fell back onto the sofa, when he realized where he was. He began the morning ritual. Today it was more for his own self than for Arjun.

'It is Friday, 11 December 1992. It's 6:30 in the morning. Your name is Arjun Oak and I am your son Ratan. This is your home, 303, Nandanvan Apartments.'

Arjun shook his head, effaced Ratan's words, and waited. He was waiting for Ratan to repeat what he'd said earlier. 'Asadullah,' Ratan said with hesitation.

Yes.

'Govardhan More,' Ratan added.

Yes. Go on.

'I don't know any more,' Ratan muttered. 'I don't remember beyond that.' Arjun's hand trembled on its long journey to his son's arm.

You will. You will remember everything.

The day had brought some respite to the city. Shops reopened. Trains ran on schedule. The BEST cobbled together a skeletal service. People considered getting their lives back.

The dead, the evicted, the brutalized, they still remained uncounted.

The urge to live was stronger.

On the streets the murderer rubbed shoulders with the parents of his victims, policemen joked with women they had widowed. Mothers and wives wandered through hospitals, morgues, police chowkis. Their eyes scoured faces, bodies, chappals, clothes, wallets, watches, rings, railway passes. Everything. Anything, that might restore the men missing from their lives. Children were silent as they played in streets scarred by gunfire. Bollywood calendars and religious posters concealed bullet holes in walls and doors. The smell of smoke became the city's new signature. They deluded themselves and called it woodsmoke. It wasn't. It was the singe in the air of charring flesh.

These things percolated slowly into the city's consciousness as the day, unwilling, fulfilled its timeless ambit.

Ratan noticed none of this. His journey to the hospital that morning was uncomfortable. Crispin was morose, even unfriendly. Ratan sat clutching his instruments case and studied his feet.

'Why did you bother to bring along that antique? I thought we're agreed you'll do the sections,' Crispin said.

'Force of habit,' Ratan replied. His chest was tight with resentment. He needed Crispin, and without quite knowing why, he needed to legitimize his daily visits to the hospital. He belonged there, didn't he?

How strange the place was these days. The towering Main Building had expunged the twin-gabled stone structure with its long roofed corridors. The old place had only three levels, each floor with a high ceiling. Every room was well lit and airy. There were no fans. Even in May, the sea breeze cooled the walls. Morning light fell like benison on the weathered stone.

Those corridors ...

Those corridors...

Every afternoon at four, Ramratan took his rounds of those corridors. There were twenty-six arches on each limb of the L. Each of these arches framed a new stack of white bundles every afternoon. The dead, swaddled and trussed, put out there to be counted and claimed. They often lay unclaimed overnight, until the municipal sweepers brought a cart around next morning. Often women sat by their dead men for hours, awaiting help to lift the bier. Dead children were easier: they carried them away in their arms.

Each corpse was swathed in a sheet soaked with perchloride of mercury. It was a surprise the nurses weren't all dead from mercury poisoning yet.

There were as many deaths from starvation as there were from the plague. British relief work was always self-righteous. Work for your measure of grain, and you will be paid. It mattered not that you were half dead already from hunger.

The work was easy, the British said. Squat in the sun and break stones with a heavy hammer. Any child could do it. Children did. And children died.

That day, fifteen of the dead had been children younger than his own. Every time he looked at a dead child, Ramratan prayed for his own.

They were safe, as safe as he could make them. Yashoda kept them safe.

But these dead children too had been kept safe, as safe as any parent could keep them.

Not safe enough. Not nearly safe enough.

Today there were forty-six, and fifteen of these were starvation deaths. He knew they'd be listed differently by the submitting officer.

Ramratan heard a cough at his shoulder. Nusser. He nodded in the direction of the lab and walked away quickly. Ramratan followed him.

Philip was in Nusser's office. He looked well. The fever following the inoculation had been brief, he reported. The swelling was painful, but nothing dreadful as he'd imagined. Aunt Alice was not quite convinced that he wasn't walking around with a mild version of the plague.

'Which of course you are,' Ramratan assured him with a grin.

'I hope both of you will join us for dinner tomorrow,' Philip said. 'Aunt Alice has been telling me about some kind of pact your fathers made with my uncle, and I'm most curious about it. What was it? A secret society? Rudy would find that interesting.'

'Nothing of the kind,' Ramratan retorted. 'These four gentlemen were not of Stalky's ilk. It is very simple, really. They decided on it in 1866, in the aftermath of what your countrymen call the Mutiny. They were troubled and horrified by everything that had happened in those ten years. There were aftershocks, everywhere. Relationships had changed. Small incidents showed how deeply hate had seeped between people. That worried our fathers. So they decided on this—*to stop hate.* I don't know what particular incident compelled them into this. They never spoke about it. That's all there was to it. Whenever they faced hate, they'd stop it. It mattered not how, or between whom, or why. They would intervene. Very often, it did not work. It caused them much grief. But that was their accord. Now we, Nusser and I, have inherited it. Mohsin Chacha is still around, and so is your uncle Lockwood. That's all there is to it. What's surprising is how often it comes up.'

'Have you ever had to do anything about it?' Philip persisted.

Ramratan shrugged and avoided Nusser's eye.

'And that Mr Mohsin? He's quite a character, I hear. A regular barnshoot, Aunt Alice said.'

Nusser drew in a sharp breath.

'Perhaps not an expression you should use to the old gentleman's face,' Ramratan said. 'My compliments to Mrs Kipling. Till tomorrow then. Goodbye.'

Before he took charge of the histopathology specimens waiting to be sectioned, Ratan had looked in on Radhika.

'Will you bring me a mirror?' she asked.

'Yes. I'll bring you a mirror.'

'Tomorrow?'

'Not tomorrow.'

'Why not?'

'Tomorrow's inconvenient.'

'The day after?'

'Still inconvenient.'

'When then?'

'I'll tell you when it's convenient.'

This morning, her bed had a canopy of fine white netting and

behind this she was a pointillist blur, like a face glimpsed through tears.

'I wanted to talk to you. To thank you,' she said. 'You saved my life, though it isn't of much use to me now. It's of no use to anybody.'

'That's not true.'

'Oh? What do you know of it?'

'Enough. I know that your life, or anybody else's, does not have to be of use. Life isn't a utility.'

'What is it then?'

'It is autonomy. It just is. Good. Bad. Beautiful. Ugly.'

'Ugly, ugly, ugly.'

'Sometimes. Most times.'

'So what does Yashoda say this morning?'

'She told me hate is a gift you do not want. So you give it away, generously. What a terrible thing to say.'

'The truth is always terrible. She suffered. She knew what that felt like.'

'No matter what I did, her pain would never go away.'

'Maybe—'

'What?'

'Nothing.'

'Maybe she saw a trace of that hate in me?'

'Yeah. It happened with me. I see now. It happened with me. Did you see him?'

'Anwar?'

'Yes.'

'Yes. I saw him. I saw the last look in his eyes, Radhika. His eyes were fixed on you.'

'And what did he see? A woman too cowardly to die.'

'A woman brave enough to live. To live past hate.'

'Like Yashoda.'

'Yes. Like her.'

She fell silent, and he sank into thought. Had she looked so deeply into him that day? And seen that submerged trace of hate. Past all else.

Past all else.

In grape-skin darkness Ramratan and Yashoda wait beneath the tree. Her face is raised to his. His, to a moon that will not appear.

It will disappoint me, he thinks. And I, her.

He would have fought a hundred men for her, but how does one duel with a dead man?

Her hand closes on his arm, and he trembles. His hands hover over her face, and she waits, her eyes opalescent in the dark.

'Do you know me now?' he whispers.

'I know you.'

'But I don't,' he whispers again. 'I don't know you.'

'So learn me!'

He traces her lower lip with his index finger. It is like touching a cloud. Against luxe satin and air tremble the ridged whorls of his fingertip. He learns her face.

His spine is aflame, each gnarl of bone a separate fire-coal.

Her fingers flutter like a moth trapped beneath his shirt. She arches back, and offers her neck. As his lips close in on her heartbeat he notices she has cast off all her jewels. Earrings, nose ring. Even her mangalsutra.

A distant voice jeers in his skull.

Widow woman! Widow woman!

Ramratan laughs, and then his eyes fill with sudden tears at her fierce insistence, her need to be understood.

That first day, shielding her from the barbs of her new family he told her, 'Don't let them hurt you. You're not a widow any longer. You're my wife now.'

Angrily, she had hissed back words that her skin whispers now:

Neither widow nor wife, I am Yashoda.

His hot tears sting her neck.

Alarmed, she frees herself and takes his face between her hands, and gazes at him in the dark.

She kisses him on the lips, and as he tastes that saline softness, he crushes her against himself, brutishly, his own need exigent and imperious.

Surely now she will hate him forever. It is all over before it has begun. Did she wait a month for this, this *mockery* of bliss?

She giggles. Her laughter bubbles and delights him. He spins her around, and the sheer silk that cocoons her unravels. A web of blue and silver, all nine yards of it, slithers to her feet.

She stops laughing. In the secret umbra of the tree she is suddenly afraid.

The moon chooses that instant to appear and streams silver across the tree.

Ramratan expects her to snatch up her fallen sari and scamper back into the house. The yard is open to the street, the house is overlooked on either side.

Instead, Yashoda steps out into the moonlight, and dazzles him.

Purblind with the blackness that haunts him, his one-eyed gaze falters, but his sight travels the country he must now claim as home.

Another man's home.

She has read him. She has read that blackness he refuses to see, and it shames her.

The brightness leaches out of her. She turns, still and marmoreal, a waxen effigy of her familiar self.

She shivers, as if that funereal march still moves just beyond her. Her breasts, her belly, swell in an ecstasy of aversion. Her thighs melt each to each, shadowing the dune so pallid and epilate, and tinged now with moon.

Ramratan is stung with grief.

He has seen her thus many times on those secret scrolls in his mind. *Venus epithalamia*, flinching before she is touched.

He cannot reclaim her unless he reveals his shame. He steps out into the moonlight and stands before her, thinking, but unable to find voice for words that must be said.

I cannot conceal myself from you. Forgive me.

It is a test. They both understand

Yashoda's face is still averted.

Forgive me.

He implores again without words.

'It will always hurt you,' she says.

'No!' He finds voice.

She turns then, with yearning, into him.

'Learn me, then! Now!' she commands.

She is sitoshna and sadhana, fire and ice, summer and winter, greeshma and hemant. He needs to know more. He needs to feel the vernal joy of vasant and the grave autumnal descant of sharad. And varsha, he wants the dance of cloud, thunder, lightning, before redemptive rain.

He needs to know *her.*

He touches her.

His fingers tell him nothing but serve to telescope his aching urgency. She is aware of her power. He must discover his own.

He tastes her. Her neck tastes of dew, her breasts of milk, her belly of apples and warm wheat.

Her thighs are comfort wings against him, fitted to his hips, coaxing him to fly, to fill the sky, to pluck the stars from her hair and plunder her moon.

But he will not. He will not. Not yet.

He will know her first.

He tastes her drupe, dripping and ripe, its seed inscribes his tongue. Her hair sweeps the fallen leaves as she curves away on the rim of rapture and then teeters over the abyss, as he delves her again and again. He desists still from the plunge, the descent. No matter what the shame, he will hear it.

He *will* hear it—now.

He keels her over the edge and she goes screaming with him, in terror, with delight. They glide together into a windy claustrum of stars and all he can hear in that discordance is her scream.

Ramratan. Ramratan. Ramratan.

Thrice.

She says it each time. His name. Thrice. No other name, but his.

His laugh resounds triumphant as she subsides in his embrace.

Ramratan.

She murmurs his name.

Again.

Again.

Could it ever be again?

It had never been like that for him.

Never with Prema.

Never.

He left Radhika's room, unwilling to break into her silence, unwilling to give himself away.

He wondered what it must feel like to be Radhika now, giving up on life and then to find it clamped on your soul like a vise.

Her willingness to endure him was a surprise. He had to remind himself she was still befuddled by shock and sedation. She was out of immediate danger, but the next two weeks would be critical in staving off sepsis as eschars formed, sealing off pockets of defenceless tissue easily macerated by even mild-mannered microbes.

Her real ordeal would begin *after* she was past all this, when she would reacquaint herself with her newly skewed body. Already, already she'd asked him for a mirror.

He knew what it had cost her this morning to enunciate Anwar's name. He had tormented her into doing that, simply by being there.

What would she do, where would she go, how would she fend for herself once she was past all this? He had no clue.

But for now, she was his.

Ratan walked back to Pathology with every intention of avoiding the mortuary. Chance made him turn that way. A flash of colour, the deep raw pink that scars a melancholy dusk. It flared up—and was gone.

What could he do but pursue?

It was the pink that carried crimson overleaf, veined with darkness, the pink of Ned Jones' *Briar Rose*. Without warning, the stone yard of the Coroner's Court had transformed itself into the thorny waste of the painting. The waiting figures, overcome by the narcosis of terror, were folded in sleep, and one of them, there, at the far left, was draped in that errant flash of pink, concealed now in her weedy cloak of black.

He heard Philip's voice.

He heard Philip's voice.

'The pater's world is all around us, but we don't see it. Just as he can't see ours. We can see Uncle John's tedious pencil productions and feel their moral strength and respect him for it. It is impossible for most people to respect my father's world. It isn't sublime. That would render it sacred. It isn't practical. That would turn it profane. So it remains an indulgence. An affectation.'

They had Ned Jones' book open on the table between them.

Ramratan had feared showing Philip his father's sketchbook. But Ned Jones' son understood his father.

Ramratan was moved to argue.

'Surely these sketches are not about myths or people or their stories. They're about colour. They're about stories that colours tell.'

'Do they appear so to you?'

'Yes, they do. I treasure them above all things because they make me see. I look at a leaf and I feel its green stain my fingertips. I look at a woman's skin and I can sense the web of blood beneath it. I know these things because of this book.'

'And, you have never seen his paintings?'

'Never.'

'They are better—more finished. They throb with colour.'

'Perhaps, one day—'

Perhaps, one day—

'Excuse me?'

A voice at his elbow startled Ratan.

He was back in the mephitic grey courtyard, dotted about with granite figures of resignation and grief.

The man who addressed him was neither resigned, nor in grief. A spare man, sixtyish and grizzled, with the air of patient intelligence that defines the successful bureaucrat. The kindly eyes that quizzed Ratan revealed nothing of what they saw.

'I was directed here by the Coroner's Court. Could you tell me where I can—' he faltered, casting about for a phrase less abrasive, any euphemism to conceal the unpleasantness of death.

Ratan disliked him instantly.

'Are you here to identify a body?' He could not have put it more brutally.

The man flinched.

Ratan's heart sank. Perhaps he was wrong, and this man was stricken, like the rest of them, by a grief too intense to make itself known to strangers. He didn't seem put out by Ratan's question.

'To find out if it has been brought here.'

'Name?'

'More.'

'*Govardhan* More?'

The name rattled the man, there was no doubt about that. His Adam's apple bobbed as he quelled the bile that seemed to suffuse his mouth. He licked his dry lips before he replied.

'No. Not Govardhan. His name was Balkrishna More. He died on Sunday evening. Jumped off a balcony I believe.'

'Yes, the body is here.'

'You—you are aware of the case?'

'Yes.'

'The police said post-mortem may be required?'

'That's correct. The law requires it in all cases of unnatural death. I did the autopsy myself.'

'Oh.'

'Are you here to claim the body?'

The man hesitated before he spoke.

'Yes, yes. I will claim the body. He must get some peace...'

His voice trailed away in some reverie.

'He appeared to have lived a very solitary life in his last years.'

Ratan recalled the emaciated frame, the sunken cheeks barbed with silvery fuzz, the clubbed nails, yellow and untrimmed.

'No family?'

'No. Never married. Never had any steady employment. Total waste. His whole life was a waste.'

'No life is a waste.'

Ratan had spoken with more anger than he realized.

'You are right. That isn't what I meant.'

The man shed his politeness, and Ratan felt a thrill of recognition.

He *knew* this man. He knew this steady brown gaze, level and intent.

'His life was a waste because nobody noticed it. I cannot

allow his death to be a waste as well. Yes, I will claim the body. My name is Joshi. You can put me down as next of kin since there are no others. G.B. Joshi. Gopalkrishna Bhimrao Joshi.'

He said this with a quiet expectation of regard.

Ratan smiled. He nodded and walked away quickly to keep from crying out, 'Kai re Gopya, how you've grown!'

The morning elapsed quickly as he fixed and processed tissues. In some murky way it had become important to keep Crispin happy, as if his being on the campus depended upon Crispin's kindness. He settled into the remembered routines with ease, not enjoyment.

After the first hour he worked mechanically, his mind worrying a faint memory that wouldn't come into focus. At noon he checked with the havaldar. Yes, he could hitch a ride in the police van any time after two.

He called Raki and said he would be dropping off the Xeroxes for Shakuntala's son and suggested they meet for a late lunch.

'Raki, one of those families is still around.'

They were at a restaurant near Kala Ghoda eating with the absent-minded dedication that indifferent food and weariness combine to produce.

'One of which?'

'One of the families she asked you to locate. Shankar Buwa Joshi's family. I met one of them today.'

'How? I mean they couldn't have walked up and introduced themselves to you as Shankar Buwa's family. Unless you found them looking for Salwebai.'

'Would they be looking for Salwebai? Why?'

'Why not? If she was looking for them, there's an equal chance they were looking for her too. Even if poor and inconsequential, she may have had some significance to them.'

Ratan thought of that paper which had left its imprint in Lockwood's book. Someone had taken it.

Raki was right. Someone may have been looking for Shakuntala, and may even have found her.

Raki awaited an answer.

'Oh? He came looking for a body and I recognized him.'

'You recognized this Joshi guy, or the body?'

'Both. The Joshi guy was little Gopya. The corpse was More.'

'*Govardhan* More?'

'You know the name?'

'The man who was nearly Savarkar, but lacked his opportunism. The Nathuram Godse of an earlier time. Best forgotten. But Govardhan is a common name, and there must be a million Mores around. So forget it. And he's been dead fifty years, so he couldn't have been your body.'

'No. This was Balkrishna, his grandson. I mistook him for Govardhan.'

Raki pondered this.

'I see. And you also recognized this Joshi—from that other time?'

'Yes. He was a kid then—nine, maybe ten.'

'You're quite sure.'

'As sure as I am about all the rest of it. You don't have to believe me, Raki.'

'What's not to believe? It's your experience. Seems real enough to you.'

'More real than—all this.'

More real than the streets outside, now filling up cautiously as people attempted to pick up pieces from a lost week.

The pace outside was more tired than cautious, as if like him, the city too had lived several lifetimes over that week. Hate is exhausting.

Which reminded him, there was something else he needed to know.

'Tell me Raki, were things that bad for women in Bombay?'

'When?'

'In the time of the plague. For widows, especially.'

'Oh. For widows? Things were always bad for widows, even as recently as my childhood. Probably still are. How can we tell? We're not likely to be widows. What do we know of hate?'

His words uncannily echoed Yashoda's. Ratan was oppressed with misery.

'Four or five years ago the postal department honoured Pandita Ramabai. Before issuing that commemorative stamp, they should have taken a quick trip to Haridwar and Benares. Or even to my cousin's, for a first-person account from a genuine Paati—bent, head shaven, half her teeth gone, wrapped clumsily in a coarse brown sari and nothing else. Not yet sixty, but a woman long dead, dead for forty years or more.

'Never mind all that. Those women are at Haridwar, and Benares and Thanjavur, and far from here. You want to know about Bombay during the plague. In the 1890s, Bombay was in the thick of what they called "reform". The reform is irrelevant. What was reformed—ah, that's everything! I'm not going to tell you any more, it wrings my soul to speak of it. You must find out for yourself. You can read it all in the words of those women themselves. Each line will make you protest—*No, it couldn't have been so bad*. Only don't stop there in denial, Ratan! Read further. Read Lokmanya Tilak. He wrote such hate against women. What compelled a man of such intelligence to be so brutish in his beliefs? Read Jyotiba Phule. He broke this terrible male silence that shames and oppresses us. Even now, a hundred years after. Yes, Ratan. There was a lot of hate. There is a lot of hate.'

A lot of hate.

Four men had sworn to break the silence against hate. He would honour that. Not for Krishnaji, but because of Yashoda.

He could not escape that oath.

He could not escape that oath

On his way back to the hospital, Ratan dropped off a copy of the Quarantine Papers at the Arts College. He left it with the watchman who said he was a friend of Shakuntala's son. Before he handed the papers over he scrawled his address and phone number on the envelope, not quite sure why.

He had a stack of reports ready for Crispin. Happily collecting them, Crispin assured Ratan, 'We'll clear the backlog in a couple of days.'

Meaning, of course, you can then get back to the gutter you crawled out from and I'll smooth the carpet over all the dirt I've swept underneath.

This irked Ratan.

'What about the Kajupada lot?' he asked. 'Finished with those?'

'Oh sure. Nothing much. Asphyxia mostly. Stampede injuries. Stove-in chest, ruptured spleen, that sort of thing. Panic. One little spark somewhere and all of them run. You know these slum folk, mindless hordes, vermin, the lot of them. Live for the day, that's all.'

'Whereas we strive for immortality? How very true.'

'Scornful, aren't we today? What's the matter, Ratan? That brain tumour bothering you again?'

'All the time, man. All the bloody time.'

On his way home Ratan caught a glimpse of Gopalkrishna Joshi again, this time in the window of an ambulance that overtook his police van. Their eyes met momentarily. So

Gopal had collected the body, and would now perform his duty to his friend.

Idly, Ratan wondered if the Joshis still lived in that mansion. On Shankarsett Road.

Joshi Sadan, Shankarsett Road.

It was, by far, the grandest mansion Ramratan had seen. Its dazzling white cupola and subsidiary chhatris of sandal-coloured brick were visible above the canopy of treetops. Although he had been friends with Damodar for years, Ramratan had exchanged no more than the most formal of greetings with Damodar's elder brother. Half-brother to be precise, old enough to be his father.

When Yashoda suggested he meet Shankar Buwa before looking for the More women, Ramratan disagreed angrily. He disliked Shankar Buwa and all he stood for. His connection, tenuous though it was, with the rabble-rousers of 1893 made Shankar Buwa directly responsible for Salim's fate.

'He is Salim's murderer,' he told Yashoda sullenly. 'Never mention his name to me again.'

'You should ensure he does not murder Khursheed as well,' Yashoda retorted. 'From what I hear, Govardhan More is always hanging around Joshi Sadan.'

'Damodar himself keeps a mile away from his brother, and you expect me to talk with Shankar Buwa?'

'Yes, I do!'

So it stayed, unresolved.

The next day a solution was forced on Ramratan.

Nusser sent for him a little past noon. His green ink scrawl was agitated. *Come at once*, it implored.

Nusser had a visitor. Some titled Englishman on an ill-timed visit? The brougham waiting in the college porch was the very last word in luxury, but lacked armorial bearings.

No Lord or Honourable had come calling on Nusser. As he entered, Nusser seemed diminished by a larger presence that dominated the room. Shankar Buwa Joshi overflowed the chair. That massive neck turned with difficulty in Ramratan's direction, but his greeting was more than cordial. The benevolent twinkle in his eyes was at odds with Nusser's discomfort. Shankar Buwa's voice was a portentous boom, his English consonants endowed with all the orotund complexities of Marathi.

'Ramratan Krishnaji Oak! I was present at your birth. Do you know that?'

Ramratan felt for his mother. She, like Appa, had loathed this man.

Shankar Buwa smiled.

'I see you were kept ignorant of the fact. After thirty-five years it is no longer relevant to you. However, it is extremely relevant to me. And, extremely relevant to my visit to Dr Surveyor. I request you, therefore, Dr Oak, to spare me a little of your valuable time and hear what I have to say.'

'Sit down, Ramratan, this may take some time,' Nusser put in.

'I have been approached by a distant relative.' Shankar Buwa tapped the floor with his walking stick.

It was a very handsome stick. Ebony. Its carved ivory grip was a prancing horse.

Tap.

'Avdaji.'

Tap. Tap.

'More.'

His piercing eyes quizzed the two of them.

'My ward, and his daughter, Dr Chitrangada is employed here. Dr Oak is aware of the fact.'

'Not quite. I didn't know Chitrangada was your ward.'

The old man glared.

'You are also aware, Dr Oak, that Avdaji More's wife and his daughter, Chitrangada, were forcibly removed to a Segregation Camp. Dr Surveyor, as member of the Bombay Plague Committee, must also be aware of this fact.'

'Dr Chitrangada has not reported for duty since the 24th. I became aware of her removal to a camp only yesterday.'

'May I ask what you have done about it, sir?'

'Nothing so far, Joshi Sahab. It is my intention to inspect the registers in all the camps this afternoon, as soon as I am free of my duties here. The camps in question would naturally be—'

'Spare me the recital. Chitrangada and her mother were taken to the Modikhana Camp. From the gleam in your eyes, Dr Oak, I think you knew that already.'

'No. You misread me.'

'You deny you knew of an illicit connection between my ward and a young Mussalman, also employed here with Dr Surveyor?'

'Certainly. I do deny it. There was nothing illicit about it.'

'Then you do not deny there was a connection between them.'

'They were colleagues.'

'Very well. Let us say they were colleagues. It is possible that you, Dr Oak, and you Dr Surveyor, may have encouraged that connection.'

'The private lives of my colleagues do not concern

me,' Nusser said angrily. 'They are both adults and their private lives are their own business.'

'Adults! Yes, Dr Chitrangada is an adult. At twenty-two or -three, as yet unmarried. In the eyes of British law she is an adult. But in the eyes of our law, Dr Surveyor, in the eyes of Hindu law, she is an object of contempt and derision. You may not be aware of this but before the British government gave us British laws, Hindu law decreed girls must be married between the ages of seven and ten.'

'I am aware that a bill may be introduced to amend that.'

'Yes. Today there are many anarchic elements. There are men and—I am ashamed to say this—women, who will bring shame and ignominy by challenging laws older than memory itself.'

Nusser broke in.

'I am sure you are not here to discuss the law with me, Joshi Sahab. Since you have located Dr Chitrangada, my first concern is about her health, and that of her mother. I trust their removal to the camp was on a suspicion that has since proved baseless?'

'I thank you for your concern. This brief discussion on Hindu law was no diversion. The matter is of utmost importance. Chitrangada has disappeared.'

'*What!*' Ramratan and Nusser cried out together.

After a minute of thought Shankar Buwa continued. 'I do not doubt you any longer, gentlemen. Ramratan Oak, I came here fully prepared to find you guilty of abetting this crime. I am now convinced neither of you knows anything.'

'What crime?' Ramratan asked.

'Ah. The young Mussalman who has seduced my ward was also interned at Modikhana. *Both of them are missing*. You may draw your own conclusions.'

'In that case, I'm sure they will return, when they are married, to obtain your blessings,' Ramratan said.

'Are you certain they are both well?' Nusser asked. 'They are both inoculated, you know.'

'Then, by the claims of this very laboratory, Dr Surveyor, you have nothing to worry about. Unless, of course there is some truth to this rumour.'

Nusser paled.

'What rumour is that?' Ramratan asked.

'There is a rumour that a new kind of plague has been manufactured in this laboratory. And it is possible, just possible, that this Mussalman boy has been approached by certain troublemakers, Muslim no doubt, to provide them with this substance. If that were so, I leave it to you to imagine what will happen to the innocent millions in this city. Now the gates are open and people are pouring in from the mofussil. The famine in the Central Provinces is worse than the press lets on. Gentlemen, I ask you, what will happen to us all if this diabolic new plague is unleashed?'

Nusser's bloodless lips moved soundlessly. Ramratan stepped into the breach.

'I have heard a different version. I've heard that Govardhan More, whose antecedents are well known not only to you, but also to the police, has been badgering Chitrangada for this "special plague". His reason? "To finish off the Mussalmans before they finish us off."'

Shankar Buwa's broad face turned violaceous. His jowls shook. His hand clenched on his walking stick. He quashed his rage with difficulty.

'Is this true, Ramratan?' he thundered. 'Has he approached the girl?'

'More than that. He has importuned her repeatedly. I have this from Sulabha Tai.'

'That man is a scoundrel. I put nothing beyond him. He has a grudge against me, now that I have refused his madcap schemes. Gentlemen, I do not hold with violence. Never have. Never will. You and I may disagree on many many things, but be assured of this, I will go to any length to prevent violence. If I have to act to prevent it, I will. But for that you will have to trust me with the truth.'

'I may have to hold you to that promise, Joshi Sahab,' Nusser said. 'My office compels me to a certain secrecy, but I will tell you this. Last night my laboratory was burgled. A certain safe was broken open, and certain things were stolen.'

'This new plague—this killer. It exists then?'

'It exists. More than that I cannot tell you. Except that Dr Khursheed Alam did not manufacture it. And that he would give his life before he will let it fall into irresponsible hands. The same is true of Dr Chitrangada.'

'You are easily persuaded of their integrity.'

'Easily persuaded?'

Nusser's voice rose sharply in anger.

'My laboratory staff have borne the entire burden of this plague. They identified the disease. They made the cultures, processed and purified the serum. They were the first to risk their lives by testing it out on themselves. Everyone praises the bravery of a soldier who faces the cannon. That's nothing compared to the courage of my young men! And this very young woman! Every day, for the last six months they have stared death in the face. One small misstep, one careless jostle, could spell the end. If you have inoculated your children, Joshi Sahab, and the plague passes them by, it is the staff of my laboratory you must thank. History will remember Waldemar Haffkine. And deservedly too. But, the real work here has been done by people who will never be honoured. The least you can do is keep their names from dishonour! To be suspected of such evil, as you suggest, is an insult none of us can endure! Any slur on my colleagues is a slur on me.'

Nusser mopped his head.

'But you haven't yet told me what I can do for you, Joshi Sahab. Do so now. Let us dispatch that, and end this distasteful conversation.'

'My apologies. I did not mean to insult you, but I seem to have. This is my request. If you have news of my ward, send word to me. I have made my position clear. I do not favour this—this connection of hers. She has brought shame and dishonour to our family. This child is dear to my brother, a constant source of disharmony between us. I did not like his encouraging her studies. Women are not meant for books. They are for the hearth, for providing heirs. But I have other obligations. My brother is important to me. His happiness is important to me. I would not like him to read this misfortune as a vindication of my opinions. I don't want him to taste that bitterness. I would like the girl safe. And yes, for his sake, I would also like her happy.'

'I will send word to you immediately, if I learn something.'

'Thank you. Meanwhile, all my resources are at your disposal. A carriage? Men? Messengers? Anything you may need.'

'You are kind, but we are well provided for. Thank you.'

'I will take your leave then. Forgive my words. I am an old man who has been important for so long that he has forgotten he is now important only to himself.'

He included Ramratan in this salutation and slowly picked his way out of the room. They watched him flip a rupee coin at the boy who held the reins of his horse.

'A big man,' Nusser commented.

'A small man,' Ramratan amended. 'A very small man.'

'A very small man.'

Ratan was speaking with Raki on the phone that night.

'After that meeting with Shankar Buwa Joshi, nothing much happened. Khursheed and Chitrangada had vanished without a trace.'

Radhakrishnan had called to let Ratan know that he was back at home.

It was such a relief to speak with Raki and not have to explain. His memory of the incidents relating to the Quarantine Papers was slowly emerging. Strangely, much of what he remembered was emotion, not event. Nusser's terror and Ramratan's dread combined to create a baffling impatience in him. He didn't want to think about it, he didn't want it explained. He only wanted to keep on remembering. His own life was the interruption.

'Nusser's letter to Police Commissioner Vincent is dated five days after the disappearance,' Raki said. 'Nothing after that. I pulled out ledgers from several months ahead. There is nothing further.'

Ratan sensed pity in the ensuing silence. It had nothing to do with the Quarantine Papers.

'All well at home, Raki?' Ratan asked hesitantly.

'Yes! My three hoodlums are running berserk. Can't you hear them?'

'Loud and clear!'

'And Ratan, Vani tells me Prema was here.'

Here it comes now...

'She's planning to go to Australia, Vani says.'

'Yes. Her lawyer has sent me the papers'

'I see.'

'Yeah?'

'You don't want to talk about this.'

'No.'

'Okay. About the plague thing ... *Is it possible?* Could they really have grown a new strain of plague?'

'Of course it's possible. Anything is possible with microbes. They fool us all the time.'

After he hung up the phone he wondered if Raki hadn't meant something else. Perhaps he was trying to say, *Isn't that exactly the kind of story a microbiologist might invent?*

Not that Raki disbelieved him. He was rationalizing the irrational. Did he blurt out the story to his wife? Did Vani play the shrink? Prema divorcing him—*Had that unhinged Ratan?* Had his overburdened mind invented this fantasy as a sort of relief?

The phone rang.

It was Raki again.

'The matter couldn't have just petered out, Ratan. Not if, as you say, they really could have grown a killer strain like *horribilis*. There are no further official records. Couldn't this mean just the opposite?'

'I don't get you.'

'When Nusser concealed the matter from Haffkine, it was their best insurance against panic. The matter didn't go public because Haffkine *did not know*. As a government employee Haffkine would be obligated to inform the British. From what you tell me of Nusser, *he* would have felt obligated to hunt down the *horribilis*.'

'Yes, that's true.'

Why was he so grudging?

Ratan realized he didn't want Raki to know more. Ramratan was supposed to keep it secret. Nusser expected that of him.

'It's up to you, Ratan. It's up to you now.'

'You aren't serious?'

'Of course I am. I've been thinking of Salwebai. She wouldn't have taken the route you have – she had no memories to fall back on. Salwebai knew something. Something that involved all the names she tried to trace. Something that mattered to those people, in the here and now. *What did she know?*'

'And here I was thinking you didn't believe me.'

'I'm irrelevant. You, Ratan, you have to do the believing.'

He couldn't recall anything else. He sat an hour in the dark, his mind a blank. Sometime later sleep claimed him.

12 December 1992

When Gopal returned last night, his brothers were waiting on the porch. The yellow fanlight, glowing from the solitary lamp in the hall, caught at Gopal's heart as he walked in from the gate. Vasu Tai had insisted on keeping the old doors, the old façade, when the house had been rebuilt.

In that diffuse light the two faces that turned at his footsteps belonged to the heroes of his boyhood. How invincible they'd seemed to a boy of ten, how strong and how courageous!

When had he discovered the truth? That their strength was mere bluster, and their courage only bravado? He couldn't have been very old then, fifteen perhaps.

These two had fallen in his eyes. But not Vasu Tai, never Vasu Tai. All his life he'd tried to keep up with her. It was understood, whatever Vasu Tai wanted, Gopal would do.

'It is all done,' Gopal said. 'Everything. As it should be. I waited for the *asthi*.'

'Go have your bath, then. We'll talk in the morning.'

It was morning now and here they were in the hall, waiting for Vasu Tai.

They had forsaken the newspaper and the first cup of tea. They had turned their backs on their children and shut the door on their wives. This had nothing to do with their wives or their children.

They heard Vasu Tai's walking stick. Gopal hurried to the door.

She looked ill this morning, pain adding to the creases on her lined face.

'Another bad night?' Gopal inquired. 'Why won't you take those tablets?'

'Why grudge me a few more days of pain, Gopya? Very soon all feeling will vanish. What happened? Did you find him?'

'Yes. At the J.J. Hospital morgue.'

Vasu took a sharp breath.

'Was it very bad?'

'He had suffered. He was like a skeleton.'

'Useless people, those Mores. Beyond redemption.'

'Balkrishna tried—'

'Tried? Who listened? They just threw him out.'

'But he had a place of his own, I think.'

'Yes, he kept that old address. In a chawl somewhere. He worked in a press didn't he?'

'All Mores worked in some press or the other. Printing handbills, that's all they were good at. Half these Ram Janmabhoomi handouts come from them. At least that's what I heard.'

'You know all the gossip, Gopal.'

'I keep my ears open.'

'Gopya, was everything done for the poor man?'

'Yes. I waited to collect the asthi. Baba would have wished it.'

'Then the matter is closed now, Gopal. The woman is dead.'

Vinayak said. 'Balkrishna is the only one who may have known about it.'

'Not so. I have more news. Yesterday I met Yaqub again.'

'What for? You should have refused to see him. We don't want anything to do with them.'

'*You* don't want anything to do with them, Ananda,' Vasu Tai hissed.

Anandrao was taken aback.

'So it's true after all …' he said unguardedly.

'What is?'

Anandrao recollected himself.

'Nothing, nothing.'

'That nothing will be something ten minutes from now when you sit gossiping with your wife. Say it out loud right here to me if you have any guts. You were always a snivelling fool, Ananda.'

'Don't make me say anything I'll regret, Tai.'

'Regret it then, if you must. Spill!'

'Very well then. Those rumours about you and that boy.'

'That *boy*? You call him *boy*? You, pitiful urchin, *you*?'

'You know whom I mean.'

'Yes, yes! I know whom you mean. Speak of him with respect, or not at all. What rumours?'

'Long ago, about the two of you.'

'What about the two of us?'

'You know. The usual. A matter of love.'

Vasu Tai smiled.

'What? Gopya, you're silent! You were my bodyguard! Why don't you tell your brother what you know? Go on, he wants to know who this old woman of eighty-two slept with, sixty years ago.'

'Tai, don't put words in my mouth. I never said anything of that sort. Nobody did. I said you had lost your heart to him, that's all.'

'Gopal, tell us what you were going to say about Yaqub. Why did you meet him?' Vinayak persisted.

'I called him. I asked him to meet me. I asked him to come to the morgue. We did Balkrishna's rites together.'

'Why did you have to do that?'

'I had nothing to do with it. He stayed.'

'You could have told him to go away. It was no business of his,' Anandrao said.

'What business was it of mine?'

'You were there because we promised.'

'He was there because *they* promised.'

'Ananda, if the man stayed, he did an act of goodness and who are you to prevent that? Gopal, go on.'

'Shafiuddin's son is dead. He set fire to himself when the news broke on Sunday. Drenched his clothes with kerosene and struck a match outside Pydhonie Police Station. Twenty-five years old.'

'Fanatic! Fanatics, the lot of them! Like the Mores, no different. Much worse. Much, much worse. Shafiuddin sent all his sons to join the Taliban. Did you know that? That's what I heard.'

'Yes, that's true. Yaqub told me Mohammad Yunus had returned from Kabul only two weeks ago.'

'And now he's dead. You know how the Taliban train these boys? Every one of them is a terrorist before he's ten.'

'Are the RSS camps any different? Have you mingled with the crowds in those lorries, Dada? I suggest you do. They keep inviting you to those maha-aaratis, why don't you go?'

'Shut up, Gopya! Speak with respect or not at all.'

'Tai, you have no idea what the Taliban does to women! It will freeze your blood if you heard their stories!'

'Anandrao, the Taliban would never recover if I told them some of our stories, stories not of women in some village or outback, but of women from families like ours. Who said power flows from the mouth of a gun?'

'Mao Zedong, I think.'

'Well, Chairman Mao was wrong. Power flows from a woman's cunt. Call it honour or call it power, that's all it is. About taking charge of a woman's cunt.'

'Really, Tai! No need to talk like a fishwife!'

'On the contrary, Anandrao. If this is how fishwives speak, more power to them. Anyway, this is how I wish to speak to you. This is how I wish to answer a seventy-eight-year-old man who questions his eighty-two-year-old sister about what she did at twenty.'

'I've had enough! I'm out of this business now! I've washed my hands of you, Tai. Don't expect me to dance attendance on you again!'

'I have never expected that. Please leave, Anandrao. All of you! *Leave!*'

Anandrao left the room with an angry look at his sister. Vinayak hurried after him. After a while, Gopal too left the room.

'Abu, why not go with them?' Yaqub asked.

He shook his head.

Today, words were difficult. He had started losing words since his voice returned to him.

'The building is empty. Everybody has left, except the men.

People are frightened, Abu. Things are getting worse. This is only a false calm.'

His hands rose in protest. He let them fall again. He shut his eyes.

'Mohammad Yunus is only the beginning, they say. Who knows what will happen tomorrow?' Yaqub said. 'Abu, I have tickets for tonight.'

'You must leave then,' he said with difficulty.

'You know I won't, Abu. I cannot.'

'I cannot either. This is my home. My voice lives here.'

The silence shrieked his question. *What news?*

'I was at More's funeral last night. With Gopal. He says the matter is finished now. Let it go.'

'No.'

'That's what I told him. There are others. It could be anywhere. She was so sure, Abu, so sure.'

'It binds us still.'

'Yes. It binds me.'

'Enough. Time for riyaaz.'

Yaqub moved away.

He tuned the sarangi, then pushed it away. He didn't need it any more. His voice rose now to a different command. It came from the subterranean darkness that lurks in every handful of clay.

Malkauns.

There was only pain. Not melancholy, not yearning. The days of concealing pain were over. What could he lose now?

'There's only one way to find out, isn't there?' Radhika asked.

Waking at 2 a.m., as if he were Ramratan on wharf duty, Ratan had reached the hospital in twenty minutes, zooming past parked police vans and guards dozing at barricades. Even the din of his passing motorcycle did not rouse them. Very few now were out on nocturnal patrol, and these concentrated mostly at the south end of the city. Dongri and Bhendi Bazaar had been identified as trouble spots. Other, poorer hellholes like Dharavi, Govandi, and Jogeshwari were ignored entirely.

Before he went to the burns ward, Ratan checked in on Hanif.

The staff nurse reported he was doing well. Yesterday, he had recognized his mother. There was a policeman posted at Hanif's bedside and Ratan did not linger.

The burns ward nurse was asleep again, head pillowed on an open ledger. Nobody noticed him slip into Radhika's room.

That scared him.

How unprotected she was!

'Is that you?'

There was no trace of fear in her voice. Annealed by her ordeal, life held no further terrors for her. Nothing would ever compare with what she had lived through, was living through. How could she ever forget?

'What time is it?'

'Half past two.'

'Don't you ever sleep?'

'Don't you?'

'No. I keep awake worrying what brings you here.'

'And?'

'And then I worry about why I bother. You are here. That's enough.'

'I come here because I have to. I can stop if you wish.'

'No. You make it easy. I feel as if I'm back. Back to being real.'

'You are real. All the time.'

'No. Not any more. I don't know what's real and what's not.'

'Part of that is the medication. Those sedatives and painkillers'

'Are you sure? Can you tell them to stop?'

'No. *You* can tell them to stop, whenever you want to.'

'You think I should?'

'Not yet.'

'Why not?'

'You need to shore up every bit of energy—you don't have enough to waste on anxiety.'

'Energy? Whatever for? I lie here like a log all day. No wonder I can't sleep at night.'

'You need energy to heal.'

She was silent a long while.

'I never thought of that. Is that why they keep pushing me to eat?'

'Yes. You have to work at eating.'

'To work at eating! What a strange thing to say!'

'I thought you may not have an appetite.'

'Yeah. Eating's hard work.'

'You have to do it, though.'

'What are you, a doctor?'

'Yes.'

'Seriously?'

'Yes.'

'Okay, then I'll listen to you. Enough! Enough about me. What does Yashoda say today?'

'You're curious about her.'

'Hmm. I feel she—It's just a fantasy.'

'Tell me.'

'I feel comfortable with her. She's become the ghost I live with. Reminds me I'm real. Strange, huh?'

'Not half as strange as what goes on inside my head. Only it's half in my head and half for real.'

'Can't be both. It's either all imaginary, or all real. Which is it?'

'Honestly, I can't tell.'

'Let me decide then. Tell me.'

'All of it?'

'Obviously. How do I decide otherwise?'

And so he began to tell her …

When Ratan was done, the small window was tinged a pale pink by incipient dawn. It was shut, but she had asked for the drapes to be left open. Her room was air-conditioned, a rare privilege in a place like this. Even without the devastation of pain and grief it was easy to feel dislocated, cocooned in a nursing net, as Radhika was. She needed that handful of sky.

The story he had been telling her was suddenly meaningless. All he wanted was to take her away from this isolation, to let her feel the mist of dawn on her cheeks.

'That's it. All of it. Half in my head and half real,' he heard himself say.

'Oh no! It's all real! Shakuntala Salwe is real, her quest is real, the people she was looking for are—or, were real.'

'Only that is real, Radhika. And the rest? I feel it. Only I.'

'It's real enough for you. Why not just let it be?'

'You mean—forget the whole thing?'

'Oh, how can you even think that?'

'What else can I do? I'm blank now. Maybe I shouldn't have spoken about it, and it would have kept popping up in my brain. Now there's nothing—nothing. How can I ever find out?'

'There's only one way to find out, isn't there?' Radhika asked.

If silence is agreement, he must have agreed.

There was only one way to find out.

'Ask.'

He began with his father.

'What happened to Mohsin Chacha?' Ratan asked Arjun.

That wasn't exactly what he'd meant to ask. He hadn't even thought about Mohsin for days.

Arjun shut his eyes in a sign of disavowal. He had nothing to say about Mohsin.

Ratan fetched Lockwood's book and showed Arjun the dedication.

He read it, translating painfully. He didn't pause to ask how the words came to him. It wasn't his own voice he heard. It was a thin cracked wheeze he remembered from another time. The voice was Mohsin Ahmad's.

Qibla Abu Bakht
Most respected child of a fortunate father

(Ilahi) hamesha shagufta baad
may you always be joyous like a rose in bloom

Dushnabad kharegul ast
(though) your enemy be the thorn of the rose

Bad chasm qayam nast
(his) evil eye will not prevail

Taraddud na shud, O Ajami
Be not anxious, O Foreigner!

The sting lay in the last word. It showed Lockwood Kipling his place.

Arjun squeezed out a smile of great irony.

'You always knew what this meant?'

Yes.

'You know why Lockwood ascribed this to Munshi Sher Muhammad?'

Yes.

'But it is Mohsin's work, isn't it?'

Yes

Arjun stared at Ratan, coaxing him to decipher his thoughts. Ratan stared back, baffled. With grave ceremony, Arjun raised a hand and ground his fist against his chest. His face remained impassive, only his knuckles pressed helplessly against his ribs.

Ratan felt that crushing weight in his own chest, and freed his father's hand gently.

'Lockwood was hurt. He did that because Mohsin hurt him,' he said.

No.

'No. It's the other way round. He couldn't bear to think I had hurt him. I *know* Lockwood Kipling. When I showed him this *naqsh* I knew he would take it as mere decoration. He never asked me what the words meant. To him it was a prayer. It fit the slot in his brain—Mussalman art is the Qur'an, Hindu art is gods with multiple arms. I knew he would never question that. And he didn't.

'The Lockwood I knew was a man without children. The Lockwood who published is the man with a famous son. The famous son had the naqsh read. And Lockwood suffered. As did I, when I read his book! Only then did I realize how small we stood in his esteem. That would never strike him. I tell you, Ramratan, to this day Lockwood Kipling is blithely unaware that anything in his book may have bruised us. Friendship was always dear to him. Somebody should have pointed out his words might wound. Who would? His wife? She has a mind like a bludgeon. His son? You're a better man than I, Gunga Din? No one told Lockwood, so Lockwood didn't notice. When he finally read the naqsh, he knew I had looked cruelly on him. I had called him ajami, alien. It was too much to bear! So he did what little boys do—he invented an imaginary friend to take the blame. He could not bear to put my name to it. Lockwood himself will never understand why he wrote Munshi Sher Mohammad instead of Mohsin Ahmad. But I do.'

... but I do.

Ratan held his father's hand prisoner until Mohsin Chacha's voice dwindled to a rustle in his brain.

'Baba, I think I know. I understand why,' he said.

What had Mohsin Chacha said of Alice?

A mind like a bludgeon.

A mind like a bludgeon.

Again Ramratan felt that sharp irritation Mohsin invariably induced in him. He could never fathom what Appa saw in him. Always temperamental, he was now grown cantankerous, spending long hours morosely staring at blank parchment.

'Not Mohsin Chacha,' he said. 'I'm not going to talk to Mohsin Chacha about this. Definitely not.'

'Why not?' Yashoda demanded.

'Because I can't take him just now, that's why. Never has a good word to say about anybody, has he?'

'Why? What did he say about Mrs Kipling?'

'Why should you assume he said anything about her?'

'Because that gets you very angry.'

'Lots of things get me very angry. Like you badgering me.'

'Oh? I only asked you once. You want badger? I'll give you badger.'

'What's the use of talking to Mohsin Chacha?'

'He might know where Khursheed and Chitra are. It is six days now, Ramratan. They have to be somewhere. Or they're dead. Maybe Asadullah found them. Or Govardhan. Or both.'

'Maybe they're in Aden now. Smuggling a deadly strain of plague into Europe—can you imagine the headlines? I've still to live down that furore over cholera—'

'*The flower of European youth likely to be struckdown by the filthy denizens of Jagannath*? I won't forget that one in a hurry.'

'You think London even notices us? The death toll here is 1,700 a week. All they ever ask is how many Europeans died.'

'Don't get bitter now, Ramratan. And, you don't

know they have the *horribilis* with them. What if Asadullah, or Govardhan—What if they've already got the germs from them? Khursheed and Chitra would be too mortified to return. They might even kill themselves.'

'First, wherever that stuff is, it is safe. Or we would have heard of a cluster of deaths by now.'

'And second?'

'Huh?'

'If they still have the *horribilis*, they're being hunted. If they've lost the *horribilis*, they're ashamed. Either way, they're in danger. You know that Asadullah has been hounding Mohsin Chacha. Bilal has warned him off several times, but he turns up every now and then to harangue Mohsin Chacha.'

'So?'

'Mohsin Chacha knows more about Asadullah than you do.'

'He knows more about everybody than anybody else does! The man is nothing but an inflated bladder of opinion. Lockwood is a good draughtsman but a bad artist, he says.'

'He's right about that.'

'And Alice has a mind like a bludgeon, he says. What right does he have to say that?'

'None at all. But it does explain Mr Kipling's book, and their son's make-believe.'

Philip surprised Ramratan by sending the carriage with a note. It arrived just as he finished work in the hospital.

Could he spare some bottles of disinfectant? There were none to be had at Spencer's, and Mr Cleghorn had pursuaded his aunt that no home should be without some.

Meeta had brought the note.

Ramratan brought out a large bottle of disinfectant.

'That isn't enough even for a Kamati's koli,' Meeta said scornfully. 'Do you know how big Kipling Sahib's bangla is?'

'You seem to have forgotten, Meeta. I spent a good part of my childhood there. This is just a precaution, it isn't meant to be sloshed about the house. But if you want some more—'

'Six bottles! Memsahib said six bottles.'

'Very well, Meeta, six bottles it is, I'll have them put in the carriage. You can wait there.'

But Meeta wasn't listening. He was scrutinizing a book on Ramratan's desk. He looked up reproachfully.

'You've left Sahib's book out on your table. It will get dusty. You should keep it carefully. As I've kept mine.'

'Oh, you have a copy?'

'Yes!'

Meeta's impassive face creased into a proud smile.

'Sahib gave Memsahib a book for me. Give this to Meeta, he said. This is for Meeta. Memsahib said she told Kipling Sahib what is the use, Meeta cannot read. But Sahib knows his servant's heart.'

'Yes, a gift of love and regard, Meeta. Mr Kipling knows you will cherish it.'

'To my last breath. My children will cherish it, and their children after that. It is a holy book for us.'

Overcome with emotion, Meeta wiped his face on his neckcloth.

'Meeta, do you still make those wonderful toys? I told my children about them. The little soldiers and the tradesmen and the busy city street. They were so lovely.'

A light gleamed in Meeta's eyes and died.

'You remember that, eh? I was young then. I liked to amuse my children. I've forgotten all that long ago.'

'A great pity. It is an art, Meeta, not a hobby. Something you should never abandon. Do it just for the joy of it.'

'What does a servant like me have to do with giving or getting joy? We are born into a life of service, and we will die so.'

'Come come, Meeta! I'll find you singing a different tune when the next festival comes around.'

Meeta permitted himself an indulgent smile. Then quickly recollecting his dignity, he said he would wait in the carriage and took himself off.

Ramratan, irritated, delayed going back for the five extra bottles. He was ashamed of his pique. For all his snobbery, Meeta had a loving and loyal heart. He had allowed that loyalty to abnegate a talent very superior compared to Lockwood's paltry skills. Had he never, not once in all those years of seeing his master's mediocre productions, felt a twinge of bitterness?

Ramratan had read Lockwood's version of Meeta's artistry. Now, tasting bile, he found the page again:

> *We once had an elderly servant of serious demeanour, respectable appearance, first-rate testimonials as to character, and hopeless incapacity for his work. One evening, with all the shyness of a youthful artist, he invited me to see a little 'picture' he had prepared in the court of the servants' quarters. I was delighted by a charming model of a fort with walls and bastions complete, in which there were camel-riders, dragoons, generals, colonels, and Rajas, all modelled in clay and painted; little lamps were lighted round the mimic scene, the children sat gazing in*

> *rapt admiration, and from the dark background of the yard sympathetic murmurs echoed my words of praise. The 'bearer's' triumph was complete when his mistress came to see and admire, but if he had been very wise he would have been content with the master's approval. For during the rest of the time he afflicted us I was often reminded that he had missed his vocation, and would be better employed in modelling soldiers, elephants, and camels, which he did well, than in trimming lamps, making beds, dusting furniture, and blacking boots in a half-hearted and wholly inartistic manner.*

Reluctantly, Ramratan sought out Mohsin Chacha.

'What is it now?' the old man asked testily. 'Some fresh effusion from Lockwood? Or from his famous son?'

'Nothing so frivolous, I'm afraid. We need you, Mohsin Chacha.'

'We? The royal "we"? Like that Londonwali chudail? Have you heard, Ramratan? The Queen Empress celebrates her jubilee while her Empire is one vast graveyard of skeletons, living and dead. My boy! Do you and I know what hunger is? Yet we are counted among the world's poorest. We do not know what the man in the next town is dying from. How can the Queen Empress, thousands of miles away? Will the telegraph tell her how hunger burns the marrow? How children walk with whitehot bones, their eyes blind, their mouths bleeding as they bite and chew their lips for want of anything else? I am drafting a letter to this Maharani of ours and inviting her to spend a week with us here in the Native Town.'

'I will sign the letter, if you like. But let's leave London out of this, Chacha. The "we" you deride are

Nusser and myself. I am here because Yashoda sent me.'

'Ah.'

'What is that supposed to mean?'

'It took a long argument to get you here.'

'I won't deny that. I need you to locate Asadullah.'

'I don't need to find that renegade. He finds me.'

'Same thing. I want you to ask him about Khursheed Alam.'

'The doctor?'

'Yes. Just mention the name, see his reaction, and tell me what he says.'

'Not a wise thing to do, Ramratan. Asadullah is a jaahil. His mind is a closed box, it sees only filth and darkness everywhere.'

'Chacha, I just need to find Khursheed. At any cost.'

'Why didn't you say so? I know where he is.'

'Take me to him.'

'Ordering me now, are you? My knees are weak, my legs give way. I don't gad about any more.'

'Please Chacha? Tell me where he is. I'll go find him!'

'No.'

'Why not?'

'Don't question me—boy! I have promised to be silent. That is enough. Go now! Go back to your corpses, you ghoul!'

Ramratan grinned, familiar more with Mohsin's ribbing than his recalcitrance.

'If I go now, may I come again tomorrow?'

'Whatever for?'

'Why? To hear you declaim from Chirkeen's *Diwan*!'[*]

تھا گرفتاری میں جو خطرہ مجھے بے داد کا
کر دیا بیت الخلا ہگ ہگ کے گھر صیاد کا

Both roared with laughter.

Nusser wasn't so sanguine when Ramratan recounted his visit.

'It won't do, Ramratan. Time is running out.'

He paced the room nervously.

'One week. I promised you one week. Waldemar will be here on Thursday. If the *horribilis* is still missing then, it's curtains for me.'

'We'll find it,' Ramratan promised, without conviction.

---

[*] **Baqar Ali Chirkeen**:
transliteration:
Tha giraftaari mein jo khatra mujhe beydaad ka
Kar diya bait-ul-khala hag hag ke ghar sayyaad ka.
translation:
So terrified was I of captivity
I saturated my jailhouse with shitty.

13 December 1992

Another Sunday morning. Ratan overslept.

Jafar rang the doorbell at ten for Arjun's massage. Ratan let him in and went out to the bazaar.

The city hadn't paused to lick its wounds. It had snapped back to normal, and seemed to have amnesia about its week-long concussion. If you asked a man in the street about the fires, the violent mobs, the burning buses, you were met with an uneasy smile that said *I was not there.*

Ratan had a visitor when he got back home. Jafar had stationed him in the living room with a glass of sherbet.

The man who rose to greet Ratan was painfully neat. His terylene shirt dazzled. His trouser creases were sabre sharp. His hair was abjectly oiled. He oozed reform from every pore.

Ratan identified him with disbelief. This was the drunk who had staggered out of Shakuntala Salwe's hut, her son Nityanand.

'I am grateful for what you did for my mother, Sahib.'

'It was too late for me to do anything. Did you get those papers? They are what your mother wanted.'

'Yes. She wanted them a long time, and finally she gets them when it doesn't matter any more.'

'They're yours now. They could be of use to you.'

'No use to me, Sahib. My mother was old-fashioned. She kept everything that belonged to the Gora Sahibs. It was our duty, she would tell me when I was a boy. I didn't listen to her! Gora Sahibs have been gone a long time, I would tell her. They're all dead now, or gone away, why bother about them? But she cared.'

'She went to a lot of trouble.'

'So did you, Sahib. When I got those papers, I asked myself, how did you find them? How did you know she had been looking for these papers? You had entered her house by accident that day, and you had found her dead. At first I thought, perhaps you had *not* found her dead. Perhaps she had spoken to you, and then something—somebody had killed her. Then I said if this were so, you would have run away. But you stayed, you called the doctor, you made certain they found me, useless drunk that I was. And then I had my answer. You found the receipt. These papers are Xeroxes. They cost money. She would have kept the receipt. You found that. You took that! You got the papers. Why?'

Ratan remained silent.

'I will tell you why. Because you are a good man. You told yourself the dead woman wanted these papers. Her drunk son will not find them for her. Let me find them and give them to him. Bas, then my duty is done. That is how you thought. Am I right? No need to speak. I am right. As you can see I am no longer drunk. I have found Jesus. Or, Jesus has found me. I have seen these papers. I am educated, fifth standard pass, and I see they are very old. No use to me, Sahib. No money can be made out of dead people. So I have brought the papers back to you. I have also brought something else I have of my mother's, an old book that she kept in my trunk. This is also from the Gora Sahib's time, I think. You keep it, Sahib, if it's of any use to you. If you find some living people who will pay money for these papers, for this book, I know you will tell me. I need money. I need a lot of money.'

'Do you have a job?'

'No job. How can I keep a job, Sahib, a drunk like me?'

He accepted a generous tip from Ratan and left.

Jafar had been listening from the balcony.

'This guy's mother couldn't have been very different from him,' he said. 'If she ran after dead people, you can be sure there was money in it.'

Jafar's words made sense.

Why had Shakuntala suddenly decided to learn more about something she'd known all her life?

Because her house was condemned to be demolished.

She would get alternative housing. She had her pension too.

It wasn't just the dread of being uprooted and displaced.

No. Her greatest need was something else.

Security. Having her son by her side.

That would cost her money. One look at the newly virtuous Nityanand was enough to reveal the relationship between mother and son. Shakuntala had kept him on a short leash, doling out money in small judicious doses. There was no doubt about it. Jafar was right. Shakuntala had needed money.

And money is squeezed out of the living, not the dead …

Ratan returned to the moment of his discovery.

Finding Shakuntala's corpse had turned his life inside out. So much, that he'd overlooked the mechanics of her death. The cadaveric spasm meant she had died in turmoil. At the instant of death, she was focused on trying to safeguard the scrap of paper in her fist.

Who had been with Shakuntala when she died?

What did he know of Shakuntala's life, really?

Just, this fragment. And its intersection with the Quarantine Papers.

Why not start there?

Vasundhara interrupted Gopal's siesta.

'Gopya, call Yaqub. Tell him I am coming there.'

'Tai, I will call Yaqub here.'

'*No*! Do as I tell you. I must go now.'

'I will go. Tell me what you want me to say there, and I

will. There's no point your going there, Tai. This is not the right time.'

'Now is the only time. Today. Within the hour. Take me there, Gopya. Don't desert me now.'

She caught his hand. Her tears scalded his skin.

'Make it a short visit then. We should be home before dark. I will tell Yaqub to expect us at four.'

Joshi Sadan, 14 Shankarsett Road.

Ratan had been cruising through Girgaum for the past hour. He had this clear memory of the place—a rolling declivity of treetops and a white cupola floating above them. A long, smooth drive that lead to an imposing porch. It couldn't possibly be there now, not among these seething streets.

But there it was.

The cupola was gone. And the chhatris and jharokas. So too, the drive. Yet he recognized the house instantly. The porch, visible in its elevation, above the low wall and abbreviated garden—he had waited there.

Ratan parked his bike against a tree and opened the gate.

Gopal Joshi watched him approach, almost as if he was expected.

He came forward to greet Ratan.

'Further formalities?' he asked.

It took Ratan a moment to realize he had been identified as a mortuary official. Why was that so humiliating? Salim had etched just that on his instruments case. Beneath Ghalib's verse, Salim had inscribed:

Ramratan Oak, surgeon to the dead.

'No, everything is in order. I am here on another matter, if you will pardon the intrusion,' he answered.

'Of course, you are welcome. But you have caught me at an awkward moment. I am just about to go out with my sister. The car will be here any moment, and I'm afraid we cannot be delayed. Do tell me what brings you here.'

'My name is Oak. Ratan Oak.'

Gopal Joshi's face tensed.

Ratan heard someone approach. Hesitant steps, the slow tap of a stick. Gopal stepped aside.

An old woman came out of the house, so frail she seemed almost translucent. The white silk of her sari twirled flirtatiously as she moved, despite her faltering gait. She measured Ratan with a level gaze, accepting his formal namaskar with a regal nod.

'The car is late,' she said and stood waiting with ill-concealed impatience. Her voice, unexpectedly sweet in one so old, betrayed a childish petulance.

But it was another voice Ratan heard.

'A very bald voice!'

'A very bald voice!'

It was a man's voice, high-pitched, peeved.

Ratan heard the words again.

'A very bald voice. Very faithful, but bald. Gamak is the soul of Karnatak gayaki. Every note must be combed out like a lock of hair, the voice must seek out its wave and curl and flaunt it. Khan Saheb has simply smoothed the surface.'

The sarangi fanned out its hundred colours.

'Listen to Khan Saheb carefully, and remember how not to sing—what is the name of that raga again?'

'Saveri'

'Aaroh?'

'Sa re ga pa dha sa.'

'Avroh?'

'Sa ni dha pa ma ga re sa.'

'Good. Now listen to Khan Saheb.'

The singer was Ustad Abdul Karim Khan of Miraj and Ramratan smiled at the speaker's arrogance. He was telling the little girl next to him that the Ustad's mellifluous natya-sangeet was simply not good enough.

The girl was about eight or nine, sitting tense with attention, her small grave face aglow with intelligence. An older boy, fifteen perhaps, seemed to mirror Ramratan's sceptic look as he quizzed his kid sister. She glared at him, momentarily distracted.

Ramratan was not much of a musician, but the Ustad's next rendition, a soulful and melancholy raga, took his attention away from the child. He lost the smoky hall, the blur of faces. All the lost spaces of his life unrolled their misty vista, and his eyes burned with tears unshed.

An audible sob recalled him to the present. The little girl had climbed into her father's lap and was sobbing on his shoulder. Ramratan noticed that as he consoled her, the father's leathery face also glistened with a track of tears.

The girl, feeling Ramratan's eyes on her, stopped sobbing and straightened up. Ramratan heard her father's whisper.

'There! If it brings tears to your eyes, it is pure. The soul knows it before the ears do. Do you follow?'

The child nodded eagerly.

'Good. Next time you will learn Saveri and sing it with such purity that Khan Saheb will weep. Can you do that for me?'

'Will he be angry?'

'Angry?'

'If I sing Saveri better than he does?'

'No, not at all! Khan Saheb is a true musician. He would be honoured to hear you.'

'Really?'

'Really.'

The child nodded and became very quiet, already dreaming of her big moment.

She was a lovely child, her large lustrous eyes full of tranquility when they were not flashing with intelligence. Ramratan felt a pang that they didn't sparkle with mischief instead.

The Ustad had ended Raga Jhinjhoti with a tremulous flourish and the air was thick with applause.

All around Ramratan hardened men had wept unashamedly. Aficionados all, they now discussed the performance with passion, reliving the last hour note by note. They hardly looked up when the next performers took their place on the dais. After a cursory look at them, the child's father returned to the impassioned lecture he was giving his neighbours.

'Baba! That *boy's* going to sing!'

The child's indignant voice momentarily stilled the audience. Yes, she was right! A boy of about eleven had taken his place between two young men, one of whom was tuning the sarangi. The child's father made some enquiries and reported to the world at large.

'From Lahore! The boys are good, I hear! Ustad Chhajju Khan's guests. Let us see what they can do!'

An indulgent murmur greeted this, and after the brief interruption, conversation returned to Ustad Abdul Karim.

The sarangi made its sweeping curtsy, the air stilled as the drone note took its stance, the alaap began with an introductory passage from one of the young men—smooth, like the liquid tumble of silk from a tight invisible roll somewhere.

'Basant Bahar? He's so stupid! He's chosen something so easy, he can't be any good,' the girl said dismissively. 'Anybody can sing Basant Bahar.'

Her small mouth pursed with scorn, her eyes jabbed the boy like shiny pins.

Ramratan too examined the boy. Slender, dark, sharp-featured, he looked as if he would be more at ease on the cricket pitch than on stage. And the girl was right. After the gravitas of the past hour, these notes were almost frivolous, a tune, not a raga.

Desh desh ki thi jang, dushman sab haar gaye!

With a grin that split his face, the boy leapt joyously off that springboard into the music.

Dushman sab haar gaye!

He sang the jod with all the cock-a-hoop brio of the playground. It was a crow of victory, exulting, derisive, thumbing its nose at the grave company. The audience, shocked into silence by the first line, waited for him to repeat it with zing, and then responded with a roar of laughter.

Ramratan cringed. It would be the end of the boy. He wanted to spring on the stage and drag the child away from these pretentious fools.

The boy, though, felt no such threat. Instead, he squared his shoulders and threw back his head and filled his chest for the tremulous meend marking the end of the first passage. The two older men acknowledged the audience with an amused salaam.

The boy's voice swung out in glee, and Ramratan's heart went exulting with him into the rush of spring.

Aa gayee basant ritu, phool khile rang rang.

How long it was since he had felt such happiness? Happiness without reason, shrill and sweet, and without cause!

A spasm of joy thrilled him, swift as the glissando of the boy's voice.

The dedans fell silent. Not a murmur, not a breath from the audience, sullied the purity of sound. Ramratan looked at the faces around him, and each mirrored his own, rapt in the wonder of the boy's exultation.

Now the two men took up the leisurely *vilambit* in one harmonious amble that turned the sunlit raga into an ache of yearning, slow and heavy like honey, amorous, melancholy. They held each note with such erotic languor that Ramratan thanked his stars Yashoda wasn't in the audience, or he would have throttled these boys for sure. He noticed his own reaction to their voices with dismay, rescued from embarrassment just in time as the boy's clear treble overtook them.

The child quickened his tempo and nudged the audience out of its trance with this challenge to the older voices. His brothers responded gamely, clearly keeping to the wings, letting the boy take up the *drut*. At this faster cadence the boy's voice shimmered as it rose and fell like a vein of mercury, streaked ahead of thought, spiralled and vibrated in every dimension, teased the whole gamut in swift geometric variations, each more dazzling than the last, and subsided in a sigh that seemed to meld into the long exhalation of luxury that escaped the audience.

There followed a long moment of complete silence.

The boy's face, drained, shrank into the shadows as his elder brother put a protective arm around his shoulder. The other brother's face had darkened. He lowered his eyes.

The audience sat silent and still.

The front row rippled as if a gust had tugged at a goffered frill. A turbaned head rose. Supported on both sides, an old man made his way slowly to the dais. The two young men rose to meet him, but were halted by an imperious tap of his cane. Once he was on the dais, the old man turned with a snarl on his two attendants, dropped the cane and swaggered magnificently.

Ramratan wondered how long he'd last, but he made it to the nervous trio quite steadily.

The boy was urged forward. He bent to touch the old man's feet, but was picked up and embraced, lifted and swung dangerously in the air.

'Pandit Uma Shankarji!' Ramratan's informant whispered to the girl. 'To this day, no musician has ever received public praise from Panditji. Not even Ramrao of Kundagol. Do you know that?'

The audience waited. The old man made his pronouncement in a raspy voice that carried deep in the tense silence of the hall.

'Basant Bahar is a raga that makes young men dance, and old men cry. Today this child Tariq Azhar has compelled me into both! I predict this boy will live up to his name. Tariq Azhar, may you always be the luminous morning star in the firmament of music!'

The hall was now agog. A panegyric, and from so grudging a maestro!

As people surged up to the dais, the boy was hidden from Ramratan's view and he found himself next to that little girl.

She looked forlorn. Her father had pressed ahead to join the throng at the dais. She smiled uneasily at Ramratan.

'You sing too, I think?' he asked.

She nodded eagerly.

'I am going to sing at this festival next year,' she said.

'Will you sing like that boy there?'

'No!'

'Why not? You can, if you practise well.'

'No!'

Her face closed like a book, her chin tilted up pugnaciously.

'I think you mistake her meaning.' The tall boy who had been teasing her earlier grinned at Ramratan. 'Vasu, why don't you tell Kaka what you mean exactly?'

Vasu turned to Ramratan impatiently.

'I won't sing *like* that boy,' she said fiercely. 'I'll sing better. Much, much better!'

The throng seemed to part, and all of a sudden they were directly in view of the star. The boy's face, shining now with happiness, encompassed them in its joy.

The two children stared at each other across the hall.

Ramratan felt like a voyeur, a trespasser, such was the fleam of their gaze. Vasu's brother saw them too, and was embarrassed. He jostled his sister's elbow. She shook him off fiercely, and tossed her pigtail over one shoulder with a haughty look. Then, turning back to the boy, she stuck her tongue out at him.

Ramratan felt the insult almost as sharply as the boy whose face crumpled and paled. He looked away and moved out of their line of sight. Vasu kept her tongue out until her brother's angry voice scolded her.

She wheeled around and glared at Ramratan. It was a challenge, Ramratan noted with amusement. A dare, a—a—sawal. That was the musical term for it. *Sawal.*

Sawal.

It was from the old woman's challenging glare that Ratan identified her.

'Vasu?'

The name escaped his lips involuntarily. She was taken aback and then laughed.

'It's been a long time since a man dared to call me by name. What makes you so brave, young man?'

'Forgive my rudeness. I forgot myself.'

'Indeed? It seemed more as if … you remembered!'

All these years, and she hadn't changed a bit.

Little Vasu, the arrogant tease. And she was holding her grandfather's cane.

'Your walking stick reminded me of a child I knew,' Ratan said.

'Really? This belonged to my grandfather.'

Her eyes swivelled away. The audience was over. The car was at the gate.

'Let me help Tai into the car, and we can talk for a minute.' Gopal said.

'Not now, not now.' Vasu brandished her cane. 'Can't be late today, Gopya!'

'I won't delay you.' Ratan smiled at her, overcome by tenderness. There were other children he saw in her smile – where had those faces gone? He looked away hastily.

Vasu Tai took Gopal's arm and got into the car.

'Go listen to what the boy has to say,' she said. 'Don't send him away. Tell him to come again, I want to talk with him.'

Gopal turned to Ratan impatiently.

'I've come about Shakuntala Salwe,' Ratan said quickly. 'I must speak to you about her. Please. You may find it's as important to you as it is to me. Perhaps even more.'

If Gopal Joshi was surprised, he did not show it.

'Is that your bike?' Gopal pointed.

Ratan nodded.

'Follow us then. If you want to talk about Salwebai, you can talk to both of us. We'll talk in Sakina Manzil.'

Sakina Manzil!

The words seared into him.

'We'll talk in Sakina Manzil. If they want to talk, we'll talk in Sakina Manzil. That's what she said, Sahib.'

Meeta stood shivering at the door. Ramratan had heard the gate open just as he was getting ready for wharf duty. He had rushed to the door thinking it might be Nusser. It was Meeta.

'She wouldn't come. She wouldn't come!'

He said it with such desperation that Ramratan began to doubt his sanity. He drew the man indoors and made him sit down.

Yashoda brought him a glass of water. Meeta drank it rapidly, spluttering.

'Take your time, Meeta.'

'It's too late already. But Sahib said not to tell her. Just to say it was about her son and to come quickly. She said who are they to talk about my son? Tell them if they want to talk about him they can come here. I am not stepping out of my house for any Mem or any Sahib. I'm not refusing to talk to them, but we'll talk here, in Sakina Manzil, My entire mohalla will stand by me as we talk, then let me hear what they have to say. I told her the situation is grave, best come with me. But she shut the door on me! Ramratan Sahib, what can I do?'

Meeta's face had lost its wonted veneer of scorn. He looked haunted.

'Tell me her name, Meeta. Tell me her son's name.'

'I don't know her name, Sahib. Women don't have names, do they? Somebody's mother, somebody's wife, that's the way it goes. Somebody's daughter, somebody's sister—'

'Whose mother?' Yashoda demanded.

'Khursheed Alam's mother.'

'But she's in the camp, Meeta. At Modikhana!'

'No, Sahib. They're all back at home. They were sent home two days ago.'

'Mr Sinclair sent you to call Khursheed's mother, Meeta? Why?'

'No. Not Sinclair Sahib. He doesn't know anything. Why? Because Khursheed is dying, Ramratan Sahib! For all I know he's dead by now, and I am too late!'

'Where is he, Meeta? I must go to him.'

'Will you tell Memsahib then?'

'Yes. Come on, Meeta, let's go!'

He pushed Meeta ahead of him to the gate. A carriage stood at the end of the road.

'Why have you left the gharry so far off?' Ramratan asked as he broke into a run.

'I didn't want him to know I was coming to you, Sahib. He doesn't understand anything, he's become like a child, he goes where he is led. You will explain, you will tell him.'

'Yes, yes! Hurry!'

Ramratan sprang up into the gharry, and noticed too late it wasn't empty.

'Ramratan?'

'Philip!'

They stared at each other in the dark.

'I had no idea Meeta had gone for you,' Philip said as he made place for Ramratan on the seat. 'I could make no sense of what he said. But I must say it's a relief you're here.'

'What's happening? Where is Khursheed?'

'Dead. Meeta doesn't know it yet. Nor does Aunt

Alice. I sent for Khursheed's mother. The lady refused to come.'

'Dead? Khursheed dead?'

'There was nothing we could do, Ramratan. We nursed them for two days, Meeta and I.'

'Chitra?'

'She died at sunset. A little after sunset. He was holding her when she died.'

Philip choked. Ramratan laid a hand on his shoulder. It shook with either fear or grief.

'Stop the carriage, Philip,' Ramratan ordered. 'Tell me now. Tell me everything.'

The horse trotted to a stop. Meeta jumped off and walked around to them. He squatted in the grass, his head in his hands, sunk in that timeless posture of grief.

Philip began to speak in a low voice, haltingly.

Philip's story began that morning six days ago when Nusser and Ramratan had left him in Modikhana Camp.

He hadn't brought drawing materials, but a good pen and rough paper was enough to start with, and he'd set up a makeshift easel. It was too good an opportunity to let pass, and he was hard at work all afternoon, quite forgetting his inoculation. Eventually exhaustion and hunger called a halt to his labours.

He returned the next day.

And, the day after.

Philip brought Meeta with him, much to Mrs Sinclair's discomfort. The old fellow had developed a liking for him and followed him around like a shadow. Meeta held the parasol, and kept the crowd at bay. Of course he always drew a crowd, nudging and jostling each other to look over his shoulder the minute Meeta turned away.

On the third day a little girl approached him, a native child, not more than four or five. She tugged at his sleeve, and he was helpless, her slave entirely, within minutes. What could he do but follow where she led?

There was a lady waiting behind a tent, little more than a girl herself by the sound of her voice. She was veiled in black from head to foot in a burqa and he couldn't see anything of her. She spoke English.

'Will Sahib meet an Indian painter?'

Yes he would.

He went with her—with *them*, for the child stuck to them like a limpet, quite spoiling the adventure. They sidled out through a gap in the fence. The girl glided down a lane that was barely more than a crevice between the imposing facades of the new commercial buildings at the edge of the Native Town. He followed her up a winding stairway at the back of a building into a third-floor apartment where a man was at work over a roll of parchment. He greeted Philip courteously, by name.

'I'd expected it all along, Ramratan, without quite knowing why. It was Aunt Alice's barnshoot.'

The girl lingered, as if to prompt some assurance from the older man.

'Leave us, Sharifa,' Mohsin ordered.

'I'm afraid you have been lured here, Mr Burne-Jones,' he said when he had closed the door on them. 'Not to meet me, though the pleasure is all mine. There's somebody here who would like to make your acquaintance.'

He took Philip inside the house.

It was a mean place, narrow and dark, quite incongruous with Mohsin's fastidious self.

Philip saw the girl first. Rather lovely she was too,

drooping listlessly in a chair pushed well away from the window. The tall man who rose from the shadows to greet him was young too, not more than twenty-five.

How wrong it all was—the small cramped room, and these two young people effacing their youth and their beauty in its sordid space.

'I see you feel like an artist Mr Burne-Jones. Unlike your celebrated uncle,' Mohsin's words were apodictic. 'It pains you to see the young caged in shadows. As it pains me to see that young lady who brought you veil her loveliness in a piceous shroud. I will leave you now, to get acquainted.'

Khursheed Alam began a lengthy introduction. But the girl Chitra cut in.

'Will you help us, Mr Burne-Jones? We love each other and wish to marry. We're both doctors and are working here on the plague—but circumstances make it impossible for us to stay. We will be killed if we are discovered. Will you help us flee?'

It sounded impossibly romantic to him. There were laws, after all, that would protect them.

'I could travel with you as your valet to London,' Khursheed said. 'Chitra goes as my wife. We will pay our passage. Once in London, I can get a job. We both can get jobs in any laboratory in Paris or in London. Our work is well known there.'

'I asked if they knew you and Dr Surveyor. I told them you were my friends. Their reaction was ... curious. Khursheed's frank face clouded. I began to feel uneasy. Mohsin then told me the rest of it.'

Philip fell silent.

Ramratan's heart hammered with painful precision.

What had happened to the *Bacillus horribilis*?

'Khursheed had a dangerous substance with him

in the laboratory. Dr Surveyor and he were the only ones who knew of it. People were trying to steal this, people known to him, and to Chitra. They couldn't tell Dr Surveyor. I'm not sure what he meant by this, but Khursheed said the substance was a secret. They planned to safeguard this substance. He and Chitra would ensure they both were removed to the Segregation Camp. Once there, they would elope. They planned to take the substance with them. No, Khursheed assured me, it was not theft. I don't know why I believed him, but I did.

'Their plan misfired. Khursheed was tracked to the camp that very first evening. Asadullah, who hunted him down, threatened to kill his mother unless Khursheed divulged where the substance was hidden. To buy time, Khursheed gave him careful directions to the laboratory. Of course this stuff—it was with him, right there in the camp all the while! Asadullah would break into the lab, so Khursheed and Chitra signed themselves out of the camp. They pretended they were going to work but came to Mohsin instead.

'They couldn't hide here. Now Asadullah was on to them, and Chitra feared for Khursheed's life. Chitra herself had been waylaid in the camp by a man she dreaded even more than Asadullah. What if he got to them too? They must escape! Discovery meant death—and not just for the two of them. If those men snatched this substance from them, it would be the death of this city.

'A mad story. But I believed them.

'"By now Dr Surveyor will be looking for us too, and blaming us for stealing the stuff," Chitra said.

'I noticed, Ramratan, they always said stuff or substance. They couldn't utter its name.'

Philip paused for breath.

Ramratan heard all this as if in a dream. He saw the two young faces aflame with joy and intelligence. Chitra's laugh, merry and carefree, mocking the chill mephitic air. Khursheed's gentle manner and kindness. The prisoners in Byculla Jail lined up for Haffkine's serum, after observing Khursheed with their sick. Chitra teasing Khursheed about his gravity. And then bursting into tears, because he had lines on his forehead from worrying too much. These last months, their eyes were clouded with questions.

He had surprised them once in a stolen embrace, and moved by their passion, had walked noiselessly away.

'So I hid them, Ramratan. I fell in with their plan. I suppose it gave me a sense of benevolence, an almost Pickwickian glow. I hid them. Actually, Meeta hid them. Somewhere in the bungalow, near what Aunt Alice calls the bobcheecawnah. The back of the bungalow is being repaired, so no one ventures there. Besides, it would only be for a week. Once they were out of the way, nobody would guess. I got papers made in the names of Noor Abbas, valet, and his wife, Aliyahbibi. They had tickets in the hold. Chitra was quite amused by the situation. I won't deny it, Ramratan, I grew fond of them both. I spent a lot of time drawing them. They were so beautiful!

'Then, everything changed. Khursheed went out one evening to meet his brother, and when he returned, Meeta was alarmed by his appearance. He called me from my room after I had retired—so far neither Aunt Alice nor the Sinclairs knew of my refugees.

'I went with Meeta. Khursheed was in a terrible state, raving, tearing at his hair and clothes, his eyes bloodshot and bulging. Chitra tried to calm him, but he turned on her violently. She asked us to leave them alone. Much against my will, I did. Meeta and I waited in his room. Luckily, Meeta's family was out of the city. We sat there for about an hour. The noises had stilled and we went in cautiously. He had fallen asleep, pillowed in her lap. She looked up when we entered, and Ramratan, never have I seen such desolation in a human face. Ah Lord, the pain in that girl's eyes ...

'Later, she told me Khursheed had been ambushed by Asadullah. She feared Asadullah had taken the substance from Khursheed, but she couldn't be sure. It wasn't on him now, anyway.

'No other word out of Khursheed. He was stricken, and the fever raged all night. There could be no doubt, it was the plague. Even I could make that diagnosis! Chitra sickened next morning. It was like a signal for him to recover—or perhaps just his superhuman will. He roused himself to care for her. Meeta did the rest. I sent him that afternoon to you for disinfectant. There was nothing else I could think of. I couldn't leave them. I had advanced the fiction I was much in demand in the barracks, to fit Aunt Alice's expectations of her nephew. Chitra worsened rapidly. The end was terrible. She died in his arms as the sun set in a shower of marigold, a drift of gold petals at the window. The dying girl looking at her lover with such yearning ... a man will happily enter perdition for a look like that. And she was gone.

'Then Khursheed did a terrible thing. I waited outside, knowing he would wish to be alone with her. He called us in with a shout—he hadn't spoken in days—we found he had swathed her body in sheets steeped with disinfectant and laid her out, swaddled like that, by the window.

'He had soaked another sheet. Readied it, for himself. As we entered he cast off his clothes. Naked and gaunt, he was spectre than man. He wrapped that soaking sheet about his body, and spread out another wet sheet on the floor next to her. He lay down on this and prepared to die. He held my eyes for a long moment.

'He had made it easy for me. All I had to do was fold that sheet around him after it was over. Ah, Ramratan, his eyes! They were so calm, so empty, and he was yet alive.

'I asked if I should send for his mother. He did not answer. I felt he had already passed on, out of a life that no longer held anything for him. Minutes later, he was dead.

'Meeta had the carriage ready. I meant to send him out alone, but now there was little point in my staying back. Meeta didn't ask me if Khursheed was dead, and I did not tell him. We drove to Khursheed's home. Meeta came back to the carriage too disturbed to summon the few words of English we shared. I had lost all sense of direction. Meeta stopped and said he'd be back in a minute. I thought he was overcome by a necessity. And then—you were here.'

Ramratan called out to Meeta.

Nusser must be told. Nusser and Mohsin Chacha. They would have to work fast, and secretly, before the house was roused. Before Alice raised an alarm and the Sinclairs screamed the place down.

It was almost three o'clock now. The best thing would be—he should go back with Philip, quietly shift the bodies out to the morgue, and then send for Nusser. He explained this to Philip.

'Straight into the gharry, you think?' Philip asked. 'Take them away right now?'

'By far the best thing to do.'

Meeta took the carriage round to the stables at the back. They alighted quietly.

Ramratan steeled himself for the hour ahead. Meeta stood back respectfully for Philip.

As they walked briskly towards the dark outhouse, Alice Kipling stepped out of the shadows.

Philip stammered a greeting. Ramratan remained silent. She ignored Philip and addressed him instead.

'You disappoint me, Ramratan. I didn't think you would accompany my nephew on his unsavory nocturnal wanderings. Surely, even a native gentleman has a duty to his wife.'

'I am grateful for that reminder,' Ramratan answered stiffly. 'I am sorry that you were disturbed, Mrs Kipling. Pray go back to your rest.'

'You would be wise to heed your own advice, Dr Oak.'

'I say Aunt Alice, he's staying for a drink.'

'By no means! Good night, Ramratan.'

Philip looked helplessly at him. Alice, stern, was waiting for him to leave.

Meeta coughed.

'Yes, Meeta?' asked Alice, her eyes still on Ramratan.

'Kipling Sahib tell me, Meeta do this.'

'Do what, Meeta? You can tell me in the morning.'

'Memsahib, please?'

'Oh don't be a tedious jokum, Meeta! Get on with it!'

Meeta looked at Ramratan

'You said you would explain,' he implored. 'You promised.'

It was up to him, now.

'Mrs Kipling,' Ramratan said. 'There's something you should know.'

'There's something you should know.'

His thoughts still far away, Ratan squinted and brought the car ahead into focus. It moved slowly, decorously, behind more leisured traffic. He guessed this was at Vasu's command. He felt strange riding his bike in the harsh afternoon sun while his skin horripilated to the clammy air of dawn from a different time. They were near Byculla Bridge now, another twenty minutes at least to Sakina Manzil.

Now, Mrs Kipling, if you will permit me...

'Now, Mrs Kipling, if you permit me, we will take their bodies away before the house wakes, and scrub the place down with perchloride.'

They had walked into Meeta's cottage, and were huddled in the long covered corridor that led to the room where the bodies lay.

'Will it then all be erased?' Alice said sadly. 'All gone with the morning sun? As if it never happened? What do you think, Ramratan?'

'No. But this is the best way out now.'

'What's best? What's best! That's all this country thinks of! And look where it's got us all. Where it got *them*. Dead before they could taste life. Who will claim their bodies from the morgue? The mother who refused to aid her dying son? The father who disowned his daughter, and published her name in disgrace? Is it to *them* you will deliver these children? How they were shamed! How humiliated, when they should have been cherished and celebrated! And you will inflict this on them all over again? I will not allow it. You will not take their bodies to the morgue.'

'Mrs Kipling! It will be an embarrassment to the Sinclairs.'

'They won't know about it.'

'Aunt Alice, what do you mean to do?'

'We still rule this country, Philip.'

'Mrs Kipling, the deaths will have to be certified.'

'You can do that, surely, Ramratan? After that, you must leave it to me. From what I hear, their families will be glad to be relieved of the responsibility. Of course, they'll be maudlin enough to grieve for the dead after destroying the living. Families generally do.'

'But Aunt Alice—'

'Philip, spare me! Good night, Ramratan. Meeta, you will stay here with me.'

'Good night, Mrs Kipling. Permit me to call on you later this morning. About eleven?'

'I shall receive you then. Philip, get some rest. You must leave early, as early as you can.'

'Where am I going, Aunt Alice?'

'On a picnic, Philip. With Mrs Sinclair, her insufferable husband and her snivelling infants. You will express a desire at breakfast to sketch the cannery and I will arrange the picnic. Mrs Sinclair will not refuse, as you will offer her one of your hampers from Fortnum's.'

'I don't sketch canneries,' Philip rebelled.

'You will this one. And like it too!' Alice retorted.

'The Sinclairs will object to viewing a cannery, I'm sure.'

'It's not a cannery, Philip. Kanheri is a rock temple. Buddhist monastery. Or it was one, a thousand years ago,' Ramratan clarified. 'It is incredibly beautiful, and the sculptures are exquisite. Please go.'

'Till eleven then, Ramratan. Meanwhile, should we leave things as they are? Meeta will sit vigil. I will explain his absence.'

A little past the hospital, they were stopped at the police barricade.

A heavy man in white hurried to the car and spoke to Gopal. He was giving directions. Ratan edged up to the car, and offered him a ride. Gopal didn't introduce them. The man thanked Ratan and got on.

'Take the first left, then the third right.'

'This is where the boy sang – somewhere here.'

'Sorry?'

Was there a music school here, somewhere?'

The man laughed.

'Not a school. Not a formal building for music, like they have these days. But yes, you're right! Many ustads have come and gone through this lane. Not any more. They've all gone now. Only my father is left.'

'Your father?'

'He was famous in his day. Ustad Tariq Azhar Sahab.'

Tariq Azhar, the luminous morning star!

'Just to your right now. That's it! Sakina Manzil.'

The teeter-totter building looked desolate. It overlooked a small segment of the main road unlike the other structures in the lane. The man dismounted and thanked Ratan. Then he turned to the car as it purred to a halt behind them. For a moment, he looked lost. His eyes leapt to Ratan for succour.

'Everybody's gone,' he said. 'My father refuses to leave. This is not a good place to be now. I am nervous. My family's gone to Azamgarh. It's only my father and me now.'

He turned away.

'Joshi Sahab, with your permission I will go to prepare my father,' Ratan heard him say. 'Our stairs are steep. Will Maa-ji –'

'Nothing wrong with my legs, Yaqub. Go, tell him I am here.'

Her low voice had the clarity of a pure note. For a few minutes, she made no attempt to leave the car.

Gopal walked up to Ratan.

'Come up with us. Then we can talk, Yaqub, you and I.'

Sakina Manzil!

Sakina Manzil!

The House of Knives. Don't people think before they assign names? Name is destiny.

Ramratan didn't go home after leaving Kipling House. He walked towards Pydhonie, past the slumbering belly of Kalkadevi.

As he expected, a light burned in Mohsin Chacha's eyrie. He trudged upstairs and knocked. Bilal opened the door. Ramratan did not step in.

'Abu's forever in one mess or another,' Bilal grumbled. 'A toddler is more easily managed. Lo! The day hasn't dawned yet, and here's fresh trouble. Talk to him yourself, Ramratan, I want none of this.'

Fehmida appeared and pushed Bilal out of the way.

'What's happened, Bhaisahab? Is it about Khursheed?'

'Yes.'

'Are they safe?'

'Yes. Very safe. They are dead.'

Fehmida's ululation brought Mohsin out of his room. Inscrutably, he heard Ramratan out, and turned to Fehmida.

'Beti,' he directed, 'fetch my shawl.'

Bilal barred the way.

'Where are you going, Abu? If you show your face there, you will shame us all! Asadullah will never leave you alone. He will hunt you down in every gali, every mohalla. Life will become impossible for us.'

'Live your pitiful life, my son, any way you want. Let me live my way. Asadullah will not have to hunt me down. I am going to him now.'

Bilal could not deter him.

Ramratan followed in Mohsin Chacha's quick light steps. There was nothing to be said. They stopped outside Sakina Manzil. It was less than a week since he had waited here with Nusser at a similar hour.

'You should go, Ramratan. This Asadullah is a dangerous fellow,' Mohsin said.

'I'm staying.'

'Very well.'

Mohsin went in. Ramratan walked behind him. The stairs were unlit. Mohsin knocked sharply on a door at the first storey. There was no answer.

'Must be in the outhouse,' Mohsin muttered. 'Let's give him ten minutes.'

Then Mohsin said in Urdu:[•]

حال یہ شیخ کا ہے قبض کی بیماری سے
پاد بھی گانڈ سے آتا ہے تو دشواری سے
تن بدن پھنکتا ہے سوزاک کی بیماری سے
بوند پیشاب کی کچھ کم نہیں چنگاری سے

[•] **Baqar Ali Chirkeen**:
transliteration:
Haal yeh Shaikh ka hai qabz ki beemaari se
Paad bhi gaand se aata hai to dushwaari se.
Tan badan phunkta hai suzaak ki beemaari se
Boond paishaab ki kuch kam nahin chingaari se.
translation:
Every fart will singe his arse,
As constipation bestows the coup de grace;
The Shaikh's bladder will burn with gonorrhea
As he squirms with intractable stranguria.

'Oh, I wish him worse.'

They waited in morose silence on the murky landing. At length a figure appeared at the far end of the corridor.

Ramratan recognized him as the drunk who had accosted him last week. He was sober today. His lungi and lota and the slow deliberate tread confirmed Mohsin's diagnoses, colonic and urethral. But this morning, there was surely more to his pain than strangury and constipation. His eyes were empty, washed clean of the present.

He frowned at Mohsin's greeting.

'We have come for Asadullah,' Mohsin said.

'He is not here.'

'Where will we find him?'

The man shook his head and tried to push past them, but Ramratan caught his arm.

'Take us to Asadullah now, or we will come back with the police.'

'Return with the fucking army for all I care! Asadullah has escaped them all.'

'He is dead, then,' Mohsin said.

'Asad laughs at death. He is a martyr.'

'Peace be on him, then. We have no further work with you.'

Mohsin turned away. Light had deserted him. Nimble no longer, he clung to the railing and hauled himself up, step by step. He stopped at the landing and traced the moulding on the dado with a trembling finger.

Ramratan took his arm, usually an impossible liberty with Mohsin Chacha. Meekly, he allowed it today.

The stairs seemed to go on and on.

The stairs seemed to go on and on.

Vasu moved slowly, a mountaineer on a bluff, planting her stick like a piton. She stopped every now and then, steadying herself against the wall.

'Gopya, imagine! I have never been here before.'

She touched the chipped moulding of fruit and swags, traced the curlicues with a thoughtful finger.

'Gopya, go on! See if he recognizes you.' Gopal hesitated, hovering to support her. She shook her head and he went on ahead. Ratan stayed two steps below her, at hand to steady her in case she faltered. Her face seemed transfigured. Pain or happiness, it was impossible to discern.

'Listen!'

She spoke to Ratan.

'Can you hear him?'

Ratan heard nothing.

She smiled indulgently, forgiving him.

Her eyes shone, her slight frame was taut and quivering. He sensed she would wait till her tumult stilled a little, till she was once more the grande dame of an hour ago.

He was wrong.

Her tumult only grew further, and a rosé stain crept up her neck. Her hair slipped its moorings and tumbled into filigree that trapped the sun.

'Listen!'

Ratan still heard nothing.

Then a door opened, and she was borne up weightlessly, lifted without effort, by a golden escalation of sound.

At the landing, Yaqub and Gopal stepped aside for her. She turned and gave Ratan her cane, and holding Yaqub's arm for support, she kicked off her shoes. Barefoot, she paused, poised on the edge of a cataract. Then she shook off Yaqub's arm, stepped across the threshold, and escaped them all.

Everything was gathered into this moment.

The scatter of lost years, the giddying spin of event, all had found focus in the blink of an eyelash. Now, this instant, his life stopped, flipped over, and began anew.

Yaqub receded.

Then the face of a stranger appeared, blurring, shrinking, sharpening into a small watchful countenance he remembered. The deaf boy who listened so carefully, he would grimace at a false note long before Tariq caught it.

That face, too, receded.

And it was now.

Now.

He kept his eyes on the floor.

Nothing breached the pinguid light on the linoleum.

He heard retreating footsteps, the footsteps of heavy men.

No. It wasn't going to be now.

The blood beat back from his skin, he shrank back into his bones. His heart clenched again. The dog piss day slunk past the window.

He kept his eyes on the floor.

The light wavered.

Tariq tensed, waiting.

There was someone in the doorway.

A white blur, a throbbing flash of light.

He was going blind. He was going mad.

This was death.

No. Not death.

Death does not roar through one's arteries like a lunatic on a motorbike. Death isn't sunshine on an old man's back.

This was either madness or blindness or both.

Now.

A white flower. A white flower, walking … Opening and closing its petals. Over one foot, then the other. Over feet he would know anywhere.

It was madness, then!

Madness swirled through him in long honeyed spirals of Hamsadhwani, gathering up, gathering up everything into–now.

He gripped the edge of the takht and rose, afraid now to look away from the floor. Willing it now. Now that madness had been conceded, willing his hallucination to stay.

The feet stopped. They stayed.

Tariq looked up.

It was now.

She was here.

Yaqub and Gopal lingered at the door. Drifts of sound from the old man's throat whirled around them. Ratan noticed the two men avoided each other's eyes.

Now another voice, husky and coarse, ran alongside the man's smooth tenor, kept pace breathily like a scratch on a record.

Gopal studied his hands.

'She hasn't sung in years,' he said with shame.

The man sang lower. She followed. Their voices formed a Möbius strip of sound, now glinting silver, now brooding dark, now twisting, now unravelling, a chiral marriage of algebra and geometry.

It was one voice now, long notes allargando, yet anomalously gathering momentum.

She took wing, clear and joyous, a trajectory that waited at apogee for his beating heart.

He roared up to her like a tongue of flame. Her answer was exultation, a carillon above his thunder. They swooped and swirled together, in long caresses of sound so intimate the three men at the door quietly tiptoed away. Their descending feet rang hollow on the wooden stairs.

Their descending feet rang hollow on the wooden stairs.

Ramratan wondered why every door they passed did not burst open with angry householders. Nobody heard them. Mohsin stopped at last.

'Say nothing to the woman, Ramratan. She is a vile creature.'

'But today she is a mother, Mohsin Chacha.'

'She'll make a good mother for a corpse. She was a bad mother for a son.'

He knocked angrily.

The woman who opened the door was about Mohsin's age.

She smiled mockingly at them.

'More ambassadors! What does my son want? Go tell him his mother says, "Repent your sin! And after Allah has forgiven you, I shall think about it."'

'I want Suhail.'

'You won't get him. Having taken one son of mine you now demand the other? You think I don't know how you abetted Khursheed in his evil ways? Go away, old man, or I will rouse the mohalla and have you beaten to a pulp.'

She certainly had roused the household.

Sharifa screamed, and Suhail came out running. His mother barred the way. Suhail thrust her aside and pinioned Mohsin against the wall.

No words passed between them. The silence was the news.

'Have you come to tell me my son is dead? You bring the news a little too late,' Khursheed's mother said calmly. 'The day before those Plague Inspectors came, my son confessed about his whore. I knew of her already, from Asadullah. Take your corpse out of my house, I said to Khursheed. Everybody heard me. Asadullah heard me. And now that good man is dead because of my son.'

'How can you be so cruel,' Sharifa sobbed out bitterly. 'Chacha what has happened? Where is she?'

'They are both dead,' Ramratan said.

'I thank Allah. I bless you, Mohsin Bhai, for uttering words that bring solace to this mother's heart.'

Suhail pushed Mohsin away, and hurried indoors. Sharifa followed him. Within moments they were back.

'Let's go.' He pushed Sharifa towards the door. 'Hurry.'

'Wait! Where do you think you are going, Sharifa? Leave my house now, and you can never enter it again.'

'She won't,' Suhail said over his shoulder. 'And I, mother, will not look upon your face again.'

He caught Ramratan's arm roughly and led the way out.

Ramratan looked back when they were almost clear of the lane. The grey silhouette of Sakina Manzil had shrugged off the mist and caught fire in the first rays of the sun.

Damodar!

His first thought as Mohsin knocked on the door in Sakina Manzil had been of Damodar and Sulabha. With no children of their own, they had nurtured Chitra with delicacy, always giving precedence to her parents. Their grief would be greater than that of Chitra's parents.

Chitra's father Avdaji was a fool, but he had the Mores, Govardhan and his crazy brother Nivrutti, firmly behind him.

Govardhan's catspaw Nivrutti was a muscle-bound halfwit. In matters involving violence, he was quietly efficient.

Ramratan had once seen him break a pup's neck when its bark distracted him. Nivrutti had paused in the act of lifting bricks, picked up the squealing animal by the scruff of its neck, and knocked back its jaw to snap the cervical spine. Then he'd flung it over the fence and got right back into the rhythm of his chore. Nivrutti frightened Ramratan. Damodar and Sulabha would be publicly shamed by Govardhan, but Nivrutti might do worse.

A searing denouncement would appear in *Kesari* before the week was out. Balgangadhar Tilak would lose no time at all. It would be just his kind of fight. As for the handbill to be circulated from house to house by Hindu Sabha members, Ramratan could read it already.

It would be plaintive to begin with, sympathizing with a simple man ensnared by a rich and powerful friend. Was Damodar Joshi not the younger brother of Bombay's wealthiest Chitpavan Brahmin?

It was a matter of regret Shri Damodar and his wife Sulabha had no issue. The shastras had provision for this tragedy. No less than eleven routes were open to the unhappy couple to redress the situation. They had ignored these time-honoured solutions and embarked instead on a scheme worthy of the low-minded. Expressing an interest in the daughter of Avdaji More and his wife Shantabai, they had subverted this humble tradesman from the true path of dharma. Under their influence, Avdaji More not only kept his daughter unmarried far beyond the age recommended by Hindu Law, he was also coerced into educating her. This 'education' did not stop at instructions to help the girl adapt to the life of a Hindu matron. It implanted in her the unreasonable expectation of a scientific career. Further, this maiden—now surely a maiden no more—made an illicit connection with a mlechcha

Mussalman, encouraged, no doubt, by Damodar Joshi and his wife.

Under these circumstances, the news of the death of Avdaji More's daughter can only be greeted with relief. An ungrateful daughter, she was in death as salacious as in life, drawing her last breath in the embrace of a mlechchha, a situation morally abhorrent to every right-thinking Hindu, and one certain to cause the deepest revulsion in every virtuous woman.

We condemn her to the torments reserved for women of her kind in the shastras, dragged by her hair through the Vaitarni foaming over with blood and pus and excrement, thence to Tamisra, Andhatamisra and Raurava, hells from which there is no escape. To her grieving parents who plead for the support of their community, we have nothing but the deepest sympathy.

The ceremonies of purification they must perform with humility will surely rid them of any permanent slur. The same can not be said of Damodar Joshi. In the interests of safeguarding Hindu purity, we strongly suggest Damodar Joshi be punished with the rite of ghatasphota...

Ghatasphota.

Smashing the pot.

The pot is life, cherished and nurtured. Smash it and consider that life stamped out, and that man an outlaw. You may not speak with him, eat with him, employ him or sleep with him. His wife may not be honoured as a matron, no blessings will be sought of her, no alms accepted from her, and no food cooked by her may pass your lips. His children will be regarded as orphans, to the seventh generation the taint of their father will mark and sully them.

He would seek out Avdaji first.

No, he would not.

With a queasy sense of cowardice Ramratan decided he would go first to Shankar Buwa Joshi.

Ramratan parted ways with Mohsin at Pydhonie. He found a rekla stirring early and persuaded the man to drive him to Girgaum.

At Joshi Sadan he commanded the watchman to announce him immediately. The man protested. His master did not rise till six.

'Wake him!' Ramratan ordered tersely. 'Or I will go in and shake him up myself.'

Shankar Buwa, it appeared, had spent a sleepless night. He sent for Ramratan immediately, received him in the courtyard, and led him into a walled garden where he tended his roses.

Dimly aware of the luxurious scent of roses, wet earth and dewy grass, Ramratan's bruised senses registered each nuance as intense pain. He had rehearsed his lines in the carriage, schooled himself to stick to facts and permit no hint of reproach in his words.

He heard Ramratan out impassively. Turning wearily away from his roses, Shankar Buwa sat down heavily on the stone bench.

Ramratan was shocked by his appearance. The man's breathing was harsh. He had turned grey. Sweat dripped from his shaking jowls. He held up a trembling hand to restrain Ramratan from summoning help.

'That mad dog Govardhan must be stopped,' he said. 'Perhaps you don't know this yet. Nivrutti is dead.'

'What happened?'

'The plague. It is very peculiar. You know Nivrutti was Govardhan's creature. He used him as a weapon.

Nivrutti went missing two days ago. I found out because I've kept an eye on Govardhan since our last meeting. When Nivrutti did not return home for two nights I sent for Govardhan. He claimed he didn't know. I had him questioned.'

Tortured, more likely.

'Did he speak?'

'Yes. He had sent Nivrutti to foil Asadullah's plans.'

'And?'

'We found both of them last evening, in the old pavilion at the edge of Gowalia Tank. Dead. They had been dead at least a day. They had bled. Their fingers and toes were black. Govardhan brought a friend of his, from your hospital. He confirmed it was the plague.'

Ramratan was horror struck, speechless at what this signified.

Horribilis was on the loose.

'Govardhan told us he had sent Nivrutti to ambush Asadullah. He knew Asadullah was after Khursheed. They were certain Khursheed had that special plague prepared in Dr Surveyor's laboratory. Is that true? What is so special about this plague? Plague kills anyway. Now you tell me Khursheed is dead too!'

Ramratan could not articulate his terror. Not heeding the old man's protests, he hurried out. He waited neither for rekla nor tram. He ran.

He had to find Nusser.

Nusser would know what to do.

'There is a restaurant just across the road. We can talk over tea,' Yaqub said. 'They also make excellent nankhatai.'

Ratan, who had eaten nothing since his rushed breakfast, welcomed the suggestion. He willed his thoughts to the present as he trailed Yaqub and Gopal.

The tea was excellent, sharp with ginger, yet not too strong and only mildly sweet. Yaqub relaxed a little, smiling at Ratan's pleasure. Gopal was anxious, his eyes kept swivelling towards Sakina Manzil.

He had to broach the subject or they'd never move past small talk.

'Shakuntala Salwe,' he prodded.

'This gentleman seems to know something about her,' Gopal addressed Yaqub. 'I said we could talk.'

'Yes, of course.' Yaqub was wary.

'I know she is dead,' Ratan began. 'I found her body. I also found all the papers she'd been searching for. Those papers led me to you, Mr Joshi. I also had the address of Sakina Manzil. The names I had were Sheikh Ishaq Ahmad—'

'My great-grandfather,' Yaqub said.

'And Shankar Buwa Joshi.'

'My grandfather,' Gopal said.

The next bit would be tricky.

'I too have some connection with these names,' Ratan said.

'We know that already. Your name is on this document.'

Yaqub placed a briefcase on the table. Gopal, after some hesitation, reached into the leather folder he was carrying. Yaqub spread a newspaper on the table.

Gopal extracted a sheet of yellow paper from his folder and laid it down over the newsprint with ceremony. Yaqub followed suit, aligning his paper with Gopal's. Each had brought half a foolscap sheet, foxed and brittle with age. It had been torn along its fold. Folded, it would perfectly fit the indent on the pages of Shakuntala Salwe's copy of Lockwood's *Beast & Man In India*.

'Here's your name.'

Yaqub's finger hovered over the words.

Ramratan Oak

He didn't write like that any more. His signature was a vicious scrawl, the 'R' had a snarl to it and the 'k' ended in a kick. This hand was deliberate but anarchic. The name ended in a punctum where the nib had ground into the paper. A faint abrasion would show if he held it up against the light.

They were waiting for him to say something.

'Ramratan was my great-grandfather,' he said.

A sigh passed between them.

Ratan had the strangest feeling that he had passed a test.

'Perhaps I know less of this matter than you do,' he said.

'Perhaps your father will know all the details.'

Yaqub, unknowing, had thrown him a rope. Ratan grabbed at it without hesitation.

'My father has been quite ill for a while now. He—he finds speech difficult. I do know a little, and you could fill in the blanks for me. This document was with Shakuntala Salwe?'

'Yes. We took it from her.'

They looked at each other and then clarified. 'We didn't steal it. We paid her.'

There had been no money in Shakuntala's bag. Ratan had searched the place.

'We took the paper, but she said she had more. She said she had proof that it was with us, and she would make that proof public.'

It?

'You know the story, don't you, Ratan?' Gopal Joshi looked keenly at him. 'Perhaps your father didn't tell you about it, and you came to the knowledge on your own.'

Ratan took the plunge.

'*Bacillus pestis horribilis*?'

Yaqub smiled.

'When I first heard the story from Abu, I was in college. I thought the name was a joke, until I learned what happened.'

'What happened? I only know they found Asadullah and Nivrutti More dead in the pavilion at Gowalia Tank.'

'Read this.'

Ratan had looked away from the paper when he'd seen Ramratan's name on it. His response frightened him. It was entirely visceral, a feeling of thirst, of air cut off, of a darkness that sucked the day out of his eyes.

'Read it.'

Ratan read it.

We, the undersigned, accept responsibility for the safekeeping of the missing vials of Bacillus pestis horribilis. We have reason to believe these vials of a malignant form of the plague germ were stolen by Asadullah Rehman and Nivrutti More. We have reason to believe that before their deaths, Asadullah Rehman and Nivrutti More gave these vials to members of their family, with every intention of causing public harm. As of the present moment, these vials have not been traced. The families of Asadullah Rehman and Nivrutti More are under our surveillance, and we take responsibility for them. In the event there is an outbreak of malignant plague caused by Bacillus pestis horribilis, we take on ourselves the onus of making reparation. We take this solemn oath in repentance for the hatred and enmity between our communities that has caused the tragic deaths of Dr. Khursheed Alam and Dr. Chitrangada More. We are aware that this strain of the plague germ is capable of extended survival and therefore extended harm. This oath of responsibility and reparation, therefore, extends beyond our lifetime. Our children, and theirs, are bound to this oath.

signed at Joshi Sadan, Girgaum, Bombay.

Suhail Shafique Ahmad & Shankar Rao Mangeshnath Joshi

On this 28th day of February, 1897 in the presence of:

Mohsin Ahmad
Nusserwanji Fakirji Surveyor
Alice MacDonald Kipling
Ramratan Oak

'So they took it off Khursheed! They stole the vials! ' Ratan exclaimed.

'We have different versions of that,' Yaqub said. 'The way I heard it, Khursheed was ambushed by one or the other ... or by both of them. The vials were taken from him, but he escaped. One vial, definitely, broke in that scuffle. Khursheed was striken. As were Asadullah and Nivrutti. Asadullah and Nivrutti quarrelled, but by then the plague was upon them, and it worked very fast. People came looking for them. Asadullah's drunken brother certainly did. Perhaps Asadullah passed on the vial to him. He later boasted to my grandmother that he had a weapon to wipe every Hindu off the face of the earth—'

'—every Mussalman off the face of the earth is the way I heard it.' Gopal smiled sadly. 'My grandfather Shankar Buwa told us this story every year, he never let us forget. He had Govardhan More imprisoned but he escaped and hid in Poona, and ganged up with those Chapekar brothers. He wrote to Shankar Buwa, a blustering document which said no prison could keep him from unleashing a weapon to wipe out every Mussalman.'

'Asadullah's brother boarded with my great-grandmother until he died. Asadullah's followers met at my great-grandmother's house when she was alive. She never forgave her sons, and her sons never forgave her.'

'We kept the covenant our elders forged. But you know they'd never have taken such an oath if it hadn't been for these four people. Mohsin Ahmad, Nusserwanji Surveyor, Alice Kipling and Ramratan Oak.'

'Yes, that's true. It was their story that moved my grandfather. Such a simple thing, really.'

'Story?'

'The story of the four. Surely you know that?'

Ratan was oppressed by shame.

'I know about the four, but the story—'

'Oh if you mean why they started doing what they did, I don't know that story either,' Yaqub said. 'My grandfather said it was very simple. He called it the Rule of Four. If four people do nothing to stop hate, within four days they will have to send out for four people. *Chaar din mein chaar logon ko bulana hoga*.'

Ratan shook his head mystified.

'Four people, Ratan! To lift a bier! Hate kills. So insidiously, we don't even see it happen. Unless you do something to stop it, someone somewhere always gets hurt.'

'So our elders only followed what these four men were pledged to do. No, one of them was a woman, British from her name. What were these people like? We never knew. Vasu Tai was closest to our grandfather, but he never told her about these four people.'

'My grandfather knew Mohsin Ahmad well, but he too didn't talk much about him or the rest of them. What about Ramratan Oak? Do you know much about him?'

'Not very much,' Ratan said, surprising himself.

Both the older men nodded. Ratan heard their thought: *It's like that with some families*.

'This plague germ was stolen from Dr Surveyor's laboratory,' Gopal said.

'Yes, he took it very badly,' Yaqub added.

Dr Nusserwanji Fakirji Surveyor.

Nusser.

Nusser.

Expressionless, he let Ramratan speak without interruption. Ramratan, drained by his breathless narrative, was surprised by Nusser's calmness, but soon he realized it was the calm of despair. This was also a man of science to whom curiosity was paramount. Nusser might end up cutting his throat, but only after he'd taken a good long look at the way *Bacillus pestis horribilis* behaved.

'Both Khursheed and Chitra died of the *horribilis*. It infected Khursheed in a few hours, perhaps even within the hour. Asadullah and Nivrutti were affected faster, they didn't even have the strength to crawl home. They quarrelled, bled horribly, and died. Exactly like those rats. Khursheed and Chitra lasted longer. Almost a day. Was that because they were inoculated? Philip hasn't sickened so far. He's inoculated too. That servant of the Kiplings, Meeta? The one who cared for Khursheed and Chitra at that bungalow? He isn't inoculated, is he? He's unaffected too. So how does this work? If our standard inoculation works against *Bacillus pestis horribilis*... Ramratan, why then, we're all saved!'

'Nusser, you're missing the point! Where are those remaining vials? Did they all break? I don't know if any glass was recovered from that pavilion. I must ask Shankar Buwa. I don't believe that Govardhan discovered his brother's body a day after his death. Nivrutti may not have gone alone. Govardhan would have sent someone to look for him when he did not return that night. I think they were both seen when they were still alive—and abandoned. We know how often that happens. So, where are the vials?'

Nusser nodded morosely. For a while he'd fooled himself into a reprieve, he was past that now.

They prepared to leave. Nusser woke the coachman, and the carriage moved out briskly.

'I'll need samples,' Nusser said. 'We'll need an autopsy, Ramratan.'

Ramratan was silent. He still had to tell Nusser about Alice Kipling.

'What will their families do now?' Nusser asked. 'The funerals will become the nucleus of a riot—have you considered that? Emotions are running high. We'll have to do something.'

Yes, they would have to do something. They would have to do as their fathers had done.

Ramratan decided to stop at home. He wanted Yashoda's comfort now.

Yashoda paled as they told her.

'What will happen now, Ramratan?' she whispered.

In silence he imagined maddened mobs and thundering horses, Salim's face shattering in a blur of blood and flesh, anger in the children's eyes, hate in their hearts.

'It's over, Yashoda,' Ramratan lied tiredly. 'We can't do anything more.'

'More? What have you done so far?'

He recoiled at the contempt in her voice.

'Nothing at all. It shouldn't be Mohsin Chacha alone bearing the brunt. What about the other three? You and Nusserbhai and Lockwood Kipling? If you ask me, Philip has done more than his uncle's share. Your fathers trusted you.'

'Easily said, Yashoda. *Stop hate*. What kind of diktat is that? How is one supposed to pull that off?'

'By not saying you can do nothing about it. By refusing to *think* you can do nothing about it. For instance, what are you going to do when the bodies are taken out? These will be very public funerals. There will be meetings and speeches and then the trouble will start. What will you do about that hate? Or what Sulabha Tai will face from Chitra's parents? Or the hate Bhauji will get from Govardhan More? The hate

Sharifa will face from her mother-in-law? Hate will spill, Ramratan, and we have to do something about that.'

'Mrs Kipling has refused to let me take the bodies out of the bungalow,' Ramratan said.

Yashoda and Nusser stared at him as if he'd gone mad.

'Yes. She wants me to certify the deaths. Then she'll see to the rest. She says she will never let their families inflict hate and humiliation on them again in death as they did in life. She was very determined.'

'I say, Ramratan, that's very high-handed of her. We'll have to get Cleghorn to intervene.'

Yashoda laughed.

'How very clever of Mrs Kipling! Of course you mustn't intervene. It is the perfect solution. You don't release the bodies to their families. You say they are infectious and unsafe. You also say they will be prosecuted if they raise a furore. They won't check on that, they'll be too frightened. Let Mrs Kipling level with Cleghorn. He needn't know anything about the *horribilis*—I gather you haven't told her, Ramratan? I hope you haven't told her.'

'No. Philip doesn't know either. He knows about it, but he doesn't know what it is. Both Khursheed and Chitra were very circumspect with him, and I decided to go by that.'

'But what will Mrs Kipling do?' Nusser asked, his voice rising in falsetto. 'Really, she's a most difficult woman!'

'We'll just have to ask her.'

'Take Mohsin Chacha with you,' Yashoda advised. 'I won't be surprised if he agrees with Alice.'

'We must see the bodies,' Nusser said. 'We must insist on that, Ramratan.'

'Yes. Or Suhail will not be convinced his brother is truly dead,' Mohsin said. 'Where is all this going to end? Your fathers and I and Lockwood, we were so confident when we made that pact, so certain we could make a difference, no matter how small the steps we took. You now are as old as we were then, but you have no such conviction! I don't know how I can persuade you boys when your own fathers have failed. I have failed with Bilal, Allah knows. But I must have faith in somebody—can't it be the two of you?'

'We must see the bodies.'

Ratan came back to Yaqub and Gopal.

'They didn't bring home their dead,' Gopal was saying. 'Neither Khursheed Alam nor Chitrangada More had a proper funeral. Strangely, my grandfather said it was for the best.'

'I know Asadullah's brother had primed the whole mohalla. They were ready to erupt when the janaazah was brought in. There was no funeral. Khursheed's mother, my great-great-grandmother, she said he would never find rest in any qabristan. She was a foul woman, happier with Asadullah than with her own sons.'

'Govardhan swore he would raze the city to claim Chitra's body, so Shankar Buwa had him arrested and thrown in jail.'

Ratan nodded, but not in agreement.

It hadn't happened quite that way.

It hadn't happened quite that way.

Ramratan used the back gate, uncertain about the Sinclairs. Had they been packed off to 'the cannery'?

Meeta led them to his cottage, through the long roofed passage from the bungalow.

'So much of space!' Mohsin muttered.

They stared out into the backyard. It was a shambles of rubble and barbed wire. The old well was redundant now, with the advent of piped water. Its wall had been broken, the ancient stones dark red and mossy, flung about like old bones.

'Malabar Hill will have electricity soon,' Mohsin grumbled. 'When will our time come?'

Alice walked briskly up to them.

She ignored Ramratan and Nusser.

'You could have trusted me, Mohsin Ahmad,' she said. 'My nephew is a stranger here. It was unkind to place such a responsibility on him.'

Mohsin bowed, but said nothing.

'I have sent Philip away. I told Ramratan this morning I will not have the bodies returned to their families. That's my final word on this subject, gentlemen.'

'A wise decision, Mrs Kipling. Will it not sit heavily on you?' Mohsin asked.

'And on you, Mohsin?'

'Not on me.'

'Nor me,' Ramratan said.

Only Nusser stayed silent. Nusser knew nothing of hate.

'Meeta will take you in to view the bodies. You will excuse me if I do not accompany you.'

The room where the bodies lay adjoined Meeta's quarters. It was at a lower level, opening directly on to the backyard. A larder probably, and rarely used.

When Meeta opened the door, Ramratan saw it was quite a large room with a west-facing window. Meeta had not tidied up yet. The two bodies lay side by side on the floor, swaddled in soaked sheets drying in patches of yellow. Only their faces were exposed. Chitra's face shone, probably washed by Khursheed in a last gesture of love. Khursheed's was a map of torment. Cracking islands of dried blood caked his chin and neck. His face had stilled in a rictus of agony, but the eyes, straining upward, were devoid of expression.

'Do you want to examine them, Nusser?' Ramratan asked in a low voice.

Nusser shook his head. It would be a further cruelty.

Mohsin averted his face. They heard him leave the room, his footsteps operose on the flagstones of the corridor, ringing out his pain.

'Meeta, tell Mrs Kipling I will have the certificates ready for you before noon. Come to my office and collect them.'

Meeta nodded, turned to leave. Ramratan put an arm around him and led him into his own quarters. Nusser shut the door on the bodies.

Meeta sank down to the floor, his head in his hands.

'You are worn out, Meeta,' Ramratan said. 'Stay here. I will go to Mrs Kipling while you rest. Shall I fetch you a glass of milk? Something to eat?'

Meeta shook his head.

'Memsahib needs me. I must go.'

'Meeta, I want to give you the plague injection,' Nusser said.

Ramratan was surprised. Would inoculation after exposure be of any help?

'Waldemar has another fraction of the serum that has proved to be of some use,' Nusser explained. 'We should try that.'

Meeta refused.

'Nothing has happened to me so far,' he protested. 'If I fall sick, I'll listen to you. You get back to work, keep those certificates ready for me. I will be there by twelve. Go now.'

Ramratan realized they were excluded. This was between the old man and the Kiplings.

Out on the road, Nusser looked to Mohsin Chacha.

'What is she going to do with them?' he asked.

Mohsin shrugged. 'Whatever she does, it will be more respectful than what their families have done to them.'

'How do we tell their families? I must see Khursheed's brother,' Nusser said. He and Mohsin left together.

Ramratan had to face Chitra's parents next. He determined to get to the hospital first and prepare the death certificates for Meeta to collect. Whatever Alice's plan, he would not let the Mores get in its way.

Shankar Buwa's phaeton stood outside the college building. Ramratan nearly overlooked him. His large frame appeared compacted and shrunk, no longer a figure of consequence. Ramratan showed him into his office.

'I thought I would find you here,' Shankar Buwa said nervously. 'Tell me, Ramratan, is it possible somehow to expedite formalities? How soon can we get the body? I will sign for it myself. Grave things are afoot, Ramratan, and I must act fast.'

His hands trembled, his cane crashed to the floor. As Ramratan retrieved it, he noticed the fine ivory head had cracked. It now bore a fissure across the muscled haunches of the horse.

Ratan trailed his fingertip on the ivory head and encountered the crack. This was no illusion.

'You're still holding Tai's cane.' Gopal smiled. 'Time we were getting back, we should be home before dark.'

'Give them a little longer,' Yaqub pleaded.

'They'll still be singing an hour from now,' Gopal said ruefully.

'Are you a musician too?' Ratan asked Yaqub.

'Oh no! I never had that blessing. My mother hated music. She made sure my brothers and I never learnt from Abu. My sister too—but her life took a strange turn when she married. Her husband encouraged her to learn music. She does not sing, though. She plays the rudraveena. They live in Panvel.'

Gopal nodded, making some connection between Panvel and rudraveena that was lost on Ratan.

'My grandfather was a musician,' Yaqub said. 'Abu's talent comes from him. Abu says he was much more gifted, though he never did get the *taalim*. Abu's guru was Ustad Chhaju Khan, but he says he learnt everything he knows from my grandfather.'

Shankar Buwa mopped his face.

'I came here directly after seeing Avdaji and his wife,' he said.

'That must have been quite an ordeal.'

'They are not human. Avdaji is Govardhan's mouthpiece, but that woman! So much hate! And against her own flesh and blood? "Throw her body to the jackals," she said. "Bring it here and leave it in the streets, let the dogs devour her."'

'People say horrible things when they are distressed.'

'I went to Damodar first. He and Sulabha are too dazed to react. They are with my wife now. I want them out of the city within the hour.'

'Where will you send them?'

'To Goa. I have friends there. They will be looked after.'

'That's a relief. It will be awful for them here.'

'Tilak has been gunning for me a long while now. This will be his opportunity. I fell out with your father because of Tilak, do you know that?'

'No.'

'I told you, I was present at your birth. Of course, at that time Tilak hadn't entered the picture. I was still good friends with Krishna. You gave your mother a very hard time, Ramratan. The dai had given up. The doctor said it was touch and go. Krishna told him, "I want my wife back, I don't care about the baby." As if it was in that doctor's hands! Perhaps it was, who knows? Anyway, they brought you out of her room a mangled lump of red, all swollen and bruised. Nestled in bloodstained rags you were left outside your mother's room, while your father hung anxiously over the doctor's shoulder, and all the women muttered doom around them both. You were just a still red lump beginning to look grey. I had three of my own. I knew what to do. I picked you up, opened your little mouth with my finger, turned you over and slapped your wrinkly bottom. What a wail I got in return! Since that instant I've always thought of you as one of my own. Even though five years later it was all over between Krishna and me.'

What did the man want of him now? What kind of repayment did he expect?

Shankar Buwa read his thought.

'Nothing. That story means nothing. There is an old bond between your father and me. I never understood what he told me then, but I understand it now.'

'Understand what?'

'That pact he made with his friends. It became their religion. I laughed then at them. I have come here not just for Chitra's body. I've come to remind you of that pact. Something will have to be done now. I cannot find Govardhan, but Avdaji tells me he has some weapon with which he will avenge Nivrutti's death. He says not one Mussalman will be left alive. My men are out looking for Govardhan, and they're shadowing Avdaji. He must have run to Govardhan with the news. Govardhan's boys will lie in wait near the qabristan. When they bring Khursheed's cortege out on the street, it will be all over with them. Ramratan, they must be stopped!'

'You'll find Govardhan.'

'Even if I do, he has a loyal following. They're all primed on hashish and armed with steel trishuls. Such a travesty of belief! My years have embittered me. I believe in nothing any more. They must be stopped, Ramratan! You must stop them!'

'I!'

'You, and the rest, who made that pact with Krishna. I owe my friend reparation. I will do as you tell me. Call the rest of them. Let them decide with you.'

Ramratan took a deep breath and told Shankar Buwa about Alice Kipling's decision.

He frowned angrily, pounding the floor with his cane.

'This is intolerable! I will not stand for it!'

'Why?'

'You ask me why? Do you expect me to allow a mlechchha to determine the death rites of a Brahmin woman? There's no redemption for that poor girl's soul.'

'Her soul? Was there any redemption in the poor girl's life? Did your rules and observances not decide her fate? Are you not responsible for her death? Who gave her honour? A mlechchha who loved her above his own life, who risked everything he had for her. Who gave her shelter? Another mlechchha, who owed her, or her kind, nothing. Who tended her when she was sick? An outcaste, a Mahar whose touch you shrivel from. Where was her own mother when Chitra was wracked by pain? What did this old man have to gain by risking his life in tending this stranger? And when she died, who honoured her body and prayed for her soul? Where were your Brahmins then? Where were her parents? Her mother wants her body thrown to the dogs. Another woman wants to give it the offices of respect. Which of them is the Brahmin? The rabid mother or the kind stranger?'

Ramratan was shouting now, his voice breaking with sobs at injustice that held a human life in thrall even after it had departed.

'You make it hard for me to decide,' Shankar Buwa said slowly. 'What should I choose? The respect of other men? Or that of my soul?'

'Is that such a difficult decision?'

'No. Merely an uncomfortable one.'

Ramratan shrugged.

'Do what you want. The bodies are not going to be released to the families. They are highly infective. They will be incinerated.'

'Where?'

'That is the hospital's responsibility.'

Shankar Buwa nodded, but he made no attempt to leave. They stared at each other like strangers. Without belligerence, without friendship.

There were voices outside.

Nusser entered, followed by Mohsin Chacha. Suhail trailed in behind them.

Shankar Buwa greeted Nusser.

'I have been told you will not release the bodies because they are infective,' he said. 'As long as everything is done respectfully, I have no objections. I speak for the girl's parents. Your decision is final, I suppose? Very well, then. Who am I to quarrel with science?'

Suhail stepped forward.

Shankar Buwa recoiled.

'You!'

The word was torn from both their throats, a syllable of inexpressible anguish and outrage.

'Why did you not tell me?' Shankar Buwa roared.

Suhail's hands rose and fell helplessly.

'I didn't know.'

They stared at each other, red-eyed.

'And if I had told you—what would you have done?' Suhail said bitterly. 'Could—*would* you have saved them?'

Shankar Buwa shook his head. Not in denial, but helplessly, overwhelmed.

'Your brother?' he asked, in a barely audible whisper.

'Yes. My elder brother.'

'I never saw him with you—'

'He did not sing. He paid for my music lessons. Secretly. Because the family did not approve. Everything I know, all I am, is because of him.'

'You made him proud.'

'It is all wasted now.'

'No. Don't say that, son. It is up to you not to waste it. In time you will understand.'

He rose ponderously, bowed to Mohsin, and ignoring the others, staggered out.

Ramratan followed him out and saw him into his carriage. Shankar Buwa sank back on the cushions.

'Krishna's son, you are no shame to your father,' he said. 'No shame at all.'

'There is bad news, Ramratan,' Mohsin Chacha said. 'There is word on the street about Khursheed. Asadullah's brother is gathering forces. Mrs Kipling's idea is a good one, and Suhail agrees.'

'What about your mother, Suhail?'

'My mother has no say in the matter. She has said too much already. I will do the *namaaz-e-janaazah* for my brother.'

'What if Asadullah's followers make trouble?'

'Then they must be stopped.' This boy too spoke with the same conviction as Shankar Buwa.

Stop hate.

'I thought you worked in the press,' Ramratan said. 'I didn't know you were a musician, Suhail.'

'I'm not one yet. Joshi Sahab is a musician. He sits with my guru, they sing together very often. That's how he knows me. I'm just a novice.'

'He seemed to think highly of your talent.'

'They all do,' Suhail said simply. 'Bhaisahab did too. I have yet to justify that. I'm—I'm too old. Singers start training when they're five or six. Even that is considered late. I was sixteen when I started!'

'What will you do now, Suhail?' Nusser asked. He had been silent all this while.

'We will go away. We will find something in Lahore. We have family there.'

'And your mother?'

'This house is hers. This life is hers. She is welcome to both. There's nothing left for me here. I will not leave my wife at my mother's mercy.'

When Meeta arrived a half-hour later, Ramratan gave him the certificates. Meeta shook off Nusser's concern and walked away rapidly.

'Isn't this the man Lockwood mentions in his book?' Mohsin asked. 'The bearer who made toys when he should have been dusting?'

Ramratan nodded.

'I wonder what Lockwood would say if he knew this man had risked his life for him.'

'Not for him, surely!' Ramratan protested.

That was a strange way to look at it. But events would prove Mohsin right.

'In remembering these old things, we've quite forgotten your question, Ratan,' Yaqub said. 'You asked about Shakuntala Salwe. You know who she is—was, of course?'

'Meeta?'

'Exactly. Meeta's great-granddaughter. Then you also know what she wanted.'

'Money.'

'Money.'

Shankar Buwa was quiet a long while.

'It all comes down to money. The man will have to be paid.'

'Meeta? Yes, I suppose a small baksheesh will be welcome.'

Shankar Buwa laughed.

'You are an innocent, Ramratan. Let it go. Perhaps we can deal with it after Mrs Kipling has left. What news of Philip Burne-Jones? He sails on the *Caledonia* tomorrow? I will see to his comfort. He has a taste for magnificence, no doubt.'

A Piccadilly dandy.

'He will be called "the Indian gentleman" for the rest of his life!'

What was that line?

Camels bearing apes, ivory and peacocks ...

Ah yes. It all comes down to money.

'Money? Shakuntala Salwe wanted money?'

'Of course! Our families have *always* paid Meeta's people. Her demand didn't surprise us.'

'How did she find you?'

They looked at Ratan blankly.

Of course.

She'd always known where to find them. She had no need to locate their addresses through the Quarantine Papers.

Then what did she need the Quarantine Papers *for*?

'She knew where to find you,' Ratan corrected himself. 'Please go on, Yaqub.'

'She needed money. Not the usual small sum. She had something to sell. This document. When she came to Sakina Manzil she told me she had been to Joshi Sadan already. She would sell it to the highest bidder. She asked me to meet her on Sunday evening. "At the old place," she said. I had no clue where she meant. I was inclined to dismiss it. Then on Sunday—when the masjid crumbled, I saw our lives crumbling too. I had to find her. I had to get the document from her. You see, Ratan, that document was something of a family legend. It had lost its meaning. It was a pretty story. It was memory. It couldn't touch our lives. And then, suddenly after Babri Masjid, it did. It became terribly powerful. I had to obtain it—at any cost.'

Ratan saw that now, with hate coming to a boil, every man could stand accused. A mosque is destroyed, hate breaks free, memory becomes weapon.

Gopal nodded.

'I—we, all four of us felt the same. Vasu Tai in particular. Yaqub didn't mention this, but Salwebai had already tracked down Balkrishna More. She didn't know about Mohammad Yunus.'

'Who is Mohammad Yunus?'

Yaqub sighed.

'Asadullah's family. His brother's great-grandson. Mohammad Yunus was one of four boys. All four disappeared two years ago. We heard the stories, they were at a training camp in Waziristan. Then Mohammad Yunus came back in July. This Ram Janmabhoomi business had him in a bad way. He wasn't a violent boy. He was inspired—like a poet. On Sunday afternoon, just after the news broke, his brothers telephoned. They mocked him. Where is your talk of peace now, they taunted. Go out and prove yourself a man! A life for a life, that's the only way, they told him. It was an ultimatum. I saw him that afternoon, that poor boy. He kept repeating wildly, "A life for a life." Keep your head, I advised him, what's happened to your intelligence? Think clearly, come have some tea with us, tell us what's on your mind. He shook me off and ran away. Poor boy! Not a mean bone in his body. He wasn't like those louts he'd grown up with! He set fire to himself outside the police chowki in Madanpura. That's why Sakina Manzil is empty. The police know Mohammad Yunus' connections. Any day now they will attack us.'

Yaqub's apprehensions were all too real.

'You should consider taking your father away,' Gopal advised.

'He won't go!' Yaqub cried out in anguish. Then, pausing to calm himself, he continued. 'To return to that evening, I reached Salwebai's cottage in the Arts College after five. Gopalbhai was already there. We recognized each other, even though we hadn't met before. She showed us the document. We hadn't talked about it, but the same thought occurred to both of us.'

'We examined the document,' Gopal said. 'It appeared genuine. It belonged to both of us. We would both buy it. She wanted twenty thousand. We haggled. Beat her down to ten. We had the money with us. We put down the money. We tore the page across, and each took one half of the document.'

By that simple gesture of solidarity, by the division of that paper, they had shown Shakuntala Salwe that her blackmail was at an end.

Blackmail.

Blackmail.

The word coiled colubrine in Ramratan's brain.

Meeta did not look like a blackmailer.

What do blackmailers look like?

'I am a poor man, Ramratan Sahib. I have done a lot for these people.'

Meeta repeated this over and over.

'Oh? I thought you said Kipling Sahib told you, Meeta do this for me?'

'That was what Philip Baba wanted. I have eaten their salt. What Philip Baba and Memsahib ask, I do. But I owe nobody else. The others should remember I am a poor man. I owe them nothing. They should remember how poor I am, if they want to be safe.'

Money, Shankar Buwa had said. The man will have to be paid. It wasn't over, not yet.

It wasn't over, not yet.

'The document was genuine, she had the money, the matter was over. But she hadn't finished with us.'

'She said the document was the least of it. She had it. She had the *Bacillus pestis horribilis*. No, that isn't what she said. She said she knew where it was. She knew who had it. She had all the proof—or she would have it in a week. Ten pissant thousand rupees wouldn't save us.'

Gopal was rueful. 'She seemed to know a great deal about those vials, more than what's mentioned here in this paper. She knew how the disease would appear, how it would kill, how it would spread. For a woman of no education, she knew a lot about the plague.'

'I think, Bhai Sahab, at that point we let our surprise show, or she wouldn't have told us how she came by her knowledge.'

'Which was?'

'Meeta had told his family that he, and he alone, knew who had taken the *horribilis*. She, Shakuntala, would show us proof—for a price.'

Then teasingly, she had shown them a slip of paper.

Yaqub had tried to grab it from her. Ill-advised. Imprudent. She grew frantic and abusive. Next moment she was convulsed in a fit, twitching, jerking, frothing at the mouth and, within minutes had collapsed in a heap before them. For all they knew, she was dead.

'What we did was wrong. We left. She may not have been dead then. We are culpable. We left.'

Gopal was more matter-of-fact. He shrugged dismissively.

'We left,' Yaqub repeated. 'It's over now. We are no longer bound by this.'

Gopal shook his head bitterly.

'Somehow I am not so sure. It will haunt us as long as we live.'

'It will haunt us as long as we live,' Shankar Buwa said. 'A document such as this is an eternal commitment.'

They were gathered in the octagonal hall of Joshi Sadan. None of them, except Alice Kipling, registered the luxury of their surroundings.

'The *horribilis* is an eternal threat,' Nusser emended. 'This germ is capable of growing spores. That means it can survive indefinitely, and under the toughest conditions. It doesn't need a freezer to survive. It doesn't even need air. Its activation is swift—both Asadullah and Nivrutti died within hours. Khursheed and Chitra lasted a little longer because they had been inoculated. Yet, that isn't the entire explanation. Philip Burne-Jones escaped completely. He was inoculated. Meeta escaped. He wasn't inoculated. While these observations are indisputable, our inferences are questionable because the chain of reasoning is far from complete. It won't stay incomplete for long. We'll soon know how microbes work, what decides disease. If these vials are found, say fifty years from now, chances are they will still cause a terrible disease. Unless we are sworn to stay responsible, we will forget. Our safety lies in keeping the knowledge of this germ alive. You, Joshi Sahib, will perceive immediately why we cannot make this knowledge public.'

'Already, there are tremors in the order of things,' Shankar Buwa said. 'I cannot say more just now, but men in high places are aware that things won't stay the same for long.'

'As long as our dear queen reigns over these shores, nothing can threaten us,' Alice said spiritedly.

Ramratan wondered if she expected them to cheer.

'Amen to that, Madam. But it cannot be for long. This is after all the sixtieth year of her glorious reign,' Mohsin Chacha retorted.

Alice looked at him sharply, but his quicksilver gaze eluded her.

'We're here because there is something to worry about,' Ramratan said. 'However fantastic these rumours may be, we cannot deny they may be based on actual fact. Govardhan's description of the vials, for instance, is accurate. Nusser tells me that's exactly how the *Bacillus pestis horribilis* was stored. Six glass pipettes in each blue glass bottle. Both bottles together are easily concealed in a man's coat pocket. Asadullah's brother talks of "glass needles full of plague". Again, that's accurate. There's no getting away from this, both these men have actually seen the vials, even if they no longer have them. And who's to say they don't?'

'I can tell you Asadullah's brother's meetings are not going to stop. He has stopped drinking. He brims over with virtue these days, and is therefore much more dangerous,' Mohsin said. 'And, Joshi Sahab, you had Govardhan thrown into prison. No, don't deny it. "Preventive arrest", Commissioner Vincent called it. But he escaped didn't he? Lately, haven't you been accompanied by bodyguards? Even when you step out into your garden? Right now, as we talk, are we not surrounded by strong men and spies?'

'Really, Mohsin Ahmad, my son will have a novel out of you!' Alice laughed.

'It will be my very great pleasure.' Mohsin bowed with great irony. 'But Mrs Kipling, you are with us in this? You agree we need some kind of commitment?'

Alice knitted her eyebrows.

'John would agree, I think. As for me, I would be content if those present here would commit to it. We cannot burden our children with it.'

'I disagree. I have no children yet, but when I do, they must share this with me,' Suhail said. 'They have a share in my brother's memory too.'

'Well, I could say the same. I owe it to Damodar and Sulabha. She was their daughter as much as Avdaji's. I have grandchildren who must be cautioned against men like Govardhan More, and what better way than to tell them the truth?'

And so they signed.

And so they signed...

Ratan, returning, focused on Gopal and Yaqub.

'Vasu Tai doesn't think it's over,' Gopal said. 'That's why she wanted to come here today, to decide what must be done.'

'It is the same with Abu. He will not let it rest.'

'Shakuntala Salwe's son is a drunk, I gather.'

'Yes,' Ratan said. He did not add that Nityanand had come into the bungalow on their heels, stumbled upon his mother either dead or dying, pocketed the cash Gopal and Yaqub had left her, and staggered out horrified, a man in a nightmare.

A meditative silence settled on them. Almost, Ratan was to think later, almost as if they were waiting for something.

Words returned to him when the air stilled between them.

'You sing better these days,' he said.

Vasu smiled.

The sadness in that smile smote him.

'I sang well today,' she said. 'I should have sung like this every day. Every single day of my life, I should have sung like this.'

'I heard you sing exactly like this every single day of my life.'

Her hand on his.

She had never touched him before.

He had felt her skin against his all his life. He covered her hand with his.

'I am always afraid to sing well in your hearing,' he said.

'I cannot remember a single time when you did not!'

'I can remember the only time I did. I remember too, what that made you do.'

'Tariq Azhar, my luminous morning star, have you never forgiven me?'

'Never!'

'Then it's only fair you have a chance to get even with me.'

He shut his eyes.

Her voice was no longer a web of mulmul, filtering each scintilla of light. It was silk. Sheer, colourless, slipping like water, so tensile it could caress like a feather and pierce like steel. Lighter than air, yet strong enough to absorb the weight of the world. It rose buoyant and toppled in free fall, the tight weave of notes scarcely perceptible in its slide.

He shut his eyes, because it was a girl's face he saw, radiant as if a lamp burned within her tender skin. No maiden could sing *Basant Bahar* like this. Muliebrity. Only a woman mellow with life, who had known and revelled in rapture, who had tasted the seasons, and learned how melancholy balances joy, only she could sing Basant Bahar as she sang it now. All this was brimming within her, all this, and he had never known.

The taste of his tears, bitter on his lips, distracted him from all he had to say to her. His eyes bled with burn. These could not be tears, nothing so thin, so ordinary and salt, could derive from such pain.

There was so much, so much he still had to say!

His lips opened and shut noiselessly in the silence. After a lifetime of waiting, his throat betrayed him.

She caught his helpless hands to her heart. Startled, he felt its vigour slap his palm as if he held it naked and glistening in his fist. He cleared his throat. He knew they would converse now, in quiet valleys between peak and abyss, in Raga Bhopali.

Their voices took up the raga helplessly, falling in with a need only those notes could meet. The narrative of their lives was in its descant, and its bones were what they were. Each sang a memory, waiting for the other to complete its essence. Old friends, their voices strolled companionably over long contemplative passages, each trying now and then to pleasure the other with a taste of something imagined, something invented, and returning always to what they were. There were places where their voices fused and melded till they broke apart breathless with unbearable joy.

Then it was all comfort, familiar caresses, old clothes, the scent of the room they sang in, the music room they had inhabited in each other's skin, all these lost years.

A noise arrested them.

They, who would never have stopped for face or footstep, stopped for a noise. A random gaggle of notes without meaning.

A dissonance. It was larger than the swell of their voices. It roared them down. With a hot rush it pounded at the door and burst in, an orange bulge of flame.

He found his feet and lifted her, backing off from the fire.

Fire!

How had it sneaked up on them from the door? There was nothing visible beyond a scarlet shimmer of heat. The room was filling with smoke. He heard a beam crash as a door caved in.

They moved to the window, cowering against the open sky, facing the slow, teasing advance of flame. The fire danced sideways, taking what it could. With greedy prehensile tongues it licked at the dwindling boundaries of their lives.

'Tariq. Are you afraid?'

'Yes.'

'Of what?'

'I'm afraid you will leave me again.'

'No. Wherever we go now, it will be together.'

He tightened his arms around her. How frail she was, lighter than a bird.

She felt his heart beat in her bones as she had always imagined it would.

'What are we waiting for?' she whispered.

Their voices took up the trailing threads of the raga again, tautened now in drut, faster, more intense, higher, sweeter, swooping lower, an ecstasy of sound absorbed in itself.

The fire pushed them further, past the cracking wall. It pushed them, out on the flaming ledge of the window, their frail bodies closer to the air, their exulting voices closer to the sky.

Who heard it first?

Ratan was never sure, it all happened so fast.

One moment they were sitting there in morose silence, the next they were out on the street, tearing madly across the teeming street as Sakina Manzil crumpled, a black shape blenching and then imploding in an orange mushroom of flame.

The image of Sakina Manzil igniting stretched forever. They stared, uncomprehending. Then Yaqub lunged forward with a cry, with Gopal hurtling after him. As they reached that doorway, a flaming beam toppled, barring the entrance. Beyond, a solid wall of heat cut off the interior.

Ratan had to use all his strength to restrain the two men. Luckily, there was no dearth of help. Both Yaqub and Gopal were quickly pinioned and dragged away to safety.

The fire brigade had been summoned.

Sakina Manzil was empty, Gopal's rescuer told Ratan. He stopped mid sentence.

They looked up. Yaqub and Gopal shook off their restraints.

Against the orange brightness two shapes stood out stark and black. They moved closer together till they were one. For one long minute they waited.

Brightness flared between them.

They fell.

A double curl of cinder floating down in an incandescent salvo of sparks.

Immediately, abruptly, the burning roof keeled over, dragging with it the building's frame. The smoking mass settled slowly over the two bodies.

Three fire engines worked through the night to put out the fire.

The restaurant owner led Yaqub and Gopal into a family room on the mezzanine. Ratan left them alone. He watched the firemen clear the area as best they could. The fallen timber lay smoking now, a grey mountain that would need better equipment to move it.

Yaqub and Gopal said they would wait. They would see things through.

'You too, Ratan,' Yaqub said, handing him both halves of the document. 'You too will have to see this through.'

Ratan reached home at midnight. The house slept. He had called Jafar soon after the fire was doused, and explained he may not get home till morning. Jafar had stayed back. He was asleep on the living-room sofa.

Arjun was awake.

Ratan knew that even before he entered his father's room. Jafar had made him comfortable, but trapped within his own silence, comfort was often the last thing Arjun craved.

Ratan shut the door after him so as not to wake Jafar and drew a chair up next to his father.

When Ratan finished his account, Arjun slept. The moon shone in at the window and made his father's sleeping face strangely youthful, a face he remembered from his other life. Ratan drew the curtain and crept out of the room.

Sleep was impossible. His head reverberated with the music he had heard. So fleeting, yet indelible. What hand had flung that fireball into the stairwell of Sakina Manzil? Beginning in the back of the building, the fire commandeered the wooden stairs, and devoured the timbered walls in its ghastly embrace.

It was done.

No. It wasn't done yet.

Shakuntala Salwe stared down at him in the dark.

Why had she wanted the Quarantine Papers?

To assemble proof.

Proof of the whereabouts of *Bacillus pestis horribilis.*

Three generations of blackmailers hadn't managed to pull that off. What made Shakuntala think she could?

He leapt out of bed and switched on his desk lamp. His hand found something unfamiliar. It was Nityanand's book.

Philip Burne-Jones.

Philip's sketchbook.

He opened it as if it was a letter from an old friend.

The first few pages bore pen-and-ink drawings of the Segregation Camp.

Here was Meeta, holding the umbrella over Philip's bowed back. The curious crowd around them was sketched with panache, in swift dynamic lines that sprung out from the blurry wash of sepia.

'You've found out,' Radhika said sleepily.

The languor in her voice quickened a swift thrill of desire in him.

'You've found out.'

'Not everything.'

'What then? No, don't tell me now. Tell me when you know everything.'

'I may never know everything.'

'You will.'

'How can you be so certain?'

'You're the only thing I can be certain about. Everything else is unreal with me now.'

'That's just the medication, I told you. It will wear off.'

'That's what I'm afraid of. What I shall find when it wears off. What *you* will find when it wears off.'

'I know what I will find.'

'You do?'

'Yes.'

A billion corpuscles in his arteries shouted that certainty.

This is what it will be. This is what he will find. This is what he wants.

In this landscape, there is a tree.

Samanea saman.

There is always this tree. He waits for her here. He waits for the moon to reveal her. He waits for her to reveal the moon.

Ratan felt her distress though he couldn't see her.

'It is all right,' he said. 'I was just dreaming.'

'You should sleep.'

'And you.'

'What would Yashoda say?'

'What?'

'Yashoda. What would she say? About you sitting here night past night with a woman you cannot see, a woman you do not know.'

'Why do you ask?'

'Because she is important to me. She's become my family. I feel safe thinking she's with me through the day when you're away. She takes care of me. Do you think I'm mad?'

'Not at all. She would be happy you feel this way. She would cherish you.'

'Really? She wouldn't think badly of me?'

'*No!* Not her. Never.'

'You knew her so well.'

'Yes.'

'You miss her, don't you?'

'Yes.'

'Is she dead?'

'Yes.'

'How did she die?'

The pain that lanced him cancelled out the world. The light leached out of his eyes.

'I'm sorry. I shouldn't have asked you that.'

He rose mindlessly, bumped into furniture, knocked over a glass of water.

'You will come back, Ratan,' she called piteously.

But he hurried out, broke into a run in the corridor, blundered down the stairs, and sprinted all the way to the porch where he had left his bike.

14 December 1992

It was 5 a.m.

Jafar still snored in the living room.

Ratan lay on his back, staring at the ceiling, his brain slowly turning the pages of Philip's sketchbook.

How closely Philip had observed Chitra and Khursheed! He had sketched them over and over again. In so doing, he had transcribed many of his father's paintings and given them new life. The passion between the lovers on the steps had the power to move, even with his weak and indeterminate colouring. Ramratan recalled Ned Jones' *Love Among the Ruins*, rich and ripe with colour, yet deficient somehow of the urgency that electrified Philip's sketch.

And that last one, recreating his father's marine fantasy.

There was something predatory about *The Depths of the Sea*. Ned Jones had painted a mermaid, buoying up a fainting man.

But Philip had transformed the painting.

Chitrangada—it *was* Chitrangada—held her lover close in an embrace that was the very antithesis of an embrace. It was the posture of yearning. Her back arched away from him, she floated away from his encircling arms. Khursheed's head, tilted in adoration, looked upward, sightlessly. They floated in a swirl of drapery seemingly lit by a blue glow within. It cast shadows on Khursheed's forehead and on the tight swaddling across Chitra's breasts.

Swaddling.

This was no embrace.

This wasn't erotic ecstasy. They weren't lovers straining against the compulsion of their lust.

These two were dead.

Philip had painted Chitrangada and Khursheed dead.

The drapery was the shroud they were cocooned in.

They weren't embracing. They were draped in soaked sheets meant to hold them together, to *bundle* them. They were unravelling now, these wet wraps dripping mercuric chloride, coming loose as their bodies hurtled *into*...

The depths of the sea?

There was nothing in the picture to suggest the sea.

As in the other sketches of the lovers, Philip had painted props that were of their time, their place. They were in a shaft that showed crumbling bricks, deep mossy cracks, dull red and oily green. The lovers were painted pale brown and the drapery grey, lit only by that central blue light ...

Later, Ratan could never explain why he waited so long. Did his absolute certainty slow him? Past that moment of incandescence there was no need to hurry. No need at all.

He left Nandanvan at nine as usual, made small talk with the havaldar, endured Crispin, worked his way through the histology sections that waited him. He did this all in a dream, as if hurrying would jostle the precarious balance of what he must soon attempt.

At twelve he called Raki, and asked to meet him at the gates of the Arts College at 2 p.m. It would take only half an hour. Could he get away?

Respice finem. Now, look to the end.

Raki waited at the gate for Ratan. He asked no questions. They walked into the campus in silence. The developer's team was back, as Ratan had guessed it would be. The earthmover was still parked at the edge of the maidan, but men bustled about with tape measure and barbed wire, marking up territories.

'Is this where Shakuntala defied that monster?' Raki asked.

'It looks scary enough just sitting there. She threw herself in its path, you said.'

'They said. When I got here, it was all over, and everything was quiet.'

'Some hero.'

'Shakuntala?'

'What, you disagree?'

There was reproach in Raki's voice.

'About her motive. If they'd waited till Monday…'

'Who? The demolition guys?'

'Yes. Raki, we have to speak to them.'

'That burly guy in the checked shirt, he's the one in charge, I think. What do we need them for?'

Ratan laughed.

'To outwit Shakuntala.'

The man in the checked shirt was prepared to indulge Ratan. He had time. Their work wouldn't begin until tomorrow. Today he had time, their surveying was all but done.

'What are you looking for, exactly? History stuff? We won't be going that deep, I think. Sometimes we do find things very near the surface. We found a copper plate once. Coins. Oh yeah! We've done history stuff.'

'Not history stuff. No. What kind of soil is this? Just mud?'

'It's never just mud. This is hard-packed earth, trucked in from Khandala Ghat, poured and flattened. A mixture of laterite and trap. Two, maybe three, feet of it. Caliche next. Scrape this out, and we'll see what lies beneath. You'll be surprised. We found a whole courtyard once, and parts of a house. We tried asking these college fellows for the old plans. They don't have any! *This* is a College of Arts and Architecture, can you believe that?'

'I do have some idea of what was here.'

'Football field, I heard ...'

'No, I mean earlier. There was another cottage, smaller than that one and already a ruin. Just wattle and daub, with a shed for firewood. Even the well was crumbling ...'

'Well? There was a well here?'

'Yes! Now that you mention it, *there was a well*. Raki, that's what she was guarding! I was thinking of a cellar, a tehkhana. But this makes sense, is so much simpler!'

Raki went into a huddle with Checked Shirt and returned half an hour later with talk of caterpillars and grave diggers, radars and magnetometres. None of this made any sense to Ratan but Raki was enjoying himself. They would check out the field with GPR, ground penetrating radar, if Ratan insisted.

Was the well in use? Did Ratan remember?

Ratan did.

The well had been dry for years. As a boy he'd watched the bhisti bring water across from Do Tanki.

Perhaps he imagined that.

'I don't know,' he told Raki.

Then Ratan corrected himself.

'No! I *do* know. This is it! It is the place. It's the only thing Alice could have done.'

Raki was puzzled, but he walked away to confer with Checked Shirt again.

Ratan's stomach growled. He hadn't eaten since the nankhatai and chai with Yaqub and Gopal yesterday.

He went to the college canteen. The din of students excluded him and a hush fell when he entered. Like a pulse interrupted, an arrhythmia, it lasted no longer than a moment, but was enough to establish his ectopia. He backed out, left the campus, and strolled over to Badshah Cold Drink House and ordered an ice cream falooda. The tukh malanga, usually a sensual delight, slipped unnoticed down his gullet. He paid and hurried back to the college in increasing panic. Had Raki and Checked Shirt packed up and gone home?

They hadn't. They were pacing the maidan, measuring out distances. Ratan waved to them and found a place to sit. He could not give in to exhaustion now.

What if it was all a mistake?

It all depended on Philip Burne-Jones. And how little he knew of the man!

That wasn't true.

Philip was a romantic, but he was also British. Alice, on the other hand—

'I hope your people appreciate the immense drain the plague is upon us,' Alice said. 'Mr Cleghorn says the loss to the exchequer is terrible. If only Indians would learn! We've ruled this country for two hundred years, and it's still as primitive as we found it. I told Mr Cleghorn, we really should look closer at what we're dealing with!'

'*Bacillus pestis?*'

'Oh, I don't believe in these things you call germs. Plague is in the air of this country. I didn't mean that at all. I meant the people. Unfortunately, we seem to deal only with nawabs and maharajas. But they don't make up the country, do they? The average Indian is not a maharaja. He is half devil and half child. We cannot ignore the first even if we must tolerate the second.'

Ramratan did not respond.

'There's news of an outbreak on the hill! Of course it's only among the servants, but how much longer before it spreads among *us*?'

The Arts College was far removed from Malabar Hill, and Alice's reception at the governor's was, at best, tepid.

'Still,' said Ramratan, 'you took the worst in your stride. You have been truly heroic.'

Irony was always lost on Alice.

'Oh? That was Philip. He was always a fool. And Meeta has been very loyal. Luckily, that's all dealt with now, and we will not speak of it any more. I'm relieved I shan't have to be polite to Mrs Sinclair after tomorrow!'

Mrs Sinclair echoed Alice, with a little more circumspection.

'Oh, after Mr Burne-Jones left things have been most difficult, Dr Oak! The servants have simply stopped listening to Mr Sinclair and self! The khansama has been using up all the stores quite without reason. Really, I shall be quite pleased to be back to the old ways. Though I hope you will watch over us, Dr Oak, even after Mrs Kipling has left. This dreadful plague—you know, she has been trying to persuade me to send the children home, but I will not agree!'

He heard no more of Philip Burne-Jones. He wrote twice over the next year, but his letters remained unanswered. By then, Nusser's condition had worsened, and with Haffkine close to collapse from overwork and anxiety, Ramratan had little time to waste on a Piccadilly fop.

Raki watched a worker trail a small red box across the field as if he were walking a strange dog. He'd forgotten he should have been back at the Archives hours ago. It was nearly sunset now.

'Checking for void,' Raki explained, falling easily in with the jargon he'd absorbed all afternoon. 'Subsurface imaging can locate a void beneath solid structures. Like concrete slabs.'

Translation?

If there had been a well here, covered over with a slab, this little red box would locate it.

Machines had never enthused Ratan.

They went into a huddle again, Raki, Checked Shirt and the man with the red box, the GPR guy. They called out to Ratan, and pushed a graph full of shadows at him.

'GPR grid,' Raki said happily, and pointed. 'The void is clearly shown here.'

'Very clearly,' Checked Shirt agreed.

The GPR guy said nothing. He unrolled the strip and suffered their adoration without protest.

'It works just like the usual radar,' Raki interpreted. 'Only difference, it scans the ground, not the air.'

'See these red and yellow bits? That's the void!'

Checked Shirt took charge.

'Now what we need to know is—how deep does it go? What does it contain? Water? Any other sort of material?'

'What are you expecting?' The GPR guy grinned. 'Bodies?' Raki and Checked Shirt laughed.

'Your void's about twenty feet—a well seems about right. No liquids, just mixed material.'

'What's the mixture?' Raki asked.

The GPR guy shrugged. He began reeling in the cord. His job was done.

'I have to talk with my men,' Checked Shirt said. 'You want this opened?'

'Yes.'

He shrugged. 'We'll need to, anyway. We'll have to fill it in.'

'Can you send me down?' Ratan asked.

They stared at him as if he'd gone suddenly mad.

'I can't let anyone else go down there till I know it is safe,' Ratan earnestly explained.

'What are you expecting? Contamination?'

To Mr Checked Shirt, contamination probably spelt radioactivity. Ratan did nothing to disabuse him.

Raki was silent, pondering all that Ratan had left unsaid. He had indicated nothing of yesterday's events. He couldn't yet bring himself to speak about any of that.

They would dig a trench, Checked Shirt explained, and approach the shaft from beneath. They would scrape the surface, some sort of concrete structure covered the mouth of the well, but he wasn't sure if they could de-roof it. Descending into the shaft wasn't an option; such walls tend to collapse. A trench was the best plan. The GPR would enable them to fashion that trench.

It all sounded needlessly complicated to Ratan. He had imagined all they had do was to pry off the concrete lid and rappel down on a rope.

Checked Shirt hesitated. There was a problem. He was in charge, and his men would do the work, but who would pay their overtime?

It would burn a hole in his finances, but Ratan agreed without demur.

'And it cannot be done tomorrow morning. It's either tonight or not at all. There will be questions in the morning. Even if we start now, it may take hours. We're used to this and mostly work nights. So, if you want to take a look you better stick around.'

'Let's go get some food,' Raki suggested.

'Don't you want to go home?' Ratan asked.

'I phoned already,' Raki said. 'You should too. Then catch some sleep.'

'Sleep?'

'Yes. You'll need sleep if you're going to be awake later.'

'How come you're so wise?'

'Because archaeology is my secret passion.'

'That guy thinks there's radioactivity in the well. You heard his "contaminant in the void"?'

'Hmm. Yes. Kadam. His name is Kadam. He's got a Geiger counter. And more. Overalls. Masks. Gloves. You're going to need all that?'

'Just the mask.'

Five days.

Philip had spent five days with them, three after Khursheed was stricken, five in all.

He'd painted them over and over in those five days. He'd painted from life.

All that time, they couldn't have been silent. They were making plans for the new life ahead of them and tidying up the old one they were leaving behind.

When Chitra fell ill, Khursheed had rallied.

What if Philip had been lying?

What if Khursheed had entrusted him with what really happened that evening in Gowalia Tank?

Gowalia *Tank*.

It was still called that though officially it was August Kranti Maidan now. The GPR guy, Kadam, would locate a void beneath a cricket pitch if he were given the chance ...

'Ratan! Wake up!'

He sprang up, alarmed.

It was dark, bitumen black. Except for a greenish flare at the edge of the maidan.

Oh heavens. No! He'd been asleep for hours. It was over, and he had slept through it all.

'They've just finished the trench. Time to move.'

Raki held out a bottle of water.

Ratan drank greedily, splashed some on his face and they hurried towards the green light.

The men had cleared a wide deep trench. The Caterpillar had backed off, leaving a small mountain of red-black soil. Kadam was down in the trench. He waved to Ratan. The walls were sloping enough for him to slide down, but they put him in a harness nonetheless and eased him down.

A small heap of gear lay next to Kadam.

'In case of contamination,' he said. 'Bleach. DDT, for infective material. In case of radioactive waste, it's best to inter without handling. We have gloves, overalls, masks. Concrete mix. Sample canisters.'

Ratan was impressed.

'The wall here is thin. We should easily break through with a pickaxe. Take that headlamp there.'

He started chipping away at what rang like stone but soon lost sonority. Ratan looked up. Kadam had set up two large lamps at the edge of the trench. Their hard white glare threw the dreaming mass of Kipling Bungalow into buoyant relief. The green wooden house seemed to float in the night and hover on a cloud of dark matter above protesting trees. He had the uneasy feeling Alice was in the studio, watching them dig up her backyard.

'Come on!'

Kadam had ripped a hole in the mudbank before them.

'You want to take the first peep?'

He handed Ratan a mask, helped him with the headlamp, and guided him to the breach barely large enough for him to squeeze through.

'Just look,' he cautioned.

Ratan looked.

The cone of light from his headlamp quivered with his every breath, danced madly, and refused to settle long enough for his vision to accommodate.

'See anything?'

'Not yet.'

He saw a great deal, actually.

Infinite gradations of brown and grey and black. He couldn't yet define any individual shape. There was a twig obstructing his field of vision. He reached in to push it out of the way. Branches, twigs, rubble, landfill for a void. That's all we'll find, he thought.

He caught hold of the twig, then reached lower for purchase. The drag suggested a heavier branch underneath.

The light from his headlamp swung and struck his hand—and shone on another hand imprisoned in his fist.

Ratan froze.

This was no skeleton in his grasp. The hand he clasped was *complete*, fingers curled into the leathery palm. A child's hand he had held as she turned to him with eyes full of dreams. A girl's hand he had seen signing her name with a flourish. A woman's hand he had found caressing her lover's neck. A mummy's hand now, a curl of dessication in his palm.

'Ratan?'

Raki was at his shoulder.

Ratan couldn't move, not yet. He couldn't let her hand go. He shifted his head, and the brightness seeped deeper. Something arched like a tree over her, something that seemed to move in the shudder of light.

Ratan drew back from the opening.

He looked up at the studio window.

Alice turned her back on him, the broad white back that had borne the brunt of it all. She turned once to look over her shoulder, knitted her strong brow at the mess they'd made of her backyard, then looked beyond that, past him, with a flash of pain.

And then she was gone.

'Ratan? Are you okay?'

'She's here, Raki. I've found her. I've found Chitrangada.'

Ratan took the pickaxe from Kadam almost violently.

There was no way he was going to let either of them go in. He warned them to stay well back until he called for them.

The wall chipped off easily. Like most old wells, more board than brick had gone into supporting the cavity. He delved well away from Kadam's opening, tearing off chunks till he could enter with ease.

He almost doubled over and plunged his hands blindly into the thick dry debris. There was no other way but to feel.

It felt as if there hadn't been a drop of moisture here since the beginning of time. Everything was coated with crumbly soil, there was nothing he could hope to *see*.

The bottom of the well was rocky and surprisingly clean. He stepped in cautiously, gingerly resting his feet in the spot he had just cleared.

Khursheed's body had toppled over Chitrangada's. She lay nestled within the arch of his torso. Both the bodies were mummified. Shreds of linen trailed from them.

Philip hadn't gone to 'the Cannery'. He should have guessed from that sketchbook. There were no sketches of Kanheri in the book.

No, Philip hadn't gone on that picnic. Perhaps he had left with the Sinclairs, developed a headache, and returned. It would be a shame to disappoint the children, he would have said, and the Sinclairs would have been grateful for a morning all to themselves.

Philip had returned to the bungalow. Philip had been *here*. Philip had wound the sheet around both the bodies.

Philip and Meeta.

Together they had hefted the double bundle, while Alice watched. And kept vigil.

It was the easiest thing in the world to do.

Meeta had stepped back after they toppled the bundle over the broken wall of the well. Alice stayed safely back.

But Philip had looked.

He had peered down as the bundle unravelled in its spiralling free fall, lit by a slanting sunbeam lancing into the depths. The shaft of sunlight fabricated satin from their damp cerecloths. A spark of celestial blue flared from what Philip had wedged between them when he bound them together, skin to skin.

It could have shattered in the drop.

In which case, he would be inhaling lungfuls of *Bacillus pestis horribilis* spores now, as he stood here in air undisturbed for a century.

It could have been ground to powder, pulverized by scree.

He scrabbled with his hands between their ligneous thighs. Nothing.

He slid his hand in the crevice between their flanks and the wall.

It was no crevice, there was a space here, a heap of soft earth. And planted in its heart, something smooth and hard and fluted, beneath the dust.

He extricated it with infinite slowness.

Khursheed's body toppled sideways.

He didn't let go.

Chitra's blind sockets stared up at him.

Rudyard's cruel line flashed in his brain.

A rag, a bone, a hank of hair.

He had it now.

Gently.

Now.

He wiped it against his thigh.

A dazzle of blue gleamed past the crust of mud.

A blue glass jar.

He shone the headlamp directly onto it.

Six sticks of glass winked back at him from the blue confines of the bottle, entire and untouched as they'd been when Nusser sealed them in.

This is for you, Nusser.

Ratan climbed up to the adit.

'Did you find it?' Raki asked.

'Yes. One jar. It's safe.'

He stepped back so that Raki and Kadam could look in. They moved away hurriedly, horrified.

'My men will let down a sling, we can lift them out easily,' Kadam said.

'No!'

'What then?'

'Let's use that concrete,' Ratan said.

'If we ever find it, Nusser, what should we do?'

'Grow it, what else?'

Nusser never had doubts about where his obligations lay.

Ramratan wasn't so sure.

'Just make certain it is with somebody incorruptible,' Mohsin Chacha said.

'Who, Ramratan, is above corruption?' Yashoda asked.

There was another voice Ratan wanted to hear.

Talk to me Appa, he willed. But Krishnarao did not speak.

He heard instead a swell of music where two voices sang as one. He heard instead the silence of lovers who had given their lives to guard this cylinder of glass, this freak anomaly of science. These lovers, who had kept a century's vigil over contagion.

What had Khursheed meant to do? Would he have sailed for England, taking *Bacillus pestis horribilis* with him? He had taken the jars from the laboratory to save them from Asadullah. After his flight from the camp, he would have restored the vials to Nusser. That's what he set out to do that last evening.

Asadullah had ambushed him. And Nivrutti attacked them both.

In the melee, a jar broke. Within hours, Khursheed had the plague. Delirious, bleeding, he must have pleaded with Philip to hand the jars over to Nusser or Ramratan after his death.

But Philip did not.

Philip trusted none of them, Hindu or Mussalman or Parsi. Nor himself. He saw *Bacillus pestis horribilis* as a medium of hate.

He had decided to bury the vials with the dead lovers.

Had Alice known?

She would have prised it out of Philip. But with the looming menace of Govardhan More and Asadullah's forces, Alice stayed silent.

Her silence was neither malice nor guilt. It was policy.

Bacillus pestis horribilis at large was an assurance of mutual suspicion, and mutual hate. Two families, Hindu and Muslim, would bear the brunt, but that was a small sacrifice for the larger good of keeping the natives aware they were simply not capable of pulling together. All that restrained them was Pax Britannica.

Alice Kipling was merely been doing her bit for Country, Queen, and Empire.

'And you, Ratan, what will you do?'

All the voices he loved were in those words, most of all the voice he hardly ever heard these days.

His father's voice.

The voice of Arjun.

Ratan took the trough of concrete from Raki. He settled the two bodies against each other, and between them he wedged the jar of blue glass once again.

He made no prayer, no plea for peace.

The concrete fell on the lovers in wet slops.

Raki kept handing him more and more. They kept pouring it in until there was no hint of shape or form any more. Nothing left of what they had seen. Nothing now but a wall, wet and glistening in the spill of light.

He heard Radhika's sharp intake of breath as he entered.

'I thought you weren't coming back,' she said.

He sat down quietly.

'You smell of soap.'

'I just showered.'

'Isn't it very late?'

'Or very early.'

'It's over, then?'

'Yes.'

'Did you find out everything?'

'Yes.'

'And?'

'And what? It's over.'

'Or is it beginning?'

When Ramratan returned home, it was almost dawn.

The stench of death hung miasmic about him as if it had claims over him too. Sadness was a stone in his belly. He did not go into the house but crouched in the shade of the raintree, repeating its name like a mantra.

Samanea saman, Samanea saman.

As if it would produce the kindly spirit of his father and heal him.

Everything in him shrivelled with revulsion. What could he offer his sleeping sons except hate and malice?

The door opened.

He'd woken Yashoda.

She walked out to him without a light and he remembered their first night beneath the tree.

'Are you there?'

She knelt beside him, kneading his temples with the wisdom of long familiarity. Tonight, it failed to lift his ache. She took his glasses off his nose and put them in his shirt pocket. She unbuttoned his shirt. I'm in no mood for this, he told her.

She left him and he panicked.

Then he heard her laugh as she caught him in a web of something fragrant and silky. He freed himself and she was there, standing out in the moonlight, not a jewel on her, no glint of gold or gemstone, hair undone, nude.

Like she was the night they both remember with pain.

Neither widow, nor wife, I am Yashoda.

The hurt still lurks in her eyes, somewhere in the irony behind her smile.

The moon gilds her, erases the years. He treasures each line, each scar, each sag, each ruck as his own. He feels life burst past his sadness as he maps her with his lips, tasting the flavours of home.

He looks up suddenly, surprises the grief in her eyes, and lets her look into him without fear, without pain. She holds his gaze for one long look, then settles around him as the earth packs close and dense and eager about the subterranean hunger of the tree.

It was neither over, nor was it a beginning.

Neither widow, nor wife, I am Radhika.

He'd shelter her now.

He would wait.

Because of the look in Anwar's eyes, he would wait.

Bombay, Maharashtra & Long Beach, Mississippi

23 October 2009

Afterword

The Quarantine Papers grew out of two journeys.

The first began with Abu's smile when he watched us puzzle over the naqsh in Lockwood Kipling's book. For what followed, our loving thanks to Shakir Ali Syed.

The second was through the eyes of a very young reporter on the city beat in 1992. Thank you, Naresh Fernandes, for sharing that experience with us.

The kind keepers of the Bombay Archives guided our manic quests with patience and efficiency.

As always, Afaaf and Ihaab make everything better.

About the Type

The Ratan Oak sections are in Didot, a neoclassical serif typeface that evokes the Age of Enlightenment and is named for the French printing family. The letters were cut and cast as type by Firmin Didot and his brother Pierre Didot used them in printing.

The Ramratan Oak sections are in American Typewriter, a serif typeface that evinces an old-fashioned intimacy. The English engineer Henry Mill patented the typewriter in 1714, but the first practical typewriter and the QWERTY keyboard were invented by the American Christopher Sholes. He was granted a patent on 23 June 1868. Based on Sholes' monospaced design, Joel Kadan and Tony Stan created American Typewriter in 1974.

About the Authors

Ishrat Syed and **Kalpana Swaminathan** are surgeons. The anonym **Kalpish Ratna** is an almost-anagram of their first names.

The Quarantine Papers is their first Ratan/Ramratan Oak novel.